UNDENIABLY FORBIDDEN

J. SAMAN

***This book can be read as a
complete standalone. This family
tree is simply a reference if needed.**

Boston World Family Tree

***This Does Not Contain Spoilers And Will Be Updated As The Series Progresses**

Fritz Family

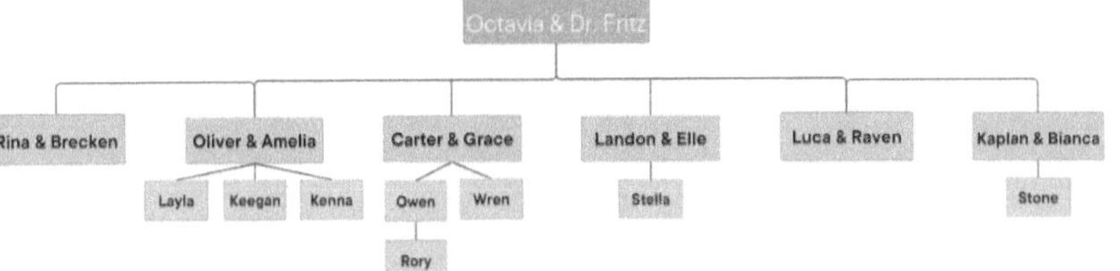

Central Square

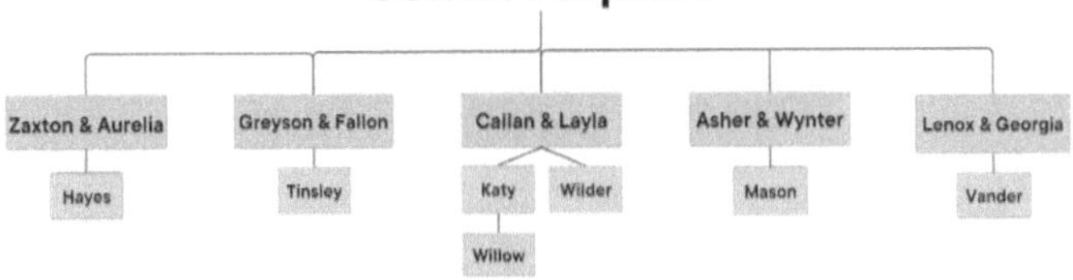

The Edge

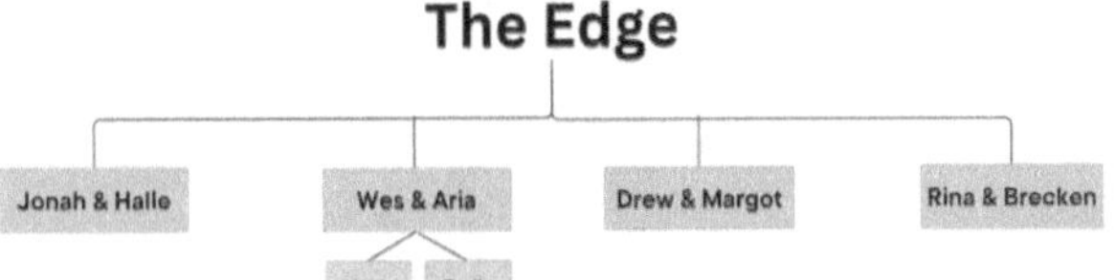

1

OWEN

A smirk curls its way up my lips, and I wipe it away with my thumb as I read the last line of his text. As one of my best friends growing up, all through our residencies and the birth of my daughter Rory, who is now six, Jack knows if I'm not at the hospital or with my family, I'm with her. My nights out are sporadic at best. But now I find myself in the unique position of sitting alone at a bar in Back Bay completely childless since my little sister Wren has graciously taken Rory for the night.

Still, I was looking forward to seeing him tonight.

> Jack: Asshole, it's Eddie, and you've met her like a million times. She has been working as a live-in nanny for the last seven months in London, and she loves kids. Just meet with her. That's all I'm asking.

Right. I know all of this, and I do know Eddie. Well, sorta. I haven't seen Jack's little sister since she was a kid. She's about twelve years younger than us and has been living abroad for art school for the last five years.

Eddie isn't so much the problem. I'm sure she's great. I trust Jack and I trust his family, and he swears once I meet her again, I'll love her, but more importantly, Rory will love her. My problem is that I'm having a hell of a time digesting the idea of a live-in nanny, though I know at this point it's what Rory and I need.

> Me: I'll meet her, and I'm sure she'll be great. Safe travels, and I'll see you tomorrow.

I stare at the screen of my phone, thinking this all through. It's difficult for me to admit that I need more help, but with Rory starting first grade and my insane work schedule, she needs more consistency and routine in her life than me shuffling her around between my family members.

"Another?" the bartender asks. I stare down at my bourbon on the rocks and debate this. I could go home and get a full night of sleep—something I rarely get—and perhaps even sleep in before I pick up Rory. Or I could call one of my cousins, who I don't get to hang out with nearly as often as I'd like, and see what they're up to.

Or, better still, I could stay and see where the night takes me.

Even if it won't go beyond tonight.

My mental debate doesn't take long. I slide the glass back toward the bartender and lift my chin. "Two fingers, please."

She gives me the sort of appreciative smile I'm interested in. "Sure." That smile grows as her head dips and she gazes up at me through her thick black lashes as she dutifully fills up my glass and slides it to me. "You're Owen Fritz, right?"

And just like that, my interest dies as ice floods my veins, freezing over any warmth or possibility I'd been building myself up to. That. That fucking bullshit.

You're Owen Fritz.

Yeah, I am.

It's why Rory still doesn't have a nanny even though we desperately need one for her. It's why it's been far too long since I've ventured out and sought to meet a woman even for a one-nighter. It's why the only people I surround myself with are my family. Recognition as a Fritz, a celebrity family of billionaires who more or less own Boston is a more effective cockblock than my little girl.

"Not tonight, I'm not," is my only reply. One she doesn't comprehend as her eyebrows slant inward and she stares bewilderedly at me. Her lips part as if she's about to question me, when mercifully the other bartender calls her name. She gives me a wistful look and then reluctantly gets back to work.

I pull out my phone, deciding maybe a night hanging out with my cousins *is* the better option when movement out of the corner of my eye catches my attention. A delicate hand wraps around my glass and then lifts it. I turn in my seat, staring incredulously as my glass touches the full red lips of the petite woman on my right. She drinks about half of it, licks her lips, and then sets the glass down, her focus entirely on her phone that's in her other hand.

I blink at her, stunned. "That was my bourbon you just drank half of."

Her head whips in my direction as if she had no clue someone was sitting beside her, and when her large, blue-green eyes meet mine, I nearly fall off my chair. *Holy hell.*

"This drink?" She holds up the glass in question and examines it. "What makes you think it's yours and not mine?" she retorts with an artfully curved eyebrow and a slight upturn to her red lips. I'm having trouble breathing. And remembering basic English. I might also be having a heart attack with how my heart is suddenly racing in my chest.

"I'm sorry, what?" Inwardly, I cringe. Has it been that long since I've been in the game or spoken to a beautiful woman who isn't a patient's mother? Yes. The answer is immediate. Yes!

Except she's so much more than simply beautiful. She's eccentric and wild, which is normally not my thing at all, but on her... damn. Long, brown hair, so dark it's almost black with swirls of pink and blue underneath, and aquamarine eyes with an elegant curve and fan of natural black lashes. Her petite nose, which feels like such a contradiction compared to her kissable, plump, bow-shaped lips, has a diamond stud in it. She's wearing a black halter top that shows off her narrow shoulders, smooth, tanned skin, and a sexy hint of cleavage from her large tits. Her ripped jeans hug her shapely hips and thighs.

She's small but perfectly fucking curvy, and hell am I here for it.

The slight smirk she'd been giving me curls into a full smile at my blundered retort and owl-eyed mystification, and if I thought I was having trouble breathing before, that's got nothing on what her smile is doing to me now.

I used to be better at this. So much better. Hell, I was fucking *good* at this once. I had a smile and swagger that could get a woman's panties off without even having to touch her. Now, after a shitty divorce and far too much time spent in the hospital treating sick kids or staying in with my own, I've lost my game. Thank God Jack and my cousins aren't here. I'd never hear the end of it.

"You said this is your drink," she answers my inane question. "Not possible. I ordered a Knob Creek on the rocks. That's what this is. Trust me, I know the difference in my bourbons well enough to taste it." Her delicate fingers swirl my glass around in a circle, the remaining amber liquid and ice going along for the ride. "You might want to work on your material. The old, *that's my drink* line has been used by men the world around."

I clear my throat and get my shit back together. Especially when her bit about that as a pickup line makes me chuckle. "I also ordered a Knob Creek on the rocks. And I believe"—I reach across the bar in front of her and tap the glass near her other hand—"this is your drink."

Her head slingshots, and once she sees I'm right, a melodic laugh bursts from her lungs. "Well, look at that." She turns back to me, a slight flush on her cheeks. "Oops. Sorry. So... that wasn't a pickup line then?"

I shake my head. "Not a pickup line."

"Thank God." She wipes imaginary sweat from her brow. "Even though you're gorgeous, that was an automatic turn-off for me. I can't stand cliché men."

I drag my thumb across my bottom lip, fighting my grin. "You prefer unexpected men instead?"

"Always." She assures me as if that should have been a foregone conclusion. "What woman doesn't?"

My jaw tingles with a smile I'm forcing myself to contain. "Like stealing someone's drink kind of unexpected?"

Her lips twitch and her cheeks flush again, and I'm utterly captivated. It's rare, if ever, since Angelica walked out on Rory and me three years ago that I've been drawn to anyone, but one look and a few sharp words and that's where I find myself.

She holds up a hand, her expression earnest. "I swear, I wasn't trying to be a drink thief. I was just a bit distracted by a text that came in. Let me buy you another round since I doubt you want to finish the one I just drank half of."

She moves to signal the bartender, but the last thing I want is for the bartender to return and start hitting on me again. Not when I have this woman's undivided attention—and she called me gorgeous.

I reach for the glass still in her hand, and when our fingers brush, a warm shockwave zings along my skin, making my palm tingle. Her sharp intake of breath infers she felt that too. With my eyes locked on hers, I take the glass from her, bring it to my mouth, and polish off the rest of it.

She sits back and folds her arms over her chest, appraising me. "It's going to be like that then, huh? Swapping spit with me before I even get your name."

I lean in, taking a deeper inhale when I catch the hint of her subtle fragrance. "Technically, you swapped spit with me first since that was my second drink in the same glass. And who says I was going to give you my name?"

She arches a challenging brow. "I think we both know you want to give it to me." She picks up her glass, takes a sip of it, and then hands it to me to do the same. I smile, a real fucking smile that feels so rare on my lips I let it linger even as I take a sip from her glass.

"What's your name?" I ask as I hand it back to her.

"Estlin."

"Estlin. That's... different. I'm not sure I've heard it before."

"Don't ask the origin. It's not a story I enjoy telling."

I smirk, tapping my thumb against the edge of the bar. "Then I won't ask."

She brushes her hair back over her shoulders, more of the pink and blue popping out and playing with the black. "I told you mine, now it's your turn to tell me yours."

And the fact that there's no mocking or hint of recognition in her eyes or voice has me saying, "Owen."

"Nice to meet you, Owen. Do you do this often? Come to bars and pick up women with overused lines?"

I chuckle lightly. "Hardly ever, actually. I'm not a man with a lot of free time. What about you?"

"I haven't picked up a woman in a bar in years."

A laugh bursts from my lungs. "Oh. Is that your not-so-casual way of saying I'm barking up the wrong tree?"

"Not even a bit." She drops an elbow on the bar and leans her head into the palm of her hand as she faces me. "But that doesn't mean I'm not already someone's date tonight."

"Are you?" I throw back at her, liking how her eyes glitter and her nose ring sparkles in the dim lighting as she boldly flirts with me.

She dips in until our faces are inches apart. "Want to know a secret?"

My hand hits the back of her barstool, and I sneak in close enough that I can practically taste my bourbon on her lips. There is no stopping the conspiratorially playful note in my voice as I say, "Tell me."

"I got stood up tonight."

I pull back so she can see my shock. "You? Impossible. What man would be stupid enough to stand you up?"

"My brother, and it wasn't quite his fault."

"I got stood up tonight too."

"Impossible," she parrots teasingly. "What woman would be crazy enough to stand you up?"

"Not a woman. Just a friend."

"I guess that means we're both alone tonight."

"Not anymore." My hand on the back of her chair finds a lock of her silky hair, and I run my fingers through it. She shudders ever so slightly, and I smile, moving until my knee brushes against hers. She hasn't moved away or asked me to stop. She's enjoying this as much as I am.

My mouth slides along the side of her face until I whisper in her ear, "Estlin, would you like to have another drink with me?"

She makes a noise in her throat when she feels my hot breath on her skin, and I slide away, noting the resulting flush on her cheeks again. I can't help but wonder if all of her blushes so prettily.

"Yes. I'd like that. But this round is on me since I drank your last one."

"I've never had a woman who isn't family buy me a drink before," I admit. "I'm not sure how I feel about it."

She rolls her eyes at me. "We can fight about the patriarchal and archaic notion that a man has to financially take care of a woman over the drink I'm buying you." She half stands up, waving at the bartender all the way down at the end. She holds up two fingers and points to each of our glasses. He throws her a wave of acknowledgment, and then she sits back down.

"It's not me being patriarchal. I believe women rule this world and do a better job of it. It's called being a gentleman."

"You're one of those guys? Hmm." The male bartender comes over and refills both our glasses, and immediately she hops off her stool and picks up her glass. "I tell you what. If you beat me at darts, I'll let you pay for my drink. If I beat you, you let me pay."

I rub my jaw, eyeing the empty dartboard she's indicating. "You sure that's fair? I'm pretty good at them."

She tilts her head, her expression taunting. "I thought you wanted to buy me a drink. Now you're tipping your hand?"

Touché.

"Okay. You're on."

"I'll be back in a few, Matty," she calls to the bartender with a wave.

The bartender winks at her, and then she saunters off toward the dartboard without waiting on me, already knowing I'm going to follow her.

Who the hell is this woman? And what is it about her—other than her looks—that has me so goddamn intrigued? I honestly don't know, but something about this ocean-eyed beauty has me anxious for more. Maybe it's the smart, no-bullshit sharpness of her tongue or her boldness or youth—since I can tell she's quite a bit younger than me—or the fact that I am so very out of practice with this.

Whatever it is, she has me on my toes, making me feel that even though she's within my grasp, I'm going to have to work my ass off to get her.

I've always liked a challenge, and I definitely want to keep this going so I can see where it will hopefully lead for the rest of the night. So, I guess it's game on.

"Matty?" I question as I come to stand beside her about six feet from the dartboard.

"We went to high school together. Take these." She hands me three red darts while she holds the green ones.

I decide not to question it. The less I know about her, the better. There is only tonight for us. No tomorrow, and certainly not the next day. Not with my life.

"Have you played before?" I ask, rolling the darts back and forth between my palms.

"Once or twice, but I don't recall it being all that difficult."

"All right. Ladies first." I wave at her to take the lead, and she shoots me a side-eye.

"Didn't we discuss that already?"

I point to my chest. "Gentleman, remember?"

She puffs a breath but relents and throws her dart, hitting the outer ring of the nine.

"Yay. That's good, right?"

I smirk. "That's good. Go again." She throws two more times in a row, hitting just outside the bullseye and the inner ring of twenty.

I squint at her. "Why do I get the feeling I'm being hustled?"

She smiles like an angel up at me since she's a solid foot shorter than I am. "I don't know what you're talking about.

Who hustles at darts?" She goes over to the board and pulls out her darts, then comes and stands right beside me.

I throw my darts and hit the inner ring of the twelve, the inner ring of the twenty, and the inner ring of the nineteen.

"Oh darn. You *are* good at this."

I stare down at her. "You're totally hustling me."

"You're paranoid."

I give her a dubious look. "Right. Sure, I am. You realize since I won that round, I just bought your drink."

Her hand lands on my chest, and I can feel the heat of her palm through the thin material of my black button-down. "Don't get mad at me."

I laugh. "Mad at you? Impossible."

"Good. Because I get free drinks here. Matty owes me from a thing a while back, so he simply added your drink to mine. The game was just a fun diversion."

"Hustler," I play, snaking a hand around her waist and dragging her tighter to me. My fingers trickle up until I find the smooth, bare skin of her back, warm and soft beneath my touch. My cock starts to thicken in my jeans, and if I shift a little to the right, she'll feel it for sure.

She rocks up on the balls of her feet until her chest presses to mine, her full, soft tits squishing tantalizingly into me. "I totally am. I'm killer at darts. I let you win because I'm generous like that."

"Maybe. But maybe not." My face dips. "If you say you let me win, then you won't object to upping the ante, right? How about we play for something real since you already bought me my drink?"

Amusement tilts up her lips into a fearless smile. "What did you have in mind?"

My gaze washes over her, following the lines of her body and then back up to her lips. Sweet, full lips I want to devour and hear moaning my name. I meet her eyes. "If I win the next round, you get a hotel room with me for the night."

Her hand slithers up my chest, past my shoulder, and to the back of my neck, where she plays with the ends of my hair. "That's rather bold of you, Owen."

I don't bother pretending otherwise. "But it's exactly what I want."

"A hotel room though, huh? Are you hiding a wife or girlfriend at home?"

"I'm as single as it gets. A hotel room is just more convenient." I never bring women home, and I have no plans to start now.

She considers this for a moment, and just when I think she's about to tell me to fuck off, she surprises me with, "And if I win the next round?"

I search around the bar, which is moderately crowded for a Friday night in this part of the city, and then shift back to her. People recognize me here. Everywhere I go in this city, people recognize me. It wasn't so long ago that my face was plastered over every tabloid out there. So if I kiss a random woman in public, it will end up somewhere I don't want it to be.

Somewhere my daughter could see it. Even worse, somewhere my grandmother could see it, and then she'll start in on me about getting married again because that's what she does.

To that end, I should go, but I'd like to take Estlin with me.

"Lady's choice." Because I have no intention of losing.

She grins wickedly. "Okay. You're on."

2

ESTLIN

I could beat him with my eyes closed. Growing up, we had a dartboard in our basement that I used to take my pent-up frustration out on, and when I was in college and living with Claude, we had a board in our flat for the same reason. Owen was right when he called me a hustler, and darts aren't my only game. So I could win this with the lights out.

But I won't.

He's too fucking hot for that.

Light brown hair, ultra-blue eyes, tall, broad, twin dimples, and smells like expensive cologne—the kind where the guy doesn't try to smell as good as he does... *yum*. I could eat him like candy for breakfast and not have an ounce of guilt for it. Plus, he was a little awkward at first—though that evaporated as fast as it was there—and looks at me like he doesn't know how to look away, which is cute and endearing and a definite turn-on.

Especially after the rock bottom hit my self-esteem took at the hands of my ex.

I could use a night of no-strings fun before the real world sets back in for me tomorrow when I meet my new boss and his daughter. Jack's flight was canceled, which means big brother can't step in and cockblock. The competitive queen in me cares that I'm going to throw the game. The lusty, I-haven't-had-sex-in-months-and-need-a-real-orgasm-not-delivered-by-a-silicone-boyfriend girl in me doesn't. Though my faith in men and partners has been brutally shaken, that's not what this is.

This is only tonight since that's all I've got the time or desire for, and he seems to be on the same page since he's talking hotel room and not his place or mine.

I step out of his embrace, and with my gaze still locked on his, I throw the darts blindly at the board. One. Two. Three. I have no idea where they landed, but judging by the dull *thud*, at least one hit the wall.

"Your turn."

His blue eyes smolder, and he drops the darts on the tall cocktail table on his right. "Fuck the game." In my next heartbeat, he snatches my hand, runs us back over to the bar, drops a hundred-dollar bill down on the counter even though I told him his drink was on me, and then runs us straight out the door before I can even so much as form a protest.

Not that I was planning on it.

I have pepper spray and my folding knife in my purse. A single girl can never be too careful. If he tries anything, I'll take him out, but I don't get the impression that's who this guy is. I wouldn't be here if I thought he was. He doesn't strike me as the type who would ever consider hurting a woman an option. He's an admitted gentleman, and I don't think that's a line or an act. After what I went through with Claude, I have a different eye and way of sizing men up, and this man isn't going to do anything other than give me a night of fun, and hopefully a hell of a lot of pleasure.

With my hand bound in his, he twirls me out onto the sidewalk, the warm Boston summer air hitting me in the best way.

"I've wanted to do this all night." In a flash, he has me

pinned up against the wall of a neighboring building, his hands cradling my face and his mouth swallowing the gasp he forced from me. Warm and firm, his lips waste no time parting mine, his tongue immediately diving in. He groans when he gets a taste of me, his hands sliding up and back into my hair, holding my head and moving it how he wants so he can explore every inch of my mouth.

He's more controlling, more take charge than I had immediately pegged him to be, and I like it. He's also a hell of a lot taller than I am, and since I'm only wearing flip-flops, I climb up onto my tiptoes to snake my arms around his neck and kiss him back. He tastes like bourbon and something spicy and feels like everything wonderful and male I've been craving.

My hands slide down over his shoulders until I'm holding onto his strong, muscular upper arms. It gives me some extra leverage to pull him tighter against me and deepen the kiss. His tongue thrashes with mine, whipping me into a dizzying torrent of lust and desire.

"There's a hotel down the street," he pants against my lips. "You still with me?"

I fucking love that he checks. "I'm still with you."

His smile cracks straight across his lips, pressing into me and forcing one of my own.

Gripping my hand once more, he squeezes it, and then we're taking off down the street, too excited for bullshit chit-chat neither of us is the least bit interested in.

This isn't leading to anything beyond tonight, and we both know it.

The hotel lobby is bright and cheerful, if not a bit too modern for my taste. I prefer older, eclectic, and well, some real art on the walls instead of this mass-produced crap, but who cares? This isn't a Paris showroom. Owen excuses himself, choosing to head to the front desk alone, and I use that as my excuse to go to the ladies' room.

"Yeesh." I snicker when I get a good look at myself in the mirror. My hair is a tangled mess, and my lipstick is smeared halfway across my cheek. I give my reflection a long pause as I clean myself up. Jitters hit my gut—the fluttery, squishy kind that makes me feel both alive and nervous at the same time.

It's been a while since I've been with someone, and my last someone shook my confidence to my core. I finally feel ready, though. Ready to restart my life and all that comes with it. That's one of the reasons I moved back to the States. Well, my brother also moving back to Boston is another.

"You can do this," I tell myself. "Put that asshole behind you and go after what you want. You own this, not the other way around."

I readjust my strapless bra and give my hips a good wiggle to make sure my jeans fit me just so. I'm uneasy, and I hate that I am. I knew I'd feel this way, so it's no shock that it's hitting me now. The first time with a new person after the last one didn't end well isn't easy for anyone. But tonight is on my terms, under my conditions, and if I need to leave, I will.

With that mental declaration, I give myself a *you've got this, bitch* wink and head out of the restroom to find Owen standing against the wall, his eyes on his phone. He slips it into his pocket, and his gaze does a slow drag up my body until he meets my eyes. He flashes me a keycard and then extends his other hand for mine.

Without hesitation, I walk the three steps and take it. Maybe it's the way he's looking at me—like I'm the most beautiful woman he's ever seen and he's still nervous I'll say no—or maybe it's that he kisses with a possessive urgency but still asks if I want this too. I don't have a reason for it, but I feel safe with him, and I let my gut be my guiding force.

We reach the elevators, the doors open and waiting, and after we step on, he presses the button for fifteen, the top floor.

The doors close, and the car shoots up. "I hope you don't have any plans tomorrow."

"Why's that?" I ask, suddenly apprehensive and hoping I didn't misread the situation between us.

He gives me a wicked smirk. "Because I plan to fuck you all night and leave you sore and exhausted."

Holy shit. Did he just say that? And why is it so fucking hot that it makes me instantly wet?

I glance up at him as the car slows and we reach our floor. "I do, actually, so I suppose I'll just have to suck it up and deal."

That smile grows and when the doors open, he yanks me into him, kissing me feverishly and walking me backward out of the car. His hands are all over me, tugging at my top and feeling every inch of my ass he can over my jeans. With a quick peek, he checks the placard on the wall that tells him which direction our room is in, and then he lifts me off my feet, forcing my legs around his waist.

His mouth doesn't leave mine, both of his hands now gripping and squeezing my ass as he devours me. His hard cock presses right against my center, and I hold tighter against him, wanting to feel more of him right where I need it.

Our room is the last one on the right, and he slams me into the wall right beside the door. Blindly, he reaches out, swipes the keycard against the lock, and misses once, then again before finally, on the third try, he snags it. The door *snicks*, followed by that mechanical unlocking sound. He adjusts me and uses one hand to open it, kicking it with his foot.

"Put me down," I tell him with a small laugh, but he shakes his head, kicks the door again so it swings wide, and then shoves us from the wall and straight into the dark room, only lit by the glow of the city outside the window. We don't make it far, barely passing the door before we're ripping at each other's clothes. My top lands on the nearby dresser, and one of my flip-flops hits the floor, quickly, followed by the other. I tear at his shirt a bit too eagerly, causing one of the buttons to go flying, making both of us laugh until urgency consumes us once again.

He shrugs off his shirt as my hands fumble for the button and fly of his pants, but he grows too impatient and spins us into another wall before we bounce onto the bed. For a moment, he stands over me, toeing off his shoes and raking in my messy appearance. And as he does, I return the favor, admiring the toned, strong lines of his tanned abs, chest, and shoulders.

I knew he had a great body. I could tell that even through his clothes but seeing him shirtless is something else.

Wordlessly, he crawls over me, kissing up my belly, over the swells of my breasts, and up to my neck. His fingers dig behind my back and unhook my bra with precision. The cups fall away from my tits, and he groans, pulling back and straddling my waist so he can take in the full picture of them.

"Fuck," he rasps, dragging a hand across his stubble-lined jaw. "Just... fuck. Look at you. You are so goddamn beautiful."

He cups my tits in his hands, lifting them, testing their weight, and giving them a firm squeeze that has me moaning and my head tilting back into the soft bed. My tits—especially my nipples—are more than a little sensitive. His thumbs drag over the stiff peaks, his smoldering gaze following the motion like a man so enthralled by what he sees that he can't force himself to look anywhere else. Hungrily, he licks his lips and dips his head to capture one nipple in his hot mouth, sucking it in deep and hard.

"Hell," I cry, raking my fingers up into the back of his hair and holding him there as he licks and sucks on my nipple and uses his teeth to scrape at my breast. My jeans are shoved roughly down my legs until they catch on my ankles, and I use my feet to finish kicking them off. Now that I'm only in my thong, he adjusts his position, using his knees to nudge my thighs apart as his mouth continues to eat at my chest.

Greedy for more, my hands run along his back and shoulders, my nails scraping across his bare chest to finish what I had started before with his pants. Deft fingers slip into the sides of my thong and shimmy it down as his face begins to chart the same course. His lips slither lower, his tongue swirling across my belly, tasting me, and fuck, *please keep going, please keep going.*

I must chant this aloud because he peers up at me through his lashes with a wicked smile that could make me come right now. He licks his lips and says, "I intend to."

That's it. And he makes good on that dirty promise as he kneels on the floor, pulls me to the edge of the bed, and spreads my thighs wide. For a half beat, he stares at my bare pussy before he slides an arm beneath my ass and lifts me to his mouth.

He doesn't bother kissing me.

There's no soft touch or introduction.

His entire mouth covers my pussy, and my hips involuntarily jerk in response. The tip of his tongue rings my opening, tasting me before diving straight in. My hand threads into his hair, holding on, because I have to fucking hold on as my eyes close and my vision sways. I don't know if it's from the alcohol buzzing through my system or the way his diabolical mouth eats me like a man starving, but I don't care.

His teeth graze my swollen clit before he pulls it between his lips and sucks, using the tip of his tongue to flick it over and over. But that's not even the best part. The sounds he makes as he eats me out, the way his hands grip my flesh, his blatant, unhinged desire. They're all so much—almost *too* much—and are making my body build and build faster than I can keep up with.

Two fingers slide straight inside my pussy and crook up until he's directly finger fucking that magic spot on my front wall. Liquid heat rolls between my legs and up through my limbs, and I just about lose my freaking mind. I prop myself up, desperate to see him, and find myself mesmerized by the powerful flex of his muscles, the bulge of his strong arms, and the ridges of his abs. His lips move against my center, wet and glistening in the dim light of the room from my arousal. And his eyes—they're just gone. Totally ransacked by pleasure and lust.

I swear, I've never seen a sexier sight than this in my life.

"Yes. Oh, god, yes. Don't stop."

"Do you like it when I touch you here?" he asks, running his finger in circles around my opening. "When I kiss you like this?" His mouth sucks and licks on my clit. "If you like getting fucked with my mouth and fingers, just wait till you feel my cock."

My limbs go weak. *Fucking hell.*

He increases the pressure, fucking me with his fingers over and over while sucking on my clit, and I come. So. Hard. All over his face as I rip at his hair. My back arches, and I moan so loudly I'm positive everyone in this hotel can hear me.

The moment my body starts to sag, he pulls away and I blink open my eyes, my chin dropping to find him licking his lips and then the two fingers he had inside me. He stands slowly like a predator, only I don't have an ounce of fear in me. I'm desperate with want. I want to feel his thick, hard cock inside me. I want him to pound me into next week. I want him to give it to me so good that I'm as exhausted and sore as he said I'd be.

He pulls out a small box of condoms from his pocket and tosses it on the bed. I raise a *care-to-explain* eyebrow. His lips curl, and he wipes his bottom lip with his thumb.

"I didn't have any in my wallet." He shrugs in an almost self-deprecating way. "I told you before, I don't do this very often. I bought them in the store off the lobby."

I love that. Like so goddamn much I can't even handle it.

"It's been a while for me too." I don't know why I told him that. Maybe it's his honesty provoking mine, or the fact that I'm suddenly a bit nervous again, but whatever it is, I want him to know.

"Good."

With his eyes on mine, he slides his pants and boxer briefs down until his long, thick cock springs free. My mouth instantly waters. His cock is fucking perfect. Opening the box of condoms, he pulls one out, puts the wrapper between his teeth, and then tears it open. I watch like a junkie about to get a fix as he rolls it on and then climbs back over me, his face hovering inches above mine, his eyes raw with need.

"I need to fuck you so hard right now. I can't handle how sexy you look like this."

His hand loops under one knee, slides it up to his shoulder, and without warning he plunges straight into me. My head throws back, and my eyes pinch shut as pleasure, hot and wind-ing, tears a path through me. *God, yes.*

"*Fuck,* you feel good. And so goddamn tight," he pants, his head straining, the veins in his neck bulging as he holds himself still.

Christ. That's because he's so goddamn *big*. All of him. A blissed-out sigh passes my lips at how full I feel.

I start to wiggle and move, making his chest press down harder into me, squishing my tits beneath his honed muscles as if to say *you don't get to control this, I do*. He pulls out and then slams back in, making my lungs empty, and another moan flees my lips.

"You like that?" he rasps in my ear, his voice strained. "Does that feel good, sweet thing? It's about to feel so much fucking better."

"Do it. Fuck me. Fuck me so good, nothing else matters." Because that's exactly what I need. I want to be fucked hard. I want to come again. I want this man—a man I'll never see again —to wipe away all memories of the one before him.

His eyebrows draw together, and his lips part on a strong exhale. One that rattles me to my core. Especially with the way he starts pounding into me.

"You want it? You want it like this?"

"Yes. More. I want more. Everything you've got. All that you promised me. Give it to me, and don't stop."

His eyes meet mine, and he licks my neck, nipping on my jaw. His hands slide up from my ass to my hips, and he fucks into me ferociously, nailing into me in a way I've never been fucked before. Upping the ante as he bends me in half with one leg still tucked between us and draped over his shoulder.

He steals my breath. Robs my soul. Shakes my bones. But manages to leave my heart untouched and unscathed. It's so perfect, so fucking cathartic, I smile, rocking my hips up into his, meeting him thrust for thrust.

"Yeah. That's it," he says, almost to himself, his eyes locked between my thighs, enraptured by the sight. "So fucking good."

And with that, he drives into me harder and deeper and with more determination than before. He fucks me like a man possessed. So dark and rude and uncaring with how he claims me. My hands shoot above my head, my fists clutching the white fabric of the duvet and holding on for dear life. I shift my foot so it's on the edge of the bed, widening my thighs and taking him in even deeper.

His fingers dig into my hips, his cock continues to plunge, and I can't do anything other than hold on. He flattens himself against me, his naked chest pressed to mine, and he wraps his arms tightly around me, holding me close. Senseless words are murmured into my ear, his hot breath rushing against my skin in endless pants.

The friction of his body like this, the way he's taking me,

hits my clit in the most perfect of ways, making me gasp and whimper and *need* like I've never needed before.

He can fuck me like this all night, and I'll never grow tired of being wrapped up in him—his sounds, his harsh breath, his scent—all consuming me.

"You're going to come for me," he demands as if the topic isn't up for negotiation. "All over my dick. And after that, I'm going to eat you out and fuck you again." He holds my body against his as he pumps and pumps, hitting my front wall and driving me up higher, to the point where I'm ready to break.

My hands fist up into the back of his head and I hold on, daring him with my eyes, hoping he's able to do just that.

His lips meet mine in a sloppy kiss, and something about the taste of him, the hint of bourbon and me still lingering on his tongue, how I've never had a one-night stand in my life, and how I'm fucking a total stranger I met a little more than an hour ago in a hotel room shoots me straight over the edge.

My body seizes, my pussy clenches, and a scream echoes off the walls before I realize it's mine. I don't say his name. That's too personal for me. But I come all over him as he said I would, and then I marvel at how seriously fucking hot he looks as he comes immediately after.

He collapses against me, heavy and suffocating in that really good way men seem to know how to do. His lips press into the soft space beneath my jaw, and then he pulls out of me, removes the condom, and heads to the bathroom to dispose of it.

The room is silent, the space between us a bit awkward, but before I can let that sink in, he's back and ready to start all over again, and all I can think is, thank God, I don't have to be anywhere important until tomorrow afternoon.

3

OWEN

I woke before dawn—as I do every morning—only instead of sneaking in an hour of workout before Rory wakes up, I snuck out of a dark hotel room, leaving a naked and sleeping Estlin behind. She was on her stomach, her head tilted away from me, the sheet up to her mid-back, but I found myself watching her sleep for a moment. The rise and fall of her body with her slow, even breaths. The spill of her dark hair interspersed with pink and blue strands. Eyes closed, lashes fluttering ever so slightly as if she were dreaming.

She is arrestingly beautiful, and being with her was exhilarating, heart-stoppingly pleasurable, and just... fun. A fun I haven't had in far too long. A fun that was selfish and satisfying and something I didn't want to give up in that quiet moment in the dark. I wanted to stay, slide back beneath the sheets, and do it all over again.

That thought is finally what made me pull away and leave. If I didn't leave then, I'd be more than a little tempted to stay. Knowing the right course, I dressed silently and left. But not before I took something of hers. A dirty keepsake to remind myself that last night happened, and the woman of my dreams was real.

Estlin is a young, gorgeous temptation I have no space for in my life.

But that didn't stop me from thinking about her all morning or from jerking off in the shower with her on my mind. I guess that's the nice thing about a one-night stand with a woman you'll never see again. Fantasy is safe when you know it won't lead to more.

This afternoon, Jack is coming by, and he's bringing his little sister, Eddie, for me to meet, or more like reintroduce myself to, so I can find Rory a nanny. That's where my attention needs to be. Rory needs someone consistent so I can give her structure and routine and some semblance of normal. Not something all that common when you're a single dad, hospital-based pediatric general surgeon.

As I make Rory's Mickey Mouse pancake with a smiling face made out of blueberries, that's all I'm allowing myself to be focused on.

"Can I go swimming at Katy's pool today?" Rory asks without bothering to look up at me as she plays on her iPad.

"Not today, Moonshine," I call back over my shoulder as I plate her pancake. "Tomorrow Katy is going to take you."

Katy Barrows is one of my best friends—my cousin, though not by blood—and also Rory's godmother. She had a baby a couple of months back, but whenever she can, she still tries to take Rory swimming. Swimming and generally being in any water is Rory's favorite thing on the planet, and I won't lie and deny that I love what a good swimmer Katy has made her.

Rory's lips pull to the side, but that's her only reaction of displeasure. I set the plate in front of her so she can see its shape before I start cutting it up into bite-sized pieces and then dousing it in an unhealthy amount of syrup.

"Clementine or strawberries?"

"Clementine," she answers easily as she fists her fork, spears a piece of fluffy cake, and shoves it in her mouth. I go to correct her finger positioning, but she pulls her hand away before I can even reach it. This girl is all gross motor but needs some definite work on her fine motor skills.

I peel her clementine and set it on the edge of her plate away from her pancake before I take the seat beside her at the island counter, sipping on my third cup of coffee today when I'm normally a one-to-two-cup max guy. I watch her for a moment as she eats and stares at her screen, rewatching the same *My Little Pony* video she has a million times over and feel like I'm doing everything wrong. As I have since she was a toddler and her mother left us because she decided having a kid and a husband was a real drag and interfering with her social life and her ability to become the best cardiothoracic surgeon in the country.

But she didn't just leave us.

She planned the whole thing out for well over a year before she filed for divorce, and I had no clue. She moved funds around, even dipping into a few of my personal accounts without my knowledge or consent. She had two PIs and a team of attorneys digging into me and my family, searching for anything they could. And when that turned up with nothing—I know because I had my good friend Vander and his father, Lenox, who are master hackers, dig into it—she wrote a tell-all book, claiming that I financially starved and emotionally abused her.

Thankfully, I found out about this before it went to print.

I sued the publisher, and it never saw the light of day, though some excerpts of her lies did leak to the media. The backlash was enormous, and I had to sue her for defamation of character. And while all this was going on, just to be a bitch, she fought me for sole custody of Rory when she never wanted her to begin with.

No, she needed to look like the victim as she went after my money and ruined my name. Money she wasn't going to get because of our iron-clad prenup.

She dragged both Rory—who wasn't even four at the time—and me through the mud, making our divorce as public as she could and not caring at all when the press followed us around or hounded poor Rory who was already scared and didn't understand why all of a sudden her mother decided she didn't want or love her.

Eventually, some of my ex's evil doings came to light—again, thank you, Vander and Lenox—and when everything made its way to the press along with the courts, she finally declared through her attorneys that if I paid her five million dollars, she'd quietly go away and relinquish her parental rights to Rory. I gave in just to get rid of her from our lives. Just to ensure she couldn't touch Rory ever again.

Since then, I feel like all I do is juggle life, and my baby girl gets caught in that.

Last year, the school I had her in for kindergarten was a nightmare. She hated it. Hated her teachers, her classmates, everything. And with that, she acted out. Throwing tantrums and having fights—nonphysical—with other kids. She'd cry herself to sleep and wake up angry, mean, and resentful. I put her in therapy and did everything I could to get her to open up to me, but she refused, shutting down and keeping her thoughts and feelings close to her chest.

But this is a new school year in a new school. And I'm determined to fix everything for her and get her back on track.

"The magic of friendship," she calls out along with the video.

"Hey, Moonshine, can you listen for a sec?"

She doesn't pull herself away from the screen, not even for a second. "What is it?"

I hold in my snicker. "Focus for a minute. This is important.

We're going to meet a new friend today. A new nanny for you. Remember?"

She pauses, food halfway to her mouth, and she peers over at me. The bite gets shoveled into her mouth, but I finally have her full attention.

"Her name is Eddie. She's Uncle Jack's sister. She might come and stay with us for a while and hang out with you. Some days, when I can't or Nonna and Baba can't, she'll pick you up from school and maybe make you dinner and help you with any homework you have. She'll be fun. What do you think?"

"You're just kidding, right?"

Hell. Even my upbeat tone and smile didn't sell it. I soften and lean forward, setting my coffee down on the counter. "No, sweetheart. I'm not kidding. We might have a new nanny living in our house and as part of our lives, helping to take care of you."

I get a slow, unsure blink. "She'll sleep in my room?"

I run my hand over my girl's soft blonde curls. "No, baby. She'll sleep in her own room in our house, but not far from your playroom."

Her eyes peer up at mine as she picks up a piece of blueberry with her fingers and eats it. "And she's nice?"

"I'm sure she's super nice."

"But we don't know her. What if she meets me and doesn't like me?"

It's days like these that I hate my ex-wife and all the little assholes in her kindergarten even more than I do on regular days. My daughter, who has the purest, sweetest, most face-value heart, is filled with distrust when it comes to strangers and new people after being chased around by the press for nearly a year after her mother left her.

I cup her face in my hand and make sure she's looking at me. "Rory, I'm positive she's going to love you. But if you don't like her or you don't want her to stay, then we can talk about it and try to find someone else that you do like and do want to stay."

Another slow, even blink as she considers my offer. "I guess that's okay. Can I show her my toys?"

"You can show her anything you want. I think she's an artist, so she can make art with you."

She shrugs, already moving on and back to her show. "Will I get to see baby Willow tomorrow when I go swimming with Katy?" Rory scrunches her nose. "She's so cute."

"She is, but I don't know if Katy is going to bring her along." I lean over and kiss the top of her head.

I take a sip of my coffee, hopeful this afternoon's meeting with Eddie goes well when my doorbell rings. Rory's head peers up and toward the door, but she doesn't move. I jump out of my seat, kiss her head again, and say, "Finish your lunch. I'll go see who that is," before jogging over to the door.

I check the video app on my phone and groan.

"I heard that."

I roll my eyes as I open the door, and my little sister Wren is there, her phone tucked against her ear.

"Yeah, I'm here, Mom. I'll call you back later." She presses the red end button and then gives me a look as she takes a sip of her enormous Starbucks. "Why am I just now hearing you're hiring Eddie Kincaid as your new nanny?"

"What are you doing here, Wren? I picked up Rory from your place two hours ago."

"Yeah, but you didn't tell me about this."

I step back, waving for her to come in. "I haven't hired her yet," I tell her with a tired breath as I walk back toward the kitchen.

"You know she was my best friend when we were kids, right?"

I pause and twist back to her. "Really? I didn't realize that," I admit. "Or maybe I forgot about it. You were always surrounded by eight thousand kids."

Wren huffs, tossing her long, blonde hair back. "That's because we have eight thousand cousins and family friends. Eddie was one of them. She's a couple of years younger than me."

"Great," I deadpan, continuing to the kitchen because I don't care all that much. I mean, I guess on one level, I'm glad Eddie is so interconnected to my friends and family. That's actually the only reason I've agreed to meet with her. "I need Rory to like her first before I can hire her. This was all Jack's idea. I guess Eddie was living abroad and is returning home to get back into her art, whatever that means. All Jack said was she was working as a nanny in England for the last seven months, doesn't want to live with her parents, and can meet the hours I require."

"Wow. You just really don't want to hire a nanny, do you?"

I shrug. "Not exactly, but what are my other options at this point? She needs more consistency with her days and routine. Plus, it's getting harder for her to be bounced around or have a revolving door of people. Hopefully, this Eddie will fit the bill. If she doesn't, I'll interview someone else."

"*This Eddie*?" Wren grabs the back of my shirt, stopping me before I reach my kitchen. "You're such a jerk," she grouses. "You can't be like that with her, or she won't want to accept the position and live here with you."

I grunt. "That's not me being a jerk." I swat her hand away. "That's me taking care of my kid. She's my priority, not Jack or you or even Eddie."

She shakes her head. "I love Rory more than I love myself, and I'm glad you're finally agreeing to hire someone."

"But?" I press when she ends it there because I can tell one is coming.

She tosses her hands up. "But nothing. I just don't want you to be... *you* to my friend."

"*Your friend*?" I scoff sarcastically. "When was the last time you talked to her?"

"I don't know. A year and a half ago, maybe? She was still living in Paris, but I heard she moved to London for a while. Still, just because I haven't talked to her in a while doesn't mean I don't care about her."

I fold my arms over my chest, staring my sister down. She's young and wears her heart on her sleeve in the form of worrying about everyone. "What, Wren? Why are you all defensive over her?"

"Because I care about her, and I care about Rory." She sighs and shifts her weight, staring down at the floor. "I want you to hire someone because I agree Rory needs it at this point. I love the idea of you hiring Eddie—or should I say Estlin since her middle name is the one she likes to go by now—so I want it to work out with the two of you because I think she'd be a perfect nanny for Rory. Promise me you'll try to keep an open mind about her. And that you'll try not to be short or gruff with her the way you can be with people."

Wren keeps going on, but I stopped listening like ten sentences ago. I blink. Then I blink again, glaring at my little sister as if she has fifty heads and all of them are speaking Icelandic.

No. I must have misheard.

It's impossible.

Jack would have said something if his little sister was supposed to be at the same bar we were last night. It can't be the same person. I just have her on my mind, is all.

I clear my throat. "What did you say her new name is?"

Wren rolls her eyes as if she's once again a teenager, and I'm far too adult to comprehend her. "It's her middle name. She's been going by it for years because, legit, what sort of parent names their little girl *Eddie*? I don't care if she's named after Edgar Degas and Edward Cummings. She's not a Cullen, but even then, that was a guy. I've always been team Edward."

"Huh?" I spit out, nonplussed. "Wren, what the hell are you saying? Her name isn't Edward or even Edgar. It's Eddie."

She waves me away. "Nothing. Ignore me. Estlin's family still calls her Eddie, and she's fine with that if that's what you're going to do."

"*Estlin*," I repeat. "You're positive that's her name?" Because I feel like I'm about to throw up or possibly pass out. It can't be the same woman I slept with last night.

"Yes. That's not exactly a name you hear all that often. Why?"

Oh fuck. Just... *fuck!* This can't be happening. Only the sick churning of my stomach is telling me otherwise. I lick my lips as my heart starts to pound a vicious torrent of blood through my veins. I can't catch my breath, and I take a step back, my hands dragging through my hair.

There's no way I slept with my best friend's little sister and the woman I'm about to hire to be my daughter's nanny. Right?

Jesus. How could I have done this? And what the hell do I do about it now?

"It's a strange name, is all." I puff out a breath, feeling like a miserable bastard. Even more of a miserable bastard than I normally feel like. "What happens if I don't hire her?"

Wren's light eyebrows pinch. "Why wouldn't you hire her?"

"I don't know her all that well."

She looks at me like I'm a moron. "Except she's Jack's sister and my childhood friend."

Wren's hands go to her hips, her expression fierce and determined. "She's not the sort of person to care about your money or fame. She dated a very famous, wealthy artist in Paris for years. She's an artist, Owen. A seriously talented one, like her mother. Rory loves art. Think of how good this could be for her."

"Right. For Rory." I lick my suddenly dry lips and try to swallow past the drought plaguing my esophagus. *Fuck!* I'm screwed. So screwed.

I can't have her be Rory's nanny. I can't have her live in my house. I can't pretend like I didn't spend all last night fucking her into multiple orgasms and watching as she came all over my mouth, fingers, and cock before falling asleep beside her. I said things to her. Dirty things. And I did those dirty things too. I told her I'd make her sore today and fuck me for wondering if I succeeded.

Did she know who I was?

Was all this some sort of game to her? That brings on a fresh wave of nausea.

If Jack finds out I slept with his little sister, he'll kill me. Rightfully so, because if it were reversed, I'd kill him if he ever laid a hand on Wren. Jesus.

"Are you okay?" Wren asks. "You're pale and... sweating." She scrunches her nose at that last one.

Am I okay? No. I'm anything but okay.

Before I can manage any sort of reply, the doorbell rings, and my heart plummets to my feet.

4

ESTLIN

The front door of the massive brick house in Brookline swings open, and just as I plaster on my professional smile, a tall, thin woman leaps out and practically tackles me to the ground. Her arms wrap around my neck, her legs around my waist, and her momentum forces me to take three steps back, and even then, I'm only saved by Jack putting his large hand on my back and stopping us.

"Oh my God! I can't believe you moved back to Boston and didn't tell me!" Wren screeches in my ear, hugging me fiercely.

A huge laugh catapults from my lips, and I squeeze her back just as staunchly. "Because last I talked to you, you were living in Seattle."

Wren pulls back and climbs off of me with a gleaming smile on her lips, all her pearly white teeth showing and reflecting off the afternoon sun. "I moved back here last year for medical school. I'm so fucking happy to see you. We're going to have to get coffee, or better yet drinks, and catch up. I missed you. And I can't believe you're going to be working for my older brother."

"Same. I missed—" I pause and tilt my head. "Wait. What?

Your older brother?" Come to think of it, what the hell is Wren doing here?

Wren belts out a *don't be ridiculous* laugh. "Yes. You're going to be the nanny for my niece, Rory."

"Huh?" Her brother? I squint at her and then turn to Jack. "You didn't tell me it was..." I trail off as a thousand sharp pieces cut into my brain so fast that I suddenly feel like I'm bleeding out all over the walkway. Owen Fritz. Wren's older brother is Owen Fritz. His name is freaking *Owen*.

"Didn't tell you what?" Jack asks.

"Uh." Only I can't answer him because suddenly, I'm locked in a standoff with the deep blue, wildly unhappy eyes of the man watching us from just inside the doorway. And yep, they're the same blue eyes—even if now they're covered by glasses— attached to the same man I shamelessly flirted with and then allowed to take me to a hotel and fuck me all night.

Jack goes in for a bro hug with Owen. "Good to see you, man. It's been too long." He slaps Owen's back, but neither Owen nor I can look away from each other.

My head spins, and a weird, almost hysterical laugh threatens. Because what are the freaking odds of this? My first one-night stand ever, and it was with my brother's best friend and my potential new boss. Life has a sense of irony, I'll give it that.

"Hi, Jack," Wren practically shouts at his back since he plowed right past her without even so much as acknowledging her.

"Hi, Wren," Jack replies in a barely polite, monotone way. Jack never liked Wren. I remember that now. He always thought she was childish and bratty. Then again, I believe Owen thought the same about me when I was twelve and he was twenty-four. Since that's how old I was the last time I saw him. Ten years ago. Well, if you're not counting last night, of course.

"You didn't tell me it was Owen Fritz I'd be the nanny for," I accuse, starting to shake as a steady dose of flight or fight—I'm definitely leaning toward flight—adrenaline surges through me.

"Yes, I did." Jack throws his arm over Owen's shoulder, all buddy-buddy.

I shake my head, positive he didn't. "No. You said it was a good friend of yours. You gave me no details beyond that other than about the little girl."

And I didn't ask because I didn't care all that much. I was busy packing and leaving the family I had lived with for the last seven months in London—the family who saved me when I needed to be saved.

So I didn't ask for details.

Knowing the single dad was good friends with Jack was good enough for me because Jack would never have me live in a situation that wasn't safe or a good fit for me.

"Is that a problem for you?" Owen asks, his voice low and cool. Possibly a bit angry or resentful. "That I'm Owen Fritz?"

I laugh. It's awkward as hell. "No. Just that you're Owen when I didn't know you were going to be Owen." I laugh again and scrub my hands up and down my face. I need to pull myself together before people catch on that I'm acting weird. Well, weirder than I normally do. "Sorry, I didn't mean for that to come out sounding the way it did. I just didn't know it was going to be you is all, and I was surprised."

He doesn't respond. He just turns and heads into his house, and Wren glares daggers into her brother's back before giving me a sheepish grin. "Sorry. He's... well, he can be a bit grumpy. Come in and meet Rory, since she's the important one."

Before I can protest, Wren grabs my hand and hauls me inside the enormous mansion without allowing me to take in any of the gorgeous details like the dark hardwood floors, arched doorways, abundance of windows and light, and crown moldings. Oh, or the piano in the sprawling formal living room.

Nope. Wren's grip is no joke. To the point where she whisks

us past Owen and Jack, only to have my arm grabbed by a strong hand, bringing me to an abrupt stop.

"I was thinking you and I should talk a bit in private first. Before you meet my daughter."

Wren slays him a pointed look, her eyes wide as if she's trying to convey something Owen isn't the least bit interested in acknowledging.

I nod because I'd like a word with him too.

Reluctantly, Wren releases my hand. "Be nice," she warns Owen, and then marches off for the kitchen, leaving Jack behind.

"I'll just follow after Wren and say hi to Rory. And what Wren said. Be nice. That goes for both of you." Jack raises an eyebrow at me, and I give him my *I'll be on my best behavior* smile that I'm pretty sure he can read through, but excuses himself regardless, clearly aware that there's already tension, but wisely choosing not to engage in it.

The moment they're out of sight, Owen uses the unrelenting hand he has on my arm to lead me back toward the front of the house and into that open living room I was initially eyeing. He has a painting over the large, stone fireplace that I instantly recognize as my mother's. I walk over to it and peer up, taking in the strong brushstrokes and use of color.

"Your mom gave it to me as a gift when Rory was born," he says from behind me.

Of course she did. That's how my mother operates. Something that should have been so easy—such a no-brainer of a situation—is now impossibly complicated.

"It's beautiful," I murmur because all of my mother's work is. I've spent my life trying to crawl out from beneath her shadow and forge a name of my own in the art world, only to have my ex fill my head with years of professional and personal self-doubt. Now I finally feel like I've put his ghost to rest, and I wonder if I truly set myself free, if I'm capable of creating something as beautiful.

It's been too long since I attempted it because what happened in Paris with Claude destroyed me and my confidence. It was easier to hide behind the two small children I was nannying for than to force myself to paint when painting felt impossible. I'm hoping that's changed. I'm hoping I can find this part of myself again.

I turn around and face Owen, his hard eyes on me. He pushes up the nose of his glasses, and why does he have to wear glasses? They're nerdy and stupidly sexy.

"I didn't know it was you, and Jack never said a thing to me about you coming out last night. I was supposed to meet him there, and when he texted to say he wasn't going to be able to make it, I texted back and told him I was going to head home and that I'd see him this morning."

He sighs, his gaze shifting to the rug. "He didn't tell me you were going to be there either. My guess is he was trying to arrange a more casual meet and greet since he knows I'm on edge about hiring a nanny." His voice is so cold, so detached. So unlike the man I met last night. But that was Owen, and this is Owen Fritz, and I'm starting to realize that distinction is everything.

I nod and walk over to the piano, running my hand along the smooth, black wood. My fingers press in on a couple of the keys, happy to find it perfectly in tune. Anything to distract myself from the man watching my every move like he can't quite decide what he wants to do with me. I'm in his house, in his space, and this was never supposed to happen.

Hell, I was never supposed to see him again. I liked that about him. What I don't like is pairing this Owen—the one who comes with my brother and his sister and my entire fucking family—with memories I was anxious to keep while wiping out others.

His hands meet his hips, and I can feel his frustration. It's practically seeping from his pores. "I knew you as Eddie, not Estlin."

"And I haven't thought about you since I was a kid, and even then, not a lot," I admit, turning back to him with an indifferent shrug. "Back then, I didn't care about Jack's friends. You were all a lot older than me and didn't exactly pay me much attention. We didn't know who the other was last night, and there's nothing we can do about that now."

He takes a deliberate step forward. "Except I can't hire you to be Rory's nanny."

Even though I already figured he'd say that, it hurts that he's so quick to dismiss me just because we slept together.

I wanted this job.

Badly.

I don't want to live at home—my parents will be all over me, checking on me, analyzing my every move and word, treating me like the child they still view me as. And while I know it comes from a place of love, in the five days I've been back, it's already too much. I've been living on my own for the last five years, so moving back in with my parents is the farthest thing from ideal. My art—*please, dear God*—will take up the majority of the mornings and early afternoons, which makes finding a job other than waitressing or bartending difficult, and even those jobs wouldn't be enough to afford a safe place in the city. Plus, I love being a nanny. I love being around children and helping to care for them.

It's what got me through the last seven months.

My parents already paid for me to attend college abroad, and I swore after that, I'd never take another cent from them again. More than that, I need to prove to them and myself that I've got this. That I can do this on my own. Room and board as a nanny were a perfect situation.

I close my eyes for a moment and swallow a heavy breath. "Why not?"

He gives me a *don't be ridiculous* look. "You know why not. You can't move in here. You can't sleep down the hall."

"It didn't mean anything," I find myself protesting with a deeply annoyed scowl now marring my face.

"That doesn't matter. Sleeping together was an undeniably forbidden line that never should have been crossed. One that will always sit between us."

I shake my head, aggravated by that. I was counting on this.

"If Jack ever found out—"

"He wouldn't," I interject. "I'd never tell him. Or Wren."

He sighs plaintively. "I'm sorry, but I don't see how this will work."

The way he says that, so pompous and arrogant, so proud and hastily harsh—it rips at me. It fills me with a helplessness I can't handle.

"So that's it?" I snap. "I thought this was supposed to be about your daughter, not you."

His eyes narrow, and he takes another sharp step in my direction, watching me with a guarded expression. "This is about my daughter—"

I snort derisively. "Oh, right. I can see that." I cut our distance by half, ready to strangle him where he stands. "Since I haven't even met her yet."

Fury bubbles beneath his surface, but he quickly reins it in. "Fine. You're right. This is about me. I don't want you living here. I don't want you working here. Last night was... well, it was a mistake, and it never should have happened. But it's not something we can undo, and you living here will be a constant reminder of that."

Hurt flashes through my chest at him calling it a mistake, but I shove that aside and press on. "It's not something that will happen again. It was sex, Owen. Just sex. We're both adults, and since it was such a *mistake*, we won't have to worry about a repeat."

That hits something in him, and suddenly he's right in front of me, grabbing my shoulders and forcing my neck to crane until I meet his flustered eyes. "What do you want me to say? That I enjoyed it?"

I squint at him. "Oh, I know you did. Hell, you stole my fucking panties, didn't you?" I bluster out a breath, trying to calm myself down. "I don't care if you did steal them or even if you enjoyed it. For me, it was merely scratching an itch."

He smirks tauntingly. "Christ, you're so young."

His eyes rove over me, and then his face dips until it's inches from mine. My belly hiccups into my chest, and I fight the urge to bite my lip to cut this tension swirling between us. What is it about this man that makes my heart race and my knees weak? I can't handle how intense this is, how I react so quickly to him when all we did was spend one night together.

"Yes, I enjoyed it," he whispers, practically against my lips. "I enjoyed every second of it, as I know you did. That's the problem. We enjoyed it. A lot. Fucking you was incredible, but it was also a mistake because now here you are, standing in my living room, and we're forced to have this conversation."

My breath hitches, and I clear it, only I know he heard it. I press on. "You're the one making more out of this than we need to."

"Am I? What do you want me to do?" He flexes his strong, irritated jaw before he blows out a silent breath. As if coming to his senses, he straightens and releases me. It doesn't matter. I feel the imprint of his hands on my skin. That should be a warning, but I won't allow it to be.

I meant what I said. It won't happen again.

"Hire me," I throw back at him.

"How can I hire you after what happened between us? How can we go from that beginning to anything else? I don't bring complications or drama into my daughter's life because her life has been nothing but that, and you are a fucking complication and a hell of a lot of drama I cannot afford."

His breath comes out in rushed pants, his chest practically against mine. He's pleading with me to see his side of this, but his side is not a luxury I have at the moment.

"I won't be a complication, and I tend to be very little drama. I don't want that either. I'm not looking to start anything with you or anyone else. We can put it behind us and act like it never happened. Last night we were two different people, but last night is over." He may look the same and, well, smell the same. His whole house smells like him, actually, and it's just as heavenly as it was last night, but the man standing before me is different, and that's what I'll focus on.

Not the way he's breathing fire down at me or the heat and size of his body when he stands this close. Not how when I woke up alone in those twisted sheets this morning, I had to make myself come because I couldn't get the flashbacks from the night before out of my head.

Last night was everything I wanted and needed it to be, and it seriously sucks that the one who gave it to me would be my new boss. It'll be impossible to forget how he kissed me like he was dying for it. Like he couldn't get enough. But I'll deal with it like I deal with everything else that I have to.

"If it weren't for last night, is there one real reason why you wouldn't hire me?"

It's the last card I've got. Because the truth is, he's all but painted into a corner with this, and I have no issues throwing that in his face.

"Jack is your friend. Wren is mine. You know my parents and my family as I know yours. Ultimately, you can do whatever you want. She's your daughter. But you'll need to come up with a damn good reason for not hiring me."

"Fuck," he bites out, running his hands up his face and

through his hair. He knows I'm right. "This is a bad idea, Estlin. A seriously bad idea. Nothing good will come of this."

I put my hand on his arm and immediately retract it when I feel his hot, smooth skin over strong, perfectly honed muscles. That wasn't a good idea. Not at all.

Note to self, don't touch my new boss. Anywhere.

"Listen, just let me meet Rory. That's all I'm asking for. If it's not a good fit after that, then fine. I'll go and you'll never have to see me again. But if it is, if she likes me..." I trail off, letting that hang in the air between us.

He licks his lips, his gaze hot and locked on mine. "You really want this job?"

I stare straight back up at him. "I really want this job. You notwithstanding."

"I don't like this."

"Get over it."

His eyebrows hit his hairline, and an incredulous chuckle bursts from his chest. "Get over it?"

I shrug. "I mean, I realize I'm incredible in bed, but yeah. Get over it. You were just okay, by the way. In case you were curious."

His lips twitch, and he shakes his head. "I'll make your life hell. I'll make you want to quit."

"Meeting you again today, I have no doubt that's true. I don't like you all that much right now either. That doesn't mean I'll let you succeed."

After an endless minute of inner conflict, he loses the battle with himself and grunts. "Fine. Come meet Rory, and then we'll see. No promises."

5

———

OWEN

The woman already drives me crazy. She gets under my skin and fights back at me in a way no one other than my family ever does. Now, we're stuck in this mess, and this mess has the power to consume us both. Why she wants this job, I don't understand. There have to be plenty of other nanny jobs she could find. Why does she have to want this one badly enough to fight me for it?

"Did you make them disappear so you wouldn't have to hire me?" she poses when we reach the kitchen and find it empty. Rory cleared her plate, her dish on the counter by the sink.

"If only it were that simple to get rid of you."

The edges of her mouth soften and tilt up into an alluring smile. "Nothing about me is that simple or easy," she retorts cheekily. "You might as well start getting used to that now."

I grunt. I'm starting to learn that the hard way. I loved the image of her I saved strictly for my fantasies. She was safe there, and I had plans to keep her there for some time. Except now everything is different, and I cannot give what happened between us any room to move or breathe within me.

Last night died the moment I learned she was my best friend's little sister.

That's how this has to go.

"Speaking of being easy, do I get my panties back, thief?"

"I don't know what you're talking about."

She gives me a side-eye. "Hmm." Surprisingly, she lets it go at that, staring around the kitchen and down into the great room beyond. "Not that I want to compliment you, because I don't, but your home is extraordinarily beautiful. I love the architecture. All the rich, classical lines mixed with modern elements are stunning."

I think so too. It's why I bought it. But I don't bother telling her that or even thanking her for the compliment. "We should find Rory and get this over with."

It doesn't take long for me to guess they're upstairs in Rory's playroom. I can hear the thumping and banging through the ceiling, which tells me Rory is doing cartwheels.

"Follow me," I grind out, heading toward the back stairs that wind up to that side of the second floor. And just as I suspected, the moment I enter the playroom, Rory does a cartwheel straight over to me and then jumps, forcing me to catch her in my arms only to immediately wiggle out and go to her kitchen play area.

"Everything okay?" Jack asks, sitting on the sofa, legs crossed, his phone in his hand resting against his knee. Wren is at the art table, sitting on the bench seat that lines the back windows, her face and body angled toward the patio, grounds, and swimming pool beyond. It's oddly silent and tense in here other than Rory, who seems to have already played with one of every toy she has in here.

"Just getting to know each other," Estlin explains with a chipper smile. "We were going over some of the finer details of what we can expect from each other if this works out." She throws me a saccharine-sweet smile.

"And did you come to an arrangement?" Jack persists, looking hopeful.

"Not yet," I answer before Estlin can. "I have my reservations."

Both Jack and Wren roll their eyes at me.

"You always do," Wren accuses caustically. "How about you give your perpetual need for control and general dic—grumpy disposition an Ativan and just go with it for once?"

I open my mouth to lay into my little sister when Rory takes me by surprise and comes right up to Estlin. "Hi," she says.

Estlin bends until she's eye level with Rory. "Hey. I'm Estlin. You must be Owen."

Rory cracks a smile. "No. I'm Rory."

"Oh!" Estlin doinks her forehead with the butt of her hand. "Rory is a much better name than Owen." She throws me a cheeky grin and then leans into Rory, whispering conspiratorially in her ear. "My real name is Eddie." She pulls back, her face pinching up as if it's a bad word.

"Eddie? That's a boy's name."

Estlin laughs, her arms flailing about her. "I know! My mom named me after a poet and an artist. Both of them were boys."

"I thought you said your name is Estlin."

"That's my middle name. But you can call me either one you like."

"I like Estlin."

"Me too." She reaches her fist out, and Rory gives her a pound before she stands to her full height and looks around the room. "This is an amazing playroom, Rory. I have to say, I'm jealous you have a whole art space to yourself."

"You could use it too. If you lived here."

Hell. Did she have to just say that? I can feel Wren's smug grin from across the room, and I don't even bother looking over at Jack. Rory likes her. Of course she does because what's not to like? Estlin is young and beautiful and obviously good with kids.

There's no way I'll get out of hiring her. I'm not sure I could have even before she met Rory.

Estlin's eyes light up and she gives Rory a beaming smile. "Really? Wow. Thank you. An artist's space is a sacred place, so I appreciate your offering to share yours with me. I love art. It's sort of my thing."

"I like swimming and gymnastics."

Estlin meanders her way around the room, taking everything in. "I like those too. I could tell you like gymnastics because you did that perfect cartwheel when I came in. Do you take lessons?"

"On Thursdays," Rory hums with exuberance. "And I go swimming with my godmother Katy a lot."

"Cool stuff." Estlin turns back to her and skips right over to her. "I have a godmother too. You know her. Her name is Rina."

Rory's eyes light up, and she looks up at me and then back at Estlin. "My aunt Rina?"

Estlin nods her head. "Yes. Isn't that funny?"

Rory licks her lips and goes over and takes Estlin's hand, then walks her toward the back window.

"Still having those reservations?" Jack asks dryly.

I flip him off since Rory's back is to me as she shows Estlin the pool we have in our backyard.

"It's heated so the water is always warm. Do you want to go swimming? We could invite Katy and baby Willow to come. That's Katy's new baby. She's only two months old. She loves me a lot. I got her first smile."

Rory continues to tell Estlin all about baby Willow, and I sigh, my chest so tight it's impossible to breathe. Outside of my family, Rory hasn't taken to anyone since her mother left.

I don't know what to do with this. I already feel guilty just looking at Jack, but Estlin swore she'd never tell him or Wren.

It'd be our secret. Our past. One we'd never mention again.

But hiring her means moving her in here. Having her sleep down the hall from me. She'll cook in my kitchen and watch television in my media room. And I'll... I don't know. Keep my distance as best I can. Stay as professional as I can. Look at and treat Estlin as a nanny and nothing more. Forget all about the woman I met last night.

Yes. All of those things.

While pretending she's not the most stunning creature I've ever seen.

It all sounds so easy when I know it would be anything but.

"I think swimming would be so fun!" Wren exclaims, snapping me out of my thoughts. "Right, Owen?"

"What?" I scratch the back of my head.

"Rory wants to have Katy and her fiancé, Bennett over to swim and hang out. We can all barbecue. Oh, and have margaritas. I bet we can even get Katy to pump and dump. Lord knows that woman could use a drink."

"Uh." I shake my head, trying to take in what Wren just said. "Yeah. I guess we could."

Because I wouldn't mind talking to Katy about this. Not Bennett, though. Although I do trust Bennett, he's friends with Jack, and not only do I not want to put him in that position, if he ever accidentally slipped anything to him, I'd be a dead man. Plus, Wren is right that Katy could use a margarita and a break from her house. She's hardly left since the baby was born.

"Do you want to?" I ask Rory. "I can call Katy and see if they're busy."

"Yes!" Rory jumps up and down like the floor is made of lava. "You can come swimming with me and meet Katy and baby Willow too?" she says to Estlin, who suddenly looks unsure.

"I'd like to see baby Willow too," Jack offers, pulling himself off the sofa and joining Estlin and Rory at the window. "Bennett is my friend from way back, believe it or not."

"Perfect! Let's do it. I'll call Katy now," Wren says to me. "I need to run home and grab some swimsuits. Estlin, you can borrow one of mine."

Something quick flashes across Estlin's face. "Um. I don't think anything you have will fit me."

"Nonsense." Wren waves that away as she heads for the door. "I have one that I think will work perfectly. Rory loves to swim. Don't you, Moonshine? It'll be fun. I'll be back in like twenty minutes." Wren leaves without giving anyone else a chance to argue about any of this. The decision is made. And if I know Wren, which I do, she's already calling Katy before she even gets out the front door.

Jack whispers something in Estlin's ear that has her chewing on her lip.

What am I missing? "Do you not swim?"

She looks back at me. "I swim. I just… usually prefer to wear one of my suits." She clears her throat, evening out her features. "It'll be fine, though. If Rory loves to swim, I'd love to swim with her. And meet Katy and baby Willow."

"I could run home and grab you one," Jack offers, and still, I feel like I'm missing something. Estlin didn't seem the slightest bit self-conscious about her body last night—not that she should be. Her body is fucking perfect, curves and all—but I can't think of anything else it could be.

"I left them all in Paris," she answers quietly, and Jack continues to stare at her as if he's about to whisk her out of here.

"I could go buy you one."

My brows scrunch. What in the hell?

"Really," Estlin assures him. "It's all good."

"You're sure?" Jack checks.

She forces a smile, urging him to drop whatever this is. "Positive."

"What am I missing?" I finally ask.

"I want to go swimming now!" Rory races over to me, calling the attention back on herself as she tears off her dress, chucks it at me to catch it, and then immediately takes off for her room down the hall.

I drag my hand through my hair, not thrilled about any of this, but it seems the plans are already in motion.

"She likes me," Estlin calls to my back as I head for the door. "She wants me to stay and go swimming with her. She wants me to meet Katy and baby Willow and she offered to share her art space with me. Artists don't do that with just anyone."

"She's six, Estlin. Let's see how the rest of the afternoon goes."

"I forgot what a dick you can be," Jack states. "Part of me gets it. She's your kid, and you've both been through it. But Eddie's right. Rory likes her, and at some point, you need to get over your shit and trust people again."

I turn back to them, knowing they're already hiding something from me, and say, "When people are fully honest and not trying to have secret conversations right in front of my face, then maybe I will."

Without another word about it, I follow after Rory.

"What suit are you wearing, kiddo?" I ask as I enter her room and shut the door behind us.

"The shell one." She's already digging through her drawer, searching for her favorite mermaid bathing suit.

"Go potty first," I tell her, taking the suit from her hands.

She nods and races into her bathroom, partially shutting the door behind her. I sit on the edge of her bed, knees parted, elbows digging into my thighs, staring down at the floor. I pull off my glasses and let them dangle from my fingers for a moment before I put them back on. Here goes nothing.

"What do you think of her?"

I hear the toilet flush and the water turn on as she washes her hands. A second later, she comes out and stands expectantly in front of me, waiting for me to help her put on her suit.

"She's pretty and has pretty hair. I like the pink and blue. And she has an earring in her nose. Can I do that too?"

I shake my head. "No. Definitely not." I adjust the straps on her shoulders. "Not until you're thirty. At least." I pull her little body on my lap and wrap my arms around her. "Moonshine, other than her being pretty and you liking her hair and nose ring, do you like *her*?"

I try to keep myself neutral, but even I can hear the hope she'll say no in my voice.

She searches my face, a frown tilting down the corners of her lips. "Do you not like her?"

Shit. I'm fucking this all up. And I need to stop. Estlin was right. It's about Rory, not about me. My distrust is too high. My lack of desire to bring someone into our home is even more so. I realize now that I had already decided, even before I knew it was Estlin and not Eddie, that I didn't want to hire someone.

It opens us up. It makes us vulnerable. And I swore I'd always protect my little girl after what her mother did to her.

But that's not what I'm doing right now.

I'm making her life harder because of my own mental hang-ups. I was taught growing up that being a Fritz is tricky. That people can be wolves in sheep's clothing and that our money and fame make us automatic targets for people to use and take advantage of. I didn't believe it so much. I had only surrounded myself with trusted family and friends.

And then I met, fell in love with, and married the wrong woman, and for the first time, I saw it all clear as day, in the most horrific of ways. But that's not everyone, and in truth, I don't think that's Estlin. I don't think that's why she's here or why she wants this job.

I clear my throat and tell my little girl, "I don't know her well yet. We just met her. But if you like her, I like her."

"I like her. She's fun."

I pull her into my chest and hug her tight, kissing the top of her head. "Okay. Then we'll spend more time with her today and see if she's the right person to be your nanny." And the Estlin I met last night will fade into oblivion. She'll no longer exist, and neither will that night.

"Do you think Katy will like her?"

That drags a reluctant smile to my lips. "I have a feeling Katy will love her."

"Good." Rory jumps off my lap. "Then I want to keep her as my nanny."

With that declaration, she swings her door open and races down the back stairs heading for the kitchen and the door that leads out to the pool. She won't go out without me, and even if she does, the gate alarm is on, and she hates the noise it makes.

I give myself a minute to wrap my head around the fact that I'm likely going to be inviting this woman into my home, into my life, and into my daughter's life, and once I think I'm somewhat resigned to it, I follow after Rory. Determined to make her happy, no matter the cost.

6

ESTLIN

Owen hates me. And he doesn't want me to be his daughter's nanny. The defiant part of me wants to keep pushing him. Wants to keep challenging him. I like his daughter, so there's that part of it too. But maybe it's best if I cut my losses. Forget about him altogether. Find a different job somewhere less... complicated.

"You should tell him," Jack suggests, and I sigh. I had a feeling he was going to go there after what Owen said before he left the room. All over a stupid bathing suit. There's no way anything Wren has will fit me, and Jack is turning my lack of suit into a fishing expedition.

My asshat of a brother whispered in my ear, "Does this make you uncomfortable?" Yes, I'm a lot bigger than Wren. Yes, my ex spoke badly about my curves to the woman he had just fucked, and I overheard it all. Yes, it sucks, and it tore me apart. I don't want to wear Wren's bathing suit, but it's not because I'll feel fat in it. Only Jack's worried it is.

"I don't want to tell him. It's none of his business, and he's not exactly giving me the warm and fuzzies to open up to him and bare my soul. Besides, I don't see how that side of my past is relevant to anything that has to do with him or being a nanny for his daughter." I smack his arm lightly. "And, dude, you all need to stop harping on it and making it a thing."

"I'm not."

I glare, folding my arms over my chest. "Does this make you uncomfortable?" I mock him. "What am I missing?" I mix it up to Owen's deep voice. "For real? It's a bathing suit. If I don't want to wear it, I won't. But now it's a thing."

"It's been a thing, Eddie. It's been a thing for the last seven months. You just won't talk about it or deal with it the way you should."

I roll my eyes. "First, that's not true. Second, not everyone copes the way you want them to. Sometimes people have their own process for healing, and it doesn't always fit into a neat little box of should and should not. Third, what happened with me and Claude has nothing to do with the fact that I don't want to wear one of Wren's bathing suits."

"I'm happy to hear that because you're beautiful, and a man should never make you feel otherwise. But it does have to do with you and Claude because you currently don't own a bathing suit because you left them all in Paris. All I'm saying is none of us saw you after it happened because you wouldn't come home, and you wouldn't let us come visit you. Do you know what that was like for us? To know what the man you'd been living with for over three years did to you and your work, and then not be allowed to see you?"

I was hiding. Okay, I admit that. I was hiding from them—especially my artist mother. Hiding from the world a bit because I felt horribly and indescribably betrayed and emotionally gutted to a degree I didn't know was possible. I didn't know how to cope, let alone go back to making art.

I also didn't trust Claude.

I left without a word or even taking my stuff, and he wasn't the sort of man to just let that go. I didn't want my family involved, and frankly, I needed some time and space to wrap my head around everything.

"I was working as a nanny and living with a family in London. Plus, I didn't want the faces. The sad, pitying eyes. The questions. I needed to sort through it in my own way and continue living my life."

"Except you didn't. You stopped living your life and turned your back on your talent."

I squint at him. "Really, Jack? Really? This is the conversation we're having right this very second in someone else's home when I'm here to apply for a job?"

He holds up a consolatory hand. "Fine. I'm sorry. I didn't mean to make you defensive about it. We just love you and want to be there for you. You've been home five days and already itching to move out."

I shift my weight and fold my arms. "Because you guys are all the fuck over me, not giving me any room to move or breathe without a mental health check or asking when I'm going to start working again. Art isn't like working in a factory, and Mom should understand that better than anyone."

"You can't outrun it."

I roll my eyes derisively, so done with this I can hardly stand it. "Slow your sanctimonious ass down there, Dr. Phil. I'm not running. I trusted the wrong man, and it's done. I haven't seen him or spoken to him since. I've moved on and am trying to start the next chapter of my life. That's what I'm doing now, and I wish you'd all let me do it and make decisions for myself. I'm not a child anymore."

He grunts. It's hard for him to understand that, and I get it. He's twelve years older than I am and has always seen me as a little girl. Plus, I did push everyone away. My castle crumbled in an instant, and everything I thought I was so sure of was gone. When that happens, all you can do is burrow down deep and rebuild your fortress, but in doing that, sometimes you block out the ones you love who try to help along with everyone and everything else.

"I'll back off. Okay?" He dips his head and meets my eyes. "You're right. You're an adult and you seem to be doing okay."

"I am." For the most part. I still haven't picked up a paintbrush or a piece of clay, but we'll get there. Progress is still progress, even if it's measured in baby steps and not miles.

He stares down at the floor. "That point aside, I still think you should tell Owen. You were living abroad and didn't know all that happened with his ex-wife."

I shrug. "So?"

"So do me a favor and Google it because even talking about what she did to him and Rory makes me feel dirty and like shit. That's how bad it was for them. You've been betrayed, but so has he. Trust isn't something he fucks around with, and bringing someone into his home to help take care of his daughter is about the most serious and difficult thing he's done since his ex. All I'm saying is, if you want this job, you need to earn his trust and be honest with him."

"He only thinks I'm hiding something now because of you. He's also my boss, not my lover or therapist. If you want him to know so badly, then you tell him."

"You know I won't break your trust like that. Just think about it."

I sigh again. It's heavier. A bit resigned. What happened to me isn't a secret, necessarily. But it's also not the sort of thing I love being broadcast. I don't like talking about it. I don't like thinking about it.

But I get his point. Trust is slippery on the best of terms in the best of situations, and this is anything but.

"I'll think about telling him. But if he's not planning on hiring me anyway, there's no point."

Jack and I head downstairs to find Rory jumping by the back door, yelling for Owen. "Dad! Come on!"

"I'm coming," I hear him call back to her, his footsteps heavy as he comes from some backroom off the kitchen. If I move in here, I'm going to need a map to help me get around. He changed into black swim trunks, a white T-shirt, and flip-flops, and is holding several towels in his arms. "Catch." He tosses a towel at Rory, and it hits her right in the face, making her crack up.

"Hey!"

"I said catch," he teases.

"That was too fast."

"Then next time you have to be faster."

She blows a raspberry at him, and he blows one right back. Their interactions are cute, and I can tell they have a good relationship. It softens me a bit toward him. Especially after what Jack just mentioned about his ex.

"I have a set of trunks for you if you want," he informs Jack, nodding over to a small table by the back door.

"Perfect. Thanks. I'll go change and meet you out there." He checks with me, and I give him a nod. I love my brother, and we're close now that we're both adults, but he's still very much my big brother, and it can be a lot, for the same reason I don't want to live at home.

"Hold these?" Owen asks, not exactly giving me a choice, as he shoves about ten towels into my arms until they partially block my vision. I make a noise but don't say anything. Instead, I adjust the towels in my arms so I can see again. A loud click is followed by a bang, and then he's sliding the back door open. "Wait!" he orders as we all start to head out onto the back patio. "You have to wait for me to open the gate."

Rory harrumphs, impatiently jumping beside the tall, wrought iron fence. Owen hands her a pair of pink goggles and then flips open a hidden lid on top of the gate and punches in a code on the keypad. Once it chimes with a flashing green light, Rory pulls the gate door, tosses on her goggles mid-stride, and then dives headfirst into the deep end of the large, in-ground pool.

"Here," Owen offers, taking the towels back from my hands and setting them down on the loungers that surround the pool. His grounds are just as massive as his house is. Private and sprawling and beautifully landscaped. My parents have money, and I grew up around the Fritz family, so I'm no stranger to their enormous wealth. But it's been a while since I've experienced it firsthand, and wow. Just wow.

The backyard has a large, green lawn with a playscape, a treehouse, a trampoline, a built-in stone firepit surrounded by eight Adirondack chairs, an outdoor kitchen with a bar area, a barbecue, a seating area that's big enough to seat at least twelve, and a pool area that also has a hot tub attached. And that's just what I can see. The lawn beyond this area goes on and on and cuts into a surrounding forest.

"Have a seat," he offers, pointing to the one beside his, even though I'm still busy taking in the grounds.

Rory's head pops up, and she starts splashing around, talking to herself, and acting something out as if she's deep in a fantasy roleplay.

He leans back on his chaise, legs crossed at the ankles kicked out in front of him, arms behind his head, and reflective sunglasses covering his eyes that are trained on the water. I take the seat beside him, holding the towel in my lap. Silence sits like a wool blanket between us, heavy and uncomfortable.

"I wasn't trying to hide anything from you," I start just as he says, "I'm sorry if I was a dick to you before."

I giggle lightly and turn to look at him, my eyebrows at my hairline. "For real?"

He shrugs up a shoulder and turns back to Rory in the pool. "Rory does like you, and you were right that I was making this more about my comfort than hers. It's not easy for me, and I'm sorry for taking that out on you."

Wow. Color me surprised. "Thank you. I like her too, for what it's worth." His honesty brings forth a little of my own. "As I said, I wasn't trying to hide anything. I had a very bad end to things with someone when I was living in Paris. A small piece of that was a conversation I overheard him having about my body. Let's just say it wasn't the nicest. With that, Jack gets extra protective of me now."

Owen lifts his shades to the top of his head, his fathomless blue eyes looking straight into mine. "That's all you're going to say about it?"

"Yes." And I leave it there, my expression giving nothing away.

He sits up a little straighter, his gaze dragging across my body, and then shifting back to the pool. "I see." His jaw clenches, and a tense hand drags over it, almost as if he's angry or frustrated. I can tell he wants to ask me more about it but won't. "It's none of my business, and I shouldn't have made you feel like you owed me your secrets because you don't."

"I know. Just as you didn't owe me an apology for being a dick, even if you were one."

His lips curl ever so slightly up at the corners, giving way to a hint of dimples, but I'd hardly call that a smile.

"I still don't want you as Rory's nanny, but it seems I might have to get over that."

"What?" I squawk, shooting upright. Only at that exact moment, my brother comes out, followed by Wren and two other adults I don't know, but can guess are Katy and Bennett, who's carrying baby Willow.

Owen stands, not answering my question, and I follow, even though a weird giddiness laced with nerves sweeps over me. It seems I might get what I asked for. And I'll have to deal with the resulting consequences.

Katy, who is beautiful with long brown hair and blue eyes, looks at Owen first and then over at me, and when she sees me, her smile grows exponentially. "Look, Bennett! She's real. Owen is interviewing an actual person to be Rory's nanny." She grabs the baby from his arms.

Owen makes a sardonic noise, rolling his eyes exaggeratedly, and I can't help my snicker.

She starts to say more when Rory's voice comes screaming from the water. "Katy!"

Katy's head whips over, and if I thought she was smiling before, it has nothing on her now. "Hey, lovebug! How's my favorite mermaid?"

"Goooood!" Rory comes bounding out of the pool, dripping wet, her goggles on her head leaving circular imprints around her eyes. "Can I kiss the baby?"

"Of course. She got so excited when I told her we were coming over to see you."

Rory's face lights up, and she runs over to Katy, only to slow her steps and cautiously approach. Katy takes a seat on a nearby chair, shaded by an umbrella, holding the baby in her arms and adjusting her for Rory. With gentle movements, Rory places the softest of kisses on the baby's head.

"Aw, she loved that."

"She's so cute," Rory squeaks, doing a little dance and bringing her fists up by her face. "I just love her."

"She loves you so much, and so do I." Katy rubs noses with Rory. "Now go show me how swimming is done." Katy bobs her head toward the pool, and off Rory goes, straight back into the water with a huge splash. She turns to me. "Hi. I'm Katy. This a-hole's best friend."

Owen grunts, but without a word, kisses Katy on top of the head and then takes the baby from her arms without asking. He sits down on the chair beside Katy and kisses the little thing's nose. I inwardly sigh and simper, my ovaries that aren't the least bit interested in making one of those things swooning at the sight of this grumpy, strong man holding this tiny baby in such a sweet, tender way.

"You still love me even if every other female in my life gangs up on me," he coos to her, cradling her against his broad chest, and yeah, that might be the hottest thing I've ever seen a man do.

"We wouldn't gang up on you if there wasn't a reason," Wren whips out, and Owen ignores her completely as he continues to murmur things to the baby.

I turn back to Katy. "Hi. I'm Estlin. It's very nice to meet you and see that Owen can be friends with a female who doesn't want to drown him in his pool."

She laughs, and so does Wren. Jack and Bennett are off to the side, but even they chuckle at that.

"See?" Owen rocks the baby and brings her up to his shoulder to pat her back when she starts to fuss. "I know it bothers you that they're mean to me, but you don't have to get upset on my behalf."

"She wasn't. She's just gassy today," Katy deadpans at him. "And tired. Like I am." She shakes her head and focuses back on me. "Sorry. I thought I understood sleep deprivation before, but I was wrong. So very wrong. Wren tells me you're an artist and have been living abroad. That automatically makes me jealous of you. Weird that we never met since I hung out with your brother way back when we were kids. Oh, and my baby daddy and your brother knew each other from their fellowship in LA."

An amused smile pulls up my lips at how she's just a bit random. I don't know if that's the lack of sleep or if this is just how Katy is. Either way, I like her.

"Yes, it is weird we never met before now, but I didn't spend a lot of time around Jack or his friends since I'm so much younger and did little else growing up other than read or paint. I'm an artist, and I went to art school in Paris, which was amazing. Now I'm back here after working as a nanny for a family in London for the last seven months. And I had no idea about your baby daddy and my brother until just before you arrived, but it's very cool that they're friends too."

"I like you." She turns to Owen. "I like her. You should hire her. Wren said you're being a butt face about it, but I don't see why. She's perfect." She shakes her head. "Sorry, I don't have the energy or time for a filter. Or to even get up and talk privately."

"Go nap," Wren tells her. "Like for real. Owen has the baby. Bennett has a bottle in the diaper bag. Go sleep for an hour or two. Please. For all our sakes."

"She's right," Owen agrees. "Go sleep in your room, and after, I'll make you a cheeseburger with extra pickles and spicy cheese the way you like it. I've got my goddaughter."

"Yes. Listen to them," Bennett demands. "If you won't listen to me, listen to them. You're not taking care of yourself as you should."

Katy groans like a kid. "He was sexier when he wasn't so overbearing."

"He's right, Kit-Kat," Owen admonishes. "You have to take care of yourself. Your room is right upstairs waiting for you. All dark with a big, comfy bed."

"My room is so far away, and it took *so* much energy just to get here. But maybe I'll crawl onto one of those loungers and shut my eyes." No sooner are the words out of her mouth than she's on her feet and going for the lounger holding most of the towels. She tucks herself in under a pile of them, and in her next breath, might already be asleep.

I can't help but laugh. "If this baby wasn't so cute, that would be perfect birth control."

"Totally," Wren agrees, pulling off her tank top, leaving her only in her bikini top and shorts. She digs into her large designer tote bag. "Here's the suit I promised you. If you want to change and swim, that is. I might. It's hot as hell out today." Wren holds up a series of strings with scraps of attached fabric that will barely cover my nipples, let alone my breasts.

"You realize that wouldn't have even fit me when I was twelve, right?"

Wren takes in the red thing in her hand that is passing for a bathing suit, and then looks back over at me with a shrug. "A little cleavage never killed anyone. And besides, it's not like any of the men here are going to look. We're talking about your brother, Bennett, who is obsessed with Katy, and Owen, who's going to hopefully be your boss and has all but sworn off women."

I bite down on my lip, fighting the blush that's trying to creep up my cheeks. "Um. Well—"

Owen shoots out of his chair with the baby in his arms, cutting off my words as he says to Wren, "She's not swimming right now." Then he turns to me. "Walk with me." That's it, but there's also no argument to be had in his tone. "Wren, keep an eye on Rory for me. Rory," he calls out.

"Yeah?" she yells as she swirls around in the water.

"Katy is resting so please try not to wake her up. I'll be right back. I'm going in to show Estlin around. You be good for Aunt Wren, Uncle Jack, and Bennett. Okay?"

She waves a hand. "Okay."

Without another word, he walks off, baby in tow, expecting me to follow him like an obedient puppy.

Wren's eyes widen questioningly at me, and all I can do is give her a shrug in return. Does showing me around mean I'm hired? He did hint at it before. So if I want this, I guess I'm following after him.

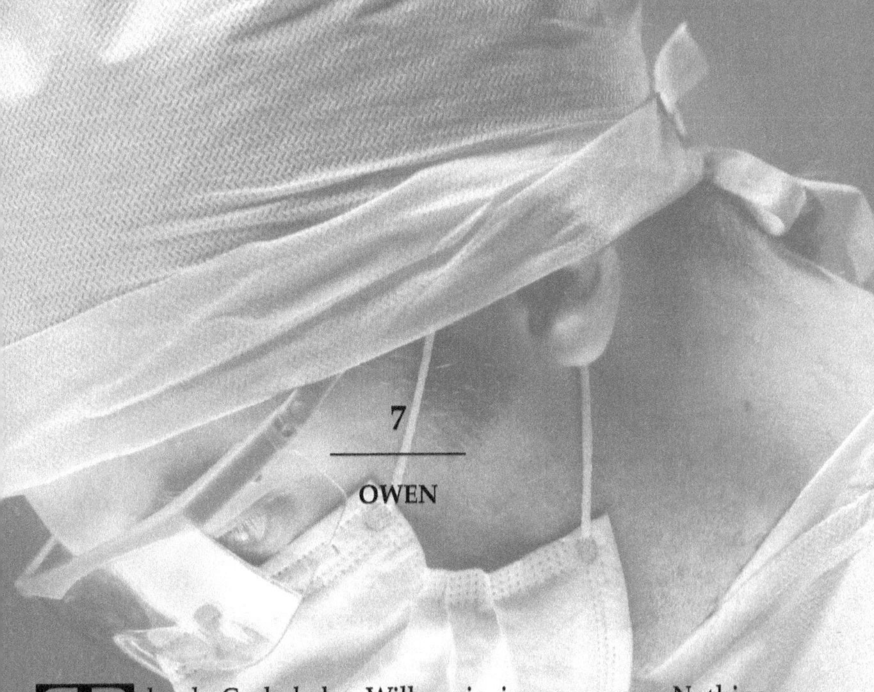

7

———

OWEN

Thank God, baby Willow is in my arms. Nothing grounds you like a sweet, little human who you love with every fiber of your being. Because Wren's words about me swearing off women and not being interested enough to look at Estlin's amazing rack if she had put on that tiny suit made me feel like a monster. Because I would have looked. And I'm positive that what I would have seen would have made me hard.

Which is why there is no way in hell I was going to let her put on that suit and splash in the water. It's also why hiring her as our nanny is a bad fucking idea. I'd have to learn how to be unaffected by her when just the hint of her smile or those blue-green eyes on mine gets my pulse racing.

Estlin follows me inside without argument. For once, her backtalk is held at bay, and she's obeying me in a way I didn't expect her to. It fills me with a sense of calm, a sense that she can be reasonable when I need her to be. She wants this job badly enough to follow me without fighting when fighting feels like her baseline.

I'm still anxious to talk to Katy and hear her thoughts on

everything, but that will have to wait until she's gotten some sleep. She may have shown up exhausted and busting my balls, but I saw her face. I listened to her and watched as she interacted with Estlin. She likes her. And Katy liking her means as much to me as Rory liking her does, since Katy is one of the few people I trust myself fully with.

She would have let me know in her way if she didn't think Estlin was right for the job.

I remove my sunglasses and grab my regular glasses off the counter in the kitchen, slide them on, and keep walking, only to pause at the sound of Estlin's voice.

"Whoa! Is that a game room?" Without waiting on me, Estlin walks straight into my game room slash man cave. It's adjacent to my office, and it's the one room in the house Rory is not allowed in. "This is awesome."

Her gaze flitters about, a look of awe on her face as she takes in my pool table, air hockey table, bar, card table, sectional sofa, large-screen TV, and finally over to the dartboard in the corner. A smile bounces up her lips, and she throws me a side-eye.

"Now I know why you were good at darts last night." She walks about the room, touching everything with a soft cascade of fingers as she goes. "This is a hell of a bar setup." She takes in the two large wine refrigerators, beverage refrigerators, and the glass shelves stocked full of alcohol. One day, when Rory is older, I'll have to do something about that, but not yet. "Damn. You have at least one of everything." She spins around and gives me a cheeky look. "Care to play for it?"

My eyebrows jump, and I shift my stance, keeping my distance from her. "Play for what?"

"The job," she throws out, as if that should have been obvious. "We can do a blindfolded bourbon taste test or play a round of darts. If I win, I get the job. If you win, I leave."

"Tempting," I tell her, only to glance down at the baby in my arms. "But I don't quite see how that will work."

"Shame. That sounded pretty fun. And obviously, I'd win, so that was in my favor." The look on her face isn't intentionally flirty or mischievous. Not the way it was last night. But I can't help but remember the same sparkle in her eye when I told her I wanted to take her to a hotel and spend the night with her.

I turn and walk out, already knowing what I'm about to do next is crazy and stupid, but lacking a solid reason not to do it other than my own shit. "You'll have full access to everything on the property," I start, talking as I walk through the back of the house. "That includes the kitchen, outdoor grounds, exercise space, indoor pool and sauna—those are in the basement and require a code to get in—media room, and anything else except my game room without permission and my office."

Estlin clears her throat behind me. "Are you hiring me?"

I cradle a sleeping Willow tighter against me as I wind up the stairs. "You were the one who told me that I better have a good reason not to hire you. It turns out, I don't. My daughter likes you. My best friend likes you. Your brother is one of my closest friends, your mother's goddamn art is hanging over the fireplace in my living room, and your godmother is my aunt. So yes, much to my dismay, you're hired." I pause and throw her a fleeting glance over my shoulder. "If you still want the job."

Estlin scoots around me as we reach the second floor, standing in the long hallway that traverses the entire house. For a second, she focuses on Willow, fast asleep and tucked against my chest, and then slowly drags her eyes up to mine. "It's impossible to have a real conversation with you when you're holding a newborn. I feel like it puts you at an unfair advantage."

"Willow never sleeps when she's around Katy, and therefore Katy never sleeps when she's around her. Willow smells her mother's breast milk and can sense her presence. She also knows that the moment she starts to fuss or cry, either her dad or her mom will come running with some sort of comfort for her, usually in the form of milk or snuggles. That's how babies are. But when I take her, I don't have milk for her. I just have a warm chest that she can sleep against, so it gives her parents a much-needed break."

Estlin does a long, slow blink, and then another. "So..." Another blink, this one both appreciative and puzzled. "You took the baby so Katy and Willow could sleep since they can't seem to do that with each other nearby?"

I nod. "Yes. I am a pediatric surgeon. Believe it or not, I do understand and like babies. Especially this one."

"You're the most mercurial man I've ever met. Nothing like the Owen from last night, though now after meeting you, I understand the reason for the hotel." She tilts her head, studying me. "I wonder which is the real you."

"Both," I answer somewhat honestly. "Only the Owen you met last night has no place in my real life, so you might as well get used to this version of me. Especially since I can never be that Owen with you again."

"I liked that Owen. He made my panties wet and my nipples hard and got me to say yes to something I never say yes to but needed badly."

I choke and take a step back. While trying not to look down at her nipples. Or remember what they taste like.

"Sorry." She laughs, brushing the long strands of her hair back from her face. "That's inappropriate. I just didn't expect you to be so... many different things. I guess it's a good thing you're not that Owen often."

"Because he made your nipples hard and your pussy wet?" I have to ask as I finally succumb and look. And yes, her nipples are hard, straining through her lace bra that sits beneath her thin T-shirt. And her tits. Fucking hell, she has the most sensationally gorgeous tits.

I clear my thoughts and focus on the baby in my arms instead. The other reason I brought her with me. So I wouldn't be tempted by the fucking temptress before me. If she's to be Rory's nanny, then I can't see her as anything but. Only my cock hasn't quite gotten the full hang of that yet, despite the little bundle asleep against my chest.

She shrugs, but I can tell by her tone and the look in her eyes that she knows I just checked out her tits and that I liked everything I saw. "Actually, because that Owen stole my panties, and I kind of liked that he did."

An incredulous laugh bursts from my chest, stirring poor Willow for a moment.

"But don't worry," she continues. "Since that was Owen, my hot one-night stand, and not Owen Fritz, my surly new boss, it won't be an issue. Let's keep going."

"Friday night is over. This is now."

She holds her hand up apologetically. "I totally agree. My apologies for even mentioning it."

"But since we're mentioning things we shouldn't be, your ex is a fucking moron, and I loved every inch of your body last night and wouldn't change a thing about it."

Her eyes bulge, and her lips part. She needed to know that because she's the sexiest fucking woman I've ever been with, and I hate that someone made her feel like she wasn't. Which only makes this worse.

I clear my throat. "But if you want this job, you can't talk about your nipples again. Or your pussy for that matter. And you can't wear bikinis like the one Wren was trying to put you in. You can't bring men home either. And when you're working, you're entirely focused on Rory and no one else."

"Okay. I can do that. So... you're hiring me?"

"Yes."

"Yay." She does a little excited hop and claps her hands.

"That's great. You won't regret it. Carry on, El Capitan." She salutes me, and I have no idea what to do with this woman.

I can't kiss her. I can't fuck her. I can't even touch her again.

So instead, I turn my back to her and head down the hallway, pointing out important rooms like Rory's and the playroom, and then down to hers—the farthest from mine for a reason. "The gym is in the basement. I use it between four thirty and five thirty in the morning. Feel free to use it any other time." I watch as she heads into her room, taking in the lines of her king-sized bed, large dresser, walk-in closet, and full en suite bathroom.

"This is beautiful." She spins back to me, standing in the middle of the room. "How much do you pay? Jack never mentioned that."

"In addition to room and board—and by board, I mean you'll give me a complete grocery list every Sunday, and my housekeeper will get everything on your list for you—you'll be paid three thousand a month plus benefits."

Her eyes bulge from her head for approximately three seconds before she manages to rein her shock in. "That's... wow. That's great."

"With that pay comes big expectations and requirements. I'm a surgeon. That means I don't have a lot of control over my hours. I can't walk out of surgery the moment Rory's school calls me or if she's sick. I also work one weekend and two night shifts a month, and one of those is a twenty-four-hour shift. It sucks, and it's not ideal, but it's reality. That's where you come in. You're on call and at her beck and call when I can't be."

"So my art..."

"Is important. But if there's an issue during the day—however unlikely—and I can't get to her, you're the one who needs to. That said, my parents and all of her aunts and uncles, as well as my friends and cousins, are always willing to help out, so it likely won't be much of an issue. I will also provide you with a car because whatever you drive Rory around in has to be safe."

She sits on the edge of the bed, twisting her lip between her fingers and staring up at me with those large blue-green eyes. I hate how attracted I am to her. She's everything wrong for me and nothing I would have ever considered before, but now, it's as if she's a light switch that's been turned on and I have no clue how to turn it back off.

"So basically, I'm her person."

"Exactly."

"That doesn't sound too bad."

I walk across the room and stare out the window at the pool below, seeing Rory swimming with Jack and Wren. "She's a great kid. I should also tell you she was having behavior issues at her last school. Acting out in class and throwing some pretty nasty tantrums at home with me. I've switched schools, but I don't know if it'll make a difference or not. Her therapist says she needs more stability and routine."

"Or perhaps some control when she doesn't feel like she has much at all."

"Perhaps that too," I concede. "But that's why I'm doing this." I turn back to Estlin. "She's missing something I can't give her, but I'll do whatever it takes to make her life the easiest it can be." Willow squirms in my arms, and I rock from side to side, shushing her ever so gently so she goes back to sleep.

"Okay." She stands. "Thank you for hiring me and putting your faith and trust in me to help take care of Rory. I know it's not exactly what you want and that this didn't start off under ideal circumstances, but you won't regret it."

"I hope not."

She rolls her eyes at me and then heads for the door, and I stare at her back as she does. "I can start moving my stuff in tomorrow—"

"Are you going to tell me the rest about the bad situation with your ex?"

She freezes at the threshold of the door, her hand going to the frame. Her head turns over her shoulder, and her eyes meet mine. "I wasn't going to, no."

For some reason that bothers me. I have no right to know. No right to ask. But that doesn't mean I don't want to.

"I'll see you tomorrow," she says, ending any further discussion on it and walking out.

~

"You stole her panties?" Katy explodes into a loud, incredulous laugh. "I'm dead. Like officially." She rolls back and forth on her back like she's having some sort of fit. "That's amazing. And so dirty. Who knew you had that in you?"

I poke her side. "Shut up."

"No, I'm serious. I never ever would have seen that coming. If someone asked me under oath if you were a panty thief, I would have sworn it's not something you'd ever consider. let alone do."

I turn on my side, running my hand over Willow's soft belly. We're in Katy's room. Or more like the room she sleeps in when she has sleepovers with me and Rory. Willow has officially gone through all four of the extra outfits Katy packed for her in her diaper bag, so now she's lying on a towel—I am not messing around—in only a diaper and a knit hat in between us.

My parents ended up coming over after Wren called them, and now, they're down the hall giving Rory a bath while I get alone time with Katy and Willow. Jack and Estlin left—thank God—and Bennett ran home to get Willow fresh clothes.

"I don't know why I did it," I admit, staring down at Willow, who's trying to figure out what her hands do. "Maybe to remind myself that I'm still human. Still a man."

"But you did and it's awesome. I'm oddly proud of you. Did you give them back?"

I shake my head and peer up at Katy, fighting my smirk. "I didn't even admit to her that I took them."

She cackles louder this time. "This is just so good."

Katy is my person. My ride or die. My thick and thin.

Never once in her life has she judged me. Our love and friendship are unconditional. When my life fell apart, she was there. But not just offering consoling words or asking if she could do anything. She was fucking *there*. In my house. Playing with my daughter. Making me dinner with her shitty cooking. She didn't care if she was photographed. She didn't care what the tabloids said about her or me. She was there with me every goddamn step of the way and even testified in court on my behalf. There is nothing in this world I wouldn't do for her, and seeing her with Willow makes me so unbelievably happy.

Katy wanted a baby for a long time and has some chronic health issues that she wasn't sure would allow for one.

"What the fuck do I do?" I roll onto my back and throw my forearms over my eyes.

"Hey! Earmuffs."

I pull one arm aside, squinting at Katy in the dim lighting. I cock her an *are you for real* eyebrow. I snatch Willow and hold the tiny lovebug above me before I drop her down to my chest and kiss the top of her head.

"Katy, she's two months old. She doesn't know what that word means."

"Now you sound like Bennett. Yes, she's only two months old, but she's super smart, you know. A fast learner. How would you feel if fuck is her first word?"

I can't help my laugh-huff. "You realize you just said it, right?"

"Shut up. I was making my case."

"Okay, fine. What the fudge do I do about this? I hired her.

She's Jack's sister. And she's young. When I met her last night, I thought she was more along the lines of twenty-five or twenty-six. She's freaking twenty-two. That's two years younger than Wren."

Katy scoots closer to me on the bed and lies down, rests her head on my shoulder, and plays with Willow's fingers. "You're talking like you're thinking about her as a woman."

That pulls me up short, and for a moment I stare sightlessly at the ceiling. "I didn't mean to. I just meant... hell, I did sound like that, didn't I? But I'm not. It was more to reiterate all the ways I feel like a dirty old man monster."

She snickers. "You're not an old man or a monster. Though after the panty-snatching, I can't say you're not dirty."

"Why do I tell you anything?" I bemoan, tossing one hand behind my head to angle myself up better while I use my other to hold Willow tighter. "She's the nanny now, and nothing more. Hell, even before I hired her, she wasn't going to be anything more. That's what last night was about. Sex. And then never seeing her again." Except now she's here, in my life, moving into my goddamn house.

Katy is quiet for a moment, watching me as I hold her daughter against my chest. Her fingers glide down Willow's back, and she makes a little screechy baby noise that has us both enthralled. "Did you have fun last night?" she asks softly.

I exhale. "Yes. I had fun."

"I think that's the problem, Owen. I think that's why you're struggling so much with it now. It's not her age or even the fact that she's Jack's sister. It's that you had fun with her. Before last night, when was the last time you had fun?"

Seconds tick like time bombs between us. "I don't know," I answer honestly. "I was a different form of myself last night. She even asked me today which version is the real Owen, and I lied and said both. The truth is, I can't remember the last time I was that guy. It's bothering the hell out of me. All day everyone told me not to be mean or such a grump to her because I'm a dic—penis and that's how everyone knows me now."

She smirks at my word adjustment. "Not me."

"You're different."

"They know you that way because you never relax. You never take it easy or take a break. You never allow yourself to have fun, and with that, yeah, you've turned into a bit of a penis." She adjusts herself, her head popping up, her face exploding into an *I've just had the best idea* expression. "Why don't you take Rory on a vacation? She has a fall break this October, right? Go somewhere. Go to Disney World or the Caribbean or take her sailing on Kaplan's yacht. Just somewhere. Away from here. A place where you both can relax and have fun."

I think about that for a moment. My uncle Kaplan, from whom I get my middle name because he delivered me at thirty-four weeks in the back of my uncle Oliver's car, is a master sailor. And with that, he'd take me and his son Stone out on the sailing yacht whenever he could. I could take Rory sailing on his yacht. I could teach her how to do that. Sailing was one of my happiest memories growing up.

"There's staff on the boat, so you wouldn't have to cook or clean. But..."

"But?" I quickly follow up.

"But it might be nice if you had extra help with Rory. So you had time for yourself too. So it wasn't just you parenting in a different location."

"Katy?" I warn, raising an eyebrow at her.

She shakes her head. "Aw, you're sweet to want to include me, but sadly, I'm unavailable. By that point, my maternity leave will be over, and I'll be starting a new trauma surgery fellowship."

"What are you doing?"

She smiles so sweetly, so innocently at me with those big,

blue eyes of hers. "Telling you that you all need a vacation because you do. And I think you should take your new nanny. Not only will this give her bonding time with Rory, but it'll also give you free time."

I stare at her. "I can't tell if you're fu—dging with me or not."

"Not. I'm being serious."

I blink at her and then blink again. "I can't go away on the sailing yacht with Estlin." Her in a bathing suit. Us stuck together on the ship in the middle of the ocean.

But I also hear what she's saying. Rory needs a break, and so do I. We haven't left Boston since she was a baby. So long ago, she has no memory of it. I'd love to have the time with Rory. And having a nanny with us—someone who could watch her so I could relax and have some free time of my own— would be incredible because I rarely, if ever, get that.

But...

"You're trying to start a fire."

"Only a bad thing if you get burned by it."

I huff. And huff again. "Cut the shit, Katy."

"Earmuffs."

"Screw your earmuffs."

"Fine." She gives me a big, dramatic eye roll. "I'm only play-ing. Don't take Estlin, even if it's a brilliant idea."

"It's not a smart move. Not by any stretch. This only works for Rory and me if Estlin is the nanny and nothing more."

"Isn't that what you just said? That she's the nanny now and nothing more? If she were a sixty-year-old instead of a gorgeous twenty-two-year-old, would you not take her on vacation with you and Rory?" She waves me away as if the answer isn't impor-tant. "Whatever. If you don't want to bring her, then don't. But if you do, I don't see the problem. If you say she's the nanny and nothing more, then what's the harm of bringing her along?"

Yes. Estlin is the nanny and nothing more. I'm determined to make her so, which means I need to treat her the way I'd treat any nanny. And if she were any nanny, I'd likely bring her along, as Katy said. Ugh. I hate it when she's right.

Willow starts to cry, and Katy takes her from me. I fall back on the bed, taking off my glasses and rubbing my bleary eyes. "It's certainly something to think about."

"Good! I think it's exactly what you all need."

Maybe.

"First, let's see how Estlin's moving in and being Rory's nanny goes, before I make any vacation plans for the three of us."

"You don't have to move out so fast," my father says without moving his attention from the tablet he's reading the paper on as he sips his coffee. "You could stay for a while. Get acclimated to life back here."

I laugh lightly. "I didn't go from living in a tiny rural town to the big city, Dad. I went from Paris to London, and back to Boston. If anything, moving back here and adjusting is easier than anywhere else I've lived."

Slowly he lifts his head and peers over at me. "You know that's not what I'm talking about."

I sigh and walk over to him, then drop into the seat across from him.

"I'm honestly fine."

"Have you painted or sculpted anything recently?"

"Making art isn't a barometer for how I'm doing. I didn't have the time or space in London, and now that I'm back here, I'd like to start again."

"So you're ready?" he checks, watching my expression.

I smile. "I'm ready. I promise."

"Good. That's so good to hear. Your mother isn't happy—"

"Did you get her to agree to stay?"

I roll my eyes at my father, whose lips twitch. "No. But she's ready," he tells her.

My mother doesn't like that answer. Not one bit. She comes over and sits beside me, facing me in her chair. "I think you should stay with us. Come work for me in the gallery. Get yourself going again in the art world, and then your talent will catch up."

"I'm going to find my own studio space," I say adamantly. "I appreciate what you're offering, but I don't want to work at a gallery. Not right now. I need to do this on my own."

She purses her lips in dismay. "You're a born artist, and the gallery is part of your family legacy. Being a nanny is a waste of your talent, and living in someone else's home is a ridiculous way to hide from us."

"I like working with children, and I'm not hiding from you. I *want* to be a nanny. It's fun, and it keeps me going. What I don't need is you down my throat about my talent, the gallery, living here, and how I need to be working again. I'll work when I'm ready."

She opens her mouth to continue when my dad reaches over and places his hand on her arm. "Enough. She's an adult and smart and strong enough to make her own choices and take her own path."

"Exactly!" I hop out of my seat and kiss both of them. "I'll be like twenty minutes away. Take a breath. It's fine."

"I'll try, but I still don't like it."

I don't argue further. There's no point. I just get the hell out the door while I can.

My family has been treating me like a baby for, well, my entire life. I'm a lot younger than Jack and the child they tried to have for years but were unable to until, miraculously, I came along.

But I'm Eddie, not Estlin to them.

And that difference is everything.

I tried to make the morning my bitch. I woke up before six, went for an intense run that had me splinting my ribs on three different occasions, came home, showered, made breakfast, packed the rest of my meager things, and now here I am, having a conversation I was hoping to avoid for the fifth time in the six days I've been home.

My mother's words sit with me as I take their extra car and... stall for like twenty minutes before I go to Owen's. I hit up a Starbucks and discovered a local gourmet grocery store, and oh, a barre studio. I'll definitely have to check that out.

This isn't who I was hoping to be here.

I'm not the girl who cowers—at least I didn't think I was, until Claude proved me wrong. But for some reason, this morning, I'm feeling a bit out of sorts. I don't know which version of Owen I'll be getting, and the thought of moving down the hall from him is, well, it's weird. There, I said it.

He went from a charming, hot one-night stand to a broody, unrelenting jerk in a nanosecond, and I haven't quite gotten my bearings. My last nanny position was more of a no-brainer and an escape than anything else. The position literally fell in my lap at the exact moment I needed to get away, and it was with people I trusted.

A couple.

Not a gorgeous single dad who I know what he looks and sounds like when he comes.

I'm second-guessing everything I was so adamant about yesterday.

"Get over it!" I snap to myself as I pull down his long driveway. "You wanted this job, now suck it up and deal. Think of how much worse it would be if he were sweet instead of a miserable, grumpy bastard."

True. Maybe Owen being a jerk is a blessing in disguise.

I park in the circle driveway near the front door and climb

out. Shielding my eyes, I squint up at the house and then spin around to take in the front yard. It's a beautiful late summer day, and I wonder if I can talk Rory into exploring the grounds with me. Jack mentioned last night on our drive home that Owen's house sits on about five acres of land, which is un-freaking-heard of this close to the city. He also said there's a creek and some forested land that's protected by the state since it's some sort of wetlands.

I check my watch: 7:55. I'm still early. How about them apples?

I don't bother glancing down or allow myself to fidget. It doesn't matter what I look like or what I wear. I'm a freaking nanny and most definitely not here to appeal to anyone. Casual and comfortable come with the gig, and my jean shorts and oversized cropped T-shirt are just that.

I ring the doorbell, and from inside, I can hear Rory yell out, "She's here, she's here!"

A smile lights my face up for the first time all morning, her excitement popping the nervous bubble I had sitting in my gut. A moment later, the door bursts open, and there are Owen and Rory, who is jumping up and down, a gleeful smile splitting her face from ear to ear.

"Come in, come in!" She starts spouting words a mile a minute, barely taking a breath. "I want to make rainbow sparkly slime and then paint a picture and I want to show you my tree house. Oh, and Daddy said that after lunch before Katy picks me up to swim, we can clean out part of the unfinished side of the basement so you can have your own art space. Isn't that awesome?"

I stumble over my own feet, and I turn, jaw agape, and stare incredulously at Owen, who is leaning against the doorframe, tall, ridiculously handsome, and stoic as ever. His eyes are on my face, intensely locked there, almost as if he won't allow them to stray anywhere else.

I blink, lick my lips, and then blink again. My impersonation of an owl must amuse him because his lips twist almost imperceptibly. "For real?"

He shrugs. "You're going to need some place to create your art, right? I heard you tell Wren that you were going to be looking to rent a studio space and that you tend to make a mess when you do art, so that part of the house should be fine."

"Wow." My hand meets my chest. "That's incredible. Thank you."

He nods, quickly dismissing the gesture as if it's no big thing when, to me, it's everything. A private place to work has been one of my main issues for not diving back into it. He doesn't even know why I need it so badly, but hell, it's beyond perfect.

He pushes away from the door. "Do you need help with your bags?"

"No. I'm good. I'll bring them in later. They're not heavy."

"You didn't bring much home with you from London?" he asks over his shoulder as he heads back into the house. I follow after him, Rory still bouncing by my side.

"I didn't have a lot of stuff to bring home," I admit.

That catches his attention, a surprised look on his face. "I thought you had been living in Europe since you were seventeen?"

Well, shit. "I had been. But when I moved to London, I left a lot of things behind in Paris."

His brows pull together for a moment, but he lets it drop as we head into the kitchen so Rory can finish her breakfast. I sit at the counter beside her, trying not to notice the strong lines of muscle pushing against fabric as Owen's tall, broad frame moves around the kitchen.

"Would you like some coffee?"

"No, thank you. I had some on my way over. Any more caffeine, and you'll be scraping me off the ceiling."

"How can you be on the ceiling?" Rory's face scrunches up as she shovels a bite of eggs into her mouth.

I wink at her. "Not literally. It's an expression."

She shrugs and then goes back to the show on her iPad and her breakfast.

"So, for today—"

"Daddy, I can't hear my show," Rory chastises.

Owen rolls his eyes. "Fine. We'll grown-up talk in my office. I have things for you to sign anyway," he tells me. "Rory, cut the attitude, finish your breakfast, and then you need to go upstairs and brush your teeth. You're done with your iPad after that show anyway."

"I know, I know, you already told me."

He drops a kiss on her head, tickles her side for all the back talk, and then waves his hand indicating I should follow him. I slide off my stool and scurry after him, needing two full steps for every one of his. Owen's office is at the far end of the house, just past the amazing man cave I surveyed yesterday and the movie theater—yes, they have a freaking movie theater. That's what you get when your home is cooler—and bigger—than a cruise ship.

"I have some papers for you to sign, and I need a copy of your license and things for tax and insurance purposes."

"Sure," I say easily as we enter his office. It's the most personal-to-him room I've seen yet in the house. Then again, I haven't been in his bedroom and have no plans to ever be. It's large for an office, more like the size of a family room. The walls are a pale blue-gray, soft and relaxing. It also smells like him in here—so rich and deeply, deliciously masculine that I find myself taking a full inhale before I can stop it.

God, does he have to smell this good? Like so good my freaking nipples pop into sharp points and my pussy clenches like a needy whore?

I take another inhale—just to acclimate myself to it—and start scanning the room wall by wall.

Floor-to-ceiling aged light oak bookshelves line an entire wall, complete with one of those cool ladder things you see in movies or high-end furniture magazines. The shelves are packed tight with books, some appearing to be old and leather bound, and some newer books with cracked and worn spines that I recognize the titles of. Many of these are freaking first editions, which again, totally turns me on and makes me wet.

In addition to the books are things like sports trophies, heavy glass medical awards, and pottery painted by Rory that says Dad in big, bold, pink letters, he has various memorabilia from all the Boston sports teams. Many of the items and photographs are signed by big-name athletes. There's some sculpture that I instantly recognize, having met the brilliant artist in Paris at an opening.

The large bay window looks out onto the grounds, and on either side of the window are several different-sized black-and-white framed photos of Rory. Some as a little baby, some with Owen, some with Katy, some with his parents and grandparents and other family members. My eyes quickly coast over each one, smiling indulgently a little at how cute she is, and then I continue over to his built-in desk with two monitors and a closed laptop on it that's bracketed by two more built-in cabinets made out of the same wood as the bookshelves.

Everything in here fills me with more questions I want the answers to. I'm curious about him, I realize, and that curiosity is not a good thing.

Off to the side is a bathroom, and then along the fourth wall is a long, gray leather sofa with a glass coffee table in front of it. Above the sofa are two extraordinary canvases, painted by my ex, Claude Morceaux, and I'm about to throw up all over his gorgeous area rug.

I stare at the paintings, unique and specific to the artist, large in how he painted them. I remember these fucking paintings. I remember him working on them. I had just moved in with him the month before, and he told me he had received a special offer from a famous gallery in New York to showcase a new collection there.

These works consumed him. At the time, I didn't care. I thought he was so dreamy, so brilliant, so everything. The way he would shut himself out from the world and be cruel and isolating and needy and so intensely focused was just part of his craft and allure, and it's what made me feel so special because he shared himself with only me.

I wrap my arms across my stomach to try and stave off the waves of nausea from taking over.

"You don't like my artwork?"

Does he know? Did Jack tell him? Or is this some psychotic, horribly ironic coincidence?

"They're stunning." Because they are. Claude is nothing if not talented. Jack was living in LA at the time, and he wouldn't know one of Claude's paintings if he tripped over it. So it's likely random that they're here, which is nothing short of karmically fucked up and a royal middle finger.

Owen folds his arms over his chest, eyes on me, as if watching me take in his space all this time is the curiosity of a lifetime. I feel my face heat, and I clear my throat and look away.

"Today is a bit of a weird day," he states as he blows past me now that he finally has my attention back. He grabs two stacks of papers from his desk and brings them over to the coffee table, then takes a seat on the couch and wordlessly expects me to do the same. I'm coming to understand Owen likes to be in control, expects to be obeyed, and doesn't like to have to explain himself more than he has to.

"Weird day, how?" I sit beside him, keeping distance between us so that we're not touching but close enough so that I can see what the papers are.

He runs his thumb along his bottom lip as he leans back against the cushion of the sofa, his body now angled toward mine. "Katy is planning to pick up Rory after lunch to take her swimming, and I agreed to play as a sub in my hockey league this evening."

"You play hockey?" I don't know why that surprises me so much. I caught a quick glimpse of the sports trophies and the air hockey table, though I didn't look closely enough to see what the trophies were all about. Maybe it's because hockey seems too wild, and that's not who Owen Fritz is.

"Yes, only not often now. I played in college. We won a national championship."

"Wow." My eyebrows bounce. "Color me surprised. That's very cool."

"Thank you. I even still have the bloody jersey somewhere to prove it."

"Bloody jersey?!" I exclaim. "Do I want to know?"

His lips twitch, his eyes glowing with haughtiness and maybe even a hint of pride. "I broke a guy's nose during a fight in the championship game of the Frozen Four."

I fall back over on the couch like he just struck me dead. "You? A fight? No way. It had to have been a mistake." This taciturn, overly conscious man could never punch someone in the heat of the moment.

"Brat," he bites out and reaches over to poke my side. Sort of like how he did with Rory when she was being a bit of a brat too. But I'm not Rory. I'm not his six-year-old daughter. And unlike Rory, I'm super ticklish.

"Ah! No! Stop!" I screech and elbow him in retort.

"An elbow? Are you trying to recreate my fight?" He nudges me back with his though not nearly as hard as I gave him.

I laugh and strike back, knocking him in the gut and delighting at his *oomph*. "Like you'd ever beat up a woman."

"Never. But when she throws elbows like you are, I'm not about to take it either." I get another playful poke, but then he's swatting at me, trying to brush off my advances as I go for his face with my hands. "That's pathetic and wouldn't hurt a fly. Like this." He takes my hands and molds them into fists, only to quickly release them so he can hold his fists up and mock box with me, showing me how I should do it.

"Is this how you broke the guy's nose?" I mimic his motion and jab forward.

He dekes left just in time. "Are you trying to fuck up my face?"

"That nose could use a readjustment," I tease.

"Thanks for the bruise to my ego. But let's not break my glasses." He thrusts forward, intentionally missing me, and I go right back at him, punching his arm without any heat to it.

"I won't. They're hot on you."

"Hot on me?!" He chuckles and I giggle in response. He's smiling more than he has since I showed up on his doorstep yesterday. "That I didn't expect." He bumps my cheek and shoulder as we continue to play fight.

"Those wouldn't harm an infant. You can do better than that. I'm not that fragile."

"I would never hit you. Not even at an eighth of my strength. I'd self-destruct if I did."

"Will you go from suck to blow?" I ask, tossing out a *Space-balls* reference.

He laughs but I knock it off his face as I cut a fist into his flank, and he retaliates by snagging a tickle on my side. He's got me in the worst, most perfect spot, and I'm a squealing, laughing mess on his couch.

"I—you have to—oh—my God—stop!"

He starts to pull back, maybe he's come to the conclusion that he shouldn't be tickling the nanny, or maybe he's just showing mercy, but either way, I don't care. The moment I catch my breath is the moment I launch myself, blindsiding him, knocking him back and sideways onto the other end of the sofa, and covering his body with mine.

Why? No clue other than that I don't appreciate being subdued or bested by a man in any physically manipulative way, and by retaliating, I can return the favor. Now I'm on top of him, breathless, and with the tail end of my giggles still lighting sparklers on my lips.

Suddenly, my eyes go stark wide, shocked as they stare directly into his. His pupils are black, deadly midnight, and wider than the full moon. His expression is pure, tormented control. Slowly, his hands go low on my hips, not sliding or touching, but holding, unrelenting as he keeps me from attacking him further.

His hands on my hips, this position, it all feels too intimately familiar to ignore. My breath exhales from my lungs, and lust pools deliciously tight in my core.

But his body is rigid, tense, and... holy shit, he's hard.

What in the actual fuck am I doing?

In a flash, I regain my goddamn senses, and in one fluid motion, I scramble off him. With a heavy bounce on the couch, I readjust my T-shirt that had somehow climbed up half of one of my boobs and my shorts that are practically straight up my ass and pussy.

Super solid way to start a new job with a boss who wants nothing more than to get rid of you.

I run my hands back through my hair and shift farther down the sofa from him. The blush staining my cheeks can't be helped, but I power on like none of that was a big deal.

"Sorry." I emit an awkward giggle. "I don't like to lose at, well, anything. Anyway, how did I never know you played hockey, let alone beat a guy up?" I throw out quickly, trying to bring us back to... who the hell knows what.

He sits up slowly and adjusts himself in his jeans as he goes. I bite my lip as he does because *fuuuck* that's hot, and right now, I'm wound tight like a coil.

One more shift and a quick combing of his fingers through his hair, and you'd never know by his features or the sound of his voice that not even a minute ago, he was play-fighting with me and then I pounced on him like a lioness.

"As you said yesterday, you didn't see me much, nor did we pay much attention to each other when you were young. And yes, a fight. I was a bit of a bruiser on the ice because I also don't like to lose."

I shake my head. "I can't see it."

His eyes lift to mine, his strong face lined with a hint of vulnerability and possibly a touch of regret. "I wasn't always this buttoned-up version of a father and doctor."

No. That I've experienced first-hand. Not even two minutes ago and most definitely Friday night.

He clears his throat and returns to the papers sitting in neat stacks on the glass table. "As it is, on the rare occasions I can make the games, Rory surprisingly likes to come and watch. So after swimming, I'd like you to bring her to my game, and then we can grab dinner out when it's over." He slides, inching to the edge of the couch and hunching forward as he picks up a pen and taps the first stack. His movements are stiff and uncomfortable, as is everything else between us. "This is Rory's schedule along with a list of numbers including my hospital, her pediatrician, and family members should you ever need them." He slides the top few pages toward me and moves to the bigger stack. "These are NDAs. Are you familiar with what that is?"

I mimic his position. "Yes. Non-disclosure agreements. I had one in my last job." And one with Claude, since I had originally worked for him in his gallery before we became lovers.

"Good. That'll make this easier. These are relatively standard, but also not. They cover everything a traditional NDA does, but they're also very tailored to me and Rory as well as my family. I'd like you to read through them and initial and sign everywhere that's indicated."

"Okay," I say a bit warily, but also not surprised he'd have something so extensive.

I took Jack's advice and went down the Google Owen Fritz rabbit hole last night. His ex—who is supermodel stunning, tall and thin and regal-looking—was seriously a piece of work, and for a while, the tabloids exploited every little gem she fed them. After everything she did finally came to light, she tucked her tail and moved to Canada.

That's how bad what she did to Owen and Rory was. The chick had to leave the country.

"I'll take a look tonight and get these back to you first thing tomorrow."

That seems to satisfy him, and he shifts them toward me. The next stack is all tax documents, followed by some sort of insurance filing for me to drive a car he's purchasing. I don't argue. It's his money and his daughter, and to him, it matters what car I drive her around in. Plus, I don't have a car of my own. I've been driving one of my parents' cars, so I suppose it just makes sense.

With my arms full of papers to bring up to my room, I stand and go to leave his office, only throwing one fleeting glance over my shoulder. But when I do, I find him exactly where I left him, sitting on the edge of the couch, knees parted, elbows digging into his thighs, face cast down, and his hands clutching the sides of his head.

For the first time, I realize what this is doing to him, what my being here actually means for him, and why he didn't want me here in the first place. Flirting with the line between professional and inappropriate strikes at a terrified and vulnerable part of his soul.

I vow here and now, if I'm going to make this work for all of us, I need to readjust him in my thoughts into nothing more than my boss. No matter how difficult that task may be.

9

OWEN

Icy wind tickles the sweat dripping down my neck and face as I skate across the roughed-up ice, adjusting my stick in my gloved hand as I go. I haven't played in months, mostly because my schedule with Rory and at the hospital hasn't allowed for it. This felt good. Necessary even to burn off the excess tension that's been sitting heavy in my limbs.

What happened this morning with Estlin in my office was a mistake.

It never should have happened from either of us, but that's not even what alarms me so much about it. It's how fast it happened. How impulsive I was to play-fight and then tickle her like that in the first place. How good it felt when she was on top of me.

After she left my office, she spent the day playing with Rory and keeping her distance from me. Any interactions we did have were polite and professional. When Katy came to pick Rory up for swimming, Estlin moved all of her stuff in, refusing my help, and I haven't seen her since as she stayed up in her room until I left for hockey.

I'm hoping what happened this morning won't happen again and that we can be adults from here on out. Adults who don't touch or tickle or tease or flirt. She's sitting up in the stands with Rory and Jack because I made the mistake of telling Jack I was playing today when he called me earlier to not only thank me for hiring Estlin but also to see how it was going.

A bump on my shoulder jostles me out of my thoughts. "Nice shot on goal," my cousin Stone, who is Kaplan's, son, says skating beside me. He also works at Children's with me, though he's an emergency medicine resident. We lost, which pisses me off because my last-second shot hit the crossbar. I never miss that shot.

"Thanks, man, but it didn't get where it needed to go."

Vander skates on the other side of me as we file toward the bench and the locker rooms so we can shower off our loss. Vander's father, Lenox, along with Zax, Greyson, Asher, and Callan, who is Katy's uncle and adoptive father, were all once part of Central Square, a wildly famous rock band. The Central Square people are good friends with the Fritzes, which means we're now pretty much one big, giant family.

"Dude, you haven't played in forever," Vander states. "Give yourself a break." He pulls off his helmet and wipes at his sweaty forehead with the hem of his jersey.

"I still played like shit. I think I'm out of sorts."

Stone gives me a devious grin as we reach the locker room and start removing our skates, jerseys, and pads. "That wouldn't have anything to do with the sexy brunette I saw watching and cheering you on, would it?"

My fingers on the laces of my hockey pants freeze for a half-second before I continue unlacing them. "You mean my daughter's new nanny?" I deadpan, throwing him an eye that lets him know I'm not taking the bait.

"Is that who that is?" Vander picks up, the other guys are

already shooting the shit on the other side of the locker room. I know them, but I'm not close with them. I only play in this league because Vander and Stone do. "I know you had mentioned you were going to hire someone, but I didn't know you pulled the trigger."

Vander has a tone and is giving me a look. One I know well from him. By day, he runs a multibillion-dollar cyber security firm. By night, he's a hacker, one of the best in the world, like his father is. And when Angelica was pulling all her shit, I used his hacking skills. Knowing him as well as I do, his tone and look are offering the same thing.

In this case, I'm not sure there's much of a need to dig into the nanny.

"She's Jack's sister," I tell him.

His eyebrows bounce. "Shit," he hisses. "That's Eddie? I didn't recognize her." Vander is only a few years older than her, though he looks like he's closer to my age, which he uses to his advantage frequently.

"That's her. Only she goes by her middle name, Estlin, now." I stand, shoving all my sweaty gear into my bag and zipping it up, leaving me in only my boxer briefs. "She just moved back from Europe."

"So she's single?" Stone presses. "Because hell, I don't remember Eddie looking like that when I met her as a kid."

"Because she didn't." Vander snickers dryly, and I'm glad I have my back to them now. I'm glad they can't see that my fists are balled up and my jaw is clenched. "So... is she single?" he presses.

"I don't think she's dating right now," I tell them.

"And how would you know that piece of information, *boss*?" Stone emphasizes, his voice taunting. "You discuss her love life as part of the interview process?"

Shit. I turn and fold my arms over my bare chest. I'm gross and sore since I haven't skated like that in a while, and I'm in desperate need of a shower. I shouldn't have said that. I did it because I don't want either of these guys sniffing around her. Not because they're not great guys and not because Estlin isn't allowed to date whomever she wants.

But because the idea of her with someone else, one of my friends, my family, hitting on her, dating her, fucking her when I can't hits a strange trigger button I didn't know I had—and definitely shouldn't have where she's concerned.

Still, I can't tell if Stone is fucking with me or not. He hasn't shown interest in anyone in a long time. He's been too obsessed with the woman he had a vacation fling with two years ago and hasn't seen since.

I do my best to play it off, to sound casual and unaffected. "I told her I didn't want her bringing men home to my house, and she told me it wouldn't be a problem because she's not dating right now."

That last part is a fucking lie, but I don't give two shits. Thankfully, they let it drop, but not before they exchange quiet looks I don't like.

"I'm gonna hit the showers. Are you guys taking off?"

"Yeah." Vander steps forward and extends his hand to give me a fist-pound since we're all too nasty for even a handshake. "Nice game out there today. Hope you can make it more often."

"Same. It was fun." I give Stone a pound as well, and then I get my sorry ass into the shower, trying not to think about if they'll run into her—intentionally or unintentionally—as she, Jack, and Rory wait for me to finish up. They'd flirt because that's what they do with beautiful women, and they're single and closer to her in age than I am.

Fuck. The side of my fist hits the tile wall as hot water cascades over me. Why do I care this much? I barely know the girl. She's my nanny. My best friend's little sister. Undeniably forbidden to me in every way.

I can't have her.

But that doesn't mean I want them to either.

Jealousy fucking sucks and makes me feel like a stupid college kid.

This bullshit needs to stop, and it needs to stop now.

I finish showering and get myself dressed quickly, knowing Rory must be getting antsy by this point and is likely hungry. I grab my heavy equipment bag off the ground along with my skates and then head out of the locker room.

"Daddy!" Rory calls out as she races over to me like I just won the Stanley Cup. She jumps up into my arms, and I have to drop my skates and bag to catch her.

I let out a chuckle, kissing the side of her face. "Hey, Moonshine. How was swimming?"

"Fun. Katy showed me how to do the butterfly stroke which she said gives me a mermaid tail when I do it."

"Cool. You'll have to show me." I set her down, noticing Estlin and Jack talking up by the exit. Thankfully, Vander and Stone aren't with them. "Are you hungry?" I ask, picking up my stuff again and walking with her to join them.

"Starving," she groans in that exaggerated kid way. "Can we go for sushi?"

I smile down at her. Katy's uncle Callan is a silent owner of one of the best Asian fusion and sushi restaurants in Boston, and whenever we go there, they spoil Rory like crazy, whether Katy or Callan is with us or not. Rory doesn't even eat sushi. She goes for the dumplings, fried rice, and chicken fingers.

"Sure. But only two chocolate mochi this time, Moonshine. Last time you had too many, and it gave you a stomachache."

She pouts but doesn't argue. Likely because she remembers that stomachache.

"Nice game, brother." Jack gives me a bro hug. "It's been a long ass time since I've seen you play."

"You were really good," Estlin chimes in, giving me a coy

smile. "Not quite the bruiser I was told about, but it was fun to watch."

"Bruiser?" Jack laughs. "You told her about breaking Vargus's nose?"

"It's my battle glory," I defend. "My one claim to fame."

Jack snorts, slapping me on the back. "Oh, you mean other than being Owen Fritz and a world-renowned pediatric surgeon?"

"Fine. My one badas—butt"—I glance down at Rory as I make the correction, but she's too busy singing to herself to have noticed—"claim to fame." I take her hand, adjusting my heavy bag on my shoulder as we reach the parking lot, but Estlin comes running around to the other side of her and takes her hand to make it easier for me.

"Well, I think it's pretty bad butt," Estlin says with a hint of a smile aimed at me as we make our way to my car, and I'm relieved to see there's no mocking or even innuendo behind that. "I've never done any butt-kicking in my life. I've never won a championship either, so I'd be bragging more than you are if I did." She helps Rory up and into her booster, shutting the back door behind her.

"No, you just won every literary and art award growing up and graduated from your high school *and* university at the top of your class." Jack pokes, but there's no hiding the pride in his voice or expression either. He grabs Estlin around the shoulders and drags her into him, hugging her right here in the parking lot, and I'm hit with a brutal pang of guilt. "I'm being a sappy bastard, but I'm glad we're both back home. I'm glad you're... well, you know what I'm especially glad for. This was fun." He kisses her forehead. "Thanks for inviting me along."

She laughs, hugging him back. "Me too. Thanks for driving us." After giving him a squeeze, she releases him and gets in the front passenger seat.

"You don't want to join us for dinner?"

"Nah," he says as we make our way around the back of the car to my side. "I've got an early shift tomorrow. My first one working back in Boston. But enjoy."

I smack his back and then head toward my door when he calls out, and stops me. "Hey, Owen?"

I turn back to him. "Yeah?"

"Take care of my sister for me."

Hell.

I don't respond, but thankfully he doesn't wait for me to. He just crosses the lot over to where his car is, and for a moment, I watch him, twisted up, unsure for the first time what the right and wrong thing is to do.

I've never kept a secret from Jack in my life. Growing up, we were impossibly close and have stayed that way into adulthood despite distance and the madness of life. Now I'm keeping this from him. A secret so invasive it tears me up from the inside out. I'm a piece of shit who fucked his little sister—the one he just asked me to take care of—and then snuck out of the hotel room like a thief.

I'm not the friend to him that he has been to me.

And I hate it.

A SOFT KNOCK stirs me out of the patient's chart I was reviewing. "Come in," I call absently, logging out of the EMR. It's getting late and I need to go to bed. Rory has already had her bath and has been asleep for over two hours and my shift starts at seven tomorrow morning.

"Sorry to bother you." Estlin's sweet voice comes from the doorway where she hovers, her tone hesitant and a little unsure. "I wanted to give you these before I forgot. I know tomorrow is going to be a bit off to the races for both of us, and I wasn't sure if I'd see you in the morning before you left."

At dinner, I told her that tomorrow she's essentially on her own here. Rory has one more week of summer break, which puts Estlin in the hot seat to keep her occupied now that Rory's camps are all done.

I shut down my laptop and spin in my chair to face her and instantly regret it. Her long hair is wet and hangs past her shoulders to the middle of her back, and her face is soft and bare of any makeup. She's wearing green cotton sleep shorts that make her full thighs look pale and creamy and an old threadbare T-shirt. With no fucking bra under it. Her nipples are gorgeous, hard peaks, and I have to force my eyes to stay on hers and not drop to appreciate the view before me.

"What is it?" I bark harshly, and my unexpected tone startles hers. It startles me too, but I can't do this. I can't have her walking into my office late at night looking like a wet dream I don't want to wake from.

She licks her lips—a nervous gesture, but it still makes my cock twitch—before straightening her spine and carrying the NDA I gave her earlier in the day across the room for me to take. As she gets closer, the smell of her shampoo and body lotion hits me like a grenade, making my jaw clench and my hands grip the arms of my chair so I don't do something stupid like grab her hips and place her on my lap.

"Just put it down on my desk."

She does, her body coming so close to mine that I can feel the heat of her skin.

Goddammit. What is it about her that I'm so fucking attracted to, and how on earth do I make it stop?

"I... uh. I was going to ask if you'd mind if I borrowed a book, but I can come back another time when you're not so... busy," she finishes, but I can see in her face she was mentally calling me a jerk or some other term I've no doubt deserved.

I don't want to be a jerk to her. She's Jack's little sister and my employee. I'm not a dick to the people who work for me, and I'm not a dick to the people of the people I care about. But with her, I'm not sure I have much of a choice.

"Go pick something out," I snap and then turn back to my desk, wishing I hadn't shut everything down so I'd have something to distract myself with while she's in here. I go for her papers, putting them all into a neat stack for me to scan and send to my attorney. I won't be able to do that until tomorrow evening, so for now, I get up and go over to the large safe I have built into the wall behind one of the drawers next to my desk.

"Yes, Mr. Darcy."

"What?"

She shrugs. "You remind me of Mr. Darcy. You know, from *Pride and Prejudice*."

My hand drags across my jaw. "I know who Mr. Darcy is." As I recall, he was a bit pompous and judgmental. Arrogant. For some reason that makes me chuckle. I haven't read *Pride and Prejudice* since high school, but I remember the basics. "Does that make you my Elizabeth?" I shake my head quickly, wondering where that came from and what the hell made me say it. "Don't answer that."

"I won't. I'm going book shopping now."

A moment later, I hear a soft laugh from the other side of the room and turn to look over my shoulder. Estlin is standing on her tiptoes, reaching for something on one of the shelves. The movement makes the muscles in her legs bunch up and it also gives me a view of the underside of her perfect ass. If she bends just a little...

"I never took you for a spicy romance reader."

"What?"

She turns, nearly catching me staring at her ass, and my gaze shoots up just in time to appreciate her giving me a playful smile, holding up a book, waving it back and forth like I should know what the hell—oh fuck. Fucking Katy. "Those aren't mine."

"Uh-huh," she plays. "Sure."

I roll my eyes and huff, turning back to my safe and making sure it's blocked as I use my thumbprint and then punch in the code to open it. It makes a mechanical sound, and then the door pops open. I set the papers in on top, then quickly shut and lock it.

I stand, close the cabinet, and turn to face her, putting my hands behind my back to grip the edge of the built-in. "Bennett's mom has cancer," I tell her. "She loves dirty romance books, and during her chemo, Bennett reads those books to her. Katy, who doesn't think I get out enough and loves to tease and torment me, brought those over. She put two on the bookshelf and two on my nightstand for me."

Estlin cracks up, taking in the book cover with new eyes. "I love that. I love that Bennett reads these to his mom, and I love that Katy gave them to you."

I don't respond. I just stare her down, wanting, *needing* her to go. "They're yours if you want them."

"Oh, I'll take them. I was planning on stealing your Hemingway that I saw earlier, but these will help tuck me into bed."

Jesus. Did she just say that?

"I think you're missing out," she continues, oblivious to how I'm now sweating. "These look good."

"I have no doubt they are, but I have neither time nor the inclination to read them. And the Hemingways on that shelf are all first editions, so if you take one and don't return it in perfect condition, I'll not only fire you, I'll kill you."

"Noted." Her hand goes up in surrender. "I'd never ever destroy a book, let alone a first edition. But now I might be too afraid to touch them."

"You can touch them, Estlin, since I know you want to."

Her eyes spark wide for a flicker of a second, and a blush

stains her cheeks. "I um. I think I'll start with this one tonight." She holds up the book in her hand.

"Good night then."

"Good night, Owen."

She tucks the book against her chest and walks out of my office. I count to a hundred, and when I figure she's had a good enough head start on me, I shut everything off in my office and go up to my room.

My dick is hard as I enter my bedroom and bathroom. I can't shut my thoughts off as I think about how she looked just now and about the book she's reading. Will she touch herself to it? Sink beneath the covers and play with her tits and wet pussy until she's a writhing, moaning, delicious mess?

Fuck. I sigh and shake my head. Immediately, I start the shower, turning it to cold. I won't give in to the temptation.

Even if it's the sweetest fucking temptation I've ever encountered.

10

ESTLIN

All I know is stepping back into my world shouldn't be as hard as it feels. Seven months ago, I was in a great place. I had a guy I loved who I thought loved me. I had finished art school at the top of my class and was trying to build a name for myself in the Parisian art world. Everything was perfect.

I met Claude a few months into starting school, and after that, nothing was the same for me. I went from being the quiet wallflower, more comfortable with a book or working on my art to being part of a social world you only see in movies.

I never went to frat parties. I never got drunk at a keg party or had a wild one-night stand with a hot football player. Yes, I realize much of this sounds like romance-book clichés, and that's obviously where I'm drawing my comparison from.

My days were spent in my art classes, my afternoons working in Claude's gallery, and my nights in his bed. We'd go out to lavish dinners and exclusive parties with his art-world friends. I got swept up in the romanticism and sophistication of being with the famous, brilliant, and much older Claude Morceaux.

I worked hard, night and day to improve my craft. A craft that my lover told me wasn't quite ready for the big-time galleries and needed more development and skill. I was determined to get there and be just as successful as he and my mother were. I took his words as gospel. His guidance as my artistic bible.

And because I was young and he was older, and because my talent was burgeoning and his was masterful, and because I loved and idolized him so much, I lost myself. I was his, not mine. Only I didn't realize that until I left him and discovered I had to rebuild myself piece by piece without knowing where to start or how to do it when I felt so spiritually and creatively empty.

And insecure. There was that annoying piece of this too, only that part didn't last nearly as long as the rest has.

All that is bound to happen when your lover cheats—though he swore he didn't—and proceeds to speak down about your body and your work with the woman he cheated on you with, and then lies about what's your work and his. As if that's not bad enough, after you confront him about all of that, he flies into a rage, and you leave. Then when you return to get your things, heartbroken beyond words and comprehension, you realize he upped the betrayal ante to epic proportions and destroyed every single piece of art you spent your blood, sweat, and tears making.

It took me too long to understand that he was far more insecure than I was and that his actions were a byproduct of that.

Clearing that away, I start into the studio when my phone vibrates in my purse with an incoming text.

Owen: What time are you done with your studio thing?

Me: Three probably. Is that okay? Your mom said she was picking Rory up to take her to get ice cream since it's her first day.

Owen: Yes. That's fine.

That's it. That's how he ends it. Ugh. He's so Mr. Darcy. Everything about him is like Jane Austen's broody hero from *Pride and Prejudice*. The money, the caring for a young girl, the haughtiness. The hotness!

I shouldn't be surprised. We've been playing the hot and cold game since I started a little more than a week ago, though over this past weekend, it turned more cold than hot. Today is only my first day trying this. It's also Rory's first day of school. Owen went in late to work so he could take her, and I took the T here because it was just easier, and I knew Grace was picking up Rory.

My first week with her went exceptionally well, and so far, I'm loving being her nanny. Her father is a different matter, but we're both getting better at pretending nothing happened between us and are very firm that nothing will happen again.

After another minute of staring at my screen and debating if I should say anything else, I shove it back in my purse, refusing to be tempted. I take a look around, unsure which way I'm supposed to go. Owen offered me a spot in the basement in the unfinished area, and Rory and I had fun setting one up. It's a great space for clay work, but not so fabulous for painting. and painting is my first and primary love.

"Are you here to check out the studio or the gallery?" comes a male voice from beside me, and I turn straight into rich dark eyes attached to a handsome, dark-skinned face that's smiling at me with blindingly white teeth.

"The studio. I didn't make an appointment, though."

"Not a problem. But you look as though you're not sure if you want to stay or go."

I laugh lightly at being so obvious that even a stranger picked up on it. "Because I'm not. You see, I graduated from art school about a year ago, and then seven months ago something not so great happened, and since then I haven't felt inspired, let alone had the desire to create anything. But I'm determined to change that because, despite everything, I do miss it." And why am I telling a stranger my every freaking inner thought?

"Ah. I see. First day back jitters. It gets easier. I promise. Where did you go to art school?" His warm smile hasn't left his face, and something about it puts me at ease.

"I went to school in Paris."

His eyes widen in appreciation. "Wow. That's very cool and different. I dream of going to Paris, but my boyfriend is more of a beach guy on vacation, and with him in only a bathing suit, I don't complain."

I laugh. "You'll have to show me pictures then."

He winks at me. "I only show him to people who make it through the door and into the studio. I can see how this would make you nervous if you've dealt with something not so pleasant. But you're here, and that's half the battle. You should stay and not go. I'm Billy, by the way. I own this place."

I blink and then sigh. "Of course you do. I'm Estlin. It's nice to meet you."

"Estlin. Gorgeous name for a gorgeous woman. What's your medium?" He puts his hand on the middle of my back and gently guides me deeper into the building.

"Painting is my main one. Acrylics, not oils or watercolors. And clay, but that's more fun than passion."

"Got it. We can work with either or both here. This is the studio."

We bypass the posh studio on the left and head right where everything is the opposite. Dirty and rough with paint-splattered concrete floors and a high open-rafter ceiling. There are about six or so people working in here, doing everything from throwing clay on the wheel to painting to sketching a nude model to working with metal.

"Right now, I have two open spaces for rent," he says as he walks me around, letting me take it all in. My blood hums through my veins and prickles my skin. I'm starting to feel it. That itch. That aching desire to create. "Each stall comes with a small safe, a sink that runs hot and cold water, and a fan if needed. If you require fire, we charge an extra fee to cover insurance and you need to provide the equipment."

"I won't need fire. The hardest thing I work with is occasionally marble."

"That's pretty badass, and our ventilation system is amazing, so if you do, dust isn't an issue. I have someone who works with wood, which I imagine marble is similar with that sort of mess."

I nod, taking it all in. "It's an incredible space."

"Thank you. I happen to agree. Still undecided? I can see your eyes swirling. In a good way."

"Definitely in a good way." I spin to him, giddy in a way I haven't been in so freaking long. I could rocket right out here with how high I'm feeling. "I'm in. But only if you show me a picture of your boyfriend."

He laughs. "You've got a deal."

"Awesome! Where do I sign?"

An hour later, he walks me out. Billy is a lot of fun, and we haven't stopped talking. It's a gorgeous day. The air is mild with a hint of the impending fall crisping the breeze. "So, are you a gym doer or a gym sign-up and never-goer?"

"Huh?"

He throws his arm around my shoulder. "Are you the sort who puts their money where their mouth is and does the work, or are you someone who pays the money and never shows up? I need to know what level of friendship I'm going to invest in here."

I snicker and roll my eyes. "I'm a doer. I'm motivated. But more than that, I'm ready."

And I am. It's the best fucking feeling in the world.

"Fantastic. Then you can be my new friend."

I prop my hands on my hips, ready to sass him back when my name is called out. My head whips around, and I see Rory and Owen standing on the sidewalk by the edge of the street.

A smile splits my face in two and I wave. "Hey! What are you doing here?"

"We wanted to surprise you!" Rory screams back. "Look!" She jumps up and down and then points at Owen, who doesn't look happy at all to be here, surprising me. It takes me a second to realize she's talking about the car they're standing in front of, and my eyes go wider than the moon and my jaw drops.

Billy gasps. "Holy shit, who is that fine fucking man, and did he buy you a car?"

I can't help my small, nervous giggle. "Best surprise ever. I'll be right there," I call back to Rory. "That's my boss," I tell Billy without giving him Owen's name. "And the car is so I can drive his daughter around safely. I'm her nanny."

"That's a hell of a good gig you've got there, but he does not look happy right now."

I turn back to Owen, his eyes fierce and intense as they flicker back and forth between me and Billy, his jaw hard and his stance rigid. "Uh, well, that's just sorta how he is. Think Mr. Darcy."

"Girl, Mr. Darcy nothing. I know that possessive look on a man. He does not like me talking to you, and he definitely doesn't like my arm around your shoulder. Good thing I didn't have my hand on your lower back, or he'd crush me in that fist he's clenching."

I shake my head, turning back to Billy. "No. It's not like that."

"Uh-huh. Take out your phone."

"What?" I question, scrunching my face up at him.

"Just do it. Take out your phone because I want you to text me, so I have your number. And don't argue with me that it's on your paperwork because I don't care."

I cock an eyebrow at him but do it anyway, pulling out my phone from my bag and texting him as he tells me his number. "There. Sent."

His phone buzzes, and he looks at his screen, smiling at me. He leans in and gives me a kiss on my cheek. "See you soon, Estlin. And if you don't believe me about your simply divine boss, take a look at his face now." With a wink and a self-satisfied smirk, Billy saunters off and I have no choice but to head over to Rory and Owen.

Hoisting my purse higher on my shoulder, I reaffix the smile on my face and skip over to them. "This is such a fun surprise. Thank you for coming to pick me up."

Owen doesn't speak, but if I thought he looked tense and displeased a moment ago, that has nothing on him now. He's so cold, so controlled, so detached, but the anger burning him up is cracking a fissure in his brutal armor.

Rory gives me a hug that I immediately return while ignoring her father. "How was your first day?"

"Fun." She starts to tell me all about it, everything from her teacher's name to the other kids in her class, to where her cubby for her backpack is, to who sits at her table. "Daddy surprised me too, and we wanted to show you the new car for us."

I stand to my full height, taking in the large, black, expensive as fuck Range Rover. "It's incredible," is all I can manage. Finally, I look over at Owen, his blue eyes blazing and his lips unsmiling. "Hi."

He doesn't say hi back.

"Thank you for coming to pick me up."

Still nothing. Okay then. That's how this is going to be.

"Grandma is going to meet us at the ice cream store."

"That's so fun. Let's go."

Without a word, Owen walks away, moving into the street and climbing into the front driver's seat with an elegant grace few men possess let alone can pull off.

Fuck. He's pissed. But... why? I mean... yeah, I'm not quite getting it. We said professional. We said we'd act like that night never happened between us.

"Kiddo, let's get you in and buckled up." Rory is oblivious to her father's foul mood as I open her door and she climbs in. We get her buckled, and then reluctantly I slide into the front passenger seat, shutting the door with a heavy click and taking in the extreme luxury of the car.

It's the middle of the afternoon, the sun is high in the sky, and traffic is light since it's not yet rush hour.

"Rory, I'm going to turn up the music back there for you," Owen tells her.

She cheers from her booster, already singing along loud and proud while I'm upfront trying not to visibly cringe or shift.

"Did you like the studio?" he asks, his voice icy and low.

"Yes, thank you. I ended up renting a space. It was nice of you to take the afternoon off to pick me up."

"Well," he says. "I wanted to surprise Rory, and she wanted to surprise you since the car came in."

Gulp. I can practically feel the tension pour off him in waves.

"Do you not like the studio in the basement?"

Oh. Is he... hurt? Somehow that doesn't seem right. I slide closer to him, trying not to breathe in too deeply. His scent, I've learned, creates a Pavlovian response in me. I smell him and I'm instantly wet.

"I love the space in the basement. The lighting is fantastic, and there's a lot of room and even an old sink that works. It's everything."

"But you plan to work here?"

"I plan to work in both spaces. I think the basement is perfect for my clay work, and the studio will be good for painting with all the natural light. I signed a monthly contract. It's been a very long time since I've worked, and since I used to solely work in the studio where I lived, I thought this might be just the separation I need."

"Why do you need separation like that, and why has it been so long since you've worked?"

Annnd I'm an idiot. "The family I nannied for made working on other things difficult since the children were so young."

I'm lying and he knows it, but he lets it slide. We're silent for another two blocks when his grip tightens on the wheel and he finally asks, "Who was the man you gave your number to who kissed you on the cheek?"

Here we go. I sit up a little straighter. "He owns the studio."

"Oh," he remarks, though there's no surprise or inflection in his voice. He's so controlled, but his animosity is starting to fissure through that control. "You met him today. As in just this afternoon?"

I grit my teeth, not liking where this is going. "Yes."

"Interesting. So you gave the owner your number and let him kiss you. Even though you had met him only an hour or so before that."

Bastard. "Yes. Did I not explain that clearly enough the first time you asked?"

"I'm just surprised, is all, though maybe I shouldn't be. You did more with me in less time. Still, that sounds like a bit of a conflict of interest to give him your number and let him kiss you, but I don't work in the art world. Or maybe a special deal is what you're after with him."

This motherfucker. "That's not what that was," I snap,

growing angrier by the second. "On either account. Why are you being like this?"

He shakes his head as if even he doesn't know the answer to that. I could tell him that Billy is gay and has zero interest in me and that the number and kiss were to prove a point, but Owen doesn't deserve that level of explanation.

He doesn't say anything else, and neither do I, and I can't help but wonder if things will smooth out between us from here or if this is the start of a brewing storm.

11

OWEN

At the end of every summer, my grandparents throw a massive party at their compound on the outskirts of Boston. It's one of Rory's favorite events, even though there aren't a lot of other kids there for her to play with. Probably because a lot of the attention falls on her, and she's doted on by everyone.

My grandmother, who would do anything to make her great-grandchild happy, goes all out. In addition to the large pool and waterslide they already have, she gets a bounce house, a magician, a cotton candy and popcorn machine, a milkshake station, and more food and specialty desserts than anyone could ever eat.

And because my grandmother likes to mess with shit she likely knows better than to mess with but doesn't care, she personally invited Estlin to join us after I made some noise about how she's the nanny and didn't need to come.

It's been three weeks since Estlin came to live with us. Two weeks since I lost my head about some asshole—who I've since come to find out is gay—kissing her. After that little meltdown, I've vowed to get my shit together.

And in these two weeks, we've fallen into a routine. School, studio, work, life. Things with Estlin have gotten both easier and harder. Easier in that I've learned how to spend the least amount of time with her as possible without it being construed as dickish. Harder in that now that I'm avoiding her and spending less time with her, I think about her more.

Everything in my day revolves around her.

She's constantly in my thoughts. If we're both at home, I'm wondering where she is in the house and what she's doing. If she's out somewhere, I'm wondering who she's with. When she picks up Rory or is in the car with her, I track them on my phone.

But it gets worse than that. I watch her.

When she's playing with Rory or in the living room playing piano—something I fucking love that she does—or simply reading in the back den that overlooks the garden, I make up an excuse that brings me near her.

Estlin is growing into a fixation. One I don't know how to stop.

She's sweet and funny and smart and considerate and adoring with Rory and is so fucking beautiful she takes my breath away. Why couldn't she have been an eighty-nine-year-old grandmother of fifty grandchildren like mine?

"What's so interesting?" Katy asks, holding Willow in her arms, only for me to immediately snatch her and tuck her against my chest. I kiss Willow's tiny head and then her cheek.

"I don't get to see enough of her." I glance up. "Or you."

"I know. But you're dodging my question."

"Rory is playing in the pool."

"Uh-huh." Katy's eyebrows bounce suggestively. "And the fact that she's playing with a stunning, partially rainbow-haired brunette who has curves that make me both drool and jealous has nothing to do with it, right?"

"First of all, don't ever talk to me about your curves. Second of all, absolutely not."

"She looks like a pinup, dude. Your nanny has an hourglass figure whether you like it or not, though we both know you do."

"Please stop," I beg. "That's honestly not helping anything."

"Fine," she grants. "You're right, and I'm sorry. I'll behave. Even if she is all anyone is talking about today."

"Oh my God! I am obsessed with your nanny!" My cousin, Keegan, one of my uncle Oliver's twin girls who is also one of Katy's closest friends, screeches at me as she flies over to us, wrapping a towel tighter around her chest, her wet, red hair spraying everywhere.

Katy gives me a *see what I mean* look.

"Straight facts," Keegan continues. "When I grow up, I want to be her. The hair, the nose ring, the badassery, the art, the living abroad—all of it. I'm legit jealous of Rory that she gets to hang out with her so much."

"Same!" Katy exclaims. "Totally the same! She's everything, right? And so nice!" She clutches Keegan's arm as if she just had a brilliant idea. "Oh, we should invite her out for girls' night next weekend."

"I'm already fifty shades ahead of you. I invited her, and she said she was in." Keegan turns to me, giving me a dubious expression. "She also said you were a good boss and nice. So I guess I'm wondering if you've drugged her or if you're blackmailing her into speaking kindly about you when we all know the truth."

I kiss Willow's cheek because it's sweet and soft, and she smells like innocence and perfection. So unlike everything and everyone else around me.

"Yes," I deadpan, rolling my eyes as sarcasm drips from my tongue. "Obviously, I both drugged and blackmailed Rory's nanny to say nice things about me."

"More like she's too sweet to speak badly about him to his

family," Stone claims as he joins us, sipping his margarita, and I need another drink. Or three if I'm going to make it through the rest of this party where everyone is obsessed with my nanny. "Or maybe things have progressed with the two of you, but you're keeping it to yourself."

"Fuck off, Stone. Don't start with that crap."

"I will take my baby back if you keep using words like fuck around her."

I smirk at Katy. "You mean the way you just did?"

Katy glares death threats at me.

"S'up, brother," Mason, who is Asher from Central Square's son and also an NFL quarterback for the Boston Rebels, comes over, not wearing a shirt because he likes to show off his man muscles whenever he can. He's got a home game tomorrow and is not drinking or eating junk like everyone else is, but I'm glad he stopped by. Until he says, "I just met your nanny. She's something else, isn't she?" He steals Willow from me, much to my dismay, and blows raspberries on her neck that make her wiggle and do her new baby smile.

Katy's eyebrows dance.

For fuck's sake.

"Why don't you start a fan club?" I grumble. "You, Keegan, and Katy can open the Boston chapter."

Mason laughs.

"What's funny?" Vander questions, joining us as he sips his tequila neat.

"Owen is being a defensive vagina about his new nanny," Stone declares.

"I am not."

"You can play it," he continues. "But you have the same grumpy, dismayed look you had on your face when Vander and I were joking about it at hockey."

"It's true," Vander agrees, tossing his tattooed arm over my shoulder. I shove him off, and he grins knowingly at me. "You should have seen him," he tells Katy, Keegan, and Mason. "I thought he was going to take his skates and slice our carotids over her."

"What is wrong with you men?!" Katy clips incredulously. "There are tiny ears present. Willow doesn't need to hear about your violence."

Stone and I give Katy a hard look, and then he pushes past her baby ears insanity as a slow, sly smile unravels across Mason's face. It's giving me the sudden urge to hurt him.

"So we shouldn't hit on her then?" he questions, and yep, he's asking to die.

"No," I answer evenly. "You shouldn't. Because Rory loves her, and I'll be forced to kill you if you ruin that for her."

"Oh. Right." Stone laughs. "*That's* why we can't hit on her."

"Like you're hitting on anyone? You're still a love-sick puppy all over a woman you spent a week with two years ago."

He squints at me. "That was a low blow even for you, asshole. Clearly, we've hit a nerve if you're taking cheap shots."

"Enough already," I bark and snatch his drink from him to finish it off before I shove the empty glass back at him.

He finds far too much amusement in this. So do Mason and Vander.

"I'm just saying there's something more than her simply being your nanny. At least that's how it appears. Or more like that's what I'm hoping is the case." Vander's expression grows serious as he rolls his tongue ring across his bottom lip and takes in my nanny, who is wet and wearing a retro bikini that goes up to her mid-stomach, and the top pushes her bouncy tits up to perfection.

"I happen to agree with him," Stone chimes in. "You haven't shown interest in anyone in far too long, and you clearly have an interest in her."

"Both of you let it go." One afternoon. I had hoped I could escape this for one afternoon. There is nowhere safe here. My grandmother asked me a thousand questions about her. My mother was practically waxing poetic about her. I thought maybe Katy would be safe, but nope. Maybe I should go find Bennett or my uncles and talk about sports or cool surgeries.

Keegan holds up her hand in surrender. "Fine. All teasing aside, it's okay to like her."

"Keegan," I groan. "For the love of all things holy, stop!"

"Just hear me out. All we're saying is, we think it'd be good for you to finally find someone and rejoin the human race. Maybe you'll smile more. Be happy. Less... grumpy."

My eyes momentarily close. They don't get it. None of them do.

"When was the last time you dated anyone?" Mason questions. "You clearly have a thing for her. Why is that so bad?"

"Let's, for argument's sake, say I do the stupid thing and sleep with my much younger, best friend's little sister. There's still the main issue of her being Rory's nanny. A nanny she likes a lot. A nanny she feels comfortable and safe with. *A nanny she does not want to lose,*" I emphasize, trying to strike my point home as I meet each of their gazes in turn. "I get that she's the first female other than my family to be around me since Angelica, but that doesn't make her right for me. Yes, she's beautiful, and I'm not blind to how sweet she is, but so what? It doesn't matter. She's a no-go. And that's final."

They have no rebuttal for that. Thank the Lord. Hopefully, I can now salvage some piece of this party without it all being about Estlin. I have a twenty-four-hour shift starting Monday morning. It's the first one since I hired her. This is what I need her for, and they know it.

She's the shiny new toy for my cousins and friends. And now Hayes Monroe, who is Zax's son is in the pool talking to her. Has no one ever seen a woman outside of this group before?

I get it. There's something about her that draws you in.

But does she have to be everywhere all the time and be everyone's obsession?

I snatch Willow out of Mason's arms, ignoring his cries of protest.

"Fine," Keegan relents. "We'll back off about her. You're probably right about Estlin not being a good idea for you. But one of these days, maybe you'll try finding someone again."

My brows furrow in annoyance. I didn't sign up for a therapy session. "I'm taking my goddaughter out of the sun," I announce and walk away with Willow.

"We just want to see you happy, brother," Mason calls out to me, and I don't bother acknowledging him. I need a break from this crap. I was happy once with someone, and it was a lie. A sham. A mirage in the desert. I won't put myself or Rory through that again.

It's simply not worth it.

I start to go toward the house when my name is called out. I stop and look over to find my grandmother giving me a smile and a wave. "Owen, darling. Perfect timing. Come sit by me and bring that sweet baby with you." My grandmother, Octavia Abbott-Fritz, the matriarch of the Fritz family and Boston's reigning queen, is sitting on the edge of the patio under an umbrella with a martini in her hand because that's how she rolls, along with my uncle Kaplan, his wife Bianca, and my uncle Oliver.

I walk across the lawn and take the open chaise beside my grandmother.

"Hey. Good to see you. It's been a while," Kaplan teases. He's a pediatric cardiothoracic surgeon, and yesterday we spent the better part of four hours in the OR together.

"Well, it has been a while since *I've* seen him," my grandmother inserts.

"I'll try to come by more often," I promise, because she's right. It's been a little since I've seen her, and that's not right.

"It's a lovely party." I lean back and shift Willow, who seems to be almost asleep, closer to my grandmother.

"Yes. It always is. Do you remember when we used to host them at the Martha's Vineyard home?"

I glance at her, smiling fondly at the memory. "Those were some of my favorites."

She pats my arm and then runs her hand over the back of Willow's head. "Mine too. Shame it's such trouble to get everyone out there now."

"Our family got very big," Oliver muses, looking at something on his phone.

A smile lights up my grandmother's face. "It did. And it continues to grow." She looks at Willow in my arms. "Rory told me she's very happy this year in school."

"She is. Changing schools was the right call for her. It's only been a couple of weeks, but the report I received from her new teacher is very reassuring."

"And things are working out with Eddie—I mean Estlin?" Oliver questions. He's good friends with Wes, Jack and Estlin's father. "She's grown up. I feel like the last time I saw her was years ago."

"Yes. She's lovely." My grandmother's eyes sparkle. "Rory seems to like her."

Inwardly, I sigh. "She does, and yes, so far things are working out well."

"I'm glad you hired someone," Kaplan agrees. "I know you had your reservations, but I think you can see now that it was the right call to make."

"It was. I know it was."

"But," Bianca chimes in with a small laugh on her lips.

"But nothing." Nothing really. "Am I..." I feel so fucking stupid for asking this, but I have to know. "Do I appear unhappy?"

"What?" Kaplan and Oliver spit out, only my grandmother reaches over and places her hand on my arm.

"Yes," she says in no uncertain terms, her green eyes holding mine.

"Why are you asking?" Bianca follows up, but knowing Bianca as I do, she has a reason for that question.

"It's been mentioned by pretty much everyone that I'm grumpy and unhappy." Even Katy hinted at something similar when she told me I should take a vacation.

"Are you?" Bianca throws back at me, and I knew it.

I shrug, not exactly knowing how to answer that. Or, more likely, not willing to face the truth.

"My short answer is, if you don't know, you likely are."

"I have to agree with my wife," Kaplan declares. "So maybe you need to figure out how you change that."

MY GRANDMOTHER'S and Bianca's words have been bugging the shit out of me all afternoon and evening. It never occurred to me that everyone saw me as unhappy. Hell, it never occurred to me that I *was* unhappy. It's just life. I'm busy. I'm cautious. I have a daughter who hasn't had the easiest time of it and needs as much of me as I can give her, and I already spend too much time away from her with my job.

Plus, I don't see how the pinnacle of happiness is found in someone else. I need to find that happiness for myself. But I also appreciate that much of my unhappiness and shit attitude have stemmed from all that Rory and I went through.

I haven't wanted another relationship. The idea of dating random women, of trying to wine and dine and deal with their bullshit isn't appealing. I don't want to wade through gold-diggers. I don't want to manage high-maintenance. And I absolutely do not want a revolving door of women in and out of my daughter's life.

Do I wish I had sex more often? Of course I do.

It's just not worth the price I'd have to pay right now.

That doesn't make me unhappy. It simply means my situation is different and unique and not a bed of fucking roses. I'd love to have more kids. I'd love to give Rory siblings. I'd love to have what Katy has with Bennett. I just don't see that happening right now, and I sure as hell don't see that happening with Estlin, who is in an entirely different stage of life than I am.

It's like I told Jack last week, happily ever after isn't in the cards for me.

"Today was fun," Estlin whispers with an almost dreamy sigh as she stares into the back seat at a sleeping Rory.

"I'm glad you had a good time." I mean that. I'm glad she came because she did look like she had fun.

She twists her head, her body tucked against the seat. "Did you not?"

"I…" I trail off, rubbing a hand along my jaw. What is it that Vander said about me? That I had a grumpy, dismayed expression. Keegan and Mason said I wasn't happy and hinted that I'm not the nicest. Even Stone got in on it. Is that what I've become? A grump? A man so miserable and wound so tight, no one wants to be around me?

Is this who I want to be?

Is this the father I want Rory to see?

I glance in the rearview mirror and quickly take in my girl. She laughed and splashed around all day. She ate garbage and ran around to the point where she wore herself out. And I didn't appreciate it. I didn't get to enjoy it with her because I was sulking like a child. Estlin is the first woman I've slept with in a very long time. That's what makes it so easy to think about her. It's not Estlin per se. It's what she and that night represent. Right?

Yes. Has to be. That makes total sense.

I flash another glance at Rory and then, with my mind made up, ask, "Do you have any plans for next month?"

"Next month?" Estlin parrots questioningly.

"I'd like to take Rory sailing on my uncle's yacht. She's never been, and I think both of us could use the break. We haven't been on a vacation in a very long time." I glance over at her and then immediately back at the road. "Rory's school break is the second week of October. Would you like to join us?"

She sits up a bit. "I don't know. You'd want me to come with you on vacation?" Her face scrunches up as if she's still unsure that's what I asked her.

"If you'd like, but there's certainly no obligation if you'd rather not or it doesn't work well for you." I pull into the driveway and down to the garage on the back side of the house. Estlin hasn't said anything else and is still silent as I turn off the car and close the garage. Unbuckling Rory as gently as I can, I lift her out of her booster seat and straight into my arms. She's dead weight, her body hanging limply, and I carry her inside and straight up the stairs.

Estlin doesn't follow me, and I wonder if she thinks the invitation was too much or somehow inappropriate. I meant for her to come as Rory's nanny, not anything else, but maybe I didn't convey that sentiment well.

Pulling back the blanket, I set Rory down on her bed and slip off her sandals. I cringe that she hasn't brushed her teeth after all the sugar she ate today, but I don't want to wake her when she's this out. Instead, I kiss her forehead, turn on her nightlight, and tuck her in.

"Good night, Moonshine. I love you so much."

My hand runs along her long hair, and then I leave her and shut the door behind me. I blow out a strained breath, look down the hall toward Estlin's room, and then turn away and head back downstairs.

I flip on the light in my man cave and go straight for my bar. A soft tap on the open door calls my attention just as I set a glass down on the bar top.

"May I come in?"

I smirk. "Yes."

Slowly, she enters and hesitantly walks toward me.

"You're very proper around me now."

"You're a gentleman, remember? Gentlemen expect manners. Even surly gentlemen."

I chuckle lightly even as the surly comment zings me. "Wiseass." I point to the stool on the other side of the bar. "Have a seat. Do you want one?"

"Yes. Thank you." She takes a seat, and I pull out another glass and set it down.

"Do you want ice?"

"If it's not too much trouble."

I inwardly sigh and go over to the ice maker and scoop some into both our glasses, only to remember something and turn back to her. "Do you actually know the difference in your bourbons?"

A smile curls up her lips. She got some sun today and now has an adorable smattering of freckles across the bridge of her nose. "Yes. At least some of them. The father I nannied for in London is Irish and big into his whiskeys and bourbons. His wife, who is French, hates them, so he and I would drink together, and we started exploring different brands and doing taste tests."

"Care to play a game then?"

"Depends. What did you have in mind?"

OWEN

"How about we have a little fun and get to know each other better?"

Her aqua eyes widen with surprise before they immediately narrow with suspicion. "Better how?"

"I'll pour us four glasses each. If you guess the right bourbon, you get to ask me a question. If you guess the wrong one, I get to ask you one. And we have to answer, no matter what."

"So, this isn't like truth or dare?"

My elbows drop to the polished wood counter, and I lean in her direction. "I'm thirty-four not twenty-two. I'm a bit old for truth or dare, and frankly, the only good thing I ever found that comes out of that game is kissing or stripping."

A blush tints up her cheeks. "And we won't be doing either of those."

"No. We won't be doing either of those. Sorry to disappoint you."

She laughs, tucking a wayward strand that fell out of her messy bun back behind her ear. "What makes you think I'd want to kiss you again? Or see you strip?"

I shrug and stand to my full height, folding my arms. "I'm

a great kisser, and we both know you've got a thing for me shirtless." I turn and start to set out more glasses before this gets out of hand and I remind her just how great of a kisser I am.

That's not what this is about.

This is us getting to know each other, getting more comfortable with each other, and her not walking on eggshells around me while thinking of me only as a fucking asshole because, for some reason, it bothers me that she does more than anyone else right now.

"What do you say? Are you brave enough to play my little game?"

She raises a challenging brow. "This doesn't seem fair to you. The odds are in my favor with this."

I shake my head. "While I appreciate your concern for me, I won't show you which bourbons I'm pouring. But you do have the advantage in that you can see my shelves, so you'll be able to narrow it down. Besides, I may not know you well yet, but I think I've already figured out you're not one to back down from a challenge."

"You're right. I'm not." She sits up a little straighter and leans her forearms on the bar top, all business. "Let's do it. But how will you know I won't cheat and watch you take them off the shelf and pour them?"

Good point.

"I could blindfold you."

Her eyes flare and my cock twitches, and I know that's the wrong path to take.

"Or you could just swivel around on your bar stool and face the other way."

She laughs, and without a word, spins her stool so she's facing the opposite direction.

I get to work, pulling four random bottles and pouring eight glasses in total. I set hers down on the bar in front of her seat and mine in front of me, and then I put everything back where it came from.

"You can turn back around."

She does, eyeing each of the glasses one by one and then slowly dragging her gaze up to mine. "You remember what you poured into each glass?"

"Yes."

"How?" she asks skeptically.

"I have a photographic memory. It's how I also graduated top of my class in both college and med school. But that's not one of your questions, so it doesn't count."

Her eyebrows bounce. "Still, I'm impressed. Okay. I believe you, and I believe you won't cheat. Here goes." She reaches for the first glass, and I do the same. With our eyes locked, we both polish off the first one, then set the empty down on the counter. She licks her lips, tilts her head, and studies the shelves behind me. "Nice one. That was Blanton's black label."

"Yes, it was. Very good. Now *I'm* impressed." I wave a hand in her direction. "Ask me anything."

Fire lights her eyes as if they're glowing from within, and she starts to swivel back and forth on her stool as she thinks. "All right. Um." She licks her lips. "What's a secret you've never told anyone?"

That every night I fall asleep thinking about you after I have to take a cold shower. But again, that's simply because of what she represents and not who she is. I'm positive of it. I'm determined to fucking prove it. But more than that, that's a secret I'll carry to my grave.

"The night Rory was born, Angelica didn't want her in the room with her. That should have been a tip-off, but I didn't think too much about it. I stood in the nursery, unable to sleep, and just stared at my little girl, thinking about everything. About all the diseases she could contract and surgeries she could require. About all the bad things she could encounter in this world and how I had no clue how I'd protect her from them. When I came to, I was sitting on the floor with my head between my knees. I'd had a panic attack and passed out right there in the nursery."

"Holy shit!" Estlin exclaims, covering her mouth with her hand.

"The nurse who helped me told me that worrying would make me a good dad, but panicking about things I can't control would clip her wings, give me an ulcer, and ruin us both. I try to remember that every time things beyond my control happen, even if I don't always succeed."

She stares at me for a long moment, only to pick up the second glass without saying another word about it. The whiskey goes straight down the back of her throat, and I follow, downing my shot.

She grimaces as she swallows and shudders. "Argh. That was rough. Jack Daniels."

I laugh. "Nope. Evan Williams. I bought it for Katy once as a joke because she had a hickey on her neck from a guy she met with that name. So now I have the bottle."

"I hope Katy's Evan kissed her better than that shot kissed me. I can still feel it and not in a good way."

"Here." I go into a nearby cabinet and pull out a container of pretzels I have and pour some into a dish. "Chase it down with these."

"Thank you." She grabs one of the twists and pops it in her mouth, chewing as she watches me carefully, not at all looking forward to my question. I want to ask her about her ex in Paris. She only briefly mentioned him, and I know she's holding something back from me. But I want to earn her trust—earn her comfort—and pushing her somewhere she doesn't want to go with me won't help that.

"What's the wildest thing you've ever done? And you can't say something easy like going to the hotel with me."

She smirks. "What if it's true?"

"It's not. No way." I fold my arms and wait patiently.

"You're pulling my answers," she accuses, but I can see there's something. She's blushing and fidgeting in her chair. "I was an artsy book nerd."

"*Was.* But that was when you were a kid. Give it to me, Estlin. The whole truth."

She puffs out a breath. "You won't like my answer," she warns as she tugs the elastic from her hair and vigorously rubs her fingers into her scalp. All of her beautiful dark hair with splashes of pink and blue tumbles around her shoulders and back, messy and wild, and I remember what those thick, silky strands felt like against my hands.

I swallow harshly and drop my gaze to the four empty glasses before us. "Try me."

"I lost my virginity at seventeen in a sex club."

"What?" I practically shout. "Seventeen?! A sex club?!"

She shrugs. "I told you you wouldn't like it. But yes, I did, and if you tell Jack—"

I hold up my hand, stopping her. "Our secrets stay between us, and I'll never tell them to Jack. But... I don't know. I don't mean to judge because I'm not. Just... explain."

She runs her finger along the rim of the next glass. The bourbon is getting to her a little. Her face has a glow it didn't before. It's the same glow it had that Friday night. It's alluring and sexy as hell. Maybe the bourbon is getting to me too because the idea of her in a sex club...

"I had just gotten to Paris. I'm young for my grade and didn't turn eighteen until the middle of October. My roommate was about to turn nineteen and was appalled that I was still a virgin. I had spent high school with my books and my art and found the boys my age to be boring and sophomoric. So my roommate took me to a sex club, just so I could see what sex was all about. I hadn't intended anything to come of it, but then

I met someone there. We spent the night talking, and I went back the following two nights with the same result. On night four, I let him take my virginity, and we continued to see each other for a few weeks after that until I stopped going back to the club."

I blink, utterly floored. "Was it kinky?" I don't know why I ask. But I do, and I have to fucking know. We weren't kinky that night. The sex was hot and a little dirty but definitely not kinky.

"The sex or the club?" Her lips twist in amusement.

"Either. Both."

"A little, and only if that's what you were after."

Jesus hell. My dick is defying the laws of whiskey. Thank God I'm standing behind the bar and she can't see it.

"Did you enjoy it?"

She leans back in her stool and throws her arms behind her head. She's relaxed and has that playful glint to her. The one that lures me in like a moth to a flame. "Yes, I enjoyed it. It was so wrong and so unlike anything I'd ever done or thought to experience. He was older, and when I learned he was married, I stopped going to see him. It plagued me for weeks and weeks. I had no clue until another woman in the club told me."

"I lost my virginity at sixteen in the back of my car. It was cramped and uncomfortable, and she didn't enjoy it despite my best efforts because she was too nervous to ever relax. Your first time sounds like a hell of a lot more fun."

Her hands fall back to the counter and cradle the next glass. "Was she your girlfriend?"

"Yes. We went to school together and dated for about four months, I think."

"Hmm." She slides the glass back and forth along the wood. "Okay. Next one."

She picks up the glass and drinks it down, and for a moment, I watch her do it, still a bit lost in what she just told me.

I lift my glass and start to drink when she blurts out, "I'd like to come."

Alcohol sprays from my mouth in a brown shower, covering every surface around me. I cough at the burn in the back of my throat and wipe my wet lips and chin with the back of my arm.

"I meant on the trip," she finishes, her lips stretching wide even as she fights her laughter. "Not like... *that*. Are you okay over there?"

I grab some paper towels and wipe up my mess, grateful that I at least didn't get her. "Awesome. And thanks for that. That was great. A lot of fun and not at all embarrassing."

"Anytime. Glad to know I can still rile you up. Oh, and that was Pappy Freaking Van Winkle you gave me, so now I feel especially bad that you sprayed it instead of drinking it."

I wipe my forehead and lean against the wall behind me. "I thought maybe you were dodging my offer. I meant for you to com—join us," I amend, "as Rory's nanny. Not as anything else."

"I know. I would like to join you." She smirks. "I didn't want you to think I was ungrateful or unappreciative of the offer. And I would love to go."

"But?"

"But... I don't know how smart it is to do that, and I'm thinking of maybe not going."

I nod slowly, taking in her words and their not-so-well-hidden meaning. "It wouldn't be like that for us, Estlin because it can't be. Still, I appreciate your honesty, and if you change your mind, it's an open invitation. Now, moving on, you answered that correctly, so go ahead and ask me something."

She stands, picks up her last glass, and drinks it. "You tried to trick me. This is scotch and I don't know what brand." I get a coy smile, and then she's over by the pool table. "Do you play or is this for show?"

"Is that your question because I'll give you points for

knowing it was scotch and not bourbon, despite not knowing the brand?"

"Not even close."

"I play. Sometimes."

"Good. Come play with me. This you'll beat me at since I suck at pool. Or we can play darts again?"

I likely should go to bed. Even if it's only nine o'clock. I should go upstairs and take that cold shower and do everything I can to not think about her the way I do every night. I haven't jerked off since she moved in here because every time I get hard and go to touch myself, I see her, and I can't jerk off to my kid's nanny. I can't allow my mind to roam and the fantasies to start.

Once they start, they'll never stop. They'll only grow and twist, and I can't do that and still have this with her.

So yeah, I should go to bed. I shouldn't be picking up my last glass, drinking it down, and then coming out from behind the bar area to join her at the pool table the way I am.

"Let's stick to pool," I suggest, even if it's so fucking stupid I want to kick my own ass. She's wearing loose cotton shorts and a tank top, and I'm going to have her bending over the goddamn table like that?

"Good. You break."

I grab a stick from the rack and hand her one.

"Thanks. Okay, tell me two truths and a lie."

I throw her a curious glance as I slide the pool cue between my fingers and then smack the white ball dead center, sending it careening toward the triangle of multicolored balls. It hits with a loud *crack,* and the balls go flying. Three balls clunk into pockets on either side of the table.

"Two truths and a lie?" I move around the table, line up, and shoot, the seven ball just missing as it bounces to the side of the pocket.

"Yep. I don't really have any good questions for you."

Estlin leans over the side of the table to take her shot, and my gaze immediately hits the floor when her cleavage spills out of the top of her tank top. The stick slides through her fingers once, and then she steadies it and tries again. Hitting the cue ball, she knocks the fourteen but misses.

I set my stick against the edge of the table and come around like the stupid asshole I am tonight and stand behind her like a cliché. Like I'm some guy in a cheesy movie making his move on the gorgeous woman he's trying to pick up in a smoky bar.

"Here. Like this," I start, lining her hips up and then helping her grip with the stick. I lean over the back of her, smelling her hair and feeling the heat of her body, her ass right up against my dick that is not at all unhappy to be in this position with her. Her breath catches, but I ignore it as I place my hands over hers and take the shot with her, showing her how to do it.

The white ball sails straight into the fourteen, and this time it goes into the pocket.

I release her and walk to the other side of the table, putting distance between us once more. Her face is flushed, and her eyes linger on the table for an extra second before she rights herself.

"Thanks," she says, her voice a little breathy, and I ignore that too.

I shouldn't have touched her like that. I shouldn't be doing any of this. But I can't seem to make myself stop either. Being near her is like a drug. A high that lingers long after she's gone. I like spending time with her. I want her relaxed around me. I don't want to be the jerk everyone thinks I am.

Not with her. Not with anyone. Not anymore.

I want to be the guy I used to be. The one she brought out of me that night. The one who took her to that hotel room and spent the night making her scream for me.

I clear my throat, ready to give her these two truths and a lie, when Rory's voice calls out to me. "Daddy? I threw up."

My head whips over to find Rory an absolute mess. This girl

has the most sensitive stomach, and I should have known better than to let her eat all those sweets the way I did. "Oh, Moonshine. Are you okay?"

I rush over to her and peel her disgusting clothes off.

"My tummy hurts."

I kiss the top of her head and then her forehead. No fever.

"Let me get a bag for those." Estlin pinches her nose and visibly holds her breath, likely unable to handle the smell of vomit, but I'm not only a father, I'm a pediatric surgeon, and a little vomit doesn't scare me off. Plus, Rory is the queen of vomit.

Estlin is back in a flash, and I put the soiled clothes in the trash bag.

"What else can I do?" Estlin asks, worry all over her face.

"Nothing. Go enjoy your evening. I've got her. Come here, baby girl." I pick her up and carry her upstairs to give her a bath. Only Estlin isn't having that. She's by my side, running ahead of me to get the bath started.

"Here. I'll give her a bath, you strip her bed," she tells me. "You seem better with the throw-up than I am."

"Thank you," I say with a smile. One she returns, and for a moment, we get lost in each other. Just staring until Rory breaks the spell with a small whimper. The two of us set to work, me stripping the bed and Estlin giving her a bath.

Once Rory's bed is cleaned up and remade, I grab some fresh pajamas and enter the bathroom, only to stop by the door and lean against it. I watch as Estlin rinses out the conditioner and gently brushes the long strands of Rory's hair. All the while Estlin whispers sweet, soft, comforting words and rubs Rory's back to make her feel better.

My chest pinches and reflexively my fist comes up to rub the ache away. I'm in deep with this girl. She's perfect. For Rory. For... me.

I get Rory out of the bath and by the time she is tucked back into bed and I'm lying in mine, I realize I didn't get to tell Estlin my two truths and a lie.

They were going to be generic. Not anything like the ones floating through my head now.

1. Hiring her was one of the best decisions I've ever made.
2. I had a lot of fun playing drinking games and pool with her tonight.
3. I'm not at risk of liking her a hell of a lot more than I should.

I guess it's pretty easy to tell which one is the lie. And that's what scares me most.

13

ESTLIN

For nearly three weeks, I've felt like the biggest fraud on the planet. I've vacillated between I can do this, and these things can take time after such a long hiatus to I'm never going to be able to paint again and I need to figure something else out for my life. It's been a rollercoaster of emotions mixed with a lot of tears and cursing. The rollercoaster I have going at home with Owen isn't helping either.

I had fun with him last weekend.

I don't know what spawned the change, but after the party at his grandparents' compound, he's been lighter. Smiling more. On Sunday, we watched his friend Mason Reyes play and beat Minnesota. Jack came over along with a few of his other friends, including Katy, Bennett, and baby Willow. I'm not a huge football fan, and I didn't want to overstep by inviting myself to watch with everyone—I am still the nanny—but he insisted that if I wanted to, I was welcome.

It was a drastic departure from the avoidance we had going before that.

I'm trying. I'm trying *so* hard. But... I'm really starting to like him. More than I did before.

But this week I've done everything I could to fully get myself back in line, including *not* liking my boss. I drop off Rory at school and immediately come here instead of going back home to the studio in the basement. Clay, for some reason, is coming back to me faster and easier than painting. Maybe because clay is different for me than painting is. Clay is sort of mindless, whereas painting is all emotion.

I've started five different canvases that have all ended up in the dumpster Billy has out back. I finally broke down and called my mother yesterday in a fit of tears, and she took me to lunch and told me that forcing it won't get me where I want to be and that I have to feel inspired first.

Tonight, I'm going out with Katy, Keegan, Kenna, who is Keegan's twin, Wren, and their friend Tinsley Monroe, whom I have yet to meet. I'm looking forward to a girls' night out. But first, I need to fucking do this shit already.

I sigh and roll my neck, staring at the most daunting of all things an artist can face. A blank canvas. Some see endless possibilities and do not panic when faced with it, and that's what I'm trying to channel.

"You're overthinking this," Billy comments, sipping his coffee and eyeing me over the rim of his mug. "I've watched you in here for weeks now, and I've given you space since every artist has their own process, but you're too in your head with this."

I huff out a breath and nod as I keep my back to him and stare balefully at my canvas. "I know."

"No, honey, you don't. That's the problem. I don't know what happened to you that led you here or to this point, but shut that bitch down and lock her ass in a closet and remember what you *love* about painting."

I glance over my shoulder at him, trying to swallow the emotion threatening to rise from within. "I let him steal it from me. I allowed him to suck the joy out of it, and with that, it turned into something I was afraid of. His opinion held too much power. He knew it, and he used it against me."

Billy blinks at me, not understanding what I'm saying, but it's true. I think that's what my issue is. In the months leading up to that night with Claude, he had criticized everything I created. And not in a constructive way, but in a negative, terrorizing way. Painting became anxiety-provoking instead of pleasurable, and when he destroyed my work, it was the final nail in my coffin.

But I don't want that to be my story, and I don't want Claude to own that piece of me because, before all of that, I fucking loved painting. It was my life's blood. I could spend hours and hours doing it without a break. I'd sweat, bleed, cry, and work myself past the point of exhaustion, but I'd still come out smiling.

Claude stole that smile and turned my work against me. It became poison, and I'm desperate to turn it back into magic.

I turn back to my canvas. Close my eyes. Take a deep, cleansing breath. Open my eyes. And step forward.

I feel Billy come in behind me, and then suddenly something large and heavy is over my ears. I jump and spin around, my hands shooting up to my ears. "What are these?"

He rolls his eyes. "They're called headphones, sweetie. Surely, you've heard of them."

I roll my eyes back at him. "Yes. Thanks for that. What are they doing on my ears?"

"They're mine and I'm letting you borrow them. Put on some music and block everything else out. Get out of your fucking head, because the only opinion that matters in this world is yours. You're an artist, Estlin. Now make some fucking art."

He drops a kiss on my cheek and then saunters off, leaving me here with his headphones. I never listened to music while I was working before, but maybe Billy is right. Maybe some music is just the thing to get everything else out of my head.

I go to my phone and sync up his headphones, and then I start blasting the play mix I listen to when I work out. It's a lot of loud, high-energy beats without a lot of words, and immediately I start bopping my head back and forth.

I have my palette all ready filled with paints, and I lift my brush and dab it in the red before I add a touch of white to it and blend them on the bottom of the palette until it makes a stunning pale rose. Energy flows through me, and that giddy high I felt when I first stepped into this studio comes swarming through me like a pack of bees.

I roll my shoulders, crack my neck, and then bring my brush up to my canvas. And for the next five hours until I have to pick up Rory at school, I make some fucking art.

I've been a ball of energy all afternoon. I picked up Rory from school, and we went for a hike around the grounds of the house, and then we had dinner together because Owen got stuck in the OR with a patient. Now Rory is sitting on my bed, helping me pick out an outfit for tonight. I have no idea what to wear. I haven't been out with a group of women in forever, and the last time I did, I was in Paris, and many of those women were more Claude's friends than mine.

"I like the red dress," Rory tells me as she bounces her butt up and down on the end of my mattress.

"You don't feel like it's too much?" And too tight. Yeesh. I can hardly breathe. I step out of the closet, standing before the full-length mirror on the back of the door, twisting this way and that.

"What's too much?" she asks, and it's a valid question even

if she means it in her childlike way and not in an existential one.

The dress is short and *tight* and shows a decent amount of cleavage with the plunging square neckline.

"This dress is too much." My old art professor and the mother of the children I nannied for gave it to me, swearing she'd never be able to wear it again. But she was built much differently than I am, and this dress shows that. "It's more of a clubbing dress than a going out for drinks dress."

Rory shrugs. She has no idea what I'm talking about. My hair and makeup are done, except for eyeshadow and lipstick, since I wanted to pick the outfit first.

"How about jeans and a cute top?"

"That's what Katy usually wears when she comes over."

"Perfect. Thank you."

Just as I start to tug my dress up and over my head, there's a knock on my door followed by the sound of it opening.

"Rory? Estlin?"

"Ah. Hold on." Blindly, I rush toward the closet, only to bump into the doorframe. *Ouch.* "Sorry. I was just getting changed." I tug and pull, but the dress is stuck somehow, and I can't get it. My arms are over my head, bound and tangled in the red fabric, while the rest of the dress is cinched around my upper body and face.

"Are you—oh."

I can feel my face turning the same shade as the dress I'm wrapped in because Owen is no doubt getting a good look at me in my strapless bra and thong with this thing suffocating me.

"Sorry! I didn't realize you were changing." I hear a bang and an "Ow" and a muttered curse under his breath like he too just walked into a wall or a doorframe. "I'm... yeah. Bye."

"Owen, don't go!"

"What?" he chokes. "No. I have to go."

"Please, wait."

"Estlin, are you kidding me right now?" He sounds like he's in pain. "You're—"

"I know what I am!" I shriek desperately. "But I'm stuck." I wiggle and fight, and somehow, I think that makes it worse.

He groans. "Can you stop moving like that? Rory is right there, and I..."

"You're what?"

He comes in behind me, his hands on my hips to stop my movement, only that's not all he does. He presses himself against me, so I feel... *oh*. Like when we played pool last weekend, he's hard. For me. And I shouldn't care or like it because I feel utterly ridiculous right now like this, and he's my boss, and we're on a good streak with each other.

But...

I lean back into him, and his grip on me turns bruising. "Don't do that, Estlin. Stay perfectly still for me, and then both of our problems will go away."

"Okay," I whisper, my heart racing in my chest and my teeth sawing into my bottom lip. "I won't move."

"Good girl." He starts to tug and pull on the dress. "What the hell is this thing made out of, and how are you so stuck in it?"

"I don't know," I wail, starting to feel some panic from it. "I knew it didn't fit me well. I knew it was too small. But I want to look hot tonight when I go out with your people because I haven't been out with women my age in a hundred years, and I..." Why am I crying? What is wrong with me?

"Shh," he hushes, his hand running up and down my spine. "It's okay. I've got you."

I sniffle, feeling so foolish for getting emotional about this.

"I'm going to give it a good, hard tug, and let's see how we do. When I do that, I want you to pull against me."

"Got it."

"One, two—"

"Just do it already!"

"I hate it when women say that to me."

I burst out laughing, and it instantly dries my tears, which is probably why he said it, but still, Owen made a joke. It's freaking adorable.

"There." He yanks with all his might, and I pull against him, and we're both struggling and twisting and moving and grunting. Except I trip over his feet, bang into the doorframe behind me again, and tumble forward. "Shit," he hisses, trying to catch me, but his hands are still over my head, and we both slam into the wall of my closet, my body pressed right up against his now.

"Sorry! I'm so sorry. Are you okay?"

"I have no way to answer that."

I'm about to ask what that means, but then I register that his hot breath is fanning straight into my cleavage. Oh hell.

"Your chest is blushing, sweet thing."

I whimper and shudder as his hands meet my ribs. Thankfully, he pushes me back instead of pulling me closer because I'm not sure I have the same level of self-control right now that he does.

"Rory?!" he calls out, and my eyes pinch shut. Shit. Rory. God, what's wrong with me?

"Yeah?"

"Estlin is stuck in this dress, and I have to cut her out of it. Can you go find your safety scissors and bring them to me? Be careful carrying them. Keep the metal part in your fist as you walk."

"I know, I know. Okay."

"I'm sorry," I murmur, feeling embarrassed and foolish all over again. "I didn't mean—"

"I know. Being attracted to your nanny sucks, and it's not helping anything."

I smile a stupid, girlish smile because he can't see it. "Being attracted to your boss isn't so great either."

A moment later, Rory returns. "Don't move now," Owen warns. "I mean it. I don't want to cut you, but this dress has seen its last day."

I snicker. "I won't move."

The sawing and tearing sound of scissors on fabric fills the room, and I hold dutifully still as Owen cuts me out of the dress, freeing me.

I take a relieved breath and sigh. "Oh my God, thank you. I thought I was going to be stuck in that thing forever."

Owen chucks the tattered fabric to the floor. "You're welcome. It was truly a bit too much my pleasure."

He winks and walks out, giving me my privacy and taking Rory with him. I snatch a one-shoulder sweater and a pair of jeans, slather red lipstick on, and decide I'm good to go. I run down the stairs and say good night to Owen and Rory.

Owen's eyes are all over me, a darkness to them as he takes in what I'm wearing along with my red lips. He frowns, his gaze hardening, and pulls out his phone, essentially dismissing me. As I climb in my car and drive toward the bar to meet up with the women, I tell myself it's for the best. That our boundaries are essential, and we've already strayed, coloring outside the lines more than once or twice.

Still, as I meet the women who are all single except for Katy, listen as they scour the bar for hot, eligible men who don't hold my attention the way my boss does, I can't help but wish I were home with him. And that is a dangerous thing to wish for.

14

———————

OWEN

Stepping out of my bedroom, I rub my bleary eyes. This week has been brutal. One tough case after another, and I have to work through Saturday, and it's only Thursday evening. The only good thing going right now is that Rory is in a good place. Estlin has been here for more than a month now, and her help with Rory has been everything for both of us.

I don't have to race over to my parents' or Wren's or anyone else's to pick Rory up. She's home and her homework is done, and she helps Estlin make food for us to eat. I used to have my housekeeper occasionally make dinners and leave them in the fridge for me to reheat, but Estlin loves to cook, and Rory loves to help her, and it's been so good for her.

And me.

I admit that my level of stress has significantly gone down.

Estlin takes Rory to gymnastics on Thursday afternoons, and I get texts and videos of them together. Other than the fact that the woman makes my dick hard morning, noon, and night, I'm managing. No more drunken games or clothing mishaps for us.

I still regret that I lost my head when Estlin came downstairs last weekend before she went out looking beautiful and sexy—after I saw and felt what she was wearing under her clothes—and I texted Katy, telling her not to let her get hit on or go home with anyone.

It was wrong. I had no place asking that, and Katy even called me out on it.

Still, my jealousy and desire for her are unlike anything I've ever battled before.

With a yawn, I stumble down the hall, still rubbing my eyes so they readjust and I can see when I catch something small and white lying in the middle of the hallway floor. What the hell is that? My brow furrows as I get close, and my heart kicks up its speed when I bend down and realize it's a pair of Estlin's panties.

Shit. They must have fallen out of her basket when she did her laundry earlier. Picking them up, I can't stop my thumb from dragging along the thin lace as I examine them. They're sexy as fuck. A sheer lacy front and crotch with thin bands that make up the sides and thong. There's a small metal circle connecting the two sides and the thong piece that I can picture sitting right up the crack of her ass on her lower back.

Fuck. I groan, my dick instantly growing hard. Again.

I either need to get laid or give in and finally start jerking off, even if it's about her. I can't handle the relentless tension in my body. How I'm always wound so fucking tight, ready to burst whenever she's around. Maybe a release would help that. Take the edge off.

The problem is, I don't want anyone but her.

Like a goddamn pervert, I bring them up to my nose and take a deep inhale.

Motherfucker. I groan again, my cock actually leaking into my briefs.

A noise comes from the stairs that startles me. Shit! I stuff the panties into my pocket and turn, practically sweating like the sinner I am.

Estlin's head pops up from the top of the stairs. "Hey!" she says with a smile as she sees me. "Are you coming down for dinner? The food's ready."

"Uh-huh."

Her head tilts, her long hair falling across her shoulders. "You okay? You have that Mr. Darcy tone to you again."

What is it with her calling me Mr. Darcy? "I'm fine. I'm coming." And I'm going to need to later before I lose my mind for good. This is the second pair of panties I've officially stolen from my nanny.

The three of us have fajitas since that's what Rory said she wanted. They're fantastic. Estlin is an amazing cook. Easy. Light. I've been trying to be more relaxed, more present, especially with Rory. She's been excited to plan the sailing trip with me. Naturally, this has Katy gloating, but when doesn't Katy?

After dinner, I head upstairs to remove my contacts and put on my glasses to give my eyes a much-needed break. Only right before I go to leave, I feel something in my pocket and remember I have Estlin's panties in there.

All through dinner with her, I had them in my pocket.

It drags a wicked grin to my lips, and I slip them out, touching them again. I go over to my bed and sit down, staring at them. I'm a fucking creep. A dirty old man. I sigh, dropping my elbow to my thigh and resting my forehead in my hand as I stare down at the tiny scrap in my hand. Being a single dad isn't easy. Working as a surgeon isn't easy. Being fucking Owen Fritz isn't easy.

All those things combined equal no sex. No relationships.

And while I'm not sure how much I miss the relationship part, more and more I'm starting to miss the sex part. I can't get that night with her out of my head. I can't get *her* out of my head. I bring them to my nose again just as the door to my room opens, and I jump out of my skin. Immediately, I shove them under my pillow and turn, trying to calm my racing heart and cool my nerves after nearly being caught twice in one night with Estlin's panties under my nose.

"Dad?" Rory comes in. "Did you want to watch the movie with us?"

"Sure," I say a little too brightly. I clear my throat. "Which one did you pick? And please tell me it's not *The Little Mermaid* again."

Rory makes an annoyed scowl but gets over it a second later. "No. Estlin said she wanted to watch *Encanto*."

"Perfect." I stand and head down to the movie theater with her. Estlin is already there, the movie queued up on the massive screen, and a bowl of popcorn in her hand.

"This is not all for you," she warns Rory. "We're sharing this for sure."

It makes me snicker. I think Rory's vomiting did a number on her.

"Aargh," Rory huffs but climbs onto the reclining bench seat instead of one of the large single seats. Estlin and I pile in on either side of her, but as they watch the movie, I can't stop watching them. The way they snuggle and say the lines together and giggle and sing along. Every day I'm near her, this feeling I've been pretending isn't there gets a little stronger, a little more persistent.

Words like nanny, best friend's little sister, and too young all start to lose their meaning.

Estlin catches me watching her and smiles. I smile back, like a fool tempting a fate I have no business tempting.

The movie ends, and I put Rory to bed as she sings me songs from the movie. "When I grow up, I want to be a pop star, an artist, a mommy, and a professional swimmer."

"Those all sound good. What about a doctor?"

She scrunches her nose. "You work too much, and there's a lot of blood."

Hard to argue with that.

"All right, pop star. Let's get you to sleep."

I kiss Rory good night and then head down the hall. I don't know where Estlin is or what she's up to, but I have no plans to find out. My shift starts early tomorrow, and I need as much sleep as I can get. Only when I climb into bed and get settled in the dark, I feel Estlin's thong beneath my pillow. And it makes for a very long, restless night.

MY FOREARM MEETS the shower wall, the top of my head tucking into it, keeping my face pointed down toward the shower floor. Toward my heavy, thick cock that's practically staring accusingly up at me. Hot water cascades down my back, and I don't have it in me this morning to turn it to cold.

I woke up an hour earlier than I normally do after a shitful night of sleep. But no matter how hard I ran on the treadmill, how many weights I lifted, or how many crunches I did, it wasn't enough. No way I can go through the shift I have today like this.

With a groan of defeat, I wrap my fist around my cock and groan again, this time in pleasure. Fuck, that feels good. And God, do I need this.

I start to pull in hard, fast jerks because not only am I too wound up to drag it out for myself, but I'm short on time. My fist against the wall clenches and my eyes close as I picture her, no longer able to hold it back.

Estlin's blue-green eyes stare up at me in a haze of lust. Her silky cunt wrapped around my cock. Her large, perfect tits bounce as I pound into her. Her sweet fucking moans cling to me as she says my name.

"Owen. Oh shit!"

"What?" I jolt away from the wall like I've been electro-cuted, slipping along the shower floor and nearly busting my ass. Estlin is in my bathroom. What the fuck is she doing in my bathroom? And at this hour. "What the fuck are you doing in here?"

"Oh my God!" She covers her eyes. "I'm so sorry. I thought you'd be working out. You're always in the gym at this hour."

"I have to be in early. What are you doing in here?"

"Right. Right. Fuck. Right."

"Estlin?!" It's both a question and an expletive. She's wearing a cropped shirt with no bra and tiny sleep shorts. *Not fucking helping anything right now, sweet thing.*

"I was looking for my panties. I'm missing my favorite ones, and I can't find them anywhere, so I thought..." She trails off, nibbling on her lip as she shifts her position nervously.

"So you thought you'd sneak into my bathroom to look for them?"

"I didn't know you'd be in the shower!" she shouts, still with her eyes covered since I'm standing here naked, though my cock isn't as happy as he was a few minutes ago.

"You shouldn't just come in here."

"I know! I know, I'm sorry. But if I asked you for them, you wouldn't have given them to me."

She's right. I wouldn't have. I would have denied it until my dying breath. And to prove that point...

"I have no idea what you're talking about."

"Uh-huh. I'm sure." She cocks her hip. "And I'm sure if I asked you if you were just jerking off, you'd lie about that too."

Shit. She saw. Of course she saw. How could she not?

"Out."

"Were you thinking of me and my panties?"

Fucking vixen. "No. Never."

Her hand falls away from her eyes, and she gives me a smug

look before her gaze travels down my body, barely obstructed by the steam on the glass door. "Suuuure you weren't." She bobs her head. "Don't worry. I use my vibrator while thinking about you sometimes. At least I'm honest about it. *Panty thief.*" She swivels around and leaves, slamming the bathroom door shut behind her.

Shit. *Fuck!*

I turn off the water and fly out of the shower, wrapping a towel around my body and racing into my bedroom with wet feet, slipping and sliding as I go. My hair is dripping all over me, and I shiver against the cool air of my room.

Estlin is now digging into my nightstand drawer, searching for her goddamn panties. And of course…

"Ha!" She pulls out the ones I stole from her the night we met. "I knew it. How many times did you put these over your face and jerk off?"

My stupid dick gives a twitch, but for once I answer her honestly, despite my mortification. "Not once."

She studies me for a moment, and when she realizes I'm telling the truth, she frowns. She doesn't like that answer. Especially after she just admitted she uses her vibrator to thoughts of me. Something I shouldn't have reminded myself about because I'm starting to tent my towel.

She moves on, thankfully not noticing that. "Where are my other panties? Those are my favorite ones, and I know you have them. They were in my laundry basket yesterday, and now they're not with my clean stuff."

"Maybe the dryer ate them."

"I put them on the hand-wash cycle and never dry them, Owen. I know you have them."

I fold my arms over my chest, and she takes me in as I do that, her gaze flicking over my shoulders, arms, and abs dripping with water. She licks her lips, her pupils darkening, and then she clears her throat and looks over toward the door, her cheeks heating with color.

"I just want them back. If you don't give them to me, I'll go through your room after you leave."

I can't have that. Not that I have a lot to hide, but I can't know she's in my room, touching my things.

With a growl of frustration, I storm over to the bed, practically shoving her out of the way as I do. I reach beneath my pillow and ball up her thong in my fist. "Here." I chuck it at her. "Happy now?"

A triumphant smile curls up her lips. "You kept them under your pillow and didn't use them? Am I supposed to believe that?" Her incredulous tone tells me she doesn't believe me for a second.

"I didn't. I had them in my hand last night, and Rory came in. I panicked and shoved them under my pillow and then forgot about them."

Her eyes narrow at me, and she does another sweep of my body. "Whatever you say, Panty-thieving pervert."

"You've proven your point. Now get out of here. I have to get dressed for work."

She skips over to the door, and I watch her ass jiggle as she does in only those little shorts. The door shuts behind her, and I blow out a strained breath. My dick hurts. My balls fucking ache. And now she knows for sure that I stole her underwear. Twice.

How do I explain that away? I'm her boss. I crossed a million lines I told her we weren't ever going to cross.

With a heavy, miserable sigh, I head for the closet to get dressed when the door bursts open again. I was in the process of taking off my towel, and when she comes in, I quickly recover myself. She catches me doing it, a wry smirk on her lips.

She tosses something at me that hits me right in the face, only to bounce off and plummet to the floor.

"There. Freshly worn. Those should help you finish what you were doing in the shower." She spins back around and slams the door shut behind her. I pick up her panties—no longer giving a fuck since she gave them to me for this purpose —and smell them.

Fuuuuck.

I groan. The towel hits the floor. And with her panties against my face, I jerk off, coming too fast and hard while imagining my tongue in her cunt. It's pathetic. Not only is there no way I'll ever live this down, but there's also no way I won't do this again now that I've started.

15

ESTLIN

"**W**ake up, wake up, wake up!" Rory jumps on my bed, startling me out of a heavy, intense, dreamless sleep. My eyes pop open, my heart rate through the roof, and I do a quick check of everything all at once.

Vibrator put away from last night? Check.

Wearing more than just underwear? Check.

Time? Because why on earth is she here—oh hell, it's after seven. Shit. My alarm didn't go off. I was up late in the basement with my pottery wheel. Painting, shockingly, since I started listening to music per Billy's suggestion, has gone swimmingly. I go to the studio most days and I'm already one and a half paintings deep. And for the first time in forever—not to sound like *Frozen's* Anna—I'm anxious to do it. Excited even.

"I'm awake," I tell her as I sit up and rub at the sleep crusting my eyes. And when I've removed it, I get a good look at her.

"What on earth are you wearing, Gingerbread?" Gingerbread is my new name for her. Simply because she loves it. Like it's her favorite cookie, and who has gingerbread as their favorite cookie?

She's wearing a bikini top with mermaid scale detail, a rainbow tutu, and mermaid fins that match her top. Her hair has about a thousand clips and elastics in it and is up in about ten different ponytails. Oh, and she has red lipstick and blue eyeshadow on.

Huh. That's a bit sus since in the six weeks I've been working here, I haven't seen any play makeup in her stuff. "And where did you get the makeup?"

"I found it in your bathroom."

My eyebrows shoot up. "Oh, did you? Well then." I reach forward and grab her, stopping her from jumping and bringing her down onto the bed with me. "Listen, babe, makeup is one of those holy things we women and a few awesome men get to wear in this world. But here's the deal. You can't go into other people's things and take them without asking. Especially their private things in their bathroom. Okay?"

She pouts, her little body sagging. "Okay."

"Next time you want to wear some of my stuff, ask, and we can see if it's okay to do that, and then I can help you do it because you have lipstick on more than just your lips."

"Sorry," she murmurs contritely. Her contrition lasts about another two point five seconds, and then she's up, jumping on my bed once again. "You need to get dressed. Into an outfit like mine. Then we can go to Dunky Donuts and get breakfast."

"Whoa. Slow down there. Dunky Donuts?"

"Yes! I want an egg and cheese, and on Saturdays, if I've been good all week at school, Daddy lets me get one from there along with a Munchkin."

"That's a very precise explanation, but I'll still have to fact-check. He hasn't done that since I've been working here."

"He does. I swear. He did it last year."

"And you want me to dress like you? I don't have a top like that." Nor would I wear it out in public if I did.

"Oh." She jumps off the bed, landing with a dull thud on the floor, and then starts racing off, yelling back, "Katy has a tutu she wears when we dress up."

That's all I get, but I'm assuming now is the time to get out of bed and get myself together. I shoot Owen a quick text, asking him about this Dunkin' Donuts thing, and head into my bathroom to do my morning stuff.

Today is Saturday, and Owen is working a shift so that means it's just Rory and me all day. I'm close to finishing my full second piece, but other than that, this week shouldn't be too bad, so I'd like to venture out a bit with Rory if she's game.

Things between Owen and me have returned to hot and cold. It's as if he doesn't know how to interact with me, and I know the panty-thieving incident yesterday morning hasn't helped. I blush when I think about how I found him in the shower, grunting and groaning with his big, thick cock in his hand, and then how I threw my freshly worn panties—panties that were a little wet after discovering him like that—in his face.

There has been no middle ground for us in the weeks I've worked for him. We're either boiling hot—all teasing and barely hidden innuendo and touching—or freezing cold, needing distance and space to maintain professional boundaries.

Still, he's trying to be nicer, more friendly and open.

Owen and Rory leave for their sailing trip in three weeks, and both have been talking about it nonstop. They're excited, and I'm excited for them. If not a little jealous. I could go, but I don't think it's smart. It'd just be the three of us. And after Rory goes to bed, it'd just be the two of us alone on a ship at night under the stars. It's terribly romantic, and the thought of him in a bathing suit, his incredible body on display with the sun on his skin...

Yeah, no. I'm not going. I'd end up climbing and wrapping myself around him like a monkey.

Exiting the bathroom, I find Rory dancing around my room, using the matching rainbow tutu as a partner. "Here. You can wear this. Do you have a shirt with rainbows on it? I want rainbows to be our theme of the day."

Did I have this much energy at seven in the morning when I was six?

"Rainbow, huh? Oh!" I snap my fingers in an ah-ha way. "I've got just the shirt." I dig through my drawer until I find the one I'm thinking of, and then I snatch the tutu out of her hand and head back into the bathroom to get changed. A few minutes later, I am so rainbow I could dance in a parade.

I'm wearing red yoga pants, my "pretty sketchy" shirt that has rainbow-colored pencils on it, and Katy's tutu. My long hair is up on top of my head in pigtails to show off the colorful strands underneath, and I'm wearing makeup that matches Rory's.

"What do you think?" I ask as I come out in a twirl to give her the full effect.

"Yay! You're perfect. Can we go, can we go?"

"You need a shirt over the bathing suit top."

"But I don't wanna."

"I know, and at home, that's fine. Out and about, you need something over it. At the very least a jacket because it's cool out today."

She makes a noise like I'm killing her vibe, and I get it. Thankfully she runs off to find something, and I check my phone to see if Owen has replied.

Owen: Yes, that's fine. Bring an extra couple of singles from the cash envelope on the kitchen counter, because she likes to give them to the homeless man who hangs out outside. No hot chocolate. I don't care how much she begs and promises. The last two times I fell for it, she threw up all over the back seat.

Me: Excellent. Thank you. And I appreciate the pro tip on the hot chocolate. I don't want a repeat of what happened after your grandparents' party.

Me: I mean with her throwing up. Not the stuff that came before it.

I pinch my eyes shut. Why the hell did I just text him that?

Owen: I knew what you meant. *Winking emoji*

Owen: I enjoyed what came before it too.

My eyes pop wide and I blink at my screen. Is he flirtexting —is that even a word—with me? No. He's just being polite. Owen wouldn't flirtext me. Except the stupid butterflies in my stomach and the tingle in my chest don't seem to agree. Or at the very least, they're hoping I'm wrong.

Shaking that off, I slip my phone into the pocket on the side of my leggings and then go down the hall to find Rory, who has put on a long-sleeves, bright pink Princess Peach shirt.

"Perfect. You're stunning. You ready to go?"

Twenty minutes later, we're sitting at a small, two-person table, getting all the looks from every patron who walks in and out. And since this is a Dunkin' in Brookline, that's a lot of people. Rory doesn't seem to care in the slightest. For every strange or squinted or even derisive look we get, she responds with a smile and a wave, and I think it's safe to say, I want to be her when I grow up.

Little kids have no problems being themselves. It's not until later that we become self-conscious and self-doubting. Think of how much better the world would be if being yourself came with no judgment.

I snap a picture of her about to eat her glazed Munchkin and send it to Owen. He doesn't reply, but I don't expect him to since he's working. I sip my iced coffee and think about what we could do today.

"Do you want to go to the playground?"

"Um. Does a bear poop in the woods?"

"What?" My eyebrows shoot up as an incredulous laugh hits the air. "Where did you hear that expression?"

"My uncle Mason." She shrugs like it's no big thing.

Shocking. And yes, that's sarcasm. I met Mason at the Fritz barbecue, but after watching him play in the pool with Rory, it's not tough to imagine he'd teach her that. My family wasn't as close with the Central Square crew as the Fritz family is.

"Ignoring the bear pooping thing, do you have a preference for playgrounds?"

"I like the one in the Common. We can go on the merry-go-round too."

"All right. Let's do it."

~

FORTY MINUTES LATER, we're making our way through Boston Common. It's a gorgeous early fall day, and thankfully not too cold with the sun shining high overhead. Rory and I are walking hand in hand, talking about a million things all at once. I negotiated the removal of my pigtails because they were killing my scalp, but the rest of our outfits remain.

I'm trying to manifest my inner *fuck 'em if they can't take a joke,* and so far, it's going pretty well.

"Why do you want to be an artist?" Rory questions. She's been asking a lot of questions only children can get away with asking for how personal and frank they are. She started with boys and friends, and now she's moved on to asking me about my art.

"I love working with my hands and seeing where my imagination can take them. With art, we get to express our thoughts and feelings without having to say them. For me, it's magic. Being an artist is just who I am."

She thinks about this very seriously for a long minute as we pass the merry-go-round and head toward the playground. "Daddy says it's okay for me to talk about my mom."

I pause because that's some serious stuff right there and crouch so we're at eye level. "And how do you feel about that?"

"I don't want to talk about her."

I give her hand a little squeeze. "I can understand how that might be difficult."

"I don't remember her, and I don't want to. She left us and was mean."

"Does that bother you? That she left and was mean?"

She shrugs and stares down at the ground between us.

"It's okay if it does."

She doesn't say anything, and I can feel her shutting down in front of me.

"Would you want to make some art with me while you're thinking about her? You wouldn't have to talk unless you want to." I tuck some of my hair back behind my shoulders so she can fully see my face.

"I don't like to think about her either."

"I get that. I do." Except she brought her up for a reason. Hmm. "All right. What if we didn't think about her? What if we just made some cool stuff together and see where it takes us?"

Her chin lifts, her pretty blue eyes flickering with interest. "Like what?"

I shrug. "Anything. We can make anything you want. Do you like painting, drawing, clay, putty—"

"What's clay?"

"It's what I use to make pottery. Like bowls, sculptures, and stuff. You don't have to do it on the wheel like I do, but if you want to, I can teach you. If not, you can sculpt it into anything you want, and then we can paint it. Then I'll bring our masterpieces to a place where they put them in a special oven called a kiln to bake, and they come back hard and shiny. What do you think?"

Her eyes brighten. "Can we do that?"

"Sure!" I exclaim. "I'd love that. On the way home, I'll stop at the art supply store to get a special kind of clay for us. It's more of a sculpting clay than what I use and easier to work with."

Rory likes this idea a lot, and as we continue into the gated playground area, she tells me all the things she wants to construct out of clay. After that, she takes off, running around and sliding down everything. I stand off to the side, mostly watching her instead of joining her since she's made a little friend.

A man—maybe in his early thirties—comes over and stands beside me. "Is she yours?" he asks, indicating Rory, who is having a pretend tea party with the other girl.

"No. I'm her nanny. Is that your daughter she's playing with?"

"My niece. I have her for the day."

I nod and smile, watching the girls. "They seem to be hitting it off."

"They do." He turns to me and extends his hand. "I'm Andy."

"Estlin." I shake his hand. His eyes do an amused sweep of me.

"I like the outfit."

I snicker. "We're twins today."

"Takes a special kind of nanny to do that."

I shrug. "She's the best and makes it easy."

We both go back to watching them play for a moment before he asks, "How long have you worked for Owen Fritz?"

That pulls me up short. "I'm sorry?"

"Don't look alarmed," he intones in a smooth voice. "I work for *Boston's Landing*. I know all the Fritz people. I was one of the reporters who covered Owen and Rory during his divorce. It's nice to see they're doing well and have moved on to be happy and hire a nanny." He gives my body another sweep. "A beautiful, young nanny at that."

The fuck? *Boston's Landing* is a social magazine that encompasses more than just Boston. It's for anything happening in New England, but it's not simply farmers' markets and the best local ice cream. They have a society section that is barely one step above a tabloid.

I blink at him, appalled by every word and insinuation coming from him. I turn back to Rory and take a protective step toward her. "Hey, Gingerbread. We need to get going."

"But I want to stay. I'm having fun with my friend."

"I know, kiddo, but it's starting to get late. Especially if we want to hit up the art store on our way home."

She looks like she's about to have a total meltdown at this. "No. I want to stay."

"What's the harm in them playing together a little longer?" the guy asks, but I see his phone in his hand. I don't know if he's recording her or if he's taken pictures or what.

I flip back to Rory. "Come on. We can come back another day. Please, Rory." My voice grows insistent on her name, and her eyes flash up to mine. I give her a look I'm praying she gets, but then the tears start, and hell, what do I do?

I rush over to her and gently pull her to the side away from the girl. "Don't cry, Gingerbread. I know you want to stay, but we really need to go. I promise I'll make it up to you."

Something catches her attention over my shoulder, and I turn just in time to catch him snapping a picture of both of us. In our outfits. With tears on her face. Right here in the park. I want to tell him off. I want to scream and shout and break his fucking phone.

But if he's press, I can't touch him. And I won't react in front of Rory like that.

Still, what an absolute motherfucker he is. She's a little girl. What kind of monster exploits that?

He gives me a smug smirk, one that tells me he knows he got me, and I stand, taking Rory's hand. Without another word about it, I give her a firm tug, and thankfully, she relents and follows after me.

"He took my picture," she utters as she wipes her cheeks and nose with the back of her hand.

"I know." We walk briskly toward the garage. "Don't look back, okay?"

"Is he following us? They've followed us before."

Her voice wobbles again, and I hate this for her. I hate it so much.

"It's okay, sweetie. I'm here with you, and I won't let anything bad happen."

The moment we get into the car and I have her buckled up, I call Owen, thankful he picks up on the third ring. "Hey. Is everything okay? I'm in surgery."

"Then why are you picking up?"

"Because you called. But you're on speakerphone, and the entire theater can hear you."

"Theater?"

"Operating theater or operating room. Whatever. We call it both."

"Ah. This can wait then."

"Hold on." I hear him say something to someone, and then a second later, he's back. "What's wrong?"

Dammit. I hate how obvious my voice is. "Owen, it can—"

"Just tell me, Estlin. I need to get back. I have an intern and a third-year resident doing an appendectomy. They should be fine, but I don't want to leave them longer than I have to."

I glance in the rearview mirror at Rory, who is staring stoically out the window, and I remember what Owen and Jack said about what the press did to them. That man taking her picture when she was at the park playing must be so traumatic for her.

"Rory can hear you," I warn. "We were at the playground in the Common. Rory was playing with a little girl, and her uncle came over to ask if she was mine. I explained that I'm the nanny, and then he asked me how long I've worked for you. He asked, 'How long have you worked for Owen Fritz?'"

Owen hisses under his breath. "Jesus."

"He's a reporter for *Boston's Landing* and covered your... situation a few years back. He took pictures, Owen. I'm so sorry. I tried to get Rory out of there as fast as I could, but I don't know how many he got."

"Is she okay? Are you both okay?"

I check the rearview again. Rory is unmoved, hardly blinking as she stares sightlessly out the window as we drive through Boston. "A little shaken," I answer, hoping he gets my full meaning.

"I'm going to finish this up and come right home." He clears the harshness from his tone. "I'm going to be home soon, Moonshine."

She doesn't respond.

"I'm sorry," I mumble, feeling miserable.

"I'll see you both soon. I have to get back." He disconnects the call, and all I know is that what started off as a great day, just went to hell.

16

OWEN

The speed, power, and inaccuracy of the internet never fail to surprise me. Appendectomies are typically quick procedures. In and out in under an hour. When Estlin called, we had just made the small incisions and placed the laparoscopic scopes. So by the time we finish, scrub out, talk to the family, and make sure everything is good with the patient, pictures of my daughter and her nanny looking like matching circus performers are all over the magazine's site and circulating to other media publications.

But it's not just the pictures. It's the headline that goes with it.

"Owen Fritz and his daughter find comfort and love with the new nanny."

There's a very brief excerpt beneath it about how Estlin was playing and keeping a careful, watchful eye, and how after all Rory and I have been through, it's gratifying to see us happy and moving forward. Estlin. It said her fucking name. Thankfully, not her real first name and not her last name either, but it doesn't matter.

It's out there. And this reporter might as well have put a target on my back.

I know him too. Andy Burkhead. He was all over us during my divorce and is one of the people who posted leaked excerpts of Angelica's tell-all book. Rory is a minor, but the laws surrounding this aren't all that clear. Trust me, I've researched it. They didn't mention Rory by name, and the paper didn't publish it for "financial gain," only as an editorial piece, and the headline spoke about the new nanny and primarily focused on that.

All of which is protected by the First Amendment.

If I call the magazine or have my attorney do it in a fit and demand they remove it—which is useless at this point considering it's creeping everywhere—that target only grows. If I ignore it, there's a chance it's a one-off and dies quickly.

This is the game. One that I've had to play my entire life growing up a Fritz in this city, though the bullshit with my ex made national news.

It's not me I'm worried about. I can more than handle myself. It's Rory, and I could tell in Estlin's voice that this impacted her. As it is, I've notified our family's head of security and my attorney just in case this escalates.

By the time I finish signing out my patients and make my way home, it's nearly two hours later. I've thought about quitting my job or taking extended time off in the past. But surgeons can't do that and stay on top of their game with their skill and knowledge. So it's all or nothing, more or less, but more than less, I feel like a shitty father for it.

Like I'm not doing enough, and what I am doing is woefully inadequate.

My phone rings through my car, and I cringe when I see it's Jack. "Hey," I answer.

"Hey. I just wanted to call and check on things. I saw the

photo, but Eddie didn't pick up her phone when I tried her just now."

"I'm on my way home. I was at the hospital all day, but I spoke with her earlier."

"And?" he prompts.

"And it's a picture and a headline. She said they were a little shaken but otherwise okay. I'm on my way home to them now."

He sighs. "Sorry. I just worry about her. We all do."

"I know, and I understand you care, but she's doing fine. Why do you all hover so much?"

Her mom has been over to check on her at least once a week since she moved in. Jack calls and comes by frequently to do the same. I don't like thinking that she's hiding something from me, but it's not the first time I've known that she is.

"She just went through some stuff when she was in Paris is all, and we didn't see her until she moved back home."

Hmm. So that means they didn't see her the entire time she was in London. "What's some stuff?"

"It's nothing. It's in the past. She's just the baby, and we hover."

Sounds like a bullshit, evasive answer, if ever there was one.

Before I can grill him a bit more, my father calls in. "I gotta go, Jack. My dad is calling. I'll catch up with you."

"Sure. Yeah. Later, brother."

He hangs up, and I answer my dad's call. "Hey. I take it you saw it?"

"Yes. We saw it," he answers. "Is Rory doing all right?"

"I don't know yet," I answer truthfully. "I'm on my way home to her now."

"And Eddie?" my mom questions. "Did you talk to her?"

"I did. She said they were a little shaken up, but I got the impression Rory is taking it hard."

My mother curses. "God, they're such bastards. It was a nice headline, by the way."

I roll my eyes as I turn onto Beacon Street. "Don't start. Please, don't start. They were looking to get clicks, and I have no doubt they got them."

"Do you want us to come over?" my dad offers.

I think about this for a moment. "I was going to take Rory to Mason's game tomorrow, but maybe I won't. Maybe we'll just do dinner at my house instead. I don't want more attention on this right now than Rory needs."

"We're good with that. You can also bring her over for dinner at our house."

"Let's see how she's doing first, and we can figure it out from there," I tell my mom. "I'm almost home."

"Call us if you need us," my dad replies.

"Will do. Bye."

I disconnect the call and pull into the driveway, scanning around, and thankful that I don't see anyone lurking in the bushes. I close the garage behind me, step out of my car, and shut the door. For a moment, I linger. If Rory had been at the playground with my sister, Katy, or anyone else in my family, there wouldn't have been a picture, and there sure as hell wouldn't have been a headline like that.

Still, I can't blame Estlin or even be angry with her for this the way I'd like to.

It's like déjà fucking vu. I can't stand my daughter being on the internet again.

I drag a hand across my jaw as I enter the house, only to be assaulted with… Taylor Swift. Or at least her music is thumping loudly through the downstairs, along with two other voices singing along. Immediately after that, I smell… something sweet baking. Possibly cookies, but it's difficult to tell because I also smell garlic and tomatoes. Sauce maybe?

I enter the kitchen but stay back by the entrance, watching the scene before me. Rory has changed her outfit and is wearing her Princess Belle gown. Estlin is in the same outfit she was in earlier, minus the tutu, and both are dancing around the kitchen. Rory is doing twirls and wiggling her little hips and butt. Estlin is using a red-stained wooden spoon as a microphone, also wiggling her hips and butt, and in those yoga pants...

Christ. That hand on my jaw comes up my face and through my hair, until I grip the back of my neck.

Estlin removes the lid from a pot on the stove and stirs the sauce, taps the side of the spoon against the rim and covers it again before she turns back to Rory to continue their concert.

A wry sort of grin hits my lips. Rory has Katy, but Rory knows that Katy is also mine. Rory knows Katy and I talk, often in private. So I'm not sure how much Rory truly shares with Katy. Rory also has Wren, but again, that's her aunt.

But Estlin is Rory's.

I see it, even if I almost hate to admit it. Rory has had an incredible month at school, and we haven't had any behavioral issues there or here. She's been excited for her days with Estlin. They do stuff that is entirely based around Rory and her wants and needs. Hell, Estlin went out today wearing that tutu because, no doubt, Rory asked her to.

It's what Rory needs.

It's why I did this.

On one hand, it hurts my heart that she's gone so long without someone... well, not a mother figure per se, but someone she feels happy with and cared for by. A female someone. Someone she can connect with and relate to. Hell, Rory doesn't even talk to her therapist. I do more than she does, and now we only meet every other week because of it.

Rory needs to open up more. She has some abandonment issues that aren't minor, and we've been working on that since her mother left. I'm not sure that's the sort of thing that goes away with therapy. I think it'll require life reinforcement, and that's what I've been trying to do for her.

It solidifies my resolve to keep things indifferent and professional with Estlin even more. Rory has already lost enough in the most egregious of ways. She can't lose Estlin, and she certainly can't lose her because of me.

Pushing away from the doorway, I enter the kitchen, coming in close to the stove where Estlin is still dancing.

"What is all this?" I question only I startle Estlin, and in doing so, she swings around at light speed with the wooden spoon in her hand that thwacks me straight in the nuts. Sharp, stabbing pain shoots up through my balls into my stomach, where I cramp and immediately want to die.

My knees hit the floor, and I double over, wincing and nauseated as I grab my guys and try not to cry like a little bitch.

"Oh my God! I'm so sorry! Are you okay?" Estlin drops to the floor beside me, her hands all over me as she attempts to turn me so she can assess the damage. "Where did I—oh." She snickers and does a crap job of covering it as a cough when she sees where my hands are. "Damn, that has to hurt."

"It does," I wheeze, my forehead meeting the cool wood floor. "Maybe you should watch where you swing that thing."

"You startled me. I didn't hear you come in. I certainly didn't mean to take out your future children with a wooden spoon." She snickers again, only to clear her throat. "Can I get you some ice? Do you even put ice on... them?" She laughs lightly as she tries—and fails—to hide her amusement at my expense.

"What happened?" Rory flies over and jumps on me, which does not help. "Daddy, are you okay?"

"I'm fine," I manage, though I'm still panting and breathless. "Estlin just hit me with her spoon is all."

"Oh no. Do you need a Band-Aid? Daddy, you're bleeding!"

"What?!" both Estlin and I exclaim.

"Look!" Rory points in abject horror at the red stain right in the center of my crotch.

Estlin shoots on top of me, practically falling on me to get a better look. Her hands go straight for my pants and graze my cock. And even though I'm in pain and my balls feel like they're about to explode, my dick gives a stupid twitch.

Her eyes round when she feels it, and I push her hands away, pinning her with a meaningful look. "It's not blood. It's sauce."

And when she realizes she just accidentally touched my dick right in front of my daughter after nailing me in the balls and covering me in sauce, she cracks, falling back onto the floor and exploding into hysterics.

"It's not funny," I grumble.

"I'm sorry," she gasps breathlessly. "I can't help it. I just... and then I." More uncontrollable laughter.

I roll my eyes as I sit up slowly, my nuts aching terribly. "Yes. You did, and then you did. And you're not sorry."

Her hands are on her face as she laughs into them. I lean back against the cabinet, drawing my knees up and staring down at my tomato sauce-covered slacks. Well, these are ruined.

"I am. Sorta. It's just funny. You have to admit that."

It is sort of funny now that I don't feel like I'm about to die, but I'll never admit that to her.

"I didn't mean to... well, do either of those things. I swear." She holds up a hand. "At least the sauce wasn't hot." Something about that sets her off again, and she cackles, rocking back and forth on the floor.

I poke her with my foot. "Are you done yet?"

"Almost. I promise." She wipes at tears streaming down the sides of her face.

"Why is she laughing like that?" Rory stares at her in bewilderment.

I shrug at Rory. "Estlin has a very strange sense of humor and a very poor sense of general anatomy."

"You're the doctor," Estlin quips, her laughter finally trailing off. "But I think I just got my anatomy lesson the hard way." She laughs some more, and I poke her in the leg again with my foot.

"Really? We're going there?" Thankfully, she's too busy laughing to see the smirk I'm failing to hide.

"Sorry. I swear I'm done now." The timer on the Alexa goes off. "Alexa, stop," Estlin calls out. "That's the cookies. Don't get up on my account," she teases, and I so want to flip her off. She hops up, slips on oven mitts, and then pulls out a tray of cookies from the oven, moving them immediately onto a cooling rack.

"Are you sure you don't need a Band-Aid?"

I give Rory a kiss on the cheek. "I don't need a Band-Aid, Moonshine, but you're sweet to ask."

"Here." Estlin offers me her hand, and reluctantly I take it, ignoring the electric pulse as I do. She helps me up off the floor, biting into her lip to contain her smile as she gives me a sheepish look. "I truly am sorry for... all of that." She swirls a finger down, indicating where she hit me, and yep, my dick pulses a little at her acknowledging him. "Are you sure you're okay?"

I nod. "Lesson learned. Next time, I'll announce myself before I come anywhere near you."

"Probably smart." She gives me a cheeky wink. "Especially if I'm armed the way I was. We decided since we had a bit of a rough afternoon that we'd make oatmeal chocolate chip cookies—my favorite—and spaghetti and meatballs with garlic bread since that's her favorite dinner."

"You did?"

"Yep. We've had the best time. Right, kiddo? You, me, dancing, singing, cooking, and baking."

Rory jumps up and gives Estlin a high-five, a smile all over her little face.

Estlin leans into me and whispers, "Don't worry, I supervised everything, and the food should be amazing despite her wanting to add in weird ingredients."

Pleasure curls deep in my chest as heat floods me everywhere, making my heart beat off-rhythm and my breath short once again. The sensation flowing through me is fucking intoxicating and utterly delicious. Just like the woman standing before me.

The woman I want to kiss into next week and pleasure for eternity for putting my little girl first and doing what she can to comfort her.

The woman I swore not even five minutes ago that I would stay indifferent and professional toward at all costs.

The woman who, if I'm not careful, I could lose my head and my heart to.

17

A week has gone by, and it's been easy. Light. What happened in the park never became an issue. By the time I woke up the next morning after a restless night of sleep, it was as if nothing had happened. Monday started the way all the rest have, and each day progressed into the next.

There were no more tabloid reports about me or Rory, though there was a photographer parked not too far from her school who snapped a few pictures of us as I picked her up. Other than that, it was all normal and fine until today.

"You're sure you won't come out with me and my friends tonight?" Billy asks, walking me to my car. He's been on my ass to meet his boyfriend and a few of his other friends, and I've been pushing him off. I don't even know why, but I have been.

"Not tonight."

"Girl, that's your favorite line."

He's right. It is.

"Maybe next weekend."

"That's your second. Does Mr. Hot Billionaire Boss man not allow you free time?"

I sigh. "He does." But I like being home with him and Rory. I know it's lame. I'm almost twenty-three, and I have no social life to speak of. I'm out of practice. Or maybe just hesitant. I didn't go out at all in London, but I chalked that up to healing and still being a bit mentally shaky.

Now I don't know what's holding me back, other than I don't have a lot of interest. I'd rather spend my Friday night on the couch with Owen and Rory watching a movie than going out and meeting someone, and I know that's a problem. I know it is.

He's my boss, and there is no being with him—not for real—so I need to stop this bullshit and start living again.

"Next weekend," I promise as I unlock the car and open the door. "I mean it. For real. And the following weekend I'm going out for a girls' night with some friends." It's something the girls like to do once a month, and it meant a lot that they invited me for another round.

"I'm totally impressed," he deadpans.

"Don't pick on me. I'm a work in progress." I give him a peck on the cheek. "Have fun tonight. I can't wait to see the pictures on Monday."

He steps back, and I climb in, but he stops me by knocking on my window. I press the button and lower it.

"We're all works in progress. But there can be no progress made if you're hiding from life."

Fuck if he isn't right.

He walks off, leaving me with that, and I head off for Rory's school. I pull up in front and hop out, going up to the back door and waiting along with the rest of the parents and nannies who pick up since we're not allowed to enter the school for safety reasons. A few minutes later, Rory comes bursting out of the doors, holding up a painting with a blue ribbon attached to it.

"I got first place!" she screams, only to immediately jump straight up into my arms.

I catch her with an oomph, staggering back a step to accommodate her weight and size. Adjusting her in my arms, I look down at the painting. "You got first place on your art project?"

"Yes!" she squeals, bouncing in my arms. "I won most creative."

I'm pretty sure every kid in the class gets a blue ribbon for something, but who gives a flippity fuck? "That is awesome! I'm so proud of you."

She jumps down and shows me her art, which is a self-portrait made out of different squares, all with a different color or pattern in them. It's seriously very cool.

"This is amazing, and your prize is well deserved. We should celebrate."

Her eyes widen to epic proportions. "Ice cream?" she hedges.

I laugh. "A small cone, Gingerbread. Small."

She groans but doesn't fight it. This girl's eyes are bigger than her stomach, and her sweet tooth is by far her largest. But she gets sick fast when she overdoes it.

I drive us across town to her favorite ice cream spot, and after both of us order, we sit down and discuss her work as we lick our cones.

"What made you go with squares?" I ask, taking a swipe at my mint chocolate chip.

She shrugs like she honestly has no clue. "We had to add a pattern and a shape, so I went with squares. My friend, Ilsa did triangles for hers, and my other friend, Jenny made a bat out of rectangles. It was weird. Who makes a bat?"

"Art is art. We never judge another's creativity."

She makes a noise. "Isn't that what critics do?"

I snort out a laugh. "Where did you hear that term?"

"In class. Our teacher told us that all art is judged by critics, but we have to make it for ourselves regardless."

A shiver runs over me. I wish someone had told that to Claude.

"That's very wise and very true. But it's still not nice to judge your friend's work. That can hurt feelings."

"I didn't tell her anyway." She continues to eat her ice cream. "Daddy asked if I wanted to go see Uncle Mason play football on Sunday or go see him play hockey."

"Which one did you decide?"

"Football is *so* boring, and it takes forever."

"You don't like football?"

"I don't know. I like the snacks in the box we sit in. Do you want to come too?"

"I'm not sure I'm invited."

"Daddy said you could come. Katy and Bennett might bring baby Willow. I might want to go to hockey instead, though."

"I'll ask your dad about it tonight. Speaking of, we should finish up and get home."

After we finish our ice cream, we head outside, still chatting away, only for me to stop dead in my tracks and my voice to cut off mid-word. It's as if my thoughts conjured him out of thin air. Icy venom fills my veins as hatred slithers through me like a nightmare.

He looks the same. Tall, handsome, and suave in that European way Americans can never pull off. His eyes rake me in, noting every detail he's missed for the last nine months, and when his eyes finally find mine again, he offers me a hesitant smile.

"How did you find me?" I ask before I can stop the words. I pull Rory close to my side, and he watches me do it, his pale green eyes missing nothing. Not my vitriol. Not my instinct to protect her from him. Nothing.

"I saw you online," he says in French. His English was never very good, and he never cared to make it better. "I have been searching for you for months, but to no avail. I have a Google name alert for you, and it led me here. It's luck that I saw you now. I was walking by and caught you in the window. I had planned to come see you tomorrow at your home."

Jesus fuck. So he was alerted to my name being in the tabloids, and he tracked me down?

"Estlin?" Rory asks, nerves and uncertainty coloring her words.

"It's okay, Gingerbread." I give her hand a reassuring squeeze. "Just stay behind me, okay? He's an old friend from Paris. That's all."

He frowns, his hands going to his hips and his chin dipping down in regret. "I won't hurt her. Or you. I hate myself for ever making you doubt that about me."

I shake my head, speaking to him in French, so Rory can't understand me. "Don't. Don't feed me lines. We were both there that night. We both know what happened."

He clears his throat and glances around at the busy sidewalk around us, filled with the Friday night traffic of people just getting off work. "I was in a bad place, and what I did was wrong. But I was never going to hurt you. I came to talk to you. I couldn't find your new number, and I didn't think you'd talk to me even if I had tried to call."

"You're right. I wouldn't have. You flew to Boston just to talk to me?"

"No, my sweet. I was already in New York, as luck would have it. I was there for fashion week and to meet with some gallery owners there. It was fate and perfect timing that brought me to you."

"Oh, a gallery owner?"

His eyes narrow, and in them, I see the resentment. The still-burning enmity. "It was a mistake. Everything that night was."

I'm going to be sick. "A mistake?" I bark incredulously. "You slept with another woman in our bed, bashed me and my work to her, lied about my work and yours, and then destroyed every piece of mine before you came after me and I ran out. You betrayed me in the worst of ways." I shake my head. "You were wrong to come here." I start to walk Rory toward the car again when he shifts in front of me, stopping us.

"Please don't go. I need to talk to you."

"Talk?" I burst out. "No. That part of us is done."

"Estlin, my darling, my love. I was wrong, and I'm sorry. So sorry. I've missed you so much."

I can't even with that. I'm not even sad right now. Just angry. "I don't miss you. I *haven't* missed you. I left for a reason."

Pain strikes his features. "We can go back in time. Together we can rebuild what I broke. With your love and mine, it'll be like nothing was lost."

Is he kidding? "No. Not ever. Go away and never come back."

"I can't." He reaches for me, and I jump back. I don't want him near Rory. "These months without you have been the worst of my life. Please. Allow me to explain."

"There is no explanation for what you did. I heard your words and saw your aftermath."

I move us around him, heading for the car. Rory is starting to get upset. She can hear it in my voice, and I don't want this for her.

"I hurt you and I'm sorry. I was selfish and prideful. I lost control of myself. I know this. That's why I'm here. To tell you I'm sorry. To beg for forgiveness. To ask you to take me back."

Is he for real? "No," I snap. "And that's final." I reach the car when he stops me again with his words.

"I know where you're living. What you're doing with Dr. Owen Fritz."

My heart races faster with every word, anxious to get Rory out of here.

"Estlin? What's going on?" Rory's shaky voice hits my ears, and I crumble, hating that I'm doing this to her.

"It's nothing. He's nothing."

"I want to go home. My tummy isn't feeling well."

I spin around and pick her up, drawing her into my chest. "I've got you, Gingerbread." I fake a smile and kiss her forehead. "Let's go home."

I stare at Claude as I get Rory in the car, begging him not to engage. Not with her around. He looks helpless and lost, as if he didn't expect this reaction from me.

I buckle her into her seat and then race around to the front, driver's side when he calls out to me. "I know you're upset with me, and I know you have every right to be. But I'm a patient man, and I'll wait forever for you. I've come this far and waited this long. I'll see you soon, my love. Now that I know where to find you, I won't be far."

Bile climbs up the back of my throat, and my hands tremble terribly. Adrenaline courses through my veins, and after I buckle myself in and start the car, I pull away from the curb, wanting to get home fast.

Doing a quick check of the rearview mirror, he's still there, watching us drive away. "Are you okay?" I ask, willing a stillness to my voice I don't feel. "I didn't mean to scare you."

"I didn't like him."

I practically scoff. "I don't like him either. But don't worry, I won't let him bother us again. I promise. Do you want some music? Should we sing this out?"

She nods her head, and I catch it in the rearview.

I turn on her playlist and pump it out loud for us as I start to sing along, hoping this relaxes her. My phone rings when I'm not even a block away. Owen. God. Worst goddamn timing, Owen!

I clear my throat and chirp through the car. "Hello?"

"Hey," he says. "I'm finishing up here..." He pauses. "Are you okay? Your voice sounds funny?"

How on earth can he tell that from one word? Do I sound that bad? Dammit!

"I'm okay," I push out, coming to a stoplight. I suck in a deep breath and then another, glancing back to find Rory, who looks pale and out of sorts.

"Estlin, take me off speaker and put music on for Rory."

I do as he says, turning up Taylor's newest album for her to sing along to like I just was. Bringing the phone up to my ear, I whisper, "How can you tell I'm not okay?"

"Because I know you. I know your voice. What happened? Another paparazzi?"

"No." I clear my throat again and lick my impossibly dry lips. I shake out my hand and then ball it up, but I can't stop my chin from trembling, and I hate—*fucking hate*—how weak and vulnerable I feel right now. "I... I'm sorry, Owen."

"What, baby? What is it?"

Baby? He's never called me that before. Not once. And he had to do it now when I needed to be strong? It unravels me, and the first of the tears start. Furiously, I wipe them away and drag in a deep, composed breath.

"My, um, my ex, the one I lived with in Paris. He, uh, he found me."

"*Found you?*"

His voice slashes through me at my word choice.

I shouldn't be this shaken up. I shouldn't be like this. It's been nine months since I left him.

"I..." I suck in my sob. "I'm sorry. Rory was with me. He saw my picture on the internet. He had a Google name tracker for me. I left with her as fast as I could. But he knows, Owen. He knows that I work for you, and he knows where I live."

"Estlin, where are you?" His urgency rings through my ear.

I sniffle and keep my voice low. "We're on our way home."

"No. I want you to pull over somewhere. You're in no condition to drive. I'll look you up on the app and be there as soon as I can."

"I just want to get her home," I plead. "She's upset, Owen. It's my fault, and I don't want it to be like this for her."

"Fuck," he growls in my ear. "I can't stand this. I should have put security with you. I should have—"

"I never told you about him because I wanted to keep it in the past. You had no clue. This is my fault."

"I knew something wasn't right," he throws back at me. "I knew you were hiding something."

"I'm sorry I kept it from you. I didn't expect him to show up like this, and I didn't react well. I understand if you want to get rid of me. That's twice in two weeks—"

"Stop it. You're not leaving us, and that's final. Did he hurt you?"

"No, and I don't think he would have. He's never physically hurt me. But I still have stuff I need to tell you."

"We'll talk about it when I get home. Are you sure you're okay to drive?"

I take a deep inhale and blow it out slowly. "Yes. I'm fine. I was just rattled, but I'm good now." The light turns green, and I lift my foot off the brake and press down on the gas, wanting to get us as far from Claude as I can. "I should have—"

"Estlin, look out!" Rory cries, followed by a blood-curdling scream that slices through the air. My head whips right just in time to see a car come plowing through the red and straight into us.

18

OWEN

Fear unlike any I've ever known slams into me with the force of a runaway train. Or a bullet. Or something equally, if not more, deadly and destructive. All I could hear was Estlin's voice, thick with tears and poorly disguised anxiety, and then my baby girl's scream. *Her scream.* A crunching bang that will haunt my nightmares for eternity pierced my ears, and then nothing.

The call dropped.

I race for the elevator as I dial her again, only it rings and rings and rings with no answer. Dread and panic rip my insides apart, threatening to cut me out at the knees. I pace the elevator, about ready to lose my absolute fucking mind, but the moment the doors part, adrenaline takes over. It has me sprinting into the emergency department, straight for the nurse's station.

"There was an accident. I need you to call dispatch and get an ambulance to this address." I pull up the tracking app on my phone and show the nurse, who is staring at me with wide, shocked eyes. "Now!" I bark when she doesn't immediately move.

She snaps into gear, getting on the phone with the police and ambulance dispatch, which is infinitely faster than calling nine-one-one.

"What's going on?" Stone comes over, noting the wild, unhinged look on my face.

"Estlin and Rory were in a car accident."

His hand hits my shoulder. "Jesus. Are they okay?"

I shake my head. "I don't know. I was on the phone with them. It just happened now."

"Yes, we need paramedics, police, and fire immediately to the scene of a motor vehicle accident," the nurse says before giving the dispatcher the coordinates. "We have at least one female and one child involved. The child belongs to one of ours." She covers the phone and looks up at me. "It had already been called in, and they're not even two minutes out." She goes back to the phone. "The child needs to be brought here to Children's. The father is already here waiting."

"No. I want both of them brought here. The female is only twenty-two." Right on the line for being able to be treated here, but I don't care, and I know no one will challenge me on it given the situation.

She relays that to the dispatcher, and I thank her, though I'm hardly able to catch my breath.

"Stay close, Dr. Fritz," she advises. "I'll keep you updated when I get a status on them."

I don't know if I can hear it. I don't know if I can hear it if Rory and Estlin aren't okay.

"Notify trauma surgery to be on standby, and let's get traumas one and two prepped and ready. I want no delays," Stone orders.

Nurses and other doctors jump into action, giving me looks and patting me on the back in a way that says they've got this. That they're here with me, and I'm not alone. I spend a lot of time down here. I'm a general surgeon, and the number of ER consults we get is staggering. So everyone here knows me personally. And even if they didn't, they know Stone, and they know my other family members who work in this hospital.

It's one of the few times I'm incredibly thankful I'm a Fritz in a family of a lot of doctors.

"Police and paramedics are on the scene," the nurse tells me with the phone to her ear, snapping me away from everything around me. "The child is alert and oriented but in a lot of pain. Suspected broken right arm. Other injuries unknown."

I blow out a breath, relieved she's awake and alert, and shattered that she's in pain with a broken arm and other unknown injuries. My little girl. My baby fucking girl. I can't handle not being there.

"What about her nanny?" I ask urgently. "The woman who was driving?"

She listens for a moment and then says, "She's refusing care. But also awake and oriented."

My hands hit my head, and I pace a circle in front of the nurse's station. Fucking Estlin. What the hell is she doing refusing care? Goddammit!

"They're ten minutes out, Dr. Fritz. Don't worry. They're in good hands."

I thank the nurse again and then stagger my way out to the ambulance bay in a daze to wait. It's like I'm outside my body watching this unfold. I can't make sense of Rory or Estlin being hurt. Stone is by my side, both of us silent and tense as every second ticks by like an eternity.

"Do you want to call anyone? Your parents? Her parents? Jack?"

I shake my head. "Not yet."

"My dad is upstairs. Can I text him?"

"Yeah. Thanks. I don't know who's on for ortho—"

"I've already called them in and they're on their way down."

I glance over at my cousin. "Thank you. I'm glad you're on

right now. I don't think I could do this without you, and it'll help Rory to have a familiar face."

"It's likely against protocol."

"I don't give a fuck. I want—no, I *need*—you in there with her."

"Either way I'd be in there. No place else I'd be."

I clutch his shoulder, giving him a squeeze, before I release him and start to pace, unable to slow myself down. Where the fuck is this fucking ambulance?

I need to know what happened. Estlin was upset. She was distraught and I told her to pull over, but she wanted to get home. I should have forced it. She was in no shape to drive, and I knew it. Once I know my girls are okay, I'm going to call Vander in on this. I'm going to get everything I can on her ex.

Sirens in the distance still my movements, and I stare off into the Boston night, listening as they grow closer, louder, more urgent. Two nurses and an emergency room attending come out into the ambulance bay, give me a fleeting glance, and then it's all business.

The ambulance pulls in, and the back doors open.

I race forward, only for Stone to throw an arm across my chest, holding me back with a meaningful look. A look that says I need to let everyone else handle this. A look I can't fucking stand.

"Six-year-old female T-boned by a car running a red," the paramedic starts as she jumps out, and they pull the gurney out of the back of the rig. "Front right side of the car took most of the impact, and the child was in a booster and restrained. Side airbags deployed on impact. Obvious right arm fracture, alert and oriented times three. Vitals have been stable with heart rate in the one thirties and blood pressure one-oh-six over seventy. Pulse ox is ninety-eight, but we gave her oxygen for comfort. She received IV saline and point eight of morphine en route."

Rory is pale with visible tears all over her face. Her right arm is stabilized in an air cast but obviously broken. Her eyes lock with mine and she starts to cry all over again. I don't know how to handle this. My little girl.

I come up beside her head as Stone and the other doctors and nurses get to work on her. "I'm here, Moonshine. It's okay. Stone has you too, and they're going to take good care of you."

"Daddy, I hurt."

I choke and quickly swallow it. "I know, my sweetheart. We'll help with that. You're going to be okay. I promise."

They wheel her inside, and I spin around to find Estlin exiting the back of the rig, refusing help, a blood-soaked pad of gauze held to the left side of her head. Her eyes meet mine, and tears immediately start to pour, the same as Rory's did.

I'm furious. A rage so acute it cannot be contained.

She races into the hospital, bypassing me and my harsh gaze. Heavy steps take her right to the edge of the trauma room.

"Miss. I'm sorry, but we need to check you out," one of the nurses explains, trying to get her into a wheelchair.

Estlin shakes her head, waving her away. "I'm fine. It's just a cut. Take care of Rory."

My hand hits her waist, my fingers clutching, gripping, a fucking vise. I spin her to face me, staring deep into her eyes for a moment before my lips scrape across her cheek to her ear. "Go get checked out. Now."

"No," she sharply hisses.

I drag her into me, holding her close, not giving two fucks who sees me do it. "You're bleeding from your head, which means you *hit* your head. I need you to go and get a CT scan, so I know you're okay. I can't..." My forehead hits her shoulder, and I bring her body tighter to mine. "I can't handle this, Estlin. I can't. I need to focus on Rory, but I can't do that fully if I don't know you're not bleeding into your brain. Do you not under-stand that I need you to be okay too? Please. For me. Let them check you out, and for fuck's sake, get a CT. Then come back to me."

Her hand meets my back, and I can feel her trembling. She's scared, but I am too. On a normal day, I can lie and pretend she hasn't become my everything, but this isn't one of those moments.

"Okay," she relents. "For you, I will."

"Thank you." I kiss the crook of her neck and release her. The nurse all but forces her into a wheelchair. "I want a stat head CT with results sent to me, and I want her assessed for other injuries as well."

"Yes, Dr. Fritz."

Estlin is wheeled off, and I don't hesitate before I enter Rory's trauma room.

Stone doesn't even spare me a glance as they ultrasound her belly. "If you stay, you're the patient's father, not the doctor."

"I'm a pediatric surgeon."

"Not right now, you're not."

Fuck. *Fuck!*

"Besides, her belly is soft and nondistended, with no rebound or guarding. X-ray and ultrasound are negative. It seems her arm took the brunt of it, so we don't need a pediatric general surgeon on her case."

I give him a look that doesn't hide my every fuck you thought as I make my way up to Rory's head.

I soften my features. "How are you doing, Moonshine?"

"My arm hurts," she whines, but she's also groggy, and I can tell they gave her some more morphine.

My lips meet her temple, and I wrap myself around her head. "I know, honey. They're going to fix your arm. You're in my hospital with people here who love you and will take the best care of you."

"Like you? Like Stone?"

My forehead presses against her temple. "Like us."

"Where's Estlin?"

"They're taking a special picture of her head to make sure she's okay."

"She sang to me."

"What?" I pull back and stare down at her.

"After the car hit us, she held my hand and sang to me. She wouldn't let me out of my seat, and I was scared and crying. She held my hand and sang to me until the ambulance came."

Fuck, if I wasn't already falling in love with that woman before, I sure as hell am now.

"She was bleeding a lot. Is she going to be okay?"

"She's going to be fine. We need to focus on you."

The trauma room doors swing open, and there is the orthopedic surgeon, Lester Falcon, along with Kaplan.

Lester comes over and stands above her, giving us both a smile. "Well, little lady, I hear you're Rory Fritz."

Rory gives me an uncertain look, and I nod at her. She turns back to him and nods too.

"Excellent. It's so nice to meet you. I'm a good friend of your dad's and great-uncle's. It looks like we're going to be taking you upstairs for a special surgery on your arm. I know that sounds pretty scary, but don't worry, we're going to take good care of you, and when you wake up, your dad will be there."

"I'm going too," I demand.

"You're not," he tells me in no uncertain terms. "You're the father, and you have no place in that OR or even in my gallery. I know you've seen orthopedic surgeries. These are Rory's films." Lester turns on the monitor and shows me Rory's fractured arm. "You see that?" He points to the jagged, misplaced parts of her ulna and radius. "Those have to be reset, and I know you know exactly how we do that. You cannot watch that."

Because orthopedic surgeries are violent as hell. Saws and screws, and yeah, I can't watch them do that to my little girl. I'd go fucking nuts.

"I'll be there," Kaplan says, putting his hand on my shoulder. "Does that sound okay, Rory? Can I watch your special surgery?"

Rory looks at me and then over at Kaplan and gives another nod.

"From up in the gallery," Lester presses.

"From up in the gallery," Kaplan agrees before he turns to me. "I'll update you as it goes."

I puff out a breath and come up to my full height, hands on my hips, as I stare up at the ceiling. "How long?"

"Three hours, maybe four, but likely not more than that."

I walk with Rory over to the elevator, along with Kaplan and Stone. Kaplan is telling her stories about when I was a kid as he tries to get her to crack a smile. Lester asks what color cast she wants, and she tells him pink. It's all standard, and she's not in pain thanks to the morphine, but I feel like she's taking my heart with her as I kiss her goodbye and promise to be there when she wakes up.

"We've got her," Kaplan promises and the doors close, the elevator climbing up into the building with Rory in it. For the longest time, I can't make myself move from this spot.

"Dr. Fritz?"

I turn to find two police officers standing behind me.

"If you have a moment, we'd like to speak with you."

A few minutes later, Estlin is wheeled back, just after I finish speaking to the police about the accident. The other driver plowed right through the red light at top speed and straight into the car. It's amazing they weren't more injured. The driver of the other car was taken to another hospital but seemed to be uninjured.

"Did I miss her?" Estlin asks as she spots the now-empty trauma room being cleaned.

"She went up to surgery for her arm."

She nods, but there's no hiding how her chin trembles and

her body shakes. Fresh tears leak from her eyes, and I come over to wipe them away, only to stop myself. Estlin isn't mine. She's Rory's nanny, though I'm having a hell of a time convincing myself of this.

"Her head CT is clear," the nurse tells me. "I had the radiologist do a stat read. It's just a nasty laceration that we'll get stitched up."

"I've got it," I tell her, grabbing all the suturing supplies and dumping them on Estlin's lap.

"Dr. Fritz?"

"It's fine. I'll do the sutures and take responsibility." I take the handles of Estlin's wheelchair and start to walk us away.

The nurse wants to argue with me but wisely doesn't. "Where are you taking me?" Estlin asks as we reach the elevators.

"My office. I can't be down here right now, and I'm not allowed in the OR. I can stitch your forehead upstairs."

"What if I want someone else to do it?" she challenges, and I can't help my reluctant smirk.

"You want an intern who has been practicing medicine for less than six months to stitch your face? We don't exactly have plastics on call here this time of day on a Friday."

She sighs. "The car ran the red."

"I know. I spoke to the police."

"So why can't I stop blaming myself? I didn't see the car. How did I not see the fucking car?"

I run my fingers through her hair. "Because you were upset before that, and the light was green."

"I still should have looked both ways, and I didn't."

The elevator opens, and I wheel her down the hall toward my office. I stop just as we reach the door, and she stands, a little wobbly but steady enough that I take her hand and lead her inside.

Her nervous, tormented eyes meet mine. "The car is totaled."

I shake my head as I shut the door behind us and cup her face in my hand so she hears me. "I don't give a shit. It's a car. It's replaceable. You and Rory are not. Even if it had been your fault, I still wouldn't care about the fucking car and only care about the two of you."

She starts to break down, crying without the ability to stop as she sits on the sofa, her face in her hands. I drag over an unused filing cabinet and place all the equipment on top of it. Opening things up and keeping them as sterile as I can.

"She's been through so much, Owen."

"She'll be fine, Estlin. She'll heal and get spoiled rotten by everyone. You've been through a lot too. I'd like you to explain to me about your ex."

She nods, and I clean my hands with sanitizer before I snap on gloves and get to work on her forehead laceration.

"I moved to Paris for art school when I was seventeen, and a few months in, I met Claude Morceaux when I applied for a job at his gallery."

I freeze and stare dead into her eyes. "Claude Morceaux?"

"Yes," she says wryly, almost as if the irony is torture. "You have his paintings in your office. I was living with him when he made those."

"Jesus Christ. Are you kidding me?" I don't know how to respond to that. Other than to burn them. I bought them from a top-rated gallery in New York. I had no clue.

She grimaces as I clean her forehead. "Sorry. The ones you have are lovely."

I give her a look, and she laughs lightly. It's the first one I've heard from her all evening, so that's something.

"Claude was a lot older, sophisticated, brilliant, and he wanted me. I was barely eighteen by then and very naive. He swooped in and swept me off my feet. For almost four years, my entire world was about him. His friends, his genius, his schedule, his moods. And let me tell you, those fluctuated like a mirror in a fun house. I didn't care, though. I was so taken in by everything that I didn't realize how toxic it all was."

"What did your family say about him? This will burn."

I inject lidocaine into her skin to numb her up. She winces but holds still.

"I don't remember Jack talking about him," I admit. "Just that you were living in Paris with a famous artist."

"That's because Jack only met him a couple of times. Jack was living and working in LA, remember? That's pretty far from Paris. We kept up mostly through FaceTime and text. Besides, Jack doesn't know about any artist other than our mother. Claude never spoke great English, but he put on all the charm for my parents. They loved him because he loved me, and I loved him."

"All right. So what happened? How did we get here?" I ask as I start to stitch her.

Her eyes fill with more tears, and she's silent as I finish her sutures and cover them with steri-strips, not speaking again until I start to clean everything up.

"He created a new exhibition. Twenty pieces of new art he was going to reveal and showcase in his gallery. It was a huge deal, and he had invited people from all over the world for the opening. He allowed fifteen critics and gallery owners to preview it in our home. We both had studio space there. The boundaries between his and mine weren't all that clear. Every time these people came, I had to leave. I didn't understand why, but I didn't challenge it either.

"I came home after being out for two hours and discovered him and a gallery owner I knew he greatly admired and respected in the studio space. Claude was shirtless, and the woman's hair was down and messy. They didn't hear me come in. They were too busy looking at a photograph of me. The woman called me fat and said she was surprised Claude would be attracted to such a woman. Claude, in turn, called me a devoted pet along the lines of a baby cow you can't help but love. After that, he went on to tear apart my work, calling me talentless, but claiming he didn't have the heart to be that cruel and tell me."

"Christ, Estlin. You heard all of this?" I can barely breathe thinking about what that must have been like for her to walk in on and overhear.

"Yep." She pops the P sound. "I was in such a brutal daze, my heart literally feeling like it had been shredded inside me, that I didn't immediately catch the issue with the art. She hated his work. Like *hated* it. But then she walked over to my work, my canvases that were on easels, and loved those. He was furious. Absolutely enraged. He told her the ones she hated were mine and the ones she loved were his, and when he went to kick her out, they saw me standing there, falling apart."

"So, this gallery owner hated his work and loved yours, but he claimed yours were his and vice versa?"

"Yes."

I reach up and wipe her tears, unable to handle them for another second. "Estlin, that's the most fucked-up thing I've ever heard."

She looks down at her knotted hands in her lap. "The entire time we were together, he told me my pieces weren't good enough to sell. That I didn't have the talent to make it. And then this gallery owner walks in and flips all that on its head."

"Claude didn't take that well," I surmise.

She laughs caustically, sniffling and drying her eyes with the backs of her hands. I doubt she even notices the mascara smeared on them. "I lost my mind. Ranting and raving, but he became *unglued*."

"What does that mean? *Unglued*?"

"I screamed about what he said about me. About the cheating. About the lying about my work to her. He had never hurt me before, but that doesn't mean I always felt safe around him. He told me my work was trash, and that all these years he was fostering a nothing-there talent because he didn't know how to let me down gently, and the sex was good even though he did think I was a fat cow.

"I left. I was distraught and needed to try to think. I had never felt so ruined and betrayed. By the time I came back to end it with him and leave for good, I found all my work in shreds and shattered pieces. He had destroyed every piece of mine. He told me that I was nothing and he knew I was all along and that he was going to make sure no one ever discovered me. That if I ever tried to sell my art in Paris, he'd ruin it time and time again. That he had that power over me because he was famous, and I was nothing without him."

My jaw locks and my fists clench. "Then what?"

"I lost it." She shrugs with a small, humorless laugh. "I was heartbroken. His words killed me. What he did with that woman was crushing, but what he did to my art was devastating. Years of my work, my blood, sweat, and tears, all gone. That was my chance. I told him he was the one who was nothing and that he was jealous and pathetic. He came after me, and I ran."

I stand, pacing toward the window, breathing hard, close to losing it myself. I want to plow my fist through the window. I want to shatter the glass. I want to break and tear and burn the world apart. But I won't. I won't even attempt it because Estlin deserves better from me.

She deserves to know that I'm safe and that I'd never hurt her. No matter what.

She was right to call him pathetic. I know what it is to be betrayed by someone you love, someone you trust. It's gutting how it terrorizes you. How it strips you of your trust and faith, especially in yourself.

All I know is that I will *destroy* Claude Morceaux.

He will never see me coming, but his life as he knows it is over.

No one hurts her like that. No one hurts my girl. Not ever. And him coming after her here? No. No fucking way, no.

My hands meet the back of my head, and I blow out a harsh, murderous breath. Resolved in not caring how dark that goes, I turn back around to face her.

"What happened after you left?"

She stares down at her hands before she raises her chin and meets my eyes. Her tears have dried, and I can see the strength and conviction in her. "I went to my favorite professor, needing a comforting place to be. I had met her husband and their children several times before." She pauses here and tilts her head. "You have to understand. Claude is like you. Well, not like you at all, actually, but wealthy and famous and powerful. He ruined my art, and what recourse did I have? My work was in his studio. I owned nothing, and I knew it'd be his word against mine and I'd lose."

I collapse to my knees in front of her, clutching her legs.

"My professor's husband told me they were moving to London, which I already knew. He asked me to come with them as their nanny. I didn't hesitate. I left everything in Paris behind and went with them. Claude never knew about my professor or her husband. All he knew was that I never came back."

"And now he shows up here because you were photographed with Rory."

She nods slowly. "Yes. He was already in New York, though."

"He'll never come near you again," I promise her.

As a man whose control has snapped, I reach up and drag my thumb along the crest of her cheek. And then I do the only thing I can do. I lean in and kiss her.

19

ESTLIN

Owen's lips touch mine, and I don't know how to make sense of it. I don't want to be kissed because he heard my sad story. I don't want to be kissed because he feels like he needs to comfort me in this way. Only his hands climb up into my hair, holding my head on either side, and he groans the second his lips part mine and our tongues touch. Like a groan that speaks to his level of need and desperation and fucking desire.

Like going months without kissing me has cost him everything, and he's tired of paying instead of taking.

I never felt safe with Claude. He was always a wild, unpredictable storm. Initially, that's what drew me to him. Like his wildness made me reckless, and it was sexy and freeing. Owen is the opposite. His cool certainty and protective strength not only make me feel grounded but cherished.

He'd rather die than hurt a hair on my head and wants to destroy anyone who ever has.

That's what this touch is. That's what these sounds are. That's what this kiss tells me.

That it's not just lust. It's life. A necessity.

This entire night has been a clusterfuck of madness. Rory, *my Rory*, is hurt. She's having *surgery*. I reacted in a way I hated in front of her. So, when she's physically recovered, I'm going to have a real sit-down with her. I owe her that.

But Owen listening to me, hearing about my past, and still being here with me...

I don't know what this is between us, but I fucking want it.

I trusted a man I was in love with, and he destroyed that trust with a betrayal unlike any other. I turned inward. I withdrew, not knowing how to be around people or trust them. But I trust Owen. And that... God, that trust... I'm not sure how I could ever go without it again.

His lips ravage mine, his tongue moving in a seductive, devouring dance.

All too soon he pulls back, his forehead pressing to mine.

"My sweet thing, I need you. I crave you. I am *consumed* with you. You must already know that as I've done little to hide it."

"But?"

He blows out a heavy torrent of air. "You are easily the most desirable, undeniably forbidden thing in my world. You don't belong to me. You belong to everyone else *but* me. I'm thirty-four, and you're twenty-two. I have a child and a career. You're just starting out with an endless sea of possibilities ahead of you. Not to mention, your brother would fucking gut me for touching you, and Rory needs you. I don't know what I have to offer you that you'd want to take, given all that."

"Then why kiss me?" I ask, trying to hide the sting of rejection from my voice.

He cradles my face and stares straight into my eyes. "You are impossible for me to resist, and I'm tired of trying. But I don't know how that works for us without us risking everything."

He's right, of course. Our lives are too intertwined. The entanglements between us too high to traverse. But I want him, and he wants me, and maybe that's enough.

"I don't care," I tell him.

"Estlin—"

I shut him up with a kiss. "I know what you're saying. I understand it fully. I'd be your lover not your girlfriend. We'd stay a secret. And eventually, with no real option for a future between us, it would run its course and fizzle out."

He licks his lips, tasting me on them, and shakes his head. "No. That's not how I want you to be with me—"

"But it's reality, isn't it? We both want this, and we both know it doesn't make sense and could never work. So we'll have some fun with it and keep it separate from everything else. It'll exist in the darkness of night and stolen moments. And because of that, it won't be real, and when it ends, it won't break us apart. As long as we're open and honest about it all with each other, then we'll be fine."

He gives me a sad sort of smile, one I can't fully read the meaning behind, but then he's kissing me again. Over and over into drunken dizziness. His teeth scrape my bottom lip until, out of nowhere, he shoots himself back and sits on his haunches, scrubbing his hands up and down his face.

"We should call your family. And Jack." His forehead falls to my thighs, and his arms wrap around my back. "Fuck. Jack. I never thought I'd be the sort of friend to lie to and betray another, but—"

"Whoa. Slow down there about Jack. Yes, you're his friend, and Wren is mine. But I am an adult, and I decide who I sleep with, not my brother."

"While I appreciate that, it's not how friends work, and definitely not how older brothers operate."

Yeah, again, he's right. Jack won't like it, and I have a feeling Wren wouldn't either. I'd remind him that it worked out for my parents as well as Rina and Brecken, since they had a similar best friend's sibling situation, but Owen and I aren't talking about forevers. We're talking about hot, sweaty, and temporary.

Maybe that should bother me, but it doesn't. It feels safer somehow. Like I have some power and control over how we do this. I run my fingers through his soft hair. It's so strange to be here with him after weeks and weeks of dancing around this.

"Do you regret hiring me?"

His head pops up and his bloodshot eyes meet mine. There is so much that weighs on this man's soul. A perpetual burden he carries that he's never learned how to shake or adjust.

"No," he answers quickly and easily without even a hint of hesitancy. "Rory loves you, and you've been so good not only with her, but for her. I won't lie and say this wasn't what I was afraid of and why I initially didn't want to hire you. That said, I think this was inevitable. We were always going to get here. It's what comes after this that scares me and fills me with worry. I'm not sure what sort of father planning to fuck my nanny makes me other than a cliché, but despite it all, I want you and don't know how to say no or walk away from this or from you."

"I don't want to walk away either, and I want you too." My fingers trickle across his five o'clock shadow and then up to flatten the crease between his brows. "Relax. It'll be fine. And no matter what, Rory will always be our priority."

Just then a text comes in. He jumps away from me and practically smashes his phone to the floor as he scrambles for it. He reads the text on the screen and sighs, rubbing a weary hand across his forehead.

"Surgery is going well. Kaplan thinks I'll be able to take her home tonight."

"That's great!" I exclaim.

He dives back at me, his lips claiming mine, working me up into a frenzy, and just when I'm panting and needing, he pulls back and helps me stand. "It is. Okay, call your parents, and I'll call mine."

Owen goes out into the hall to call his parents, and I call mine as I start to pace his office, looking around. He has a picture of Rory on his desk, and off to the side on a cabinet thing, he has pictures of his parents with Rory and another of Katy, Rory, and him in his backyard.

I was right about my mother birthing a kitten. She is totally nuts, even as my trauma surgeon father tries to talk her down.

"Oh my hell!" my mother screeches into my ear. "Eddie Estlin Kincaid, what the absolute fuck do you mean you were in a car accident after you saw Claude?"

"Breathe, Mom. My CT was normal. It's just some stitches." And likely some bruising, though I haven't seen how bad off I am.

"Breathe? You want me to breathe? How can I possibly do that after my baby was in an accident?"

"Dad," I whine like a teenager. "Tell her to breathe."

"Breathe, Aria. Actually, chill the fuck out. If she says she's fine, she's fine. Though I would like to talk to Owen or at least see your CT."

My mother makes a disgruntled noise into the phone. "Does your head hurt?"

"Not yet, but if you keep screeching at me, it will."

She's not amused. "Not funny, Eddie. My baby is hurt."

"It's fine, and I'm fine," I promise. "Owen numbed me up, so we'll see once that starts to wear off. I'm sure he can give me something if I need it."

"I just can't believe Claude did that."

"He didn't," I explain, dropping into Owen's desk chair and spinning around to look out the window at not a whole lot. "I got upset when I saw him. It was a total shock since I didn't expect him to turn up out of the blue, and I wasn't prepared. A guy ran a red light and plowed straight into the side of the car."

"Flippity fuck nuggets. Come home. Please?"

"No. I'm honestly okay, and I want to be there when Rory goes home and wakes up tomorrow."

"Fine. I'm not happy about it, but I get it and I respect it. Tell your boss we're coming over tomorrow morning. He'll have to deal."

The door opens and Owen walks back in. I roll my eyes in that teenage way while I make a face that conveys my mother's level of sanity. His lips twitch and he walks over to me. "I'm sure Owen will be okay with you coming over to check on me tomorrow."

"May I speak with them?" he asks, and I hand him the phone. He does his best to put them at ease and relays my CT results. Before he hangs up, he says, "I'm having it taken care of."

My eyebrows scrunch and my eyes narrow, but he ignores me, listening to whatever my parents say in reply. The moment he hangs up, I poke his side. "What was all that, *I'm having it taken care of* stuff?" I mock his deep, surly voice.

His arm wraps around my waist, and he hauls me up into his chest. "You're my girl now, and I take care of what's mine. But even before you were, there was no fucking way I wasn't going to handle this situation with your ex."

I squint even as I swoon just a bit at him calling me his girl. "What does *handle* mean?"

He kisses me. And kisses me. And kisses me. Damn him! I was trying to ask stuff here and now... ugh, *fine*. He can handle it.

"We should grab something to eat and then get you and Rory home." His words end there, but there is no mistaking the promise in his expression or tone. He plows his lips back into mine, his hands twining up into my hair, until I'm once again breathless. "I love your hair. I can't stop touching it. And your body..." His palms rake down my sides, skimming past my breasts and over my round hips. "There is no woman alive who is sexier to me than you are."

And I'm dead. Officially.

Pulling back, he grins as if he knows exactly what saying

that just did to me. His thumb wipes along my bottom lip before he sucks it back into his mouth.

"You taste like candy. Like you're fucking mine."

"That's because I am yours." It's true, and denying it or saying anything else is pointless.

Especially when he snarls, "You better fucking be. Your lips are swollen. I only wish I had all night to appreciate them. And make the other set just as swollen and wet. But you hit your head and need to rest, so it'll have to wait."

Je-sus.

"You can't say things like that to me and then expect me to rest and not either sit on your face or use all my vibrators."

He chokes. "*All* of your vibrators?"

I give him a cheeky smirk. "You'll meet them soon. We can play a game with them. Who can make Estlin come harder and faster?"

He shakes his head but walks me toward the elevators. I make a pitstop in the restroom and nearly shriek in horror when I see myself. My hair is a hot mess of stringy chaos, half of it chunked with blood, the other half all over the damn place. My face looks like something out of a dark romance novel, with mascara crusted beneath my eyes and streaked down my cheeks.

Why didn't Owen tell me I looked like this, and what was that man doing kissing me the way he was kissing me when I did?

Because he doesn't care about that, he cares about you, hits my brain and I try to shut that bitch down since I'm trying to be his lover and not in love.

I clean myself up as best I can, and as I exit the bathroom, he's texting on his phone, but when he looks up, he chuckles at my perturbed expression. "What? You're beautiful," is all he says with a shrug like it didn't matter how scary I looked.

We get into the elevator and head downstairs. The elevator

is crowded, and he keeps his distance now, the harsh reality of the real world versus fake and forbidden versus accepted bearing down on us.

"Jack is working a shift tonight," he explains as we reach the cafeteria. "I told him you're okay. He's going to come by tomorrow with your parents and mine."

"Sounds like a great time," I deadpan. We eat quickly, anxious to get upstairs to the surgical waiting room. The moment we step into the elevator and find ourselves alone, he presses me against the wall and kisses me. His tongue slips into my mouth like I'm his first drop of water after weeks of drought before he drags his lips along my chin and the column of my neck, where he starts to suck on me. "You better not give me a hickey," I pant, my hands holding onto his shoulders, so I don't collapse.

"Nowhere visible," he promises with a dark roughness to his voice. "But your body is going to be covered with the evidence of my hands and mouth."

Shivers chase down my spine, fighting against the heat of my skin. Every brush of his fingers, every swipe of his tongue, every flutter of his lips only makes me crave more.

"I should have known it that night."

"Known what?" I murmur, my eyes closed, utterly lost to him.

"That once was never going to be enough with you."

My heart hiccups in my chest, but I refuse to give it credence. He said it before. What we're doing is forbidden, and with that, it can only ever be this.

My eyes open, and I suck in a breath when the car slows, and we reach the surgical floor. He releases me and stands, his expression giving nothing away as we enter through a back way, Owen swiping his badge and navigating us along. Just before we reach the Post Anesthesia Care Unit, or PACU, Kaplan stops us.

"They're wheeling her in now. I was going to text you, but I wanted them to get her settled before you see her."

Owen looks like he's about to burst through the doors, but Kaplan steps in front of him.

"She did great, okay? The surgery was very successful with minimal bleeding. They did dissolvable stitches and put a cast over it to keep it stabilized since we all know kids will outsmart splints and slings."

"She's really okay?"

"She is. Go see for yourself."

Owen throws his arms around Kaplan, hugging him fiercely. "I owe you and Stone."

"Right. Yeah. We'll be sure to collect on that," he teases sarcastically and smacks Owen's back. "No sailing."

"No sailing," Owen agrees, stepping back. "I'll have to do something else with her."

Kaplan says good night to us and then walks off, leaving us to enter the PACU and find Rory.

"Why no sailing?" I ask as we walk through the long, rectangular, brightly lit room on our way to her bed.

"She has a cast, and since it's over a surgical site, they couldn't use a waterproof one. Not to mention, she'd need two good hands for sailing."

"She's going to be pissed about not being able to swim or do gymnastics."

"Yes, she will be." We reach her bed, and his breath dies in his lungs at the sight of her small body, pale and tucked under the blanket with a large pink cast on her arm. "Oh, Rory." He slides into the seat beside her bed and kisses her forehead so tenderly my heart aches with a sudden, unexplainable pang.

I want them to be mine.

And I'm not sure they ever will be.

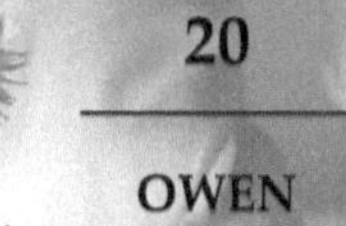

"How do you feel about Disney World?" I ask Rory on our ride home. She woke up cranky, which is normal for a child post-op, and in true Rory fashion, immediately threw up. After sucking on some ice chips and managing to keep a bit of slushy down, she rebounded quickly and then asked when she could go home. She's sitting in her booster in my car, looking anxious and unsettled, with Estlin beside her.

"Disney World?" she parrots like the words don't make any sense.

"Yeah. You know, Mickey, Minnie, rides. You can still go on rides with your cast, and we've never been to Disney."

"Can I meet the characters?" she asks, finally perking up a bit. "I saw a YouTube video where you can eat in Cinderella's castle and meet the princesses."

A smile tugs up the corner of my lips, some of the tension in my limbs ebbing along with it.

"Absolutely. Whatever you want. I'll call Donna tomorrow."

"Who's Donna?" Estlin questions.

"Daddy's assistant."

"You have an assistant?" I catch Estlin's raised eyebrows in the rearview mirror. "How did I not know this?"

"Because Donna is not my assistant specifically. She's one of the assistants for my family."

Estlin snorts. "Oh, and how many assistants does the Fritz family require?"

Brat. "We have five. But, in fairness, there are a lot of us, and my grandparents alone require one. Think of all the charity and social events we attend."

"Okay, fine." She holds up a hand. "I'm pulling back my judgment. Especially if Donna can set Rory up with a meal with the princesses."

"Donna is magic," Rory explains to her. "At least that's what Daddy says."

"Because she is. So we're on for Disney?"

"Yes! Disney! I want to meet Belle and Elsa and Minnie."

"Great. It'll be fun, and maybe we'll go sailing in the spring."

"Will you come too?" Rory asks Estlin, who emits a soft laugh. She wasn't planning to come with us, but now everything between us has changed.

"Uh. I'm not sure."

"I'd love it if you came."

She throws me an eyebrow through the rearview mirror, and I rub my thumb along my bottom lip to hide my smile.

Rory is silent after that, and I don't push her. For one, she's exhausted and likely still feeling the effects of the anesthesia. For another, I have so many things racing through my mind right now, it's hard to figure out where one ends and the other begins.

I don't know what I'm doing with Estlin other than knowing that staying away from her is impossible. But I have a very strong suspicion I'm setting myself up for the fall of a lifetime. She wants this to be a fun, casual fling, and I'm not sure I have that in me. I ache with wanting her. It's been weeks and weeks of crawling, miserable, burning desire. So the thought of having her, of making her mine, has me so twisted up that I have no bearing on right versus wrong.

It's a dangerous game to play. One that could cost me everything, and no matter what, I'll likely lose. But at this point, as selfish as it is, I'd rather have her for however fleeting it may be, than not ever again.

Then there's her ex to deal with.

I've already sent Vander a text telling him I need to meet with him.

If her ex knows she's living with me, I need to know what he's up to and what his plans are where she's concerned.

But for now, I focus on getting my little girl home. She could use a bath, but considering her eyes are droopy and she's absolutely wrecked, I simply take her up to bed, help her get changed, brush her teeth, and tuck her into bed.

"Does your arm hurt?" I ask, sitting on the edge of her bed and running my fingers through her tangled hair.

"No. It just feels weird."

I lie down beside her and take her in my arms. "Are you okay?"

She snuggles into me and my eyes close. Tonight was terrifying.

"I guess so."

"It's okay if you're not."

"I know. You always tell me that."

I grin at her tone. "I tell you that because it's important you know that you don't always have to be okay. It's okay not to be okay."

She's quiet for a contemplative beat. "I was scared. I didn't like that guy, and I couldn't understand what he was saying. He talked funny. Whatever it was, it was mean to Estlin. I could tell.

And then the car hit us, and I was scared again. It hurt a lot. Estlin made it better, but she was bleeding and…"

"You were scared?"

"Yeah."

"Wanna know something?"

"What?"

I adjust myself so she can see my eyes, even in the darkness of her room. "I was too. Really scared. All night, I was scared. It's also okay to be scared."

Her eyes fill with tears, and she hugs me, and for a few minutes, I hold her while she cries against me. My girl is always so brave. Always holds in so much. I can't remember the last time she shed any of that. I don't want to ruin this moment, but I also don't want to be the dad who pretends everything is great when it's not.

"You can talk to me," I say softly. "About anything. Anytime. Middle of the night or middle of the day, I don't care. I love you more than anything in this world, and no matter what, no matter what you ever tell me, that will never change. I'll always be here to listen and to help if I can. I hope you know that."

Slowly she raises her watery eyes to mine. "Do I have to talk about stuff?"

"No," I tell her. "You don't. But it helps sometimes when you do. If you ever wanted or needed to, you can always talk to me."

"Is Estlin ever going to leave us?"

Shit. That question. I lick my lips and tell her the only truth I know. "I hope not. But if she's ever not living with us as your nanny, she'll always be in our lives to some degree."

"Okay." A pause. "I'm mad I can't swim."

My lips twitch, and I kiss her head. She smells like the OR, and I hate it. "I know. It sucks."

She giggles through the end of her tears. I don't normally speak that way in front of her. "Can I say that?"

I smile, kissing her again. "Nope."

"Not fair," she protests even as she snuggles closer, her body growing heavy.

"If you need me, call out for me and I'll be here. You're the most important thing in my world."

"I love you, Daddy."

My chest clenches impossibly tight. "I love you, Moonshine. So much. Forever and always and into eternity." I kiss her again, never wanting to let her go. Within minutes she falls asleep, and I slowly peel myself away, climbing out of her bed without disturbing her. She looks so peaceful, but I know her mind is still unsettled.

I set up her old baby monitor so I can hear her if she needs me, and I can see her if I need to, and leave her room. Heading down the hall, I hesitate outside of Estlin's door. She already said good night to Rory, and they talked for a bit before I came in. I should likely let her rest. She's been through a hell of a lot too.

I tap lightly on the door, and just before I'm about to let it go and head for my room, the door swings open, and there she is.

"Hey," she says softly, still wearing the same blood-covered shirt, and without thinking about anything else, I take her hand in mine and lead her toward my room.

She's crazy if she thinks she's only a lover. Only temporary. I don't know what I'm doing with her, and she's clearly not there with me yet, so I have to play this cautiously, but I have no intention of letting her go or giving her up. If that's what she needs for now, I'll do my best to play along given the circumstances, but I won't be able to maintain these pretenses forever.

"What are you doing?" she asks as I walk her straight through my bedroom and into my bathroom.

"Taking a shower with you."

Opening the glass door, I turn on the water to hot, flipping switches and nozzles until water sprays everywhere, filling the bathroom with steam. Estlin is eyeing me, but she starts to lift her shirt, and I stop her with my hands, pushing hers away and finishing the task for her. Her eyes cling to mine as I undo her pants and slip them along with her underwear down her hips and legs. I help her step out of them and then reach around her to remove her bra.

This is about her, but I can't stop myself from taking her in. From devouring every stunning inch of her skin. Reaching behind my head, I pull my shirt off and undo my pants. My cock springs free and then pulses when I see her staring at it with her eyes visibly darkening.

"You can't look at me like that."

Her gaze casts up to mine, a smirk on her full lips, as I lead her into the shower. "Why not?"

"Because right now isn't about that." I bring her under the water, and she sighs, standing in between the multiple streams. "This is about me trying to take care of you."

"Isn't that what I'm asking you to do?"

I grin and give her ass a little smack that makes it jiggle. I groan. I'm so hard for her right now, my dick could cut a diamond. Especially as water cascades down her body.

"I like your shower. Mine is pretty great too, but this is next level."

"You can use it whenever you want."

She throws me a squinty side-eye. "Don't tempt me with things I'll take advantage of."

I kiss a trail along her wet shoulder as I come in behind her, shampoo in my hands. She wiggles her ass against my cock, and I hiss out a curse. "Don't tempt me with things I plan to take advantage of."

"There's no fun in that."

I work the shampoo into her hair, massaging her scalp and making sure to avoid her sutures. She emits a soft, little moan, and I have to bite my lip to stop myself from responding. The way I burn for her is like nothing else.

"You keep doing that and I'm going to come."

She giggles. "You weren't so quick on the trigger last time."

"Behave."

"Joy sucker." She flashes me a look. "Oh! I could be that too."

I laugh. A real fucking laugh that has my shoulders shaking and my body relaxing.

"Thank you. I seriously needed that."

Her voice sparkles with laughter. "Same. Definitely same."

She washes out the shampoo, and then I'm back with conditioner, repeating the motion until she takes over for me. Her fingers glide through the silky strands, removing the last traces of the conditioner as I lather body wash in my hands and start on her shoulders and then down her back, massaging her muscles as I go.

"Owen, you're killing me with how good this feels."

My mouth comes to her ear as I reach around and massage her breasts and hard nipples. "Is it making your pussy wet?"

"So wet," she moans. "Oh, god. My tits are crazy sensitive, so if you're not going to fuck me right now, you seriously need to stop."

I squeeze them firmly before pinching both of her nipples and giving them a small pull. "Sweet thing, you were accosted by your ex and then in an accident where you hit your head."

She's panting. "All the more reason to live in the moment. Please," she begs, reaching around and grabbing my aching cock.

"You need to be fucked that badly?"

She nods against me. "I'll be such a good girl for you. I promise. I'll follow all the rules. Whatever you say. But please, I need to come."

"Hmm. How good?" One hand coasts down her front, over

her soft belly to the top of her smooth mound as my other continues to play with her tits. She parts her legs wider for me, and my hand slips between them, gliding along her wet slit.

"I'm yours to do with as you please."

Fuck. She has no idea what that does to me. Her begging, her submission, her trust. It feeds my need to dominate and control. "I hope you know what you're asking for from me because if we go down that road, there will be no going back."

I swirl my finger around her opening and her knees buckle. "Good. That's what I want. Surprise me, Doctor. Don't hold back. Don't treat me gently. I want you to make me feel strong yet owned."

It's in this moment I know I'm already well and truly fucked. Because while she wants me to own her body, she already owns all of me. She is someone I won't recover from. A woman I'll always pine for even long after she's gone.

In a flash, I spin her around and press her into the marble wall. She shivers as my forearm hits the cold stone beside her head, and I lean in. With my eyes on hers, I shove two fingers inside her. Her back arches and her eyes close. Sweet, soft lips part with a whimper as my teeth scrape up her jaw.

"Don't you see how strong you already are? You don't need me to make you strong. You're doing it all on your own."

"Some moments I feel that more than others."

Isn't that the truth for all of us?

I start to pump into her, hard and fast. I'm going to make her come, and then I'm going to take her to bed. My bed. If only for a while.

Everything we're doing right now is wrong, but maybe that's part of what makes it feel so good.

She gasps, her hands clutching my biceps.

"If you want me to own you, sweet thing, I will. All of you will belong to me."

She doesn't say anything. She's too worked up. Too close.

Her eyes are pinched shut, and her lips are parted to accommo-date her extra breaths. Her wet skin is fucking rose-colored and brimming with heat. I didn't get to appreciate this the first time. We fucked in a dark hotel room. Strangers after a release.

Now everything is different.

My mouth crashes down on hers, immediately parting her lips and wasting no time kissing the hell out of her. Her pussy is so tight around my fingers, and I can't help myself as I rub my cock against her hip. I'm dying to be inside of her again. Twisting my wrist, my fingers find her front wall, fucking against her spot, and when my thumb finds her clit, she starts to lose it.

"Ah!" she cries, loudly and with abandon. She's pressed into the wall, her hands scraping at me, her knees bent. "Owen, holy shit. I'm right there. Don't stop."

I thrust my fingers faster, pounding them into her pussy and flicking her clit with tighter circles. It's messy and wet and noisy and I fucking love it. Her face is art, but I need to see her pussy as she comes for me.

Pulling away, I drop to my knees in front of her. Keeping my fingers where they are, I suck her clit between my lips before she can even open her eyes to figure out what the hell I'm doing.

"Oh fuck! Jesus, Owen."

Her hand dives into my hair, gripping the back of it and holding me tightly against her. I've missed the taste of her cunt, and because of that, I swirl my tongue inside her, gliding up along with my fingers as they continue to fuck her. She's barely hanging on, all words and curses and thrashing movements.

I keep my tongue inside her, fuck her deeper with my fingers, and then use my thumb to rub her clit until she comes. Hard. All over my mouth and fingers. Her screams echo off my bathroom walls, and I have to squeeze the base of my cock so I don't come on the spot.

Her body sags, sliding down the wall until her ass hits the floor in a heap. Her eyes are still closed, and she has the most gorgeous, sated smile on her lips. I pull my fingers out and paint her lips with them. She licks them reflexively and then grabs my hand and drags them inside her mouth, sucking them as I know she'll suck my cock.

I groan and throb.

Her eyes blink open, and I wipe some of the wet strands back from her face, making sure her stitches are clear and intact.

"Hi, beautiful. Where'd you go?"

"Someplace magical," she hums and then grabs my dick. "Now it's your turn."

21

ESTLIN

Straight facts: I don't think I've ever had orgasms like the ones I've had from Owen. Is that even a thing? Can a person have different orgasms with different lovers? I'll admit, my experience is limited. Before Claude, I had one lover, if you can even call sex club dude a lover.

Three men is hardly a wide enough audience to draw from and make a proper comparison.

But right now, I don't care. In fact, I wouldn't care if I never had another lover other than Owen because his orgasms are top-notch. Five out of five stars, a hundred percent of reviewers would recommend and repeat. I don't even know what I'm saying. I'm in some sort of alternate universe right now, and my body is a pile of wasted material.

Owen picks me up off the ground as if I weigh nothing, tucking me tightly against his chest as he shuts off the water and wraps us both up in towels. I'm exhausted and my limbs feel heavy—injured or not, your muscles do not appreciate being in a car accident—and I could go to sleep just like this. Only I can't look away from his blue eyes that try in vain to hold back the storm of emotions brewing within him.

Those are not the eyes of a man who wants to go to bed to sleep.

I move a little in his grip, wordlessly asking him to set me down, and he complies, walking toward the bed in only his towel. He's quiet now, with a lot on his mind. Maybe a little too much. Things are about to change between us. I'm going to have a fling with my boss.

For some reason, that makes me inwardly giggle and outwardly smile in the most ridiculous and ironic of ways. I'm so going to get my heart broken. Again.

But it won't stop me. Even knowing the future pain and the aftermath, it won't stop me. No more hiding. No more cowering or rolling over and playing dead. My revenge will be exacted by becoming everything Claude feared I'd be. I don't want to play it safe. I want to be wild and dangerous and undeniably forbidden.

Still, I start to shake a little as I walk into his room, nerves racking through me. I turn and find Owen sitting casually on his bed, arms behind him, hands pressed into the mattress, eyes locked on me. He's testing me, I realize. He wants to see exactly where I am, both physically and emotionally. He wants me to make the choice.

Do I stay or do I go?

Do we do this or end it here?

I drop my towel on the floor and inch toward him. Just when I get within touching distance, his hands shoot out and tug me until I'm standing between his parted thighs. He's still wearing his towel, but that won't last much longer.

His face is level with my breasts as he sits up, his hands trickling up the backs of my thighs until he's gripping the soft flesh of my ass. It's the first time he's shown any impatience, and it breeds my own. I want to devour him until we're both too spun up to think of anything else but each other. I want Owen to come undone, and I want to be the woman who brings him there. The one who pushes him to the brink of his sanity.

My fingers weave into his thick, wet hair, gripping the back that's gotten a little long. His face tilts up toward me, and all the words we had before seem to have evaporated between us. My heart races at what we're about to do, and I know he can hear it.

My shins bump into the fabric frame of the bed as I step closer, a little restless.

I bend just as he tilts up and our lips brush. A soft, teasing kiss before he tilts his head and deepens it, his tongue seeking mine. I press my thighs together, the tension building to such an extreme within me, I have no choice but to try and relieve it, but he won't allow it. His hand slips between them, prying them apart, and then dragging me down on top of his thighs until I'm straddling him.

I whine, the stupid towel trapped between us.

Pressing my knees into the bed, I rise, practically shoving my tits in his face as he undoes his towel. His mouth captures my nipple, and I whimper, gripping his hair a little tighter. I sit back down, straight on his hard length, and instinctively, my hips roll. His hand squeezes my hip, letting me know he likes that, but then he takes over, rocking me back and forth as his mouth comes back down on mine, kissing me as we grind against each other.

I lose my breath. The hard feel of him, how his hands are everywhere now—in my hair, on my breasts, rolling my nipples, squeezing my hips—is nearly more than I can handle. His mouth trickles a string of kisses down my neck, sucking and licking and biting as he goes.

Heat spreads through my body as he whispers into the shell of my ear, "I can't wait to feel this hot, little pussy wrapped around me again."

He has no idea. I need him inside of me, and I need it now. Too much foreplay in the form of avoidance and teasing and scandalous touches. I'm *burning* for him. The feel of his cock sliding through my folds, toying with my opening, and pressing hard on my clit is almost too much to take. If I have another orgasm now, I'll be done. My body won't be able to survive it, and I need him.

I shift my hips and grab him, ready to put him straight inside of me when he stills my hips. His eyes, dark and feral, hold me in place. "I don't have any condoms here."

"What?" I blink, not understanding him.

"I don't bring women home, Estlin, and we used all three that I had purchased the night we were together in the hotel."

"Okay. So?"

He blinks at me. "So I don't have any condoms," he repeats as if I should be computing this faster.

I shake my head. "I'm on the pill, and I've been tested."

"I've been tested too, but..." His jaw locks, his gaze hard and penetrating. "Are you sure you're okay with this?"

I wrap myself around him, bringing our foreheads, noses, and lips together. "Yes. I'm sure."

He curses under his breath and then guides me down... slowly... slowly... and then, all at once, he thrusts up into me. A moan rips from my lungs, and his mouth quickly covers mine, attempting to stifle the sound. He flips us over until I'm beneath him, and he has me pinned to the bed.

"Rory is all the way down the hall, and yes, my house is big, but that doesn't mean she can't hear us."

I pant and bite into my lip. "I'll be good."

"Can you be quiet?"

I don't know, so I go with, "I can sure as hell try."

He smirks against my lips, slides out of me, and then pistons back into me with the same force he did the first time. And just like then, a loud, uncontained moan wrenches through the air. *Oops.*

"Didn't think so."

"It's not my fault," I protest. "It feels really good when you do that."

"If you can't be quiet, then I'm going to have to get creative with how and where I fuck you."

My pussy clenches, and another moan slips out. God, I'm such a hussy for him and his filthy mouth and dirty promises.

He punishes me by biting my lip and pumping into me with hard, deep thrusts. It's not my fault. It's truly not. I told him I'd be a good girl for him, and I know I'm not. He should punish me, and he should keep doing it because his brand of punishment is so, *so* good. My body is his to do with as he pleases.

Every piece of me.

My mouth, my tits, my limbs, my pussy, my ass. All his.

Bracing his hands on either side of my head, he stares down at me, alternating between my face and where we're connected. He's gritting his teeth and clenching his jaw and I can feel it as he bunches up the comforter in his fists. Sweat collects on his skin, despite the shower we just took. He's barely hanging on, and it's so insanely sexy, I'm not sure I can hold off my own orgasm much longer.

"I haven't fucked anyone bare"—he pants—"in a long time."

"I've only used condoms before."

"Always?"

I nod, because even though I was on the pill, Claude insisted on them, saying he was too paranoid about getting me pregnant to trust the pill. Yet another thing that should have been a red flag for me. "Always. Make me messy, Owen. I want to be dripping you all night."

"*Fuck*," he snarls, his head throwing back and his eyes pinching closed. "I've wanted you for two months, Estlin. Every fucking second of every fucking day, I've wanted you. Now I finally have you and I'm taking you bare, and you go and say that?"

"Yes." I grab on to his firm ass, pushing him in deeper. "Because I've wanted you too, and I need it just as much."

With a roar, his hands move everywhere, all over me, and then he rolls us until I'm back on top. My blood thrums hot through my body as he uses his cock in me like a weapon, thrusting up and up and up until all I can feel is him.

His large hands grab my tits, squeezing the hell out of me as he commands, "Fuck me. Ride me. Bounce on my cock until your sweet pussy gushes all over me. Make me feel it, Estlin. Don't hold back."

His eyes rove over every inch of me, eager to see what will happen next.

My body takes over. His command I turn into action. I ride him, bouncing and rocking and taking pleasure on him. With him. I'm gonna fuck him how I need to fuck him. It's the only way I'll survive this. Our contract might not be written in stone or blood, but it's there.

It says in frank fucking letters, do not fall in love with me.

And that goes both ways.

So I do as I'm told. I fuck him. Being the good girl I want to be. I rock and use my knees on the bed and my hands on his shoulders as leverage to push up and down as he watches, his eyes all over my bouncing tits and my pussy that swallows his cock whole.

"I'm gonna fuck your tits. Not tonight. But definitely tomorrow."

That's when I come. The thought of him fucking my tits, of him coming all over them, pushes me over the edge. I lose my rhythm the moment the waves start pounding into me, deep and warm and merciless and just fucking everywhere. His mouth takes mine as I shake all over, sparks of light flashing behind my eyes. I collapse against him, and he holds me as he pounds up and up, straight into me, until fireworks explode behind my eyes again and I feel his body tense. He comes hard, fucking me until he can't take it a second longer, and his head flies back in ecstasy. His groan is louder than he intends, but he's unable to control it, even as he bites my shoulder to try.

I'm utterly spent. Completely boneless. A useless heap of a woman. He might be there with me, minus the woman part. I think I broke him. I poke his side, and all he does is grunt. I'm good with that response because I can't even find the strength to get up and pee or brush my teeth. He wraps his arms around me and holds me tight against his chest. I'm leaking his cum, but neither of us cares enough to fix that.

And that's how I fall asleep.

Me on top of him, him inside of me, lost in the euphoric bliss of this man.

A man I'll never be able to keep as my own.

THERE'S A SOUND. It's loud. Kinda distinct. Definitely relentless. *What the hell is that?* My mind is fuzzy, my limbs are each weighted down by fifty-pound weights, my vagina ran a marathon last night, and my head is *throbbing*.

"What is that?" I groan to myself until fragments of last night jackhammer into my consciousness. Claude. Car crash. Rory's surgery. Owen telling me it's game on for us. The shower. His bed. HIS BED! The door. Fuck! THE DOOR!

I jolt and simultaneously roll, falling out of bed and landing painfully hard on the floor in a massive heap. "Ow. Shit!"

"What?"

"Owen, that's the door!"

"What?"

"Stop saying what." I scramble to my feet and tear the top sheet from his bed. "That sound is the front door of your house, and I'm naked in your bed."

With wide eyes, we both take a second to absorb the magnitude of this just as the door rings for a fourth time, and then we hear it. The door opens. The alarm sounds. Someone punches in a code. The alarm shuts off.

We exchange *oh shit* looks, and then I bolt out of his room like my ass was lit on fire. I fly down the hall, my feet getting tangled in the long sheets, and I nearly eat shit twice. I don't care, and I don't stop or slow down.

"Owen?!" his mother calls out.

"Eddie?" That's mine.

Fuck. *Fuck!*

I scramble into my room and slam the door shut a bit too loudly. I wince and freeze, listening. Then I turn and look toward the Alexa clock on my nightstand. It's eight in the goddamn morning. What the hell are they doing here at this hour on a Saturday freaking morning and how on earth did we allow ourselves to not only sleep in so late but have me fall asleep in there?

Without bothering to focus on anything else, I motor into the shower and wash off a night of sex with my boss. I can't believe I fell asleep in his bed. God, that was stupid. Rory could have come in and found us. What was I thinking, and why didn't he force me out of there? Argh!

I finish up at light speed and then dress in the same fashion. A brush through my hair and across my teeth, and I'm good to go. Only I race out of my room with my shirt on backward. Crap! I flip it around in the hallway and then tear down the stairs to find Owen already down there wearing nothing more than a white T-shirt, gray sweatpants, and his glasses with his hair in wild disarray.

Is he trying to kill me?

Him in his glasses is my own personal Kryptonite, and the white T-shirt with gray sweatpants is straight out of the lady porn handbook. Something he proves as he tosses me a knowing smirk. Even as my brother claps him on the shoulder and the two of them start talking about who cares what. Rory is hardly awake as she embraces everyone and shows them her cast. She's still rubbing her eyes and wearing her pajamas.

"Oh, hey!" I exclaim. "I didn't hear you all come in. I was in the shower. In my bathroom."

And yup, I just said that. And yup, I get glances that match just how ridiculous and hopefully confusing that is.

Moving on.

I go over and hug everyone. That is, until my mother gets a look at me. "Oh my hell, your face!" she screeches.

"Mom! Language!"

She winces. "My apologies, Rory."

Rory doesn't seem to care as she shrugs while yawning.

My mother takes my face in her hands, tilting me this way and that. "You haven't seen this yet, have you? I'm going to unalive him." She glances down at Rory, as if saying it that way makes it okay.

In fairness, no, I haven't. I raced through that shower like an Olympic athlete after gold.

My mother whips out her phone, pulls up her camera app, and points it at me. Half of my face is deep black and blue. I look like I was in a boxing match and lost. It's bad. Not to mention the neat line of stitches on my forehead near my hairline.

"You should have seen the other guy," is all I can manage.

"Not funny, Eddie," Jack growls, his gaze locked on my bruise and cut. "You have no idea how scared we were."

My dad cups my face in his hand, tilting it this way and that, and then examining the sutures in his very clinical, medical way. "He's right, Eddie. None of us slept much last night. Why do you think we're here so early? We needed to see that you're okay for ourselves, not just be told that you are."

"I know," I tell him, feeling guilty. I put them through it

when I ran away to London and refused to see them. Now this. "But truly, I'm fine. My head is a little sore, but that's all."

"At least the stitches look good," Jack comments. "Nice work on that, my friend."

Owen is standing off to the side, his eyes locked on his coffee mug. Speaking of feeling guilty, it's written all over him. He feels like shit for fucking his best friend's little sister. He can hardly meet Jack's eyes. Is this how it will go for us? Owen's guilt, Jack's ignorance and overprotectiveness, and my... I don't know what. Last night was amazing, but was it stupid with how we woke up this morning?

I want Owen like nothing else, and that's probably why we should stop. Before it gets out of hand and there's no going back.

"No more ugliness or talking about unpleasant things," my mom chirps. "Let's go shopping. Eddie needs new clothes anyway. I'm tired of seeing her dress like a starving artist."

I snort. "Thanks, Mom."

"Yes!" Grace chimes in, grabbing my arm. "Let's all go shopping. We'll invite everyone and see who can make it. Rory, what do you say?"

Rory gives us all an eyeball and then turns to her dad. He shrugs. "If you're up for it."

My mother crouches down to meet Rory head-on. "I was thinking of a ladies' brunch out, some shopping, and maybe a trip to the art supply store." She glances up at me. "On me, of course." She gives me a wink.

Oh, does my mother know how to sweeten a deal?

"Yay!" Rory jumps up and down. "I'm going to get dressed. I want waffles!"

"There is no brunch without waffles," Grace calls out to her. "Rory, hold up. I'm coming up to help you. Aria, you send out the mass text."

"I'm already on it." Her fingers are flying across her screen. "I can't wait. This is going to be so much fun!"

22

ESTLIN

Rory holds my hand as we walk into Stella's restaurant. Stella is a family friend to Katy and also Owen's first cousin. It all gives me a headache. The family dynamics are next level. Still, the brunch is everything. Rory orders a massive Belgian waffle with chocolate sauce, whipped cream, and strawberries. I spend a good five minutes cutting it up for her since she can't with her cast. I order a breakfast pizza that has me moaning and groaning just as hard as I did last night with Owen.

Speaking of... the moment I catch my breath from all the estrogen around me—all of freaking Owen's family—I text him.

Me: That can't happen again.

He replies immediately.

Owen: Which part? You coming bare all over my cock, us fucking into the wee hours of the night, or you falling asleep in my arms?

I pause. I hesitate. I chew on my lip until my mother tells me to finish my breakfast like I'm Rory's age. Did I fall asleep in his arms? Because… that's intimate. That's not the stuff of flings and easily forgottens.

I nibble on a bite of my pizza, already feeling uneasy.

Me: Maybe this was a mistake.

Owen: Too late, sweet thing. I have no plans to go back. But I do have plans to own your body again all night tonight. Good thing tomorrow is Sunday, and we can sleep in.

My face heats to volcanic proportions, and I have to take a hasty sip of my water. Thank God these women don't know how to stop talking, and no one is paying much attention to me. A quick glance around the four tables we have shoved together proves this, and I return to my phone, no longer hungry now that my stomach has imploded on itself.

Sweet thing. He's been calling me that, and I might be low-level obsessed with it.

Me: This is madness! Do you not feel all that we're risking?

Owen: I do. Don't discount that. But I've decided I want you more. Are you not there with me?

Ha. I laugh and garner a few odd looks. Am I not there with him? I am so all the way, no turning back there with him. *That's the freaking problem, Owen!* I decide not to go there and focus on the sex since that seems the safest territory in this minefield.

Me: I want what you promised me last night. I want you to fuck my tits and come all over me.

Owen: You're making my cock hard in front of your brother.

Me: I don't care. I want to take it down my throat the next time I see you. I'll drop to my knees. Just. For. You.

Owen: Fuck, sweet thing. You're going to kill me with talk like that.

Me: Good. Maybe that's exactly what we both need. But this can only be sex like we said. No more falling asleep in your bed or your arms.

Owen: After Rory goes to bed, be on your knees for me. I'll tell you where to go. And be prepared. I have no plans to go easy on you.

My pussy clenches and I stifle a moan, only to realize entirely too late he never addressed my point about this only being sex and no more sleeping together. The fact that he's texting that in front of my brother is so not how I thought this would go. I expected him to retreat.

Honestly, I think part of me was almost hoping for that. Like, hey, we scratched the itch, and it was good, but probably not smart to do it again.

Except I'm starting to learn that's not how Owen Fritz operates. He's too methodical for that. He works with a plan, and right now, his plan includes me.

After breakfast, we go shopping, but when you're with about a thousand women who not only like to talk but also shop and look at *everything*, it takes forever. The Copley Mall is packed, and my stomach is so full I can hardly stand it. The notion of shopping is almost a bit too much. Especially with the curious, glaring looks I keep getting because of my face.

That's another thing. Not my face necessarily, but Claude.

I know Owen said he would take care of it in his very take-charge, alpha-male way of his, but it's not his problem to solve. It's certainly not something I want him involved with. I was upset in front of Claude—and Rory—yesterday afternoon and it's been eating at me. I don't want him to affect me anymore. What we had is over, what he did was terrorizing, but I'm in my moving on, I've got this era. That means I need to face him and what he did to me. No more running and hiding from it.

But for right now, I sort of just want to go home, get into pajamas, and read a book or maybe play the piano for a bit. I want to relax and chill out, but I also want Owen and Rory there. All that will have to wait.

I find a cute pair of jeans and a cashmere sweater in Saks and head toward the changing area when I overhear Katy's agitated voice.

"You need to stop talking about this," she demands. Baby Willow is tucked into a carrier against her chest, fast asleep. "Not only is Rory right over there"—she points to the other side of the store from where I'm standing—"but do you even know if that's what Owen wants? He hasn't shown any interest in dating, and he is not the blind date type."

That catches my attention, and I stumble over my own feet, tripping forward and practically slamming straight into the changing room wall.

"Oh my gosh! Estlin, are you okay?" Keegan and Bianca come running over to me.

I wave them off. "Oh yes, I'm fine. Just a bit clumsy."

My mother purses her lips. "You're not clumsy. You've never been clumsy a day in your life. Are you sure you don't have a concussion?"

I can feel my face starting to heat as a half dozen women—many of them in the medical field—stare at me.

I wave them off too. I must look like I'm swatting at flies. "Oh, yes. I'm fine. Probably just something in the rug."

Only Katy isn't buying it. I can see it in her eyes. And

considering how close she and Owen are, I wonder if he's told her about how we initially met or if he'll tell her about what happened last night.

"I'm just going to try these on." I hold up my stuff and then head straight into the dressing room, which allows me to eavesdrop on the small group of women consisting of Grace, Wren, Bianca, my mother, Katy, Keegan, and Rina.

"I don't see how it can hurt to try," Grace admits almost whimsically. "He's been in a much happier place over the last couple of months. This might be the right time to strike. Owen may be resistant to meeting new women, but this woman is perfect for him. She's a doctor and a single mother."

My gut clenches before it does a freefall. They're going to try to set Owen up. With someone who is perfect for him. Since I'm not.

"I agree," Rina exclaims. "She's amazing. So sweet and kind. She's one of my favorite doctors that I work with. And her daughter and Rory already go to school together."

"Okay." Bianca is all thought. "All of this is true. But Owen is Owen Fritz. That's no joke."

"I don't think she cares," Rina admits. "Her ex-husband was some sort of tech guy, and she did well after their divorce."

"Well, that's good," Grace practically cheers. "I know he worries greatly that someone will only be after him for his money the way Angelica was. But how do we set them up without making it seem like we're setting them up?"

"He's not going to like this," Katy protests.

"No," Keegan agrees. "He won't. But that doesn't mean it wouldn't be good for him to meet someone new. Someone he could potentially have a real future with."

That stings. She has no clue, but wow, did that hit hard. Just when I thought my gut couldn't sink any lower, it surprises me by plummeting into a newly formed chasm designed just for it. I have one leg shoved into these jeans, the rest of me all but naked, my eyes wide and troubled as I stare at my reflection in the mirror while listening.

"He leaves for Disney in a few weeks, so maybe after that," Rina offers.

"We can make their meeting an accident. Like Katy invites him out and I happen to be there with her," Keegan suggests.

"That's smart, Keegan," Grace agrees. "So it doesn't seem like we're ganging up on him or shoving it down his throat."

Katy makes a noise in the back of her throat. One that tells me she's not on board with that idea. "I don't want to be part of this. It goes against my code with him. You'll have to leave me out of your scheming."

"Don't you want him to be happy?" my mother asks.

"I do. More than anything. But I won't be called a traitor and lose his trust in me either."

Jealousy slices into me like a hot knife through butter. I must make a noise. Some sort of strangling and deranged or shattered sound. Because suddenly my changing room is infiltrated. I shove my other foot in and rip the jeans up my thighs, buttoning them up and then throwing on the sweater like a teenager caught making out with her boyfriend.

"Oh, Eddie, I love that outfit." Grace gives me the smile of a lifetime.

"Yes. It's definitely a keeper," my mother agrees, adjusting the sweater on my shoulder.

"We were just talking about this woman we'd love Owen to meet and get to know. But you know him. He's tricky. Do you think he'd be adverse?"

How on earth do I answer his mother? I do everything I can to keep my features even and neutral. As it is, I can feel Katy watching me like a hawk, gauging my reaction, and I can't meet her eyes, or she'll see right through me.

I clear my throat. "I honestly couldn't say. He doesn't talk to me about that sort of thing."

Not a lie.

"Right." Grace rolls her eyes at herself in a self-deprecating way as she touches a hand to her shoulder. "Of course not. I hope that didn't make you uncomfortable. I just want to see him happy again. Settled."

"I get that. I'd like him to be happy too." It's all I've got. Even as I stare down at the jeans that suddenly don't quite seem to fit me right. Maybe that's how this is. I don't quite fit here. Owen said it last night. We're in completely different places that could never line up.

There is no way things will work out for us in the long term.

But that doesn't mean I don't want them to.

I shouldn't. And I shouldn't be jealous of this woman who they think is so perfect for him. Maybe she is. Maybe a Brady Bunch situation is exactly what he and Rory need. I don't want to be selfish, and I don't want to be in the way of him having a real future with someone.

Doesn't stop it from hurting, though. Not even twenty-four hours in, and I'm already hurting. Just great.

My day didn't improve much other than the two men in the makeup department who redid my makeup and covered my bruised face with gusto. Despite the pretty makeover they did on me, my mood hasn't improved. It all boils down to one thing.

I need to stop sleeping with Owen.

I like my job. I like working with Rory. I like living there. I don't want to ruin the good thing I have going, and if this continues, despite the lame-ass promises we've made, it'll turn bad. I know it will. He'll meet his woman, and he'll like her, and he'll end it with me, and my heart will break. I have to nip this in the bud now.

My plan is to speak with him about it, but when we get home, Jack is still there. In fact, he hangs out all afternoon, through the evening, and into the night because that's just the way things go for me right now.

"Eddie, come play darts with us," Jack calls out to me as I try to race toward the stairs and go to my room now that Rory is finally asleep. "Did you know that Eddie is killer at darts?" His question is tossed at Owen, who responds with a smirk.

"I think she mentioned it once."

Oh, did I? Did I *mention* it? I might be a little bitter and riled up right now. Jack and Owen opened two bottles of wine tonight, and I had my lion's share. It's not helping me.

"Careful though," Jack teases. "She doesn't like to lose."

Owen's lips bounce. He's finding that far too amusing, which frankly shocks me. Maybe his humor is from the wine like my bitterness is. "Do you bet?"

"Not unless there's something I want," I bite out, and then immediately regret it. Ugh.

"You can't be that good?" Owen challenges, lit with humor, all at my expense.

"Oh, trust me, I'm that good." I shove both of them out of the way and then go over to the dartboard in his man cave.

"Want to bet on it?"

Is he trying to fuck with me using that voice in front of my brother? "What'd you have in mind, *boss*?"

The side of his mouth hitches up at my sneer. "If I win, you paint me some new artwork for my office, but you let me pay you for your work."

For some reason that makes my breath hiccup. He's talking about replacing Claude's paintings. With mine.

"You've never seen my work," I throw at him.

"I've peeked in the basement a bit. You brought home two canvases the other day. Your art is exquisite and I'd like it on my walls."

I fold my arms to stave off the flutter his words elicit.

"And if I win?"

A spark flares in his eyes. "Lady's choice."

This motherfucker is going to play like that? "Sure. Sounds good."

Jack chuckles under his breath, thinking our back and forth is simply a little friendly sparring. How wrong he is.

"Ladies first. I am a gentleman." Owen pans a hand toward the board and then goes and pours each of us more freaking wine. Soon they'll be dragging me up and off the floor. Or out of a cage fight with how my anger is brewing.

I roll my eyes. "I beg to differ on that," I grumble under my breath and snag three darts. And because I'm in a mood right now, I chuck all three in rapid fire, hitting the bullseye or the ring just around it each time. Jack bursts out laughing as he accepts another glass of wine from Owen.

"You're up."

Owen isn't smiling anymore.

I snatch a proffered glass from his hand and cross the room to sit on the couch, kicking my legs up in the air before crossing them at the knees.

Owen clears his throat as he yanks my darts out of the board. With his eyes on mine, he lets them fly, the darts going everywhere. Sort of how I did with him that night in the bar when I intentionally lost. It's killing me. All of this is.

"Looks like you won," he says without bothering to check. What is he doing?

"Fabulous."

My phone vibrates in my pocket as I take my first sip.

Owen: What's going on with you?

I glance up quickly, but Jack is now at the dartboard, saying something to Owen and paying me no attention. I go back to my phone.

> Me: Nothing. Just a long day of shopping.

It takes him a couple of minutes to respond since now he's playing a round with Jack.

> Owen: I can't exactly kick my best friend out.

Inwardly, I huff.

> Me: This has nothing to do with Jack being here.

> Owen: Then clue me in, because there's something that you're fired up about.

> Me: I'm not fired up. But there is something I need to talk to you about, only I can't do it over text, and I can't do it with Jack here.

> Owen: This wouldn't have anything to do with what Katy told me earlier about my family trying to set me up, would it?

I feign ignorance.

> Me: I have no clue what you're talking about.

> Owen: Best wishes

> *Confetti pops and crackles down my screen*

> Owen: With your lie.

I start to crack up. That's the equivalent of Owen making a joke, which automatically makes it funny even if it's not. I love this side of him. Even if the joke is at my expense.

"Why are you laughing?" Jack questions.

"Just reading a funny post about men's impotency."

Jack winces and turns away, not wanting to question me further on that.

> Owen: Katy knows about you and me, and she also told me about the woman they want me to meet.

> Me: Why would I be upset about that? You're free to meet whomever you want.

> Owen: I never said you were upset. You just did. All I asked was what was going on with you.

Oh. Well, oops.

> Me: I don't care if you date the woman they all think is perfect for you. In fact, you probably should.

He doesn't reply for a moment as he loses to Jack by a landslide. Jack finds this hilarious as he comes over and sits by me on the sofa, tossing his arm around my shoulders. "What are you going to ask for?" he questions me.

"Hm. I don't know. It'll have to be something good." I scrunch my brow and look up at him. "What do you think I should ask for?"

"You should ask for a raise." Jack cackles, sipping his wine. He stands and goes for the pool table, rolling the cue ball back and forth along the felt. "Or maybe for Owen to take you with him and Rory on vacation when they go."

I choke on my sip of wine, struggling to swallow it down and wincing as it burns a path up my nose, then down my throat as I finally do.

"I'd love it if Estlin came with us to Disney. I know Rory would as well, but I don't think Estlin wants to join us."

Argh.

"Then the raise it is," Jack teases, shooting the white ball until it bounces off the walls of the pool table and flies back toward him.

"You're right," I toy, glancing casually back over at Owen. "That's a good one. Considering all I do around here, perhaps a raise is in order. Right, Mr. Darcy?"

"Mr. Darcy?" Jack questions. "You call Owen Mr. Darcy?" He laughs loudly, his head going back and everything. "Fuck if that isn't perfect for him."

"Maybe we should play poker instead," Owen suggests. "Double or nothing." He unbuttons the buttons at the cuffs of his sleeves and proceeds to roll them up to his elbows as if he's about to get dirty. Why does that have to be so hot? Why can't he look and feel and smell like a dude who had a twelve-pack too many at a tailgate party and passed out in his own vomit?

"Great!"

Jack. For real? Why won't he go home?

He has an amazing new apartment in a fun part of town. He's a single guy. If I were him, I'd be there or out doing the Saturday night single-guy thing. But no. Jack is acting like we're going to do this all night and then get into our pajamas and have a sleepover.

My phone buzzes in my lap.

> Owen: Why would I date her when I only want you?

Shit. My heart thunders, and my palms grow sweaty. I glance up to find him staring straight at me with a penetrating gaze I can't ignore.

> Me: You can't say things like that to me.

> Owen: Why not if it's true?

He's not playing fair. Owen is older and more experienced,

and I can toss out all the snark and bravado I want, but there's no scenario where going up against him doesn't backfire on me.

I stand and set my glass down on the side table. "I think I'll go up to bed instead."

"Nonsense. Stay."

"Yeah," Owen agrees with Jack. "Stay." He puts his hand on my lower back and guides me over to the round card table he has, but just before he releases me and I take my seat, he pinches my ass. Hard. Like a warning. And I have a bad feeling this night is about to turn on me.

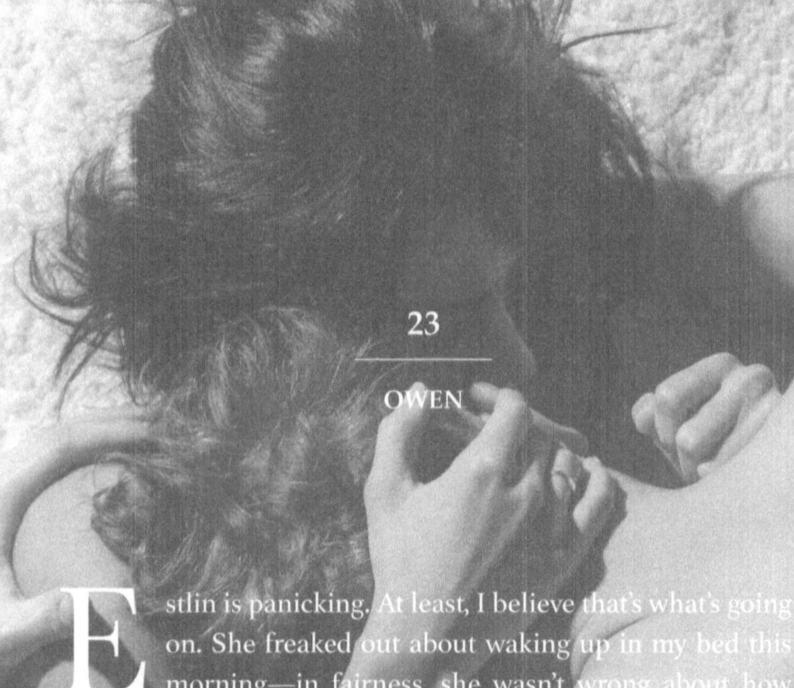

23

OWEN

Estlin is panicking. At least, I believe that's what's going on. She freaked out about waking up in my bed this morning—in fairness, she wasn't wrong about how ill-advised that move was—and then she couldn't fly out of the house and away from me fast enough. She was losing her mind even before she overheard my mother and her squad try to plan my love life for me.

But the fact that she reacted the way she did to that tells me last night was more than we bargained for her too.

At least I got the heads-up about it. That's why Katy is my person.

Katy: There's this incredible single-mom doctor who is beautiful, sweet, and kind. She works as an intensivist with Rina, and everyone thinks she'd be perfect for you. If I didn't already believe you were in love with your nanny, I'd agree. But since I do, I'm texting to inform you that plans are in the works to hook you up with this woman, and your nanny didn't seem too happy about it.

I didn't reply other than to tell Katy that I love her and to thank her for the heads-up. I didn't bother to acknowledge the in-love bullshit. That's simply how Katy works. It was a fishing expedition. One I didn't feel like being the bait or even the fish on. I was too hung up on the *Your nanny didn't seem too happy about it* part.

Estlin had already texted, trying to reaffirm our boundaries, and when I set all this in motion at the hospital yesterday, I understood the need for them even if I didn't fully want them.

Then last night happened.

Yes, the sex was fucking hot. We had been a dormant volcano finally allowed to erupt, and erupt we did. It lived up to every second of its promise.

But after that? After I came inside her—bare, I might add—for the final time and she proceeded to pass out, I couldn't fall asleep along with her. It wasn't that she was in my bed when I knew she shouldn't be. It wasn't that I had spent the night fucking my much younger nanny and I felt all kinds of wrong doing it.

It was her.

Estlin.

Asleep in my arms.

Her cut and bruised face and sweet body and sassy mouth that had finally been quieted.

It. Was. *Her.*

I was thunderstruck. Caught in what should have been a panic-inducing realization, only I wasn't panicking. It was as if finally the pieces of my life fell into place and everything I had stopped searching for had not only found me but was asleep in my arms. The words, *never stop chasing her* and *never give her an excuse to go,* were running through my head. I waited for all my fears and ghosts to come barreling back through me, but there was nothing left of them.

The only things, as it turns out, I'm afraid of are losing her and how trying to keep her will upend the steady state of my life.

I stole her panties—again—something I'm not even sure she's aware of yet. I want her to sneak into my room to try to find them again. I want her to discover me in the shower jerking off to fantasies of her. I want her to be so crazed with lust that she strips down and joins me. I want to fall asleep with her laughter in my ear and the smell of her hair across my face.

I want this to be the beginning, not the end.

I've got it bad.

It's terrifying and problematic and just a fucking mess. But life isn't always as cute, cozy, and neat as we'd like it to be. I've come alive since she entered my life, and I don't want to stop now. She's afraid, and her fear makes her run. I can't blame her for that. Not after all she's been through. But if she gives this a chance, she'll see all that we have the potential to become.

"Why don't you deal?" I offer to Jack, who has been here all day and night. I know Estlin is already done with him. It's her brother, and she's anxious to pick a fight with me before she attempts to end this. But having Jack here, despite what I'm doing with his sister, is great. He's been in LA since the end of our residency, and now he's back. Time with him is precious.

But it also solidifies that I can do this.

I can have both.

It doesn't have to be one or the other.

I can be a good friend to him and take care of his little sister. Just as he asked me to.

I can be her guy and his best friend.

I'm determined to be.

I just have to figure out all the logistics of it first. Those are the real fuckers.

Jack deals us each five cards, and I take a sip of my wine. I have no idea how many glasses this makes, but I'm not driving.

Jack, I'll likely have to shove into an Uber to get him out of here so I can be alone with his sister. Speaking of...

With my cards in my right hand, I slide my left hand beneath the table until I find Estlin's knee. She jolts at the contact, her body slamming up and jostling the table.

"You okay?" Jack asks without bothering to look up from his cards.

"Yep. All good." She grips my hand, trying to pry it away. I don't relent until she gets her nails involved.

Trying the next tactic, I pull out my phone and text her from beneath the table since that seems to be the only way she'll communicate with me right now.

> Me: That's not how you looked when you left this morning.

> Estlin: Two hot dudes did me over.

Inwardly, I chuckle.

> Me: They did a nice job, but you're beautiful no matter what. Are you in any pain?

> Estlin: Nope.

That's it. This girl. She's going to put me through my paces, but maybe that's what I like so much about her. Nothing has ever been easily won with her. I've had to work for everything she's ever given me.

Jack shuffles his cards around, and I do the same, discarding two, and then immediately return my hand to her leg, only this time I go a lot higher than her knee. My fingers splay, and my hand covers her thigh. Sexy fucking thighs I want to be wrapped around me later. She tenses but doesn't pry my fingers away this time.

Eventually, I'll tell Jack. I will. Once I've won Estlin over and

I know precisely what I'm risking his friendship for. I can't do that alone, and I can't do that until I'm positive she's with me.

Which right now, she's not even close to being.

Jack slips me two cards, his gaze intent on his hand, and I use his distraction to my advantage as I slide my hand up Estlin's thigh until I'm cupping her pussy through her leggings. Thank God she's wearing these things. Thin, easily accessible, can-feel-my-entire-hand-as-I-feel-her-entire-pussy, leggings.

She wheezes out a curse, only to suck that breath immediately back in.

"You won't always win at everything," Jack quips to her, assuming she's upset about her cards.

"So I'm learning."

Jack laughs and finally peers up, noting Estlin's stunning flush. "That wouldn't be a lie crossing your lips and staining your cheeks, would it?"

I chuckle. How can I not?

"Um. Well. Yeah. I think I fold." She chucks her cards onto the table as if they're burning her hands.

"Wimp," I chide, pressing two fingers to her opening and then moving them back up to her clit. I start to rub her, and her thighs clamp shut, but she's still not pushing my hand away.

"Oh?" She reaches over and grips my hard cock. Only she doesn't just grip it. She *squeezes* it. Squeezes the life from it. Siphoning all of the blood from it and thrusting it back up into places it doesn't want to be.

I cough and hiss and am forced to abandon her pussy in order to rip her fingers from me before I pass out or throw up. She tosses me a triumphantly smug grin and wink and then goes back to her cards, leaning back since she's already sitting this first hand out.

That's how it goes for about three hands.

My hand wanders and plays. Hers punish. By the time we hit round four, I'm fucking done. I need her now. I do an exaggerated yawn. The one that's universally used as a non-verbal cue to get the fuck out. Jack doesn't get the hint. He's two games up because both Estlin and I are distracted in our back-and-forth.

"I fold," I announce.

"Me too." Estlin smacks her cards down on the table.

Jack groans, chucking his cards in frustration. "For real. You're not even trying."

"I'm going to bed." Estlin stands up quickly, and in doing so, my hand smacks into the edge of the table. I get a smirk from her. One she's going to pay for.

I stand slowly, letting her know she's not getting away with that. "I'm beat as well."

"You guys are lame."

I shrug. Estlin points to her makeup-covered face.

Jack makes a noise, but then he stands up and stretches out his long limbs. "Fine. Maybe there's a bar and a woman with my name on them."

Estlin mocks like she's vomiting. "Ew. Gross."

Jack laughs, and I refuse to let him leave here with his car, which means he'll be back tomorrow morning. But I don't care. It gives me tonight with his little sister.

His Uber arrives, and the second the door shuts behind him, I immediately have Estlin pressed against it.

"What are you doing?" she gasps, swatting at me as I press myself into her. She's an angry, feral little kitten. She needs to get over it.

In one smooth motion, I scoop my arm beneath her upper thighs and lift her off her feet, dropping her fireman style on my shoulder. She yelps, and I smack her ass as I march back toward my man cave. I slide her leggings down, exposing her ass and pussy, and then shove two fingers straight into her.

"All day long, I've thought about you and doing exactly this."

"Ah! Oh my god. What the hell are you doing?" Her breath catches, and she shakes her head as if she wants to protest, but we both know she won't. She's spent all day thinking about me too. She's wanted this just as much as I have.

I walk her over to the long sofa in here and set her down on the soft leather. Without hesitation, I climb over her, taking her hands and pinning them above her head when she tries to get up and leave.

"I don't think so." I grind into her, pressing her deeper into the couch. "If you have something to say, go for it, but you're not running. Not from me."

I lock her wrists in one hand and use the other to finish pulling her leggings over her curvy hips and thick thighs. Kicking off my shoes, I use my feet to finish the job and stare down at her, taking in the sight before me. Christ. Will it ever get easier to see her like this and not immediately feel like I'm about to blow my load?

"I don't want to do this."

I glance up at her and shift until my face is inches from hers. "Really, Estlin? Really? Do you actually mean that, or do you think that's how you're supposed to feel? Because your body tells me you want this. Hell, I can smell how fucking turned on you are right now." I grind against her. "And you sure as hell can feel how much I want you."

She looks away, and I release her wrists, pulling back to give her the escape she's pretending she needs. She doesn't move, and I think part of her hates that. She's too locked in her twisted thoughts, just as wild and crazy about me as I am about her, and she hates it.

My fingers hook into the sides of her panties, and I tug them off. "Take off your shirt and bra."

"And yet you're fully dressed," she accuses defiantly, her tone is nothing short of sharp and cutting.

"It's not an even playing field between us," I admit, shoving her feet wider and her thighs apart. "I can't promise it'll ever be. I can't fathom a time will ever come when I won't worship at your feet. When I won't feel a million miles beneath you and nowhere ever deserving enough. But I'll always be honest. As much as I can be," I amend because I don't think either of us is quite ready for my full, brutal honesty. "But if you give me an inch, I'll give you a mile, and if you give me your trust, I swear, I'll make it so you never regret it."

Her fingers slide into my hair and glide down to my jaw, her gaze unwavering. "What happens if I get attached? I don't want to lose this job. I love Rory, and I love being here. But I hated hearing how they wanted to set you up with that woman, and that tells me a lot. It makes me afraid that if this continues, I'll grow attached and you'll break my heart, even if unintentionally. I know I said a lot of things last night, but I don't know if they're words I can live by anymore. Doing this with you is already messing me up."

I shrug. "Good. Then we're on the same page as each other." I roughly cup her jaw and stare into her eyes. "I wasn't lying. It's you. It's only you. No one else. I don't care about who my mom wants to set me up with. She's not you. I have no plans to break your heart, Estlin unintentionally or otherwise. As for your job, Rory loves you." *And I think I love you too.* "It's yours until you tell me otherwise." I pause. Take a deep breath. Nervous in a way I'm not sure I've ever been. The power this woman has over me. "So what do you say? Can we try and see how it goes?"

Her breath holds high in her throat, and her gaze slingshots up to the ceiling. She's trying to hold off. She wants to keep this easy and risk-free the way she said we would last night in my office. But that was before, and this is now. And truthfully, I never agreed to her terms. I just didn't argue with them.

That's always been my problem. I'm all or nothing. I don't know how to do in between. It's how I got into trouble with my ex. I fell for her and was blind to everything else. All the warning signs that were blaring right in my face.

That's not Estlin.

And something tells me Estlin wants me to fight for her. She wants to be mine, she's just not sure how it all works yet. Truth be told, neither am I. So we have a lot to figure out. What couple doesn't? Is that what we even are? Or are we stuck in some sort of purgatory of not quite a fling and not quite a relationship?

She has a litany of questions burning her tongue. Words she's stubbornly refusing to set free.

Fine.

She won't read the fine print or ask if I've fallen head over heels in love.

It's probably safer that way. At least for me. My answer may be yes, and that answer might cost me everything, and maybe, just at this moment, that's not the right one to give.

So I put my hands on her inner thighs, push them apart, and then shove my tongue straight into her. She wants to be stubborn, but I'd love for her to try while I'm tongue fucking her.

"You don't have to worry about being quiet this time," I tell her, licking a circle around her clit. "My man cave and office are soundproofed. Scream all you want. I'll be the only one to hear you."

24

"Open your knees wider for me, sweet thing," Owen says in that cool, authoritative tone he's used on me once or twice. I want to protest. I want to keep up the fight. I'm not even sure why at this point, other than it feels like I have some control over this. I was honest about how I felt, and then he flayed me open, and now I don't know what to do with myself.

His words...

His powerful, heartfelt fucking words that he spoke straight into my soul. Damn him for doing that to me.

I open my thighs wider, cool air sliding up along my legs and straight over my damp pussy. A shudder rolls through me, but he doesn't touch me again. Not with his mouth or fingers, only with his eyes that are trained straight on mine. I realize he's waiting on me. He asked me to take off my shirt and bra, and I'm still dressed from the waist up.

He's waiting for me to make the choice. Stay or go. Trust him or don't. Continue or stop.

It's not an even playing field between us. I can't promise it'll ever be. I can't fathom a time will ever come when I won't worship at your feet. When I won't feel a million miles beneath you and nowhere ever deserving enough.

My heart stutters in my chest. I guess I know which way I'm going.

With my breath held in my lungs, I pull my shirt up and over my head before I reach behind and unclasp my bra. His expression is tight, nearly unreadable except for his eyes that smolder with arousal. No one has ever looked at me the way Owen does. No one has ever made me feel more desired or beautiful.

My skin crackles with anticipation, my nipples painfully hard, and my breasts heavy.

He makes quick work of his clothes, his hand reaching behind his back to tear off his shirt seconds before his jeans meet the floor. His hard cock smacks his rock-hard lower abs and I feel my pussy pulse at the sight.

His finger circles a wide arc into a tight spiral around one nipple and then the other. I whimper, biting into my lip, my legs anxious to close so I can press my thighs together. I want him to do that on my clit. With his fingers and tongue and even his cock. He continues to play with my breasts, lifting and squeezing, pinching and pulling as his other hand trickles down my belly.

"Your tits are so fucking responsive."

I can only nod as I lick my lips and wait for more.

"Do you remember what I said I planned to do tonight?"

Ha! Do I? I've been craving nothing else all damn day. That's probably half of what made me so fucking nuts.

The tips of his fingers tickle my smooth mound and then glide down, following the same motion with my clit as his fingers on my breasts did. I gasp and then sigh. My head falls back before I prop myself up, anxious to watch him. Heavy with lust and pleasure, I struggle to keep my eyes open when they're so anxious to close.

The tip of his tongue rolls along my clit, and he smacks my inner thigh, jolting my eyes wide until they lock with his. This look on him. This cocky, arrogant boy, all deliciously dimpled, I-own-every-inch-of-you look. I fucking love this look. It's the one that promises he's going to do dirty, dirty things to me.

With a smirk, he pulls off his glasses and tosses them onto the coffee table, and I legit nearly come just from that move alone. As it is, my pussy clenches so hard, I think I pull a muscle.

My hips begin to rock, seeking, *needing* more of him. He doesn't make me wait. His mouth devours me with a wicked French kiss that has my toes curling. Pleasure spikes through me, and I start to pant, my hands flying over my head, fisting, searching for anything I can grab onto, but I come up empty.

"I need a headboard."

He smiles as he kisses my inner thigh, his long body half on and half off the couch. "So I can tie you to it?"

Oh! I hadn't thought of that.

"So I can tie *you* to it," I throw back at him.

He nips at my soft skin before licking the sting away. "Sweet thing, if you really want to tie me up and fuck me, I might not stop you. But I much prefer having you at my mercy."

"Oh, god, yes," I cry as he works my pussy with his tongue as if proving his point. His hand abandons my breast to hold my thighs so I stop squirming. It's impossible, though. The way his tongue circles over my sensitive bud, round and round, tighter and fucking tighter until the hot swirls are almost too much for me to take.

Lord have mercy, I'm close, and god, do I need this.

Just as I reach my peak, everything is gone. His tongue, his breath, his fingers. All replaced with the cool air of nothing. I whimper in disappointment, which makes him chuckle softly. My head flies up, and I throw him my most murderous glare.

"Women do not appreciate being toyed with."

"And yet you have so many toys upstairs. A whole arsenal of them, so I find it difficult to believe you."

I squint. "How would you know about my arsenal?"

"Other than you telling me? I did my research."

I gasp and then moan as he licks me again. "You what?!"

He smirks and blows cool air across my pussy. "You taunted me with them. And you have a history of digging through my drawers. You didn't think I wouldn't return the favor, did you?"

My jaw unhinges. I'd be ready to strangle him if my orgasm wasn't still hovering on the edge of release. "I'm indignant."

A loud peel of laughter flees his lungs, his head flying back. "Who says that?"

"I just did." I smack his shoulder. "You shouldn't have gone through my stuff."

"Ditto. But I actually didn't do that. I just wanted to see your reaction. You'll have to show me what you've got because I'm dying to use them on you."

Oh my hell. This man.

He flies up and kisses my lips, licking them with a smile on his. "You're so fucking cute. My sweet thing, are you ready for me to make you feel good?"

I start to argue, but he calls me *his* sweet thing, and then his tongue slides in my mouth while his thumb rubs my clit, and I'm utterly lost to him. His stubble scratches my skin as he works his way back down my body, only to grip my waist and lift my pussy back to his mouth.

He takes a deep inhale of me and lets out a low groan of appreciation. My fingers twine into his hair, holding on even though I'm lying lengthwise on the sofa. He's all over the place, the angle a mess for him, and I have no idea how we'll manage sex on here.

"I want you to beg for me."

I bite back a moan and then swallow my pride. I want to beg

for him too. I want to make him so hard he can't think straight. "Please, don't stop. I was so close."

"I know." That's it, but it's his way of saying I don't get to run the show. Not tonight. Not ever. Holding me tighter in his grip, his fingers wet against my thighs, he eats me with a greedy, unrelenting pace. Licking me in my tight hole, along my slit, against my folds, around my clit. He hums, satisfied with all he's tasting and yet voraciously hungry for more.

My head falls slack, and I try to hold still as he focuses his tongue on the sensitive part he's now sucking straight between his lips.

"Ah!" I gasp, ripping at his hair. He grunts as I bury him tighter between my legs. His fingers thrust in and out of me with short, shallow strokes. Enough to drive me crazy. "More," I beg. "Deeper. I need it deeper."

He cups my breast again and then smacks it, making it jiggle and bounce. "Beg me," he demands, gripping the hell out of it.

"Please. Please. Please." I keep my hand in his hair, trying to wrench him in tighter. I'm so close. Doesn't he know how close I am?

"Please what?"

My eyes pinch tight. I can't. I can't. "Deeper. Harder. More."

My words spring him into action, and in my next heartbeat, he's moving me, his back now lengthwise on the couch and my body somehow over his. "Sit on my face. Take what you need from me because I need to taste you like this."

His hands squeeze and lift my ass, and then he moves me over his mouth, making me ride his face as his mouth ravages my pussy like it's the last thing he'll ever eat. I stare down at him from above, mesmerized by the sight.

His hand climbs up through the canal of my breasts and circles my neck. He gives it a squeeze for one deliciously long moment. Just long enough for me to gasp in both breathlessness and shock, and that's when I come. His possession is my trigger, and my pleasure spirals out of control, beating me with pounding, gorgeous waves of ecstasy as I fuck his face while he groans straight into me, fucking the air behind me.

"Mine," he whispers directly against my cunt. "Mine, mine, all fucking mine." He gives me another swirling, wet lick.

Oh god. I could come again just from him whispering that straight into me.

One finger rings my entrance, and I wiggle and shift, rising up onto my knees because I'm more than a little sensitive. That finger dips down and finds the tight ring of muscles at the back.

"Holy fuck!" I cry as he pushes straight in. My back arches before I fly forward over him and grip at the arm of the couch directly above his head. "Owen! Ah!"

He starts to pump, and I start to pant again, his eyes glued to the motion of his finger, his face dark with lust. "Christ, your ass is fucking tight." Each word is rough and jagged, almost like he's choking to get them out. "It's going to look so hot stretched around me when my cock fucks it."

I gasp as his tongue starts to play with my clit again, his finger continuing to pump in and out of my ass, and it leaves me winded.

"But right now, Estlin, I'm going to fuck your tits." His bossy dominance takes over everything, and I find myself nodding. Wanting that. He flips me onto my back, and suddenly he's over me, pressing my tits together and spitting between them. But it's not the spitting that has me moaning even though that's so fucking dirty and wrong, I can't help but love it. It's him shoving straight into me, wetting his cock with my pussy that's already come for him.

He pulls out, leaving me breathless and needy, and then he's forcing my tits together as hard as he can. His cocks slips through the tight fist he's made of them, and he groans like a man on the brink. He slides in and out, his grip constricting, his thumbs rubbing and pulling hard on my nipples.

He licks his lips. "Open your mouth, sweet thing, and taste my cock as I fuck your tits."

I do, licking the tip of his dick that's wet and tacky from being inside me. It makes my pussy convulse like the needy, desperate whore she is for him.

He fucks me, his eyes raw and just gone as he watches his cock slip in and out of my tits.

"I can't handle how fucking hot you look like this. You have the sexiest fucking tits."

And just when I think he's about to come all over them, he pulls out, readjusts himself, and slams straight into me, covering me with his body as he does.

I scream at the intrusion. At the rapid pace he immediately sets. At how good and deep it is from this angle.

Strong arms wrap around my back, hugging me against his chest, his sweaty forehead pressing to mine as he pumps in and out of me. With every thrust, the base of his cock presses against my clit. It's a lot. It's so much. He's all around me, his scent all I can smell, his heat all I can feel. He consumes me, swallowing my every breath while tasting like me.

"Mine," he whispers against my lip as he fucks me. "Get used to it. It's not about to change. You belong to me now."

He licks my lips and nibbles on my bottom one, his breathing growing choppier the closer he gets. One hand grabs my thigh on the narrow couch, hoisting it up and over his ass to deepen the angle. His eyes roll back, and he groans as he fucks deeper into me.

"God, Estlin, the way I need you. The way it feels when I'm inside you." He pushes in and up, hitting me exactly where I need him to. I gasp, my nails digging into his shoulders, my orgasm right there, so close I can feel it tingling my skin and tightening my core. "This isn't stopping. It's only just fucking beginning."

And with that declaration, he unleashes himself. Hard. Punishing. Pounding. Skin slapping against skin, mixed with groans, grunts, and serrated cries. Sweat covers us both from head to toe as he grits his teeth and clenches his jaw. We nearly fall off the couch, his foot on the floor for leverage and to hold us in place.

It doesn't take me long. Just another couple of thrusts, and I come apart at the seams, my body rolling and my mind shattering. I test the sound barrier of his walls and sag into the leather that's now sticking to my skin.

A lazy laugh tickles my lips, my eyes closed, my breathing heavy.

With him on top of me, it's easy to focus solely on what he's saying and ignore everything else. And by everything else, I mean reality. The problem with reality? You can't hide from it forever.

25

—————

ESTLIN

"What in the haunted happenings happened to your face?" Billy yells at full blast, practically across the studio, so naturally every head turns in unison to take me in. I guess my makeup didn't do the trick. The problem with bruises? They get uglier before they get better.

Today I'm like a dark bluish-purple with some tints of green to it, and because gravity is a motherfucker, this bruise goes practically all the way down to my chin.

"Hi, Billy!" I wave. He's not amused.

With his lips pursed, he marches across the studio and grabs my shoulders. "Did he do this to you?"

"Who?"

"Your hot boss."

I laugh and then laugh again. "No. He did the stitches, though. I was in a car accident."

I don't mention Claude. First, his name is known. He's a famous, world-renowned artist like my mother is. Second, while I consider Billy my friend, we're not that close yet. Our gossip and chit-chat are mostly superficial.

Billy takes my arm and walks me toward my space. "Are you okay?" he asks in a low voice. "Like for real?"

I smile at him, deeply touched by his concern. "Yes. For real, I'm okay. It looks a lot worse than it is."

Owen ordered me a new car that he said is being delivered later today. When I fretted over this, he told me the other driver's insurance took care of it quickly. There were cameras in the intersection that caught him speeding right through the red. Plus, we're talking about Owen Fritz here, and I doubt the insurance company wanted any part of that more than there already is.

Our accident made the news, after all, but seems to have died down quickly.

"Damn, girly. It's a nasty bruise despite the coverup." He tsks, shaking his head as we reach my area and I uncover the painting I have been working on. I go over to the sink to fill up a pail with soapy water. "What was it like having the hot doctor's hands all over you?"

The pail drops out of my hand and lands with a loud clank in the sink, soapy water splashing up and landing all over my face and chest. I sputter and then choke out a laugh. Only me, I swear. Shutting off the water, I grab some paper towels from the roll beside the sink and wipe my face and chest down.

Gross.

And there goes my bad makeup job. Ugh.

I turn my head slowly to find Billy giving me a look. "What? It slipped."

"Uh-huh. And that blush? Those things just form on their own for you too?"

Shit. I hadn't realized I was blushing. Probably because I couldn't feel the heat under all this damn cold water.

"It's nothing."

"Oh, honey, it's something. And I can't wait to hear every last sordid, forbidden detail of—"

"Estlin?"

Immediately, I freeze at the voice cutting Billy off. I spin in a slow circle, my heart already hammering in my chest. What the fuck is he doing here? And how did he find me?

Billy's eyes are wide as he takes in Claude standing on the edge of my space, his dark eyes scrutinizing my canvas in a way that's more than just a little familiar. My instinct is to cover it up, but I won't hide from him. I'm proud of my work.

"What are you doing here?" I snap and then shake my head, only to repeat the question in French.

Billy takes a protective step in my direction, noting the alarm on my face and in my voice. Claude notes this too and doesn't like any of it.

"Is he your lover?"

I want to laugh at that, but I don't. "That's a rich question coming from you."

He sighs, his gaze roving all over my face. "I saw the accident on the news. Are you all right? It was my fault, yes? I caused you to be upset."

"Estlin, do you want me to ask him to leave?"

"Excuse me." Claude transitions to accented English. "My manners." He extends his hand to Billy. "I'm Claude Morceaux, Estlin's former lover and mentor."

What a pompous jerk. I can't believe I used to swoon and simper at his feet like he was the god he thinks he is.

Billy does a slow blink, clearly recognizing the name, before he turns back to me. He lingers for a beat on my face and then returns to Claude without extending his hand. "How fabulous for you, but this is still a private business, and we protect our clientele."

Oh, Billy. I love you so much.

Claude's jaw tics at the brush off, and his hand drops to his side. He doesn't like it when people don't bow and kiss his ring. He narrows his eyes before turning and facing me once more, switching back to French. "Estlin, my love, can we please go somewhere and speak without distractions and useless people interfering? I mean you no harm. You know that. We can stay somewhere public if you prefer."

I sigh. And realize I'm truly not afraid of him. He no longer has power over me. But that doesn't make me stupid, either.

"Billy, would you mind giving me a few minutes alone with him?" I look Billy straight in the eyes to let him know it's okay.

"Sure. But I'll be right over there." He points to the center, an open space that has chairs, tables, and picnic benches.

"That's perfect."

Billy gives me a kiss on the cheek, glares at Claude as if to say *if you try something I will fuck you up*, and then moves about five feet away. It doesn't matter. He won't understand us anyway.

"What do you want, Claude? Why won't you go?" I ask and then turn my back dismissively on him as I refill the pail with more soapy water so I can get my brushes squared away. He needs to know he no longer holds my attention.

Claude moves closer to me, and I hear Billy clear his voice loudly. The sharp sound makes Claude stop in his tracks and curse under his breath. I hold in my snicker.

"This is not the place for this conversation."

"Tough shit. I don't owe you anything, let alone a private chat, simply because you want it."

"Fine. We'll speak here. I wanted to tell you that I'm sorry. About everything."

His tone catches my attention, and I stop what I'm doing and face him, leaning my back against the edge of the sink and folding my arms.

"I was... selfish and immature." He heads over to my canvas that is still very much a work in progress. He pans a hand toward it. "Your work was growing, and I knew the second it was discovered, you'd take off and leave me behind in your dust. I was jealous. I needed that showing to do very well, and I…" His face dips toward the floor in shame, his hands going to his hips. "I did whatever I could to secure that."

"Like sleeping with that woman."

He nods, finally fucking admitting it.

"Like saying awful things about me, my body, and my work."

Another nod, though neither of these were posed as questions.

"Like claiming my work was yours and then destroying it."

His face slowly rises, remorse lining his features. "Yes. I did all those things. Every last deplorable, unforgivable one. And then I chased you out the door in a rage that still makes me cringe when I think about it. I never would have hurt you, my love. Not ever. Your face that night has been burned into my mind for the last nine months, and then when I saw your fear the other night…" He shakes his head, his eyes clouding over with emotion. "Never have I felt such guilt and self-loathing."

Huh. This is not at all where I thought this conversation was going to go. I was expecting more of the, *I know where you live and what you're doing* bullshit.

"I'm glad," I tell him plainly. "Because until I moved back here, those months were hell for me. It took me a long time after what you did to get myself right again, but part of that was on me. I gave you too much of myself while accepting too little in return."

He winces again, his hands going to the back of his head, and he nods slowly. "*Oui.* Yes, this is true. If it helps, I have been nothing without you these nine months. I haven't been able to work. I don't sleep well. I miss you, and I regret everything I've done. You were an angel, my darling. The piece that kept me intact."

I shake my head, my hands gripping the sink behind me. That makes me so angry, and he'd never understand why because he's a taker and not a giver. Or, hell, even an equal participant. That's what he's doing here. He feels like shit and wants me to make him feel better. This isn't about me, it's about him.

As it's always been.

"I can't and won't be that piece for you again. Being that piece for you meant that I allowed you to take those pieces from me. More than that, I don't want to go back. I've moved on. I'm happy now."

His expression falls along with his hands by his sides. Did he truly think I'd go back to him? Is he that arrogant? I almost laugh. The answer is yes and always has been.

"So this is it then?"

I nod resolutely. "Yes. I wish you the best, Claude, and I appreciate your apology. What you did was wrong, but I think I forgive you. If you hadn't done that, I might never have left, and I wouldn't be standing here so tall on my own two feet. I would have stayed in your shadow, and that was a very dark place to be."

A swell of pride washes over me. It's true. Every word I just said to him. Evidently, I needed this level of closure because now I feel calm. Whole. Like he had still been holding onto a few of those remaining pieces all this time, and now with his apology, I finally have them back.

But more than that, I'm the woman I was always meant to be.

The one I've always *wanted* to be.

He crosses the space, ignoring Billy's noise, and cups my face in his hands. "I will always love you, my darling. Thank you for the wonderful years you gave me. I look forward to seeing your art everywhere." He leans in and kisses each of my cheeks and then my lips before I can stop him, only to pull back just as quickly. A wan smile splits his lips as he looks at me one last time and leaves.

I blow out a breath only to suck one immediately back in. Owen is standing on the other side of the picnic benches, his expression hard like I've never seen it before. Shit. He saw Claude kiss me goodbye. And he's seriously not happy about it.

"Well, it doesn't look like you'll be getting any work done today," Billy quips, and if my heart wasn't thundering so hard in my chest, I'd laugh.

"It seems not."

"Hi, I'm Billy Williams. Please no comment on the redundancy of my name." He holds his hand out to Owen, who shakes it.

"Owen Fritz."

Billy nods, and I wonder if he knew this all along and never said anything.

Satisfied with Owen's response, Billy comes over to me. "Go ahead. I'll cover your canvas back up and clean up the water for you."

I force myself away from Owen. "Thank you. You're an amazing friend." I give Billy a hug.

"Honey, I work for gossip and details, and now you owe me a lot."

A snicker creeps out of the back of my throat. "Promise."

I grab my bag, throw it over my shoulder, and head over to Owen. I want to reach out and take his hand, but I can't, and I don't even attempt it.

"Hi," I say in a soft voice. "What are you doing here?"

He had the day off today, but I didn't expect him to come by.

"Katy took Rory to the science museum for the afternoon, and I was going to play in my hockey league. I brought your car for you. I was going to drop it off, but..."

But then he saw me with Claude.

And yeah, he's not happy with me at all.

"Thank you. I'm glad you're here."

"Are you?" he bites out, squinting accusingly at me, only to catch himself, turn, and walk toward the exit of the studio. I follow after him, because there is no way I'm letting him leave like this. "Goddammit, Estlin. You make me feel like a fucking hot-headed college kid."

I laugh. I don't know why, but I love that.

His head rolls over his shoulder, catching my eye. He pushes up the bridge of his glasses—his universal *I'm pissed* move—and glares. We stop in the empty foyer between the gallery and the studio. "You think this is funny? I'm not a jealous guy, but you make me insane with jealousy. He gets to talk to you. He gets to look at you. He gets to fucking touch you, and I can't."

"What do you want me to do? You're my boss, my brother's best friend, and your sister is my friend. This is so much more than complicated. It can't happen. Not like this."

"It's already happening because we can't stop it. After all that asshole did to you, after what happened two nights ago, you let him fucking kiss you? Do you know how badly I wanted to chase after him and rearrange his face? Do you know all the things I was going to do to make sure he'd never hurt you again?"

He spins around and shoves open the door, stepping out into the cool, sunny afternoon. Parked by the curb is my new car, identical to the last one. I stop us. "But you didn't."

"No," he barks, unlocking the car and opening the passenger side door for me. "Of course I didn't. I'm Owen Fucking Fritz. I'm a pediatric surgeon, but more importantly, I have a daughter who doesn't need her father getting arrested. Trust me, if it weren't for her, he'd be dead. Now get in the car."

Is it bad that I love this side of him? This jealous, riled-up, take-charge side?

Dutifully, I climb into the passenger's side, and he closes the door behind me as I get my seat belt on. He got coffee-colored leather this time, and I like it a lot more than the black we had last time.

He climbs into the driver's seat and slams his door shut. Before I can open my mouth or say anything else, he grabs my face and crashes his lips against mine. I gasp into him, my hands covering his. Immediately, his tongue plunges into my mouth, and he kisses me good and hard, a punishment, before he tears himself away.

My face heats, and I turn toward the windows, but they're darkly tinted, and no one on the sidewalk seems to be looking into the car.

"What the fuck was he doing there, Estlin?"

I take Owen's hand and bring it onto my lap, twining our fingers and holding it tight. "He came to apologize. It was closure and goodbye and nothing more."

"And the kiss?"

I shrug, trying not to smile. "He's French, Owen. They do that. I didn't want it, and he didn't exactly ask for permission before taking it. But it was goodbye. I promise."

"You don't want to be with him?"

My already thundering heart goes haywire. I nibble on my lip and stare down at our joined hands. "No. I don't."

He takes his other hand and lifts my chin until I meet his eyes again. "Tell me the truth."

I swallow impossibly hard and repeat the words he said to me last night, even if they terrify me to say. "I only want you."

After the sex on his couch in his man cave, we went back up to his room and showered together. He took me in there again, only slower and sweeter, and then he forced me into his bed, waking me with kisses when his alarm went off early. With regret in his eyes, he walked me down the hall to my room and then went to work out.

I don't know what's happening, but it's already a lot.

"Owen, I don't know what you meant when you said you

were going to do stuff to make sure he'd never hurt me again, but I don't want you to risk anything for that. He's gone from my life, and I forgive him. If he hadn't done everything he did, I wouldn't be here with you. I wouldn't be the artist or woman I'm starting to become."

The only remaining regret I have is that he destroyed my work.

He blinks at me, surprised. After a beat, he licks his lips and glances out the windshield. "I started something I don't think I'll ever be able to undo. There might never be a time when I don't want you." He looks back at me. "What are we going to do about all of this?"

I shake my head, at a loss. "I honestly don't know."

"I want you as mine."

"And I want to be yours."

A smile tilts up the corners of his lips, making his dimples pop, and his blue eyes sparkle behind the lenses of his glasses. Fuck, I've got it bad for him. Like, I'm totally and completely gone on him.

"But it's still new, and I'm not ready to get other people involved in it."

His gaze flickers back and forth between mine. "You want to keep this a secret."

It's not a question, but I nod anyway. "For now. Between our families, there's a lot at stake for us."

He knows I'm right. The amount of tumult, pressure, and scrutiny that would be thrown at us would be unreal. It could tear us apart before we even begin.

"All right," he says slowly in a low tone. "We'll stay a secret, and the rest we'll figure out as we go."

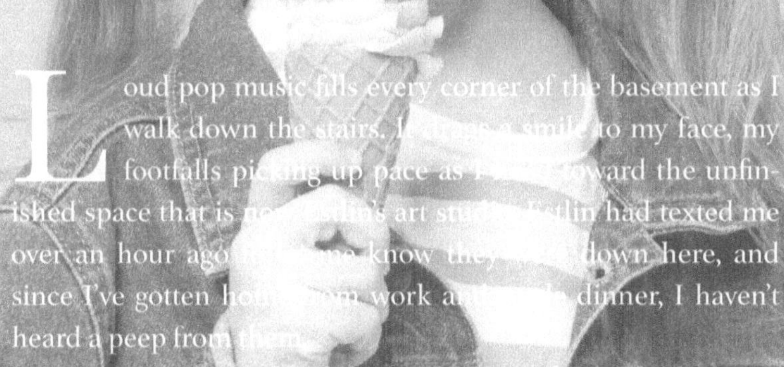

26

OWEN

L oud pop music fills every corner of the basement as I walk down the stairs. It drags a smile to my face, my footfalls picking up pace as I head toward the unfinished space that is now Estlin's art studio. Estlin had texted me over an hour ago to let me know they were down here, and since I've gotten home from work and made dinner, I haven't heard a peep from them.

Rory's boisterous laugh hits my ears, striking a higher note than the song that's currently playing. It shoots a quick smile to my lips and a lightness to my heart. My girls are busy, both vigorously working on their projects. Along the wall is a rack filled with so much pottery, I have no idea where we'll put it all. When Rory isn't at school, she's down here, but now with her broken arm, she's painting Estlin's pieces instead of creating her own.

Estlin is at the wheel she has down here, wearing a filthy old T-shirt and tiny shorts. Her hair is pinned up on her head in a tight bun, but despite the restriction, a few flyaways managed to escape. Estlin has been working hard during the day. I know she mostly does pottery here and paints at the studio, but she's brought home about three paintings already that are just sort of sitting in the corner, leaning against the wall, covered in cloth.

I'm not sure what she plans to do with them—I'm not even sure if she knows—but they're stunning. I want to buy them from her, but I know she won't sell them to me, and I refuse to allow her to gift them.

It's been a week since the accident. A week since Claude left and returned back to Paris. I know because I'm having Vander casually watch him. Estlin asked me not to do anything to him, and I'll respect her request only because the fucker apologized and said he'd leave her alone.

That doesn't make me stupid or complacent though, and if she thinks I won't protect her, she's mad.

The tip of Rory's tongue is curved along her upper lip, her eyes narrowed in concentration as she paints the eyes of the ceramic cat she's working on. I hate to interrupt, but dinner is nearly ready.

"Peter, a boy from my class is also going to Disney World," Rory notes without removing her focus from her art. "Do you think we'll see him there?"

Estlin, who is covered in gray clay, works her hands on the inside and outside of whatever the hell she's making as it spins around on the wheel. "I don't know. Do you want to?"

Estlin finally agreed to come with us to Disney World. Both Rory and I worked on her, and her initial reason for not wanting to join us is now moot, so she was out of excuses.

Rory shrugs. "Not really. He called me a Fritz princess."

Estlin's lips twitch. "In a mean way or a nice way?"

Another shrug. "I don't know. I didn't like it." She pauses and turns to Estlin. "Why do so many people care that my last name is Fritz?"

Good question. I fold my arms and lean against the doorframe, watching them unobserved.

"Because your family is special," Estlin tells her simply. "You have a very big family with a lot of very talented, special people in it. And because of that, it's made them famous."

Rory scrunches her nose. "If I'm a pop star one day like Tinsley is, do I have to be famous?"

I hold in my snicker.

"Well, that sort of comes with being a pop star," Estlin explains, partially standing as she makes the cylindrical thing taller. "Do you not like being famous?"

"I don't like people taking pictures of me."

I can't blame her for that.

"Sometimes we have to live with certain things if we want something badly enough. So, if you want to be a pop star badly enough, if it's your passion, then people taking photographs of you unfortunately comes with it. But it's a necessary sacrifice for the thing you really want. Does that make sense?"

"I guess. Like when Daddy told me I have to go to school if I want to be smart and do all the things I want to do one day, but school is *so* boring."

A whisper of a smirk curls up Estlin's face. "Yes. Exactly that. And he's right. You have to go to school because being smart and learning stuff is cool."

Rory huffs but quickly changes the topic. "My friend, Evie got a new baby brother."

"Oh, that's fun."

Rory pauses and looks questioningly over to Estlin. "Do you like having a brother?"

"Sure," Estlin says absently as she works. "It's nice. He's a lot older than me, though."

"Like my dad is?"

Estlin looks up and finally notices me, a wry sparkle hitting her eye. "Yeah. Like your dad is," she says, staring directly at me, raising an eyebrow that makes me chuckle.

Now that I'm busted, I push away from the door and enter

the room. "Do you want a brother or sister?" I ask Rory. I don't even know why. I shouldn't be asking that. I haven't thought about having more kids in a very long time and sort of put that dream on the back burner to be forgotten.

Rory thinks about this with the same level of thought and consideration she gives to her outfit choice in the morning. "I like baby Willow. But would I have to have a new mom?"

I practically choke on my tongue. "What?"

"Sarah Jane in my class has a new mom. She said she's nice, but I don't know if I want a new mom too."

I blink, my breath lodged in my chest. I have no freaking clue how to answer that. Estlin and I aren't anywhere near that level of discussion, and yet I can't help myself as I glance over at her to gauge her reaction to that. She's no longer looking at me. Her face is back on her art, but there is no hiding the hint of a blush staining her cheeks and how hard she's trying *not* to look at me.

I walk over to Rory and stare down at her painting as I answer. "Maybe one day you'll have a new mom. But it would only be someone who is nice to you. Someone who loves you. Someone who you would want as your mom."

"Someone who wouldn't go?"

Shit. This got heavy fast. "Someone who hopefully wouldn't go." I crouch, pulling on her long, blonde braid. "Are you hungry?"

"Starving!" she exclaims like she hasn't eaten in a hundred years.

"How about you go wash up and change your clothes. You have some paint on them." I kiss the tip of her nose, and then she runs off, easily persuaded when it comes to food and an outfit change. Knowing her, she'll be up there for a bit figuring it all out.

I approach Estlin and sit behind her on the long stool she has set up.

"That was intense." She giggles, throwing me a look over her shoulder as she continues this thing, curling the top so it starts to roll down. "I never know what to say when she asks questions like that."

"Me neither, and I have a degree in pediatrics." My hands go to her hips, finding the soft skin above her shorts and beneath her shirt. She shudders ever so slightly and gives me a little wiggle as if to say *don't touch.*

It doesn't stop me. My hands continue to climb higher up her ribs, my fingertips gently trickling as I go.

"Are you trying to recreate a *Ghost* moment here?"

I laugh. "Alexa, play 'Unchained Melody.'"

The song that was playing cuts out, and then the soft tapping beat of "Unchained Melody" comes on, followed by the singer's croony voice.

Estlin snorts as she attempts to ignore me while she works on her masterpiece. "You're not going to make me get a bowl haircut next, are you?"

"Fuck no. I love your hair." It's purple underneath now. Darker near the roots and fades into a lavender on the ends. "And hopefully I won't die either, so this recreation is all about the sex and not the story."

"You're pushing limits here," she reprimands as my hands cup her tits. "And you're going to make me mess up."

"I thought we were recreating a scene here. Don't I get to cover you in wet clay and fuck your brains out?"

She sighs but not in dismay. She sighs because I'm dragging my thumbs over her hardening nipples through her bra.

"You don't have time to fuck my brains out."

True. I don't. I likely have ten minutes at most. Abandoning her tits, I slide my hand up her inner thigh, going straight into her shorts.

"Owen. Shit," she hisses when I pull her panties to the side and start to run my fingers up and down her slit. She's wet. She's always so fucking wet for me.

"Sit on my lap," I tell her, kissing the back of her neck as I continue to play with her pussy. "Sit on my lap and put your thighs over mine. I want to make you feel good."

"I'll get you dirty," she warns.

"Sweet thing, I'm always dirty with you. I swear, half the time I walk around rock-hard because I'm thinking about you. Even if it's not about sex, I'm still hard because it's you on my mind."

She shuts off the wheel, the thing slowing down, her clay piece twirling, and now a bit lopsided thanks to my distraction. I expect some shit for it, but she's quiet as she does what I asked. My fingers slide out of her, and I help her sit on my lap. She spreads her thighs wide on either side of mine and leans back, the top of her head tucked beneath my chin.

The song continues to play, and it makes me chuckle. I don't remember much about the movie—I haven't seen it in a hundred years—but that scene is memorable. "I'm hotter than Patrick Swayze, right?"

"I can't answer that. *Dirty Dancing* was my favorite movie growing up."

My head dips, and I nibble on her neck, punishing her for that answer, as my hand dives into the front of her shorts and I slip two fingers straight into her. Her back arches against me, her dirty hands gripping my thighs and staining my pants. The thought of her handprints on me makes me so fucking hard I can hardly see straight.

"I want you to suck me off tonight," I tell her. "After we put Rory down, I want your mouth on me."

"God, yes," she moans as I pump into her, using the base of my thumb to roll her clit at the same time. "Can I do it now? Please?"

"Baby, I don't think we have enough time."

"I'll be fast."

I lick along her pulse. "I want to make you come."

I continue to finger fuck her, increasing the speed and loving how her wet cunt grips my fingers. She's so soft and tight and warm. It's fucking heaven.

Without warning, she stands up and spins around on me, then straddles the ends of my thighs, closer to my knees.

"What are you doing?" I rasp, watching as she pulls the crotch of her shorts and panties to the side and then takes my hand and puts it right back on her, rubbing my fingers up and down around her clit. Holy shit. I stare, mesmerized by her hand guiding mine. It's wickedly hot and so goddamn erotic. Only she doesn't keep it there. It's more to show me what she wants, because now she's going for the button and zipper of my jeans.

"There is no way you'll be able to get your hot little mouth on my cock like this."

She shakes her head. "No. I'll have to do that later." Her blue-green eyes meet mine, and she gives me a coy smile. "Perhaps you'll come upstairs and find me on my knees with my hands behind my back waiting for you."

I groan. This woman is going to be the death of me.

Especially as she digs into my jeans and boxer briefs and finds my hard dick. "Until then, I want to jerk you off and watch you come all over me."

Motherfucker.

"We have to do this fast."

She nods as she starts to ride my fingers that are back inside her. Up and down, she moves, undulating against me. My thumb rubs her clit, and she starts to jerk my cock in earnest, keeping up the same pace my fingers are. It feels out of this world good and looks just as hot. Her small, dirty hands working my big dick from base to crown, twisting me, and just about blowing my mind.

"How do you do it?" she gasps, her eyes momentarily closing. She's soaking my hand, the smell of her arousal hitting me and making me lick my lips. Her hands continue to jack me off, both of them working me hard. I don't have any lube on me, but her hands are still slippery and wet from the clay, and it's enough. More than enough.

"Do what?" I manage just as the song finishes and cuts off.

"Make me insatiable? I've never been like this. Craving it all the time. I can't get enough of you, Owen."

"Good." I increase my pace, really fucking into her now. It's so wet and noisy, both of us moaning and grunting. "I'm going to keep you like this. My little sex slut who can't get enough of my dick."

"Oh god," she moans. "Yes. Fuck. I'm so close. Tell me you're close too. I want to watch you come all over me. I want to be your dirty slut covered in your cum."

Jesus hell.

"Fuck, Estlin. I'm..." I can't even get the words out before I start shooting my load all over her. She aims it at her belly, shorts, and shirt, and I spurt everything I have in thick, white ropes. She watches, utterly enraptured, and the sight of me coming all over her pushes her over the edge. Her pussy convulses on my fingers, squeezing them like a fist as my thumb presses in hard on her clit.

She cries out—never one to be quiet—and I stifle the sound with my lips, kissing her as she continues to come all over my hand.

When she finally relaxes against me, I smile against her and slowly pull my fingers out of her, then lick them one by one.

I kiss her again so she can taste herself, and then slowly help her to stand. Tucking myself back in, I straighten myself up. "I need to go wash my hands, change my pants, and check on dinner and Rory."

"And I need a minute to come back down from space and then get cleaned up before dinner."

"Go." I kiss her lips. "Before we're busted by my six-year-old."

She giggles, and I smack her ass and then head for the door. Never have I been this happy. I can only hope it lasts and be exactly like Rory said—that Estlin will be someone who doesn't go.

27

OWEN

Rory hasn't been on a plane since she was an infant. So everything right now for her is both new and the most exciting thing ever. I can only hope that trend continues all week. Estlin and I keep our distance in the airport. She is the dutiful nanny, and I'm the dad, and that's how we've been in public for the last few weeks. In private, she's mine. Sleeping in my bed and with me every chance we get.

I have to keep reminding myself to have patience. To allow this thing between us to grow naturally. It's been less than a month. A lot can happen between two people who will tear them apart, and me acting hastily is dangerous, especially where Rory is concerned.

Estlin and I have both been burned by people we loved and trusted.

That should make me more cautious, only it doesn't. It makes me want to grab her with both hands and never let go. She doesn't care about my money. She doesn't care about my name or my family's name. She adores and cares for my daughter as if she were her own. Her people are my people.

But then there's the flip side of that coin.

Estlin is young. She very likely doesn't want to be permanently tied down to a man who works long, strenuous hours and has a kid. She's just starting her career and exploring her talent. Something she should feel free to dive into and chase. Her brother will sever my balls from my body, and while I could almost handle that, the thought of losing him—someone I've been close with my entire life—when I don't think his sister is ready to be any sort of permanent fixture in my life is foolhardy.

So here we are in the airport with an excited Rory and Estlin, who hardly looks at me, while I can't help but stare at her. It's her birthday on Thursday, and I bought her things. Things I couldn't help but buy her, so we'll see how it goes when we get there. My grandmother offered me the family jet, and I declined, but now I'm sort of wishing I hadn't. I could have been able to touch and stare freely at Estlin.

"Daddy, can I get candy for the airplane?"

I snap my gaze away from my nanny and down to my daughter. "How about some pretzels?"

You'd think I just asked her if she wanted to be mummified alive. "*Pretzels?*"

"They're going to give you breakfast on the plane," I coax, only that's not selling her either.

"Rory, can I tell you how not fun it is to throw up on an airplane?" Estlin tosses at her. "And with your stomach and the fact that you haven't been on a plane in a while, I might not test those waters just yet, kiddo."

Rory pouts. "But they have the sweet and sour gummy snakes I like. I saw them in the store we just passed."

"Rory, my girl, it's all about the peanut butter M&Ms," Estlin counters.

"Okay." Rory shrugs. When it comes to candy, she's an equal-opportunity eater.

I sigh, feeling myself relenting. I have a bad feeling this will be my baseline all week. "Fine. Go. But three of each Rory, and if you throw up on the plane…" I trail off. I have no real threat that follows that up. She could throw up on the plane, and there isn't much I can do about it. Everyone around us will have to deal.

Yeah, maybe I should have taken the jet. Eighty percent of my family does, but it's not really who I am.

Estlin throws me a look that tells me she's already onto me, and then she takes Rory to the store to buy who knows what. I'm almost better off not knowing. My phone buzzes in my pocket, and I slip it out as I take a seat at the gate.

I answer, "Why are you calling me again? I already spoke to you this morning. Don't tell me you're still—"

"Ah! Yes, I'm still freaking out! It's my first day back after the baby and I'm a mess, Owen!" Katy screams into the phone so loudly about a half dozen people nearby hear her. "You're my person, and anytime I freak out at Bennett, he just tells me he's got the baby and not to worry."

I slip in my AirPods and shove my phone back in my pocket. "Aw, Kit-Kat, I'm sorry. You're right. You can call to freak out on me as much as you want. I remember that first day. It sucks."

"Totally sucks! And Bennett is all, we're fine, we're good, we don't need you. Doesn't he get what he's saying?"

I snicker. "No. He doesn't. He's trying to set your mind at ease so you can do your other job without being upset or worrying."

"I miss my girl and my guy."

"I know. But think about the surgeries. All those trauma patients who need you."

She sighs. "I'm scared, Owen. It's been three and a half months since I've done this. What if I fuck it all up, or worse, kill someone?"

"Not gonna happen," I tell her firmly, watching Rory and

Estlin as they walk through the store, looking at all the bullshit they have in there. "I took four months off after Rory was born, and I was still a resident. You're a fellow. You'll be fine. I promise. You are an incredible surgeon."

She sucks in an audible breath. "Okay. Yeah. I totally am. I can do this."

"Yes," I agree. "Take it one shift at a time. You'll see Willow when you get home this evening, and she'll be all smiles for you. A little separation is good for her and for you. Healthy even."

"Thank you. I needed to hear that. What time does your flight take off?"

"We board in about ten minutes. My girls are shopping for sugar."

"Aw. How cute. You're calling them your girls. Remember, you are not allowed to go out and buy a ring unless I'm with you."

I make a show of rolling my eyes to no one but myself. "I'm not proposing."

"Yet."

I fall forward, my elbows digging into my thighs as Estlin and Rory hold hands, laughing and chatting, likely about all the extra candy Estlin bought her that I'm not supposed to know about.

"Probably not ever," I admit. "She's twenty-two."

"She turns twenty-three in three days. Did you get her a gift?"

My hand rubs against my mouth. "I did. She's going to think I'm crazy."

"For her? Yes. That's the point."

"Katy!"

"Do you love her?"

I sigh, wiping my forehead. "You already know I do. But loving her doesn't change our reality."

"Just like how I want to be home with my baby and my guy, but instead I'm here."

"Exactly. But you get to go home to them, and they're all yours. She's not mine. Not really. You're the only one who knows about us, and we lie to everyone else. I want to make her fall as in love with me as I am with her, but I'm not sure that's what's best for her."

Katy is silent for a beat. "You can't say shit like that to me, Owen. I'm still nursing. I'm postpartum. Therefore, I'm fucking hormonal." She sniffles. "And if she's not as in love with you as you are with her, then she's nuts. But I think she is. I think you're worried about the wrong things. Yes, she's young, but so what?"

"So I'm a lot."

Katy laughs. "You are that, my friend."

"You know what I meant."

"I do. But have faith. Don't make decisions for her that she needs to make for herself."

Have faith. Not my strong suit. "They're returning, so I can't talk about it. Just go be with your patients and know that Willow will be fine. She has me as her godfather, after all."

"Ha. Yes. Bye."

She hangs up on me, only to immediately text me. I pull my phone back out from my pocket.

> Katy: Congrats.

> *Confetti pops like splatter paint across my screen*

> Katy: On finally taking a vacation and falling in love.

I roll my eyes. I can't stop it.

> Me: Happy birthday.

Estlin stands before me. "Are you ready? They're starting to call our flight."

"THERE'S THE CASTLE, there's the castle!" Rory is screaming at the top of her lungs and jumping up and down as we walk through the front of the Magic Kingdom. She's been off the walls since we landed and has screamed the same thing about five times now, including as she ran through our three-bedroom suite like her ass was on fire.

I haven't told her we're having dinner in there tonight with the princesses and that I set up a special dessert thing where we can watch the fireworks. As much as I wish we were sailing and not hot and sweaty surrounded by fifty thousand people, Rory is the happiest I think I've ever seen her.

I reach out and take Estlin's hand, holding it—really holding it—for the first time as we walk. She glances down at our joined hands and then nervously back up at me.

I lean into her so only she can hear. "Rory won't notice or think anything of it. She's six, and I'm also holding her hand."

"But..."

"No one here knows us, baby. Let's enjoy it."

I spent too much of the plane ride down thinking about it. How can anything real develop out of a lie? How will we know what this actually is until we test it? Maybe I'm rushing this. Maybe I don't know how to slow down. But I need to know sooner rather than later because it'll only get that much harder and more painful to end it.

So I put myself on the line and say, "I want you here as my girlfriend as much as you are Rory's nanny. If not more."

"Is that what I am?" she teases with a sly smirk. "Your girlfriend?"

"No. You're a hell of a lot more than that to me."

That catches her off guard, and she stumbles over one of the cobblestones in the center of Main Street. After that, the subject of us drops, but my hand doesn't. We go on rides, and Rory does exceptionally well with her cast. Estlin had painted her a magical fairyland on most of it, and the rest is covered in signatures from her classmates.

It's pretty cool-looking, and on every ride we go on, she's sure to show the attendant and tell them she has a broken arm. Rory makes us go on Small World back-to-back, and we get stuck in Mexico the second time. That song will never leave my head. We go on Mine Train and the Under the Sea Journey with Ariel and Friends. We meet Minnie and Daisy and fly on Dumbo. Rory refused to go on the Haunted Mansion—too scary—or into the Hall of Presidents—too boring.

She eats a pretzel shaped like Mickey and talks me into buying her a princess Minnie. After that, I take her over to the castle and surprise her with the Bibbidi Bobbidi Boutique. She races in, and then she and Estlin spend a solid ten minutes picking out which princess she wants to be. She settles on Aurora with Cinderella's hair, and Estlin and I find a quiet place to sit outside as we wait for them to makeover my little princess into her fairytale dream.

Estlin leans her head against me, watching the families

pass, children laughing and screaming and even some crying. Parents smile, are happy, frustrated, and exhausted as they reach their breaking points.

"I'm glad you came with us," I whisper into her, wrapping my arms around her and dragging her back into my chest.

"Me too," she says lazily, her head tucked in against my shoulder. I'm hit with the craziest vision. Being here and holding Estlin like this, only she's pregnant with our kid, my ring on her finger, and my last name as hers. It's so unexpected that it knocks the wind from me, and I momentarily grow dizzy.

I met her three months ago in that bar, and at the time, this right here was the farthest thing from my mind. But now it's all I can think about.

"Are you okay?" she asks softly, her fingers grazing over my hand that rests on her lower belly as I hold her.

"Just tired," I tell her. "It's been a long day."

"It has. And we have a week of this." She laughs.

"Estlin..." I start and then stop. What am I going to say? Why am I even doing this?

She twists and stares up at me with those ocean eyes of hers and her cheeks that rosy shade of red that drives me wild. She leans in and kisses me. Softly. A kiss that's not driven by lust but by something else. Almost a longing. A need for this closeness and this stolen vacation where everyone thinks she's here to be the nanny so I can get a break and relax a bit too.

She pulls back and gives me a smile that robs me of my ability to breathe. Just as the thoughts in my head feel like they're about to explode out of my mouth, an attendant comes out the door, looking for us. My princess is ready.

Rory is a vision in pink as she twirls through the castle's anteroom while we wait for our turn with Cinderella. There is magic, exhaustion, and hunger rippling through the air.

Upstairs, you can faintly hear the clinking of glasses, and thank God they serve alcohol here.

Our turn is called, and Cinderella is all grace and poise, despite the thousandth child she's seen. She holds Rory's hand and smiles kindly at her as our picture is taken. Estlin tries to bow out, but I won't let her. I bring her in—and there you have it—our first not-quite-a-family picture.

We eat dinner, and the princesses fawn and oooh over my girl, who is in seventh heaven. I won't lie and say I don't get misty-eyed because I do. My little girl is becoming such a big girl, and I hate myself for not taking more moments like these before. One day, I'll be begging for her time. I have the money, and I have the time off I can take. I can do it, and I plan to from now on.

After dinner, an escort leads us over to a special pavilion off the castle where an exclusive dessert service is with a perfect vantage point for the fireworks. There's an assortment of special sweets and cordials, and I pick up a chocolate concoction and hand it to my queen.

She smirks but takes it in her hand as Rory piles up a plate with one of everything.

"My girl, remember your stomach."

Rory throws me a withering glare but then stares balefully at her plate and sighs. I can only hope she's starting to learn her limits. She offers me something from her plate, and then Estlin. Both of us take one thing but Rory proceeds to devour the rest, her body still buzzing despite the late hour and long day. I suppose we should never underestimate the power of adrenaline.

The outside lights grow dark, and through the sound system they have out here for us, a narrator comes on and starts explaining the magic of Disney and its characters, and Rory is enraptured. I reach around for Estlin's hand, taking the small, fragile thing in mine, suddenly finding myself wondering what her ring size is. And just where the fuck is that madness coming from?

Am I trying to die a slow, painful death?

Forgoing her ring size and whether or not she'd say yes if I dropped down to one knee here and now, I pull her sweet body into mine, my chin on her shoulder, my mouth by her ear.

Nearby, the castle lights up in green and purple lights that glow and flash all around us. There's literal magic in the air. And as the first crack of fireworks explodes over our heads and Estlin and Rory ooh and aah at them, I lean deeper into Estlin, holding her closer, no longer able to ignore nor deny just how badly I want this to be my forever.

28

ESLTIN

Epcot is an amusement park designed for adults. I'm
sure of it. There is alcohol in every country, great
food, and limited rides. I've seen at least a dozen
people walking by with shirts that say, "Drink around the
world" and I agree it's a smart plan. It's only about fifteen coun-
tries or so. How difficult can that be?

Owen thinks I'm nuts. He asked me where I wanted to go
for dinner for my birthday, and told me he'd take me anywhere
in Florida I wanted. He offered to fly us down to Key West for
the evening or to go to a posh restaurant in Miami.

I told him I wanted to go to the pizza and Italian restaurant
in Epcot since that's the park we're in today. So far, I also think
it's my favorite park, but tomorrow we're at Hollywood Studios,
so we'll see after that. I've been drinking my way from country
to country, which Owen finds hysterical. Especially when I
order the equivalent of a keg cup of champagne in France.

It was a bit of a sucker punch to the gut when we got to
France, the area was made to look just like Paris, and it does. I
miss Paris. I loved living there, Claude notwithstanding. So the
keg cup was necessary. Rory and I went on the Ratatouille ride,

which was super cute. We've done rides most of the day, my favorite being Guardians of the Galaxy, and hers was naturally the Frozen ride.

But now we're in Italy, sitting in the piazza as I finish my champagne—sixteen ounces of champagne isn't something you rush—and watching Rory run up and down the stairs of the fountain before we're ready to head into dinner.

Owen's holding my hand, something he's been doing this entire week, and I cast Rory a quick glance before I plant a kiss on Owen's cheek, which never fails to make him smile. It's been heaven here. The three of us are a unit, and Owen and I are a couple.

We haven't talked about it.

Neither of us asking or wanting to know what this means because it might very well mean nothing. But I want it to. I want it to mean everything. I don't want to pop this magical bubble. I want it to stay and grow and never allow anyone to burst it.

I get what that would mean.

Dating a single father isn't small-time. There is no casual or in-between. I'm only twenty-three, and the notion of being a mother—even an eventual stepmother—feels daunting and above my pay grade. But I'm not sure how much I care. I adore Rory. I love spending time with her. I love being the one she turns to with questions, and I have the best time making art and cooking with her.

So... I don't know.

Maybe what feels so wild and undeniably forbidden... isn't. Maybe I can be his Elizabeth, and he can be my Mr. Darcy after all.

Standing, I toss my cup in the trash, and then Owen stands too. "Ready for dinner?"

"You bet."

He snickers and shakes his head, but then we're led inside

the adorable Italian eatery with warm, earth-colored walls, alfresco paintings, and Romanesque sculptures built into the walls. It smells like garlic and cheese, and Rory immediately jumps up and gives me a high-five with her good hand.

I throw Owen a smug, gleeful look that continues to make him shake his head at me.

"What?" I shrug. "I don't need you to toss your money around at me. This makes me way happier than any fancy restaurant ever could."

I earn a kiss for that. Straight on the lips. Thankfully Rory seems to be too busy taking in everything to notice.

"Come on. Let's go eat."

And eat we do. Holy hell, I pack in so much food I'm not sure I'll be able to move again.

Rory and I split the manicotti and a pizza with mushrooms and prosciutto because we couldn't decide which one we wanted between the two of them. Owen gets the tortellini, which he seems to love.

Then we're onto dessert of tiramisu and cannoli, but it's delivered to the table with all the staff singing happy birthday to me along with a sparkler in the tiramisu. Rory jumps up and sings along with them, and I can't help but get choked up.

This might be the best birthday I've had.

"Did you make a wish?" Rory asks, dipping a piece of the cannoli in her chocolate gelato and crunching down on it.

"I did. I wish—"

"You can't tell us!" Rory shrieks. "Then it won't come true."

I laugh at how adamant she is about it and make a motion of locking my lips and throwing away the key.

"Should we give her our gift?" Owen questions and my shocked gaze catapults over to him. I wasn't expecting a gift. He's been nothing but generous on this trip and hasn't allowed me to pay for anything—even things that were just for me and not related to being a nanny like my champagne.

"Yes!" Rory comes racing over and jumps on my lap, making me oomph. "This is from me and Daddy."

"Oh my gosh! Thank you." I'm choking up even before they hand it to me. He pulls out a wrapped box from the backpack he's been carrying around all day with all of Rory's stuff in it.

"We hope you'll like it."

I shake my head. "Whatever it is, I already know that I love it if it came from both of you."

Rory chews on her lip, her small hand tucked under her chin as if she's nervous. I open the paper and then gasp.

"You got me an Apple Watch?"

"You don't seem to ever wear a watch, and anytime you check the time, you do it on your phone," Owen tells me. "But more than that, when you were in the accident, your phone flew out of your hand, and then I couldn't reach you. This way, you'll be able to make emergency calls or just be able to answer the phone when I call."

I smirk, throwing him an eyebrow. "So this is actually a present for you."

He chuckles. "Do you like it?"

"I love it. It's perfect. I've always wanted one but never bothered to get it. Thank you. Thank you both so much."

I kiss Rory's cheek and then Owen's, blown away by what a thoughtful and generous gift this is. After dessert, we watch more fireworks the way we did the first night in the Magic Kingdom. Owen is all about paying for extras, and we have the best seat in the house for them. Rory is mesmerized, and after we work our way out of the park along with a million other people, she is so exhausted—suddenly hit with the extent of this day and the week we've had—Owen has to carry her to our waiting car. She sleeps across his chest as we're driven back to our hotel, and then we're whisked up to a glorious penthouse of three bedrooms and walls of windows and endless luxury.

Traveling Fritz is nothing to sneer at.

He takes Rory to the end of the hall and tucks her into bed. She's out.

And because she's so out, he finds me lingering in the hall, not quite sure what to do with myself. He smiles. "That bedroom is entirely for show. I don't know why you continue to pretend otherwise night after night."

"What if she wakes up and finds me in yours?"

He shrugs as if he no longer cares. Vacation Owen isn't the same as Boston Owen. He's not thinking rationally.

"Come here, sweet thing. It's just us right now, and I have another birthday present for you." He scoops me off my feet and brings me to his chest, bride-style. It never fails to shock me how easily he picks me up and carries me.

I squeeze his biceps, making him laugh.

"I don't think I've ever seen you smile as much as you have this week. Vacation looks good on you, Dr. Fritz."

He peers down at me, smiling as light as air as if to prove my point. "It's been a good few days."

I sigh and rest my head against his chest. "It has been. And Rory hasn't gotten sick."

He groans. "Please tell me you didn't just jinx that."

I slap a hand over my mouth, horror striking my features. "Oops. No, I didn't. I swear."

"Christ, I hope not." He sets me down on the edge of the bed, and steals a kiss. Just a light peck. A taunting brushing of our lips that has me trailing after him, desperate for more as he pulls away. He stands to his full height peering down at me with hooded eyes, only to kneel in front of me. "I got you something else. Well, two things. I couldn't pick which one to get you, so I got you both."

I shake my head, not understanding. "But the watch—"

"Is from me and Rory. These are just from me. One is here with me. The other is at home because it was too delicate to travel with."

I swallow slowly, nerves skittering up through my stomach and across my skin. "Okay," I manage. "Owen, you're freaking me out with that tone and expression of yours."

He gives me a wan smile that doesn't reach his eyes. "I don't know how you're going to respond to them. But regardless, I want you to have them."

I place my hand over my racing heart and nearly pass out as he slips a small black box from his pocket and rests it in his hands on my lap. I can't swallow. I can't speak. I can't even blink. He's not... he can't be...

He opens the box, and a bemused laugh tickles past my lips. "Wow."

He laughs. "You were worried, huh?"

I blink at the stunning diamond earrings in the box and then back up to him. "Did you know I'd think—"

"That I was proposing? A hundred percent. It's why I got on my knees."

A cackle explodes out of me, and I smack his shoulder, wiping at a random, errant tear beneath my eye. Is it weird that I might be a touch disappointed he didn't? Argh.

"You bastard. You totally got me." I snatch the box from his hand and bring them up closer. "Jesus, Owen. These are..." Words fail me.

"You don't wear earrings very often, but I know you have them pierced."

"Much like the lack of a watch, and more than ten outfits, I've been lazy with myself."

"Do you like them?"

"No." I shake my head, and his expression falls a bit. Good. Now we're even for the stunt he just pulled on me. "I freaking love them. They're incredible."

"Yeah? I was worried you'd tell me they're too much."

I snicker. "Oh, they're too much. Way too much. And I have no idea how I'll explain them to everyone."

"Easy. I'm Owen Fritz. That's explanation enough."

I roll my eyes. "Now you sound like Mr. Darcy again."

That changes his entire expression. "Well, it's funny you should say that because the second thing I got you..." He pulls out his phone, unlocks it with his face, and then scrolls through something I can't see until he finds what he's looking for and hands me the device.

"What is—" Words die in my throat as I squint at the screen. "Owen." I lick my lips and shake my head, my body trembling a hell of a lot more than it was just moments ago. "No. These aren't—"

"First editions? Yes. They are. Originally, Pride and Preju-dice was released in a limited run of only fifteen hundred copies and printed as three volumes instead of one."

Tears well in my eyes and then start to plummet like rain drops, one after the other, down my face. "I can't..." I clear my throat, but it doesn't matter. There is no clearing this away. "I can't accept these. They're too much. The earrings, the watch, these books. Owen, I can't—"

"Shh," he hushes against my lips. "You can. They're yours. I want you to have them. You've been calling me Mr. Darcy from the start, and now you're my Elizabeth, and that's all there is to it." He kisses me. "Let me spoil you, Estlin. I'd buy you the world and tuck it in your pocket for you to always have and keep with you if I could. You deserve everything, including all of these."

He takes the box from my hand, removes one earring, and then pushes it into the hole in my ear, securing the backing before he repeats the motion with the other ear. He just put my earrings in for me. The man bought me diamonds and incred-ibly rare first editions, and while they're both unimaginable on their own, they have nothing on the man kneeling before me.

The man I've fallen so helplessly in love with.

I set his phone down on the bed and trail my fingers up his

neck and across his face. He's not wearing his glasses today—he prefers his contacts and regular sunglasses at the parks—and so I have free range of him. My lips come in, kissing both his eyelids and then along his cheeks.

His hands stay at his sides, but there is no hiding the burning need building in his gaze.

I start to lift my shirt, bunching the fabric up an inch at a time, exposing more skin the higher I go. His palm skims up the curve of my hip, and I quake, anticipation hot and heavy in my limbs and the short, shuddered breaths I'm having trouble controlling. A devilish smirk lights his face as he continues to trail his hand upward as if to say *if you won't do it, I will.*

My stomach dips when he reaches the edge of my bra, his finger gliding along the underwire of one cup and then across to the other before traveling up over the lace to find my nipple. I hold perfectly still, allowing him this exploration until I can't take it a second longer, and pull my shirt up and over my head.

"Those too," he rasps, pointing to my shorts.

I stand, forcing him back, but instead of shimmying out of my shorts, I saunter like an alley cat toward the window that has the curtains drawn back, unhooking my bra as I go. It slides off my shoulders and drops to the floor as I reach the cool glass. His silhouetted reflection prowls toward me, and anticipation swirls like a drug through my veins. Reaching back, he pulls his shirt up and over his head, tossing it to a nearby chair.

He moves in behind me, the heat of his chest warms my back, and I shiver.

"They're beautiful on you. Exactly how I imagined them."

The diamonds sparkle in my ears, not too large and not too small, but perfect. Made for me. Like he is.

His mouth dips to my ear, his eyes catching mine in the window. "Hands on the glass," he whispers, and I swear, I have a baby orgasm just from that.

Shakily, I press my palms into the glass and push myself

back into him. Warm, soft, wet lips start a sensual path along my neck and shoulders as he reaches around and undoes my shorts, letting them slide to the floor in a pool around my feet. His middle finger skims over the center of my panties, back and forth in a tortuous rhythm with barely enough pressure, designed to drive me crazy.

His chest lands in the center of my back, his mouth sucking and kissing and biting at me until I'm panting and wiggling against him. I look down and watch as he lowers my thong to the floor, and now I'm standing naked in the window with nothing but these earrings in my ears, high up above with water and sprawling lights in the distance. He starts to rub my clit, his ragged, hot breath on my skin.

I feel beautiful and sexy with how he's touching me. With how he always touches me.

It's as if someone has been keeping him away, and now that he's been set free to touch me however he wants, he doesn't know how to hold himself back. His blue eyes are feral, locked with mine, and I can't look away. I don't want anything other than him.

He dips one finger in me, pumping it in and out, and then adds a second. My fingers curl against the glass as his curl inside of me.

"I need you," I whine. "Please, I need you."

He continues to fuck me with his fingers as he uses his other to undo his shorts. I feel the hard ridge of his cock spring free, and I moan, my eyes closing. The way I'm addicted to all things Owen Fritz should make me feel some sort of shame, but all I feel is wanton and frenzied.

"Here?" he whispers against me, and I don't care. I just need it.

"Yes." I gasp with a jerky nod as he pulls his wet fingers from me and starts to swirl them around my clit in dizzying circles. I'm so close, but I want to come on him. I want to feel him inside of me as I do.

He keeps playing with my clit, even as he tilts me forward a little and lines himself up. I hold in my breath, anxious for that first thrust that never fails to blow my mind, but instead, he teases me with it. Fingers on my clit and the head of his cock toying with my opening. My eyes roll back. It's so much, but not enough, and it has me floating. My legs shake, and on my next breath, he pushes inside me with a wickedly hard thrust.

And because he's been playing with my clit all this time and because he's so big and thick and fucking perfect and because I fucking love this man with everything I am, I come. The glass holds my weight as I plaster myself against it and grind into him, pushing into his fingers and deeper on his cock and it doesn't stop. It just goes on, and I can't breathe or see anything other than the sparkles of dazzling light behind my eyes.

My forehead lands on the window, and I sigh, a small giggle on my lips. He chuckles too, and gives my ass a smack that makes him groan. I'm a curvy girl. I've always been a curvy girl. I got over feeling self-conscious about it when I came to accept this is just who I am, and I'll never be a tall, slender model type. But for a bit, after Claude, I couldn't help but feel girlish insecurity about my body.

But Owen fucking loves my body. Every inch of me.

His cock starts to slide out, and I wince, my walls thick and swollen and sensitive. More than that, my legs are mush, barely holding me up. He laughs some more and then pulls out all the way.

"No," I protest. "Please no."

"Oh, my sweet thing. I'm far from done with you."

He spins me around and cages me in against the glass. My back hits it with a small bang that rattles the pane, and I arch, crying out, only for him to bite my bottom lip in warning. His hands drag along my thighs, and he hoists me up, forcing them around his hips. I run my hands along his biceps that stretch and bunch, but then he's back in me, and that's all I know.

The way he grinds against me, moves his hips, holds me up, buries his face in my hair, and groans into me, anchors me to him. My arms snake around his neck, and I hold on, able to do little else as he fucks up into me, harder and harder with each delicious thrust. My thighs grip his hips, and my nails drag over his hot flesh. I might be dying with how good this feels. The contrast of the cold glass and the heat radiating off his body and the feel of him against me and inside me are everything that is magical between us.

I tell him that and he bites my chest before he starts sucking.

"You're giving me a hickey," I accuse.

"Mmm," is his only reply, but he's busy taking me, rocking into me so deep I have no idea where he ends, and I begin.

My orgasm is already starting to build, and I know he's getting close too. He's straining, grunting into me, sweating.

"Estlin," he moans. That's it. Just my name. For a man who is so vocal and dominating during sex, that's all I'm getting tonight. Sounds and my name. But, oh, is it good. "So. Fucking. Tight."

"Right there," I plead desperately because he's hitting the perfect fucking spot inside me. Pounding into it. My pussy starts to spasm, my toes curling to the point of cramping, digging in and forcing him deeper with a push of his firm ass.

I've had orgasms before. A lot, even. I've been blessed with good lovers who liked to give in the bedroom. But this one? I don't know how to categorize this one. It's more. It's extra. It's... love. It's freaking love, and I feel it swell within me from the roots of my hair to the pink nails on my toes.

It's Owen. This man. The one who would turn over the world for his daughter and for me. The one who reminds me there isn't anything better out there because better than him doesn't exist.

He's it. My guy. And it doesn't matter that I'm twenty-three and he's thirty-four. It doesn't matter that he's a successful doctor and I'm a struggling artist. It doesn't matter that he's a single dad and I'm the nanny. Or even that he's my brother's best friend and I'm his little sister's.

Nothing matters but us.

I must tell him that. I must say a thousand different things because after he's come inside of me and we're still and quiet against the glass and he's still inside of me and I'm leaking him, he can't force his gaze from mine. It's intense. The sort that would make your heart pound. The kind that makes your breath quicken and your stomach flip.

"You mean that?"

Shit. I honestly don't know what I said.

"Which part?"

He's not amused. "You said nothing else matters but us. Did you mean it?"

I gnaw on my lip, finding my brave. "Yes. Nothing matters but us. The three of us. I want you both."

He loses focus as he starts to tremble against me. Suddenly my feet end up on the floor, but he's still around me, holding me, lifting me again, and then bringing me into the bathroom so we can shower off the long day and the sweaty saltiness of sex.

Neither of us says much else. Our minds drunk on exhaustion and catatonic with thoughts. I shouldn't want him and Rory the way I do. But that doesn't stop me. It's them for me. My home. My love. No matter the risk.

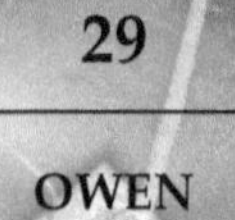

29

———

OWEN

Hollywood Studios is an enormous park. Considering we're on day four of one after the other, I've about had it. I wouldn't have minded a day off where we sat by the pool, Estlin in a bikini, but with Rory's cast, that's not advised. So it's been parks. And more parks.

I'm going to need a vacation from my vacation, and I only have one kid.

Though Estlin did in fact jinx us last night as Rory threw up after breakfast this morning.

We're moseying along the shops. Rory is munching on a pretzel and Estlin is eating popcorn, and with the hot sun beating down on us, I think we all need a break.

"Daddy, I want to go on the drop ride."

Estlin's eyes burst open wide, and then scroll up to the large pink tower not too far from us. "For real?"

She shrugs. "I bet it's not too scary."

"Oh, I beg to differ, but if you're game, I'm in."

"I might sit that one out."

Estlin smirks. "Wimp."

"I hate drops."

"I think it looks fun."

"I'm with Rory. It looks fun."

I rub my thumb along my bottom lip. "Then go have fun and report back. I'll get you a drink for when you come off it."

Estlin gives me a look that says *if I could kiss you right now I would.* "You've got a deal."

Rory drags her off, and for a bit, I head through a recreation of Old Hollywood, going through shops and enjoying the bursts of air conditioning as I come to them.

Estlin texts to let me know they're next in line, and I head toward the spot where the margarita stand is. I get in line behind three drunk college-aged women who are chatting about who cares what. As is required anytime we're in line for anything now, I pull out my phone, but it instantly starts ringing against my palm.

"Kit-Kat," I answer, more than a little happy to hear from her. "How's it—"

"Something is wrong with Willow."

Immediately, I freeze, ice filling my veins, even as I shuffle dutifully forward. "What do you mean?"

Katy makes a panicked noise. "I don't know. I mean, I could be nuts. I could be. She didn't sleep well the last two nights and I just started back to work and—"

"Katy, cut the shit and talk to me."

She sobs. Katy fucking sobs into the phone, and I'm starting to lose my mind.

"Bennett is in a board meeting. He had to go, and I had the day off. He told me to have him paged out of it if I need him, but I don't know if I'm crazy or not."

"Katy. What the fuck is going on?"

I don't even care about the perturbed looks I'm getting from the teeny-bop group in front of me. I glare hard, and they shrink, turning immediately away from me.

"She's super fussy. I mean, fussier than normal. And she's

not eating. Not nursing or taking a bottle. Plus, her legs hike up like she's in pain." She squeaks out short, choppy breaths. "Her belly looks distended to me."

"Any vomiting or diarrhea?"

"No. If anything, she's constipated."

Sweat clings to my brow, my eyes flittering around at nothing. I wish I were there. I can't stand this helpless feeling of being too far away.

"Katy, can you take a set of vitals on her?"

She sniffles, and I hear Willow crying in the background. "I don't..." She sucks in a breath. "All I have is my stethoscope and a thermometer. What kind of mother am I?"

"You called me, didn't you? Grab your stethoscope and check her temperature. I want to know if Willow has a fever and what her heart sounds like, and then I want you to tell me if she has bowel sounds."

"You're thinking bowel obstruction?"

"I'm not thinking anything yet. I want to hear what you have to say."

"Next?" the guy behind the counter calls. "What type of margarita would you like?"

"Shit. I'm interrupting your vacation. I'm sure this is—"

"Katy, I need your report in two minutes," I bark into the phone before I turn to the guy. "Whatever you have that's strong."

He pours a large cup—like we're at a freaking keg party cup—of a margarita, and I pay the man and then head out into the mass of Disney-goers.

"Where are we, Kit-Kat?"

She sniffles into the phone, and Willow is a screaming mess in the background, which is only flustering Katy more. "Temperature is a hundred point one. Her heart rate is about one fifty with no murmurs. Her belly is tense, and I can't tell if I'm hearing bowel sounds or not because she's so upset."

"Katy, I need you to think like a doctor and not a mother," I tell her, spotting Estlin and Rory as they come off the ride, laughing and smiling with each other. I flag them over and Estlin immediately notes my panic and moves briskly, practically dragging Rory behind her.

Katy sobs. "I don't know how, Owen. This is my baby."

"If it were Rory, what would you tell me to do?" I trail off, leaving that hanging.

She sucks in a series of breaths. "I'd tell you to take her to the hospital."

"Yes, you would. So you're going to do that now. You're not to drive, Katy. I fucking mean it. I want either Bennett to do it, or I want you to call Callan or Layla or any of your other thousand relatives to pick you both up and take you. If no one can, you call an ambulance."

"What's wrong?" Estlin mouths.

"It's Katy," I reply just as silent.

Worry covers Estlin's face as we start walking.

"You got me on that?" I check when Katy doesn't say anything.

"Yes." Katy sniffles again and then clears her throat. "I texted Uncle Cal, and he replied immediately to say he's on his way. He's at the hospital too and is going to go get Bennett out of his meeting first." Katy is emotional, but she's also cool under pressure—she's a trauma surgeon, so it goes with the territory—and it's a relief to hear she's getting herself together. Plus, a tense belly on a baby who was premature at birth worries me.

Estlin grabs the cup from my hand and chucks it into a trash bin as she and Rory start walking toward the exit along with me.

"Good. That's a relief. It's okay, Katy. You're doing everything right. We'll be there in four hours or so."

"No!" Katy cries. "No, Owen. You're on vacation. You're in Florida. I just—"

"It's not an argument we're going to have. I will be there in four hours. Check and see if Stone is working in the ED tonight. We'll be home soon."

I disconnect the call and blow out a breath, trying to get my own frazzled nerves under control.

"Baby Willow has a very bad tummy ache," I tell Rory while throwing a meaningful glance at Estlin. It might be nothing, but my gut is telling me otherwise and I've been doing this long enough to know the difference. "Are you okay if we head home tonight instead of tomorrow?"

Rory doesn't even hesitate. She grips my hand tighter, and that's that.

"What about my stuff?" she asks after a minute as we speed walk toward the exit of the park.

"I'll have someone pack up our stuff and ship it home."

That's how it goes. I make phone calls and send texts. Donna assures me she's got it covered, and she does. I wasn't lying when I called her a magician.

Within forty minutes, we're stepping onto a private plane, our bags already arranged to be packed up and shipped home. We'll also be greeted by a helicopter at Logan Airport that will take us right over to Children's. I offer to have a car waiting to take Estlin and Rory home, but Rory tells me in no uncertain terms that if baby Willow is at the hospital, that's where she'll be too.

When we're an hour into our flight, I get a text from Katy telling me that they're at the hospital and that Stone and his team were waiting for them. They're about to do an ultrasound and run some blood. Stone chimes in and creates a group text with Mason, Vander, Keegan, Kenna, Wren, Tinsley, and me to provide updates. Another hour passes, and Katy informs us they're going to take Willow into surgery within the next hour for a bowel obstruction.

Katy may be a trauma surgeon, but this is her baby.

It's exactly how I was when it was Rory on that table.

I text her back to let her know that I'll be there and will join mid-surgery. Then I text my surgical team, every freaking doctor and nurse I know, and tell them that this baby is my goddaughter and that she needs everything we can give her. My heart is racing out of my chest, and yet I do everything I can to stay calm and composed. Not so easily done, but Rory is scared, especially when I tell her Willow is getting surgery like how she did, only on her tummy.

I promise her that I'll take care of Willow just as Kaplan and Stone took care of her.

She seems relieved by this, but then destroys me when she asks, "Daddy, do you promise baby Willow will be okay?"

Here's the thing. In medicine, there are no promises. No guarantees we can make, and as doctors, we're taught to never promise an outcome to a patient's family. But this is my little girl. The thought of letting her down or disappointing her in any way breaks my heart.

I bring Rory onto my lap, hold her tightly against me, and kiss the top of her head. "I will do everything I can to make her so. That I can promise you." It's all I've got, and it's the best I can do, but I refuse to let her worry more than she should.

Estlin is quiet, and the moment we touch down in Boston, as in the second the airplane doors open, I race the three of us to the waiting helicopter. Rory and Estlin have never been on one of these, but as part of my residency, I worked with the pediatric medevac crews around the city.

Rory is wearing massive headphones on her ears, and to her, right now, this is an adventure. I give her full marks for bravery. Going up in a helicopter is a lot scarier than the ride she went on earlier today. Fifteen minutes later, we reach the helipad at Boston Children's Hospital, and I fly out of the helicopter leaving Rory with Estlin. My feet hit the elevator, and one of my regular scrub nurses is there waiting for me.

"It's intussusception. No sepsis or leaking. The team made their first incision thirty-two minutes ago and are proceeding laparoscopically."

"They're going to have to deal with me coming in and taking over."

She nods. "They already know."

I blow out a breath and scrub my face. "How bad is it?"

"She's likely going to need a small section of her small bowel removed unless a miracle can be performed, but nothing she can't recover from."

"Well, let's see if we can work a miracle."

Bowel obstructions of this nature are common in premature babies. Willow was born at thirty-four weeks. So was I. In the back of my uncle Oliver's car, to be exact. Kaplan delivered me and revived me when I came out blue and not breathing. There is no rhyme or reason why one baby gets obstructed and another doesn't. That doesn't mean as parents we don't blame ourselves for everything.

Katy is already on a tear about it even when on some level she knows better. I have to fix this for her. For Bennett. For our families. And for Willow. This is my goddaughter, and I don't think I have it in me to tell her mother that I had to remove a piece of her bowel, no matter how unobtrusive the loss would be.

I scrub in, listening as a resident comes out and gets me up to speed.

A moment later, I'm entering the OR, getting gowned and gloved up. Ready to work that miracle because I won't accept anything less.

"Good evening, everyone."

I glance up at the gallery and find Stone, but he's not alone.

He's surrounded by all of my uncles, with the exception of Rina's husband Brecken, who is not a doctor. I glare at Oliver and shake my head. He's essentially Willow's grandfather or great-grandfather or whatever he likes to call himself. Regardless, he shouldn't be up there watching. He's not a surgeon, but that doesn't matter.

If anything, it might make it worse.

I point to the exit, indicating he should go.

Oliver doesn't give a shit. He flips me off, and I chuckle.

"Don't worry," I call up to them since I know they can hear me. "I've got our girl."

The doctor who was working the laparoscope shifts to the left and I take over, focusing my attention on the surgical field before me on camera and not the patient on the table. Willow is so small, her anatomy tiny, but I've performed surgeries on babies half her size.

Still, time is of the essence.

The less time we can have Willow under anesthesia the better.

Regardless, I don't plan on leaving this room until my goddaughter is as perfect as I left her.

30

ESTLIN

I'll admit, I haven't spent a lot of time in surgical waiting rooms. But I have to imagine none of them are like this one is right now. It's standing room only for Katy and Bennett, and of course baby Willow. Rory is sitting on Katy's lap, tucked tightly into her. Beside her are Layla and Callan, Katy's adoptive parents. Bennett and his mom are on the other side, and all around them are every member of Central Square, their kids, including Mason and Vander who are very close friends with Katy and Owen, plus every Fritz on the planet, along with Octavia and Dr. Fritz senior.

Everyone is waiting with bated breath for word about Willow, but the moment Rory and I walked into the room, Katy's eyes, which were already brimming with tears, overflowed. Relief like I've never seen struck her features.

She knew it meant Owen was with Willow.

I feel strange being here. I'm not even sure why. In this room, to everyone here—except Katy, who knows—I'm the nanny. Yes, I grew up with some of the people here. Yes, I know them as friends. But it doesn't feel like that right now. The division feels wider.

Or maybe what felt so important before, no longer is.

The secret we've been keeping that once felt like freedom between us now sits on me like a weight. In the short time Owen and I have been sneaking around, everything between us has changed. And fast. Practically overnight.

My phone vibrates in my pocket, and I slip it out to see it's Billy.

> Billy: Don't be mad at me, and remember how much you love me.

> Me: What did you do?

> Billy: *Devil smile emoji*

That's it. Nothing else comes in, and I wait and wait. What the hell? I glance over at Rory and find her still tucked in with Katy, so I leave my perch in the corner of the waiting room and step out into the brightly lit hall. It's quiet out here, the hallway all but empty, and I walk a few feet down.

Just as I go to text him back, my phone rings in my hand from an unknown number with a two-one-two area code, which I know to be New York City. For a beat, I debate answering it, almost worried it's Claude, though instinctively I know it's not. Curiosity wins out, and my finger slides across the screen.

"Hello?" I answer softly, glancing around to make sure I'm not disturbing anyone.

"Hello." A strong male voice booms through the speaker and into my ear. "I'm looking for Estlin Kincaid."

"Speaking."

"Estlin, may I call you Estlin? My name is Alfonzo Williams," he continues before I can answer him about my name. "I run the Broad—"

"Gallery in New York," I find myself finishing for him,

though I don't know why. Maybe it's from being in shock that he's calling me. The Broad Gallery is internationally known. It's *the* premier gallery in New York and brings in some of the biggest names in the art world. Claude had been trying to get in there for as long as I knew him and even before that. My mother had a show there decades ago, and it's part of what launched her career.

I don't know why he's calling, but whatever the reason is, just talking to him has me winded.

His warm chuckle fills my ear. "Yes, I see you've heard of us."

"I can't tell if you're being ironic or not."

"Billy said I'd like you. He's my nephew. Did he tell you that?"

I blink about sixty thousand times at the taupey-cream walls. "Um. No. He didn't."

"Well, he doesn't like to pass that around. In fact, he only shares with people he feels I should know about. Tonight, he shared your work with me."

I think I'm going to throw up. As it is, I'm shaking so badly I practically fall against the wall, needing support because my legs are anxious to give out on me.

"He did?" I manage.

"He showed me two paintings you have here, but he did hint that you had others. Was he mistaken?"

I shake my head, my free hand covering my mouth, almost wanting to cry at that question. I bend in half, pressing the phone tighter to my ear. "I have two others." Claude destroyed fifty pieces of mine. Fifty. It was years and years of work. I had forgiven him, but at this moment, I think I might want to kill him again.

"So four pieces total?"

"As of right now, unfortunately, that's all I have other than some of my clay pieces."

"No, I don't deal in pottery despite how beautiful it can be. Okay." He pauses, and I can tell by his tone he's thinking, possibly reconsidering this phone call. Shit. I can't offer him anything more than what I have, but hell, I wish I could. It's excruciatingly painful. An old scar someone just sliced back open.

"Those other two pieces. Do you have pictures? I'd come to see them, but I'm heading back to New York as we speak."

My eyes pinch closed in anxious regret. "Not at present. They're at home, but I can send you pictures by tomorrow morning."

"I think we could do something with your work, Estlin. I know talent when I see it, even in two paintings. I believe Billy was correct about you, and I remember your mother. She was as young and talented as you are. I launched her career. She received many offers after her showcase in my gallery."

"I know," I say, my voice half-gone because I do know. She hit the *New York Times* with that showing. It launched her into every place she deserved to be within the art world.

"I'd need at least twenty pieces."

I collapse into a squat, breathing hard. Shit. *Twenty pieces.* How on earth can I do that?

"By when?" I squeak because I can't even believe he's entertaining me.

"June? Say June first. I'd love to do this as a summer event, and I think that would bring in the buyers for you. I'll need you to come to New York with the pieces you already have. You'll sign some contracts that give me exclusive rights to the reveal and sale of your work, and we'll discuss your other pieces as well as your vision for the collection."

I right my body, about to lose my mind, but not stupid enough not to sell myself and grab onto my dream with both hands. "Absolutely," I answer quickly. "When would you need me to come to New York?"

"Next week for certain, and then several times in between as you deliver your pieces per the contract we would sign. I think a forty-five percent commission is fair, and if you search around, you'll find that number consistent with the current rate in the market."

I don't get into that yet. I have to talk to my mother and likely a lawyer. I might be young and have done so many things wrong in my life, but I won't be stupid or naïve and trusting about this.

"You want me to come to New York next week?" I think on this but not really. My mind is spinning too fast. My dream all but smacking me in the face. "Sure. Yes. I can do that. Whatever you need."

"Excellent. I look forward to meeting you then. I'll have my assistant get in touch to work out the particulars. Have a good rest of your evening, Estlin."

"Thank you, sir. You too."

We end the call, and I fall forward, panting, unable to catch my breath as wild giddiness and pure, unbridled joy sweep through me. Holy shit. Holy freaking fuckity shit. The Broad Gallery. The fucking *Broad Gallery* is going to showcase me. I emit a squeal and quickly cover my mouth, only to jump when a hand meets my shoulder, jostling me out of my thoughts.

"Hey," Jack says, his voice dripping with worry. "Are you okay?"

My neck twists, and I peer up at him, my eyes brimming with tears that start to fall. "Jack, I just spoke to the owner of the Broad Gallery."

His eyebrows pinch together, and he blinks at me as if he's searching for how he knows that name. "That's in the *New York Times* article Mom has framed, right?"

I nod. "Yep."

"Wow. Did she get you a call with them or something?"

That question shouldn't sting, but it does. I push it aside, choosing not to focus on the fact that my brother doesn't believe I could get this on my own.

"No. I have a friend who is the nephew of the owner. He showed him two of my pieces today, and the owner just called me now with an offer to do a showcase in the gallery this summer."

"Jesus, Eddie. That's amazing. I can't believe it." He stares dumbfounded at me because he actually *can't* believe it, and no doubt my family will be the same way. It's been like this my entire life. They're proud of me, and they talk about my accomplishments and talent, but they all still view me as a little girl.

I'm Eddie, not Estlin.

A meek thing incapable of taking care of herself. A child feeding off her mother's name and fame.

It's part of why I allowed Claude to hold me down and accepted his criticism of my work as gospel. No one believed in me the way I needed them to. I had their support and their pats on the back, but they never thought I could go out and conquer the world on my own. Maybe that's why I didn't want them to come see me in London.

I didn't want to prove them right.

I straighten my spine. "Thanks. It means I'll have to go to New York next week to review and sign a contract and return there several times over the coming months since he wants twenty pieces total."

"New York. Wow. That sounds like a lot of work. Are you going to move there?"

"You're leaving us?" The high-pitched, distressed words slice through my euphoric, bitter, and scattered thoughts.

My head flies left and then down to find a distraught Rory, blue eyes big and wide and overflowing with tears.

"Oh, Rory." I cover my mouth, my hands still trembling. "No, sweetheart, I'm not moving to New York."

"But Jack just said you were."

"I was invited to show my paintings at a gallery there, and with that, I will have to make some trips to New York. That's what he was talking about."

"But he said move there. I heard him."

I crouch. "Honey, it'll just be some trips for a few days here and there—"

Her cheeks turn red, and more tears start to spill. "No!" she cries loudly. "You can't leave us."

I run my hand across her cheek, wiping her tears. "If I go, it's just for a short time—"

"No!" She stomps her foot and swats my hand away. It's late, and it's been a supremely long and emotional day for her. She's at her end and is now on overload.

"Rory—"

"You can't leave us! You love us. You can't go when you love me and my dad."

"What?" I gasp and straighten, throwing a quick glance at Jack, who is suddenly very interested in what Rory has to say.

"I saw you and my dad kiss. That means you love him, and he loves you. You can't leave us." She runs off before I can respond, and I watch her go, a sick knot of dread twisting up my stomach. Oh shit. This is bad. Rina exits the waiting room just in time to catch a crying and hysterical Rory.

Jack steps in front of me, cutting off my vision of them. "What the fuck did she mean when she said you were kissing Owen?"

Jesus hell.

I blink up at him. "Jack, calm down."

Rage excites his features. "Do not tell me to calm down, Eddie. Tell me she's mistaken. Tell me she's a little girl and didn't understand what she saw. Tell me you weren't kissing my best friend. But more than that, tell me you haven't been fucking him behind my back."

I blow out a breath. What the hell do I say?

"We care about each other."

"How long, Eddie? How long has this been going on?"

He's really not going to like this answer.

"About a month."

"A month?" he bites out incredulously, fury staining his cheeks. "A fucking *month*? So all those times I was with you, with him, you were fucking each other right under my nose?"

I stare down at the floor. I don't even know what to say. "It was new, and we didn't know what it was, and—"

"And fucking nothing," he growls before he storms off. It's only a half-beat after he's tearing a path down the hall that I realize Owen is at the waiting room door delivering the news about Willow's surgery. And Jack is headed straight for him.

A sheen of sweat covers my brow, and I wipe it away and throw out the paper towels I dried my hands with after scrubbing out. That was undoubtedly my best work yet, and it didn't go unnoticed. I got a round of applause from the OR team as well as from my family up in the gallery.

I saved Willow's bowel.

She had intussusception, which is when a part of the bowel slides into the next, creating a telescoping effect. I was able to fix this and reperfuse the area of her bowel that had been obstructed. And let me tell you, the nurse was right when she said we'd have to work a miracle to make that happen.

I kissed Willow's forehead and then let them wheel her to the PACU, feeling exhaustion deep in my bones but also elation unlike any other. There will be no wiping the smile from my face anytime soon.

With hurried strides, I head for the waiting room, anxious to give them a full update. I have no doubt my uncles went in, but they told me they'd let me be the one to deliver the news to

Katy and Bennett. I can hear my family and Katy's people from down the hall as I approach. My fist raps on the doorway and a million heads simultaneously swivel in my direction.

Katy leaps to her feet and races over to me, Bennett hot on her trail. "She's fine." I grab Katy's shoulders and hold her steady because she was about to plow straight into me. "The surgery was very successful, and your best friend is officially a god."

She laughs. Sorta. For about a half second before she breaks down and collapses against me, her forehead in the center of my chest. "Are you sure?"

I wrap my arms around her and hold her against me, kissing the top of her head. She's shaking uncontrollably, and I can't help but get choked up. Katy's tears, like Rory's and Wren's, unravel me.

"I'm positive, Kit-Kat." I throw Bennett a small smile, his hand is on my shoulder, his other rubbing Katy's back. I love that Katy has him. No one deserves happiness more than she does. "I fixed the intussusception and was able to reperfuse the bowel. Her scarring should be minimal to non-existent, because, again, I'm a god. In a few days, it'll be like nothing happened to her."

"I don't even know what to say," she sobs into me. "Thank you doesn't come close."

"We don't do that anyway," I tell her, kissing the top of her head again and holding her closer. "And I did it more for me than you because I love her more than I love you."

Katy snicker-sniffles and smacks my arm. "I love you. Even if you love her more."

Bennett envelopes himself around both of us and holds on tight. "I fucking love you too."

I pat his back. "I'm glad, brother. Just name your next kid after me, and we'll call it even."

Katy laughs lightly against me before she pulls back. She grabs my face and kisses both cheeks, and then she and Bennett race off toward the PACU.

Just as everyone else comes over to ask questions and give hugs, my shoulder is slammed hard enough to push me into the wall of the hallway. Before I can make heads or tails of anything, Jack is right up in my face.

"I thought you were my friend, but you're a real piece of shit fucking my sister behind my back." He shoves my shoulder again, smashing me into the wall the second I try to right myself.

My eyes widen in stunned disbelief before they narrow into slits. "Really, Jack? You're doing this here? Now?"

He blusters out a noise, his fists balled up at his sides, and I can tell he wants to take a swing but is holding himself back. Barely. "What? You don't want your family and friends to know you've been screwing your nanny? Do you have any clue what you've done? Or has it all just been a good time for you? A mindless divergence and a way to blow off steam?"

I shake my head, fury tingling my spine and hardening my gut. I'm ready to pounce all over that when I hear Estlin call out.

"Jack, stop!" she cries, racing over, but she's held back by Keegan and Wren as Vander, Stone, and Mason now stand in between us. Mason is practically right in front of Jack, all six-four, two-hundred-twenty pounds of NFL quarterback. He's not saying anything, but he doesn't have to. His size and expression say it all.

Only the muscle isn't necessary.

At least for me.

I have no plans to hit Jack, and if he wants to take a swing at me, I won't stop him. He has a right to be pissed and a right to confront me, but this is the wrong place and the wrong fucking time for it.

"I won't stop," he seethes at her before turning his wild eyes back on me. "Did you think I wouldn't find out? Did you think I wouldn't care when I did?"

"What's going on?" Wren questions, glancing back and forth between me and Estlin, her brows knit together. Not to mention, we've grown a crowd. Including my grandparents. Awesome. I don't see Rory, though, which is a relief, but where is she if she's not in the room with everyone else or with Estlin?

"Can we go somewhere else and talk about this?" I ask meaningfully because I don't know where my daughter is right now other than knowing she's here with everyone else, but Jack doesn't give two shits. Yes, he knows these people, some better than others, but they're not his people the way they are mine.

"No. We can't." He turns to Wren. "What's going on is your brother has been messing around with my little sister." He snarls before turning his unrelenting gaze back on me. "And from the looks of it, I'm not the only one you were keeping this from."

Well, there you have it, folks. Not the way I was planning to come clean about all of this, but it's too late now because everyone heard that—including my grandmother—so I guess this is how it's going to happen.

"Is that true?" Wren asks, and I can't tell if she's upset or hurt or just simply curious. Silence falls flat and heavy like the end of a bad joke over all of us. I sigh and throw my family a surreptitious glance, wordlessly apologizing to my grandmother, especially for what she's about to hear. There are few people in my life I never want to disappoint, and she's one of them.

"Yes. It's true," I answer everyone, though I'm staring Jack directly in the eyes.

Jack charges like a bull in a china shop, only to be shoved back by Mason.

"I'm not saying you can't be pissed, but I'm telling you now, no one is getting physical here," Mason asserts calmly.

Jack's temper isn't diminished as he starts to pace in a circle, too riled up not to move.

"She's your nanny, you bastard," he seethes at me. "She works for you. She's twelve years younger than you are." He pauses and glares at me like he's ready to charge once again. "You took advantage of her. She was vulnerable, and you took advantage."

I shake my head, fuming at that accusation. "She's not a child, Jack. She's a grown woman, and I certainly never coerced or expected anything. And screw you for assuming that about me. I'd never take advantage of a woman, and you know it."

"Except she works for you, so what was she supposed to do?"

I shrug, suddenly feeling like being a dick because the fact that he thinks so little of me hurts like nothing else. "Say no."

In rage, he charges forward again, only to be stopped by Mason and Vander, who each grab one of his shoulders.

"Not happening," Vander states calmly. "You two can talk it out, but I'm not letting you throw fists. There are sick children and their parents in this hospital, and they deserve your respect. So be a fucking adult and get your shit under control."

Jack growls, running frustrated hands through his hair and steps back.

"Jack, just let it go," Estlin pleads, keeping her distance from both of us as she stands by Wren and everyone else who is watching us. I'm not sure how that makes me feel, but right now with Jack so riled up, it's probably the smart play. "This isn't the place for this, and frankly, it doesn't concern you."

"Doesn't concern me?" He's indignant. "How does you screwing my best friend not concern me? Do you even know what you're doing with him, Eddie? You think he cares about you?" He practically laughs derisively. "He just admitted he's messing around with you. That hardly sounds serious to me. You're nothing more than some fun to him because Owen doesn't do more than that anymore. He's not looking for serious and he's not looking for happily ever after. He doesn't believe in them anymore. Hell, he told me so not even two months ago."

"You have no clue what you're talking about," I say, refusing to raise my voice even when I want to shout it at him. "We're not simply messing around. You twisted my words. You have no idea how much I care about her. Why are you—"

"Care about her?" He laughs sardonically, starting to pace again. "Bullshit, you do. If you cared about her, you would have been a man and come and spoken to me about it instead of keeping her like your dirty secret from everyone. Do you have any idea what she's been through? The last thing she needs is another older man preying on her while taking advantage."

I step forward, only for Stone's hand to hit my chest. I brush him off, throwing him a fleeting glance to let him know I'm in control. He shifts to the side and lets me through, and I stand in front of Jack despite our heavy audience flanking us.

"Preying on her?" I bite out in a low, cool tone. "You think you know everything, but you know nothing. You still call her Eddie and treat her like a child. She's been living in my house for the last two months, Jack. I'm with her all the time. I treat her like the smart, incredible woman she is, and have nothing but respect for her."

I sigh and twist to look at Estlin. This week on vacation with her and Rory was the best time of my life. This is not how I wanted to tell either of them. Not even close.

I turn back to Jack and, on a heavy breath, say, "I'm sorry. You're right that I should have told you. From the very start, I should have, because even though we said it was going to be casual, I never was with her. She was more for me the first night I met her, and that's only grown."

Jack blinks at me. "First *night*?"

"She was at the bar the Friday night your flight was canceled, and so was I. Only you never mentioned that to either of us. Did you?" I accuse. "You all but told me to go out and have a good time."

"You motherfucker—"

Mason catches Jack mid-launch, and just as I go on the offensive, Estlin steps in and shoves Jack back and out of Mason's hands.

"Enough!" Her hands plant on his chest, and she holds him steady. "Stop it. Do you think I need you to pick my battles and fight my wars?" she asks, and he sputters, staring down at her. "I love you, Jack, and I get that you're upset because Owen and I didn't feel the need to include you in our sex life, but I'm tired of being treated with kid's gloves. Owen is right. You still call me Eddie even though I've been going by Estlin for the past five years, and you hover over my every move and word. Part of that is my fault. I've let you and everyone else treat me that way because I never had the courage before to stand up to it until now, and I knew it came from a place of love. And yes, Claude was older, and he was manipulative, and I was young and easily taken in. But Owen has never treated me that way. Not once. He has been nothing but open and honest with me from the start. He's done nothing but try to protect me—from himself, from Claude, and anyone else."

Jack's hands go to his hips, and he's breathing hard. "Edd— Estlin, don't you see that he's not serious about this with you?"

"Not serious? You asshole, I'm in love with her."

"*Love?*" Jack chokes reflexively like he's hacking up a hairball.

Everyone freezes, including Estlin. The silence so resonating, my heart starts to pound faster, blood thrumming through my ears as if to make up for it.

"You know, I'm thinking we should go home," my grandmother muses, drawing everyone's attention to her. "It's late, and Katy and Bennett need their space and time with baby Willow, and there are things that need to be worked out without an audience witnessing it." She slowly walks over to me, unreasonably spry for a woman her age. I expect any manner of disapproving look from her, but she surprises me with a warm, loving smile. "Good night, my Owen. You are a brilliant surgeon and a man I am very proud of. Don't worry about Rory, she's with Rina." She kisses my cheek, wipes at the lipstick stain she left behind, then leaves, a trail of people following her, including all my uncles and aunts and most everyone else except for our small circle.

It's an incredible move and a gesture that speaks volumes about her love, faith, and trust in me. It's also one I'm insanely grateful for. Once everyone else has gone, I walk into the now-empty waiting room, and the remaining crew follows.

Now it's my turn to pace, but I quickly get over it and take Estlin's hand, bringing her to me. I said the words, and I won't take them back. They're hers now to do with as she likes, but I was tired of holding them in. Tired of her not knowing when it's all I think about. Wanting more is going to bring me to my knees, but here it is.

My heart in my hands and my life on the line.

"I knew the world wouldn't see us as we are," I murmur as I face both Estlin and Jack. "They'd see that Estlin is younger and I'm older. They'd see that I'm her boss and she's my daughter's nanny. They'd see and think so many things that didn't speak to us. But the truth is, she walked into my life, and I forgot everything else but her." My heart batters mercilessly in my chest, and my palm grows slick against hers. "What else is there to say? I love you."

Her eyes sparkle up at me, and her other hand lands on my chest over my racing heart. "I love you too. Even before you gave me my birthday presents."

I laugh at that, the sound relief and strain glued together as one. Thank fucking Christ for that. Now if Jack wants to kill me, at least I'll die a happy man.

"You?" Wren checks almost as if what I'm saying isn't computing. "You're in love. With Estlin. And she's in love with you." She does a slow owl blink at both of us. "And you met... before you hired her?"

"I met her out at the bar, and we had some fun together. I liked her immediately. She just... clicked for me somehow. But the next day, when she and Jack came to my house, it felt like everything was falling apart. I hired her because I had no choice, and Rory adored her. I tried to stay away. I tried to resist her. But she's impossible to resist." I look straight at Jack. "She's everything to me. *Everything.*"

Silence falls across the room again, only to be broken by Mason. "Are you going to try to kick his ass, or are you done with that?"

Jack emits a mournful noise, his hands locked behind his head, his elbows butterflied out, but his eyes are still hard as fucking stones on me. Me loving his sister doesn't erase that I kept it from him and lied about it. Fine, I'm pissed he thought so little of me, so I guess we're even.

"Probably not," he admits.

"Good. Because I think we should go too." Mason nods toward Stone and Vander, and Keegan nudges Wren as she puts her purse on her shoulder. Mason slaps my shoulder. "You good?"

I nod. "I'm good." Hell, minus Jack and Rory off somewhere, I'm fucking great.

"All right." He gives me a hug. "We'll catch up tomorrow, brother. Nice work on Willow."

"Thanks, man."

I exchange similar goodbyes with everyone else, and then it's just the three of us. Minus my daughter. I'm glad she's with Rina, but I'd like her here. It's late, and I want to take her home.

"And what of her work?" Jack throws out at me.

Her hand flies up. "Oh, come on, Jack."

He shakes his head at her. "No. This is important. You say you're in love, and I'm happy for you if that's true. Still fucking pissed, but happy. Except she was in love with a guy who didn't let her work take center stage for her the way he should have. You know she has an offer from a gallery in New York. Are you going to force her to stay here and continue to work as Rory's nanny because that's what you need her for?"

I didn't know about the offer from the gallery, and I feel a bit blindsided by it. For a moment, I trip over my thoughts. Over my words. His comment about forcing her to stay acts like a sucker punch, and I'm winded at the thought of losing her.

"I hope she'll stay, but I'd never force her to," I start slowly. "She works every day on her art, either in the studio we made for her in the basement or in the studio she pays for. I think her talent is amazing, just as I think she's amazing. I'm not here to ruin her life, Jack. Did you miss the part where I said I love her? I'd never stand in the way of her dream. Not ever." I turn to her. "You got into a gallery in New York?"

She nods. "Yes. The Broad. Billy's uncle is evidently the owner, and he showed him a couple of my paintings. He called just before you came out of surgery."

Well, that last part is a relief. For a moment, I was worried she was keeping it from me. "Hell, baby." I cup her face, not caring about our audience. "I'm so proud of you. That's fantastic."

"There are a lot of details to work out about it."

"Then we'll work them out," I promise her. "Whatever you need, we'll make it happen."

"I wasn't worried about it," she teases. "I knew you'd be happy and supportive about it. But Rory's upset. She overheard me telling Jack and thinks I'm leaving her. I'm not. I never will. It's like I told you in Florida. I want us. All three of us."

I kiss her because I have to fucking kiss her.

Jack makes a noise, and I pull back.

"I don't know what else to say." I shrug. "Your lack of faith in me as a man hurts like hell. I get that you're angry we kept it a secret, but you should know me well enough to know the sort of man I'd be to her. Yes, it's new for us. We have a lot to work out. But if she wants me, I'm hers. That's all I know and all I can tell you. Other than that, I'm totally, completely, incoherently, wildly, truly, madly in love with her."

Estlin's palm cradles my face as she reaches up on her tiptoes to kiss my lips again. "That was a lot of adjectives."

I scrunch my nose. "Too many?"

"I was hoping for a few more."

I laugh, my forehead falling to hers. "I'm a doctor and hardly known from my poetry."

"I'll take it because I feel the same way. With just as many adjectives, if not more."

I swallow thickly. "Then that's all that matters." My gaze flows upward to Jack. "What do you say?"

Jack steps forward and extends his hand to me. I reach out and grip it. Immediately Jack pulls me in and clasps my shoulder. "You'll take good fucking care of her."

"I promise."

"Don't ever lie or hide shit from me again."

I nod just as Rina brings a puffy, red-eyed, and a sad faced Rory back to us. Immediately, Estlin bends and picks her up, fiercely hugging her. She's a mess, her head drooping to Estlin's shoulder, her eyes already starting to close. It's more than a little late at this point, and it's been a long day, and she's emotional.

"I'm not going anywhere, Gingerbread," Estlin promises her. "I love you, and I love your dad. There may be times when I have to go on a trip, but I'll always come back to you."

"You swear?"

Estlin kisses her head. "I swear."

"Forever?"

"And ever. I promise."

I kiss both my girls. Time to take them home.

EPILOGUE
ESTLIN

"Ready to go home, Moonshine?" Owen asks, pulling her from my arms. Thank God, because as much as I love her, she was a heavy, dead weight.

"Can we go back to Disney World?" she asks sleepily.

Owen chuckles and I giggle lightly. "Maybe in a couple of years," Owen tells her, adjusting her in his arms and reaching out his hand for me to take. It's a gesture that speaks volumes, and Jack is silent as he watches us.

Just before we reach the door, Jack calls out, "If you're not good to her, I'll kill you. But if this is what you both want, then I'm happy about it."

Owen gives Jack a firm nod, and then we leave, heading out into the cold, dark night and climbing into a waiting car. I hadn't thought about how we were going to get home, but Owen thinks of everything.

Rory is belted into a booster seat and is out almost immediately.

"Poor baby. She had a long day."

I run my fingers down her hair.

"We all did." He gives me a tug until I'm closer to him as the car drives us through Boston. His hands are back on my face and in my hair, and then his lips are pressing to mine. "Everyone knows now."

I smile against him. "That they do."

"I might have to fire you."

I laugh. "No way in hell you are. I could change my mind about you any second, and I'm not losing out on a good job over a man."

"We'll negotiate then."

"A raise for me? Sure. I'm happy to negotiate that."

He smiles and then kisses me, his mouth moving voraciously over mine. His fingers toy with the diamonds in my ears as his tongue twists with mine. I don't need the diamonds, and I don't need the fancy books. I only need him and Rory to make me happy, and now that they're truly mine, a light giddiness sweeps through me.

Is it possible to ever truly get everything you want in this world? The guy, the kid, the work? I don't know, but right now I have a high unlike any other. I love that this is the start of us.

Twenty minutes later, we're home, and Owen is carrying Rory to bed.

"The number of times I've put this kid to bed without brushing her teeth makes me feel like the worst father."

I snicker. "They're baby teeth anyway."

He shakes his head as he kisses her forehead. "Night Moonshine. Love you."

I bend over her bed and drop a kiss into her hair. "Night Gingerbread. Love you."

Owen's eyes glitter up at me, brimming with love. My chest flutters at it, my fingers prickling with that ooey-gooey adrenaline burst I get whenever I'm near him. In my next breath, he scoops me off my feet, never one not to carry me if he can. I love that about him.

I love everything about him.

Even when he's being a surly jerk, he's still *my* surly jerk.

"You know this is your room now," he murmurs against my neck as he brings me straight to the bathroom. Yeah, I'd say it's safe to say we could both use a shower right about now. The man saved Willow's life tonight. He got us on a private jet and then into a helicopter and swooped in to save her.

"You saved baby Willow today," I tell him in awe, ignoring the part about how this is my bedroom now. "You're a hero."

He rolls his eyes at me as he peels off his scrub top followed by his pants. He doesn't see it, and maybe that's another thing I love most about him.

"Come here." His hands attack my clothes until I'm as naked as he is, and then I'm lifted once again, my legs wrapped around his as he brings me into the shower. He washes every inch of me, and I do the same with him, both of us silent and tired, but unable to stop our smiles as we catch each other's eyes in between rinses.

My hand grazes his cock, and I feel the hard length of it twitch against me. It makes my mouth water, and I drop to my knees.

Owen's eyes snap wide and slingshot down at me. "What are you doing?"

I smirk up at him as I grip him in my fist. "What does it look like?" My lips part, and then I suck him straight down my throat.

"Jesus Christ," he hisses out, his eyes closing and his head falling back. Firm fingers twine into the wet strands of my hair, and he holds me there with the head of his cock pressed against the back of my throat. It makes me choke and gag a little and I reflexively swallow.

A groan shreds from his lungs and heat races through me.

"Sweet thing..." It's all he's got as his grip slackens and I slide off, only to take him back down just as deep, swallowing each time I go. I do my best to flatten my tongue and breathe through my nose, but Owen is thick and long, and it's a struggle. With my hand still clenched around him, I pump him into my mouth, sucking and swirling the head of his cock as I do, paying extra attention to his slit and the sensitive underside.

He unravels at the seams, one hand slapping into the marble wall, the other still firmly locked in my hair, guiding me along. Strong hips piston forward as he mindlessly starts to fuck my mouth, groaning and grunting and moaning with every swallow and lick.

It's deliciously erotic, and nothing makes me happier—or wetter—than watching this strong man lose his mind in me.

The tile digs into my knees, and water is rushing over my back, but I don't care.

I continue to feed his cock into my mouth and then use my other hand to cup his balls.

"Ah, fuck. I'm gonna come, baby." He tries to pull me back, but there is no way in hell that's happening.

I look up, and our eyes lock, his a dark maelstrom of pleasure, and I grip him tighter and suck harder.

It drives him wild, and he pumps faster, watching me suck him off and gag with saliva dripping from my chin and tears running down my cheeks. On a loud roar, he cups the back of my head and holds me there as he shoots himself into my mouth. I swallow him down, taking in every drop he gives me, and then licking him clean when he's done.

"Fuck, I love you."

I giggle at that even as his hand curls around my arms and he hoists me back up. His lips slam down on mine, and he kisses me with abandon as he walks me back into the tile wall. His hand finds my clit, and he rubs me in tight circles. This man does not do slow, and he takes my already worked up body to new heights.

Just as I'm about to come, he flips me around and sinks straight into me. "Ah. Oh my hell."

His chest presses against my back, his hands cup my tits and hold them firmly. I feel his lips dip by my ear, his breathing harsh as he pants, "Mine."

My eyes close as pleasure curls through me. "Forever," I manage.

Something about that sets him off. His teeth rake down my neck, roughly biting into the soft flesh of my shoulder. He starts to pound into me, holding me up and against him by tits that he manhandles in the best of ways. Squeezing and pushing and pulling. It's exquisite and brutal and everything I need from him.

His cock slides in with deep, powerful fucks, pressing right against my G-spot with each go. I'm short and he's tall, and I lean my face against the wall, arched up on my tiptoes as he sinks into me, all the while his mouth ravages my neck and shoulders.

His hand clasps my wrist and pulls it behind me, followed by the other one until he's locked them between his body. It puts me at his total mercy, binding me without rope. One hand slips to my hip, his fingers digging in for leverage, while his other goes back to abusing my breast.

I've never been fucked like this. Taken so absolutely where I'm surrounded and helpless and consumed. It has my pussy convulsing, squeezing his cock, and hungry for more.

Hard, deep, drowning thrusts nail me into the wall as his hand holds my hips back for the perfect angle. I'm going to come. I can feel my orgasm rising like the start of a tsunami.

"That's it," he bites sharply at me. "Take what I'm giving you. My cunt. My tits. My body. You're all fucking mine now, sweet thing."

"Owen—" I'm about to announce I'm coming like the warning before the wave hits, but it's too late. It washes over me and drowns me in its sweet, intoxicating pleasure. I cry out, moving and jerking, but to no avail with how he has me pinned. It heightens it somehow, bringing me to a level I had no idea I could reach.

His grip on me tenses, and he stills, coming with a muffled bellow as he smothers his face in my neck.

With ragged breaths, he slips out of me and turns me around, gathering me in his arms. He holds me for the longest time, just hugging and breathing and tickling me with the lightest of kisses.

Once we're both back on planet Earth, he shuts off the shower and wraps us both up in towels. We brush our teeth, and I put on a pair of panties he stole from me along with a T-shirt of his, and then I'm in his bed with the lights off and him wrapped around me.

"I meant it," he whispers in the quiet darkness.

"What?" I question with a yawn.

"I want you to move in here with me. Into my room. Into my bed." He pauses for a quiet beat. "Is that too much too soon for you?"

"No. I want that too. I like your shower."

He smiles against my skin, drawing one of my own to my lips.

"I love you," I say softly because I said it before when we were in the hospital, but it didn't count. Not fully. I love you needs to be spoken like this. When you're just two people and there's nothing but vulnerability between you.

"I love you." He blows out a breath and holds me tighter. "God, Estlin, I love you so much. I love how you love my girl. I love how I think about you all day and still can't wait to be with you. It's the real deal. We'll figure out the rest. I don't care about anything else. Everything changed between us the moment I had you in my arms again, and I'm never letting you go now that I've got you."

"I meant what I said. I'm not worried about it. I know that

what we have is real, and I know that others will have opinions. So let them. They're not here, and they can't hurt us."

"So I can hold your hand in public?"

I roll over in his arms and look up into his dark eyes. He presses me against him, removing any space between us.

"You better. You're Owen Fritz. I have to stake my claim and let the world know you're off the market."

"I might need to marry you one day. Get you pregnant and give Rory siblings."

Holy shit. My heart takes off into a sprint. "I might be okay with that."

His lips press to mine, and then he's inside me again, our limbs intertwined, our breathing one, and I know it's how we'll be for the rest of our lives.

The End.

WANT MORE of Owen and Estlin's HEA and a deleted scene? Scan the QR code blow.

Want to know about Owen's parents Carter and Grace? Turn the page for chapter one of Doctor Mistake.

DOCTOR MISTAKE
CARTER

The second my pager goes off, I know it's going to be bad news. Nothing good is ever paged at the end of your shift. I stop in the middle of the hall—my back sore and my neck stiff after four-teen hours on my feet—to check the pager when a nurse comes barreling down the hall.

"Dr. Carter, they need you in the ED stat. They have a thirty-three-week pregnant woman with severe painless vaginal bleeding."

"Previa?" I question, reading through the page that says the exact same thing she's telling me.

"Don't know. She's not our patient."

"Tell them I'm on my way."

Without another word, or even so much as a complaint since my shift technically ends in ten minutes, I run for the elevator, hitting the button. Just as the doors open and I step on, Grace Hammond, my resident—and my younger brother Oliver's best friend—steps on beside me.

"You got paged too?" she asks, her voice soft and slightly melodic the way it always is even after a long day of delivering babies and performing surgeries. She leans back against the wall, folding her arms over her chest.

"Yep," I reply, shifting slightly so I'm not so close to her. So the scent of her floral, coconut shampoo doesn't infiltrate my senses. I hate being so aware of her. Still I can't help but surreptitiously take her in. Grace's blonde hair is wrapped up in a tight bun; her blue scrubs a shade darker than her luminous eyes that never seemed dulled by the grueling hours or the fluorescent lights.

I look away, chastising myself for the tenth time today.

"I thought you were off at seven."

"I am," I tell her. "But I got paged, so that's how it goes."

"Previa?" she guesses, clearly having the same thought I was. Heavy, painless vaginal bleeding in a pregnant woman in her third trimester can be signs of a lot of things, but a placenta previa—where the placenta covers the cervix—is usually at the top of my differential diagnosis.

"Probably, but we'll see once we get in there. She's not a patient on our service."

Just then, the doors to the emergency department open and we're immediately greeted by Margot, my sister Rina's best friend and a nurse here in the ED. She starts talking a mile a minute, setting off at a good pace as she updates us on the patient while we head toward the trauma room.

"Thirty-year-old thirty-three-week pregnant woman, G1P0 presented complaining of heavy, painless vaginal bleeding. Vitals so far are stable, but she's losing blood as quickly as we can give it to her, and her heart rate is tachy in the one thirties. Her blood pressure is a little low but holding at 96/62. Stat ultrasound confirms baby is not in any distress, but the placenta presents very low. Likely the cause of the bleeding, but since we can't do a transvaginal ultrasound, difficult to tell if it's a full previa. Patient reports no prior knowledge or diagnosis of a previa."

"Alright," I say, as we approach the trauma rooms. "Have you notified the OR yet?"

"Yes. They're already on standby and so are peds and the NICU. They're just waiting on you."

"You look a little flustered, Margot," I comment dryly, noting her flushed cheeks and messy dark curls. "All going smoothly down here?"

She flips me off without missing a step. "It's July, Carter. Do you know what that means?"

I laugh under my breath as does Grace. "New interns," Grace replies, because yeah, we have them too, though Grace seems to like her newbie, Dylan. I hate July. And August, for that matter.

"Yes," Margot expels dramatically. "New fucking interns who think they're God's gift to medicine and that nurses are placed on this earth to do their bidding. I had to literally smack one of their hands away because he was about to attempt a pelvic exam on this woman. Can you imagine?" She looks to each of us, horror in her brown eyes. "Did he not realize that sticking his hand into a bleeding vagina with a high likelihood of a previa could possibly cause a placental rupture?"

This is why Margot is a kick-ass nurse.

"Obviously not," I comment. "He'll quickly learn that nurses save lives that interns attempt to collect. Thank you for that." And I mean that genuinely. I can't count the number of times nurses have not only saved my ass, but the asses of fellow doctors.

"Any time. Though I highly doubt it will be the last today I have to stop one of them from doing something stupid. The patient is in here." She points to the door, and we stop in front of the trauma room. "Her name is Marissa, and she's scared shitless. Her husband was at a conference, and we were finally able to get through to him. He's on his way now."

"Thanks," Grace says, spinning around pushing open the

door of the trauma room with her back as she talks to Margot. "You still coming tomorrow night?"

"I think so. I have to see what time I get off. Rina will be there for sure though. Same with the other girls."

Grace gives Margot a wink and then we plow through the doors, straight into action. I nearly have to shove two interns out of the way—Margot wasn't kidding with how fucking inept they are—and then Grace and I get to work. We assess the mother's condition as well as the fetus's. Within minutes we determine that yes, she's losing too much blood from her previa to be stopped down here or even at all.

We have about ten minutes max to get this baby out of her before the mother goes into shock from blood loss and the baby goes into distress.

"Marissa," Grace soothes, coming right up to the patient's face, hovering over her and gently squeezing her shoulder. "We're taking you up to the OR now. You're going to deliver the baby."

"No," Marissa cries through her oxygen mask. "It's too soon."

"Unfortunately, we don't have a choice. We need to do what's best for both you and the baby, and that's delivering it. I know you're scared, but we'll be with you every step of the way. Don't worry, we're going to do everything we can for you both. You're in excellent hands."

Grace gives her that warm smile, the one that always gets through to patients, and then we're moving. Margot and another nurse are pushing the gurney as we all head for the elevator at a quick pace.

"You scrubbing in on this or is someone else taking over for you?" Grace asks me.

"I'll take it. I've come this far." We all step onto the elevator, the doors shutting. "What are you doing tomorrow night with my sister?" I question softly as my eyes cling to the glowing numbers as we ascend.

"Girls' night. We even managed to force Amelia to come."

Amelia is Oliver's girlfriend. Oliver and Grace have been best friends since infancy. And forever, people just assumed they'd be a thing, but it never happened. They view and treat each other as siblings.

You'd think that would have made Grace an unofficial part of the family and I guess in a way it has. But not for me. I went away to college and then medical school. Did my residency down in Virginia Beach, only returning to Boston last year as an attending.

So I wasn't expecting it. Her.

It had been years and years since I had seen Grace.

I wasn't expecting her to be... fuck, everything that she is. Smart. Beautiful. An insanely talented doctor. Funny. Sarcastic. Beautiful. I might have mentioned that once already, but hell does it bear repeating. As someone who has already been down the road of wanting someone you know you can never have, craving her the way I do is like a kick in the teeth.

On a daily basis.

"And Tony doesn't care that you're having this girls' night?" I try to keep all the bitterness from my voice. I try very hard, but Margot's head flies sharply in my direction, her gaze discerning as she cocks an eyebrow, so I'm not sure I quite hit my mark.

Tony is Grace's fiancé, so yeah, again, never gonna happen between me and her.

"He's got some work dinner thing he's going to."

"Right. Of course he does. Can't make partner without putting in all the hours."

Grace rolls her eyes at me, but it's true. The bastard is never around. At least not that I've noticed.

"Uh-huh. What time did your shift end this evening,

Doctor? Fifteen minutes ago, is it now? And you're, oh look, heading into surgery."

"Different. Medicine is a noble profession. Chasing ambulances, and then going after the doctors who saved the life of the injured, isn't."

Before she can lay into me for that, the elevator doors open and now we're back in game-on mode. We race down the hall while the OR nurses take the patient and prep her for surgery. By the time we walk into that OR, she'll be under anesthesia because we don't have time to wait for an epidural or spinal block to take effect.

Grace and I don scrub caps and boots before going about the process of scrubbing in.

"Do you feel you're ready to take point on this?" I ask, lathering my hands with antiseptic soap, washing every inch.

"Without a doubt," she answers confidently, scrubbing vigorously beside me and refusing to meet my eyes.

She's pissed at me for the Tony comment, but I don't care. I don't have to. I'm the attending and she's the resident and that's how our dynamic works. If we weren't in the hospital, she'd mouth off back to me until her face was red, but not here.

"I can have that baby out in under ninety seconds."

"I'm going to time you."

Now she meets my eyes, glaring blue fire into me. I smirk before I can stop it, thankfully she can't see it behind my mask.

"You do that, Carter." She presses her foot onto the pedal, rinsing off the soap.

"If you can do it safely in eighty seconds, I'll buy you something special for your birthday."

She shakes her head, her arms bent at the elbow, sterile hands held up and out in front of her. "You're such a condescending dick," she murmurs under her breath as she plows past me, headed for the OR.

"What was that? I'm not sure I heard you correctly."

"I said you're such a considerate doctor," she yells at me over her shoulder, and now I can't stop my laugh.

But the second we meet the OR floor, all humor is gone from my lips.

"Hi, Dr. Fritz," Angelica, one of the nurses, says to me, batting her long lashes at me flirtatiously as she goes about tying my gown and helping me with my sterile gloves. "I'm so glad you're in here performing this surgery. I know the patient is in the best of hands with you as her doctor."

"Actually, I'm the one doing the surgery, Angelica," Grace smoothly interjects. "Dr. Fritz is simply here to supervise me. So, if you're ready to get back to work, I'd like to start." With the patient fully prepped and ready, Grace gets into position, holding out her hand. "Ten blade, please."

The scrub nurse obliges, and all other commentary ceases as Grace sets to work while I watch on, here to jump in at any time if needed, but I already know I won't be. Grace, while only heading into her third year of residency, is as competent as any fourth year or attending. She's by far the best OB-GYN resident in the hospital.

Just as she makes the incision, the pediatrics and NICU teams roll in. The patient is holding her own, getting another unit of type-specific blood while Grace works diligently and methodically to get the baby out. That's actually the easy part. The fastest part. After that is where the real work for us begins.

Especially with a case like this. We have to remove the placenta without causing more damage or further bleeding.

"How's my patient doing, Larry?" Grace asks the anesthesiologist just as we get a couple of beeps on the monitor.

"Blood pressure dipped a little, but I'll get it back up."

"That would be greatly appreciated." Grace locates the fetus, working with skilled, precise movements. "If you're not too bored over there, Carter, maybe you could cauterize that bleeder for me?"

"I've got it," the nurse says, doing her job.

"I think Dr. Fritz is well beyond cauterizing bleeders," Angelica simpers. "I've seen him perform the most complex of surgeries with ease."

"Hey, Larry?" Grace cuts in once again, completely ignoring Angelica who has always been a flirty kiss ass. "Did Dr. Fritz ever tell you why he decided to become an OB-GYN when the field is predominantly female providers?"

"Here we go…" I mutter.

"Yes. Here we go." Grace extracts the baby, blue and wet, handing him directly to the waiting pediatric team. They immediately start working on him. "Time of delivery, nineteen-thirty-two." She glances up at me. "Seventy-eight seconds, Carter. I believe you owe me one hell of a birthday present."

"I'll let you use the robot in my next surgery."

She shakes her head. "No way. I want something better from you, Doctor. Something real I can sink my teeth into."

So do I, I think and then quickly shut that bitch up. "A steak then?" I offer. "Since we know Tony won't be around to take you to dinner."

I get a death glare for that.

"Wait, back up," Larry jumps in, before Grace can unleash more of her wrath. "Why are you an OB-GYN, Carter? You that into pregnant chicks and pussy?"

Grace, as well as every nurse in here, throws Larry a scathing look.

"I'm going to pretend you didn't just say that, because it makes you sound like a total misogynistic asshole," Grace barks while she goes about removing the placenta and tying off any active bleeding vessels. "But no. He actually walked in the room when his mother was in the throes of delivering Rina and after that decided birthing babies was his life's calling."

I hate that story.

It always makes me sound like such a pussy—pun intended.

Plus, Rina works in this hospital as an ICU nurse, so I know this will somehow funnel back to her, which never fails to make her laugh at my expense.

Speaking of... all the nurses, right on cue, start oohing and awing, humor dancing in their eyes. The NICU team who have an umbilical line placed and are giving the baby—who is pinking up and half crying—oxygen to help him along, are also joining in on the dig my resident just took at me.

She's not dumb either. Grace has to know I'll punish her for this. Professionally speaking, of course. I'm not actually allowed to punish her the way I'd like.

My comments about Tony must have really pissed her off this time.

Still, when you're engaged to a total dipshit, douchebag who takes you for granted and is never around, you should learn to get used to people making disparaging comments about him. Even Oliver can't stand the guy and Oliver generally likes everyone.

"That true, man?" Larry inquires, not bothering to hide his chuckle.

"Yes, it's true, and now I'm one of the top surgeons and OB-GYNs in Boston that you" —I point at Grace— "have the pleasure of learning from and watching in action. Just wait till you see what I have in store for you tomorrow, Dr. Hammond."

Grace peers up, likely to say something else that will boil my blood when pediatrics cuts us both off. "Five-minute APGAR is six. We're moving the baby up to the NICU. Have someone page us when mom is awake."

They roll out and we finish our surgery, everyone quiet as the team works, the tension in the room so thick you could cut it with a scalpel. Just as Grace finishes the last stitch, I turn and march out of the room, tearing off my surgical gear and going straight for the sink to scrub out.

Then I slink back, tucked in the corner along the shadows.

Two minutes later Grace comes out, glances around and when she doesn't spot me, she sighs. In relief or regret, I cannot tell, but she goes for the sink, rolling her neck until it pops as she begins to scrub out. And when her hands are lathered in soap, and she has nowhere else to go, I move in behind her, towering over her with my height. I take a deep inhale, marveling how she still manages to smell sweet and clean after a day spent in the hospital and my cock twitches in my scrubs.

She feels me behind her, not touching her but merely inches away, and she stiffens. "I thought you'd gone."

"Not quite yet," I whisper, my lips dipping down till they're hovering by her ear, watching as goose bumps dance across her neck. "Pull another stunt like that and I'll have you running scut along with the interns for the rest of your residency. As it is, tomorrow you're on postpartums. No surgeries."

"Carter—"

"The proper response is yes, Dr. Fritz. Anything else is completely unacceptable."

"Yes, Dr. Fritz," she grits out through clenched teeth, and I grin, making sure she feels it on my lips. That's how stupidly close I am to her right now. So stupidly close I feel her sharp intake of breath and quickly force myself to get control and step back.

I shouldn't have done that.

Each time I give in just an inch, I lose ground on forcing her into her neat and tidy role in my life. Brother's best friend. Resident. Engaged.

Off-motherfucking-limits.

"Good work in there, Doctor. Keep it up and I will take you out for that steak."

With that, I turn and leave the hospital, needing to clear my head. Clear it of her.

Because that's all I can ever do with her. Even when the desire for more is growing increasingly unbearable.